Malory Towers Collection 4

Other Enid Blyton School Stories Collections

The St Clare's Collection 1:
The Twins • The O'Sullivan Twins • Summer Term

The St Clare's Collection 2:
Second Form • Third Form • Kitty

The St Clare's Collection 3:
Claudine • Fifth Formers • Sixth Form

The Malory Towers Collection 1:
First Term • Second Form • Third Year

The Malory Towers Collection 2:
Upper Fourth • In the Fifth • Last Term

The Malory Towers Collection 3:
New Term • Summer Term • Winter Term

The Malory Towers Collection 4:
Fun and Games • Secrets • Goodbye

The Naughtiest Girl Collection 1:
In the School • Again • Is a Monitor

The Naughtiest Girl Collection 2:
Here's … • Keeps a Secret • Helps a Friend • Saves the Day

The Naughtiest Girl Collection 3:
Well Done • Wants to Win • Marches On

Enid Blyton

Malory Towers
Collection 4

Written by Pamela Cox

Hodder
Children's
Books

HODDER CHILDREN'S BOOKS

Fun and Games first published in Great Britain in 2009 by Mammoth
Secrets first published in Great Britain in 2009 by Mammoth
Goodbye first published in Great Britain in 2009 by Mammoth
This edition published in 2016 by Hodder & Stoughton

1 3 5 7 9 10 8 6 4 2

A CIP catalogue record for this book
is available from the British Library.

ISBN 978-1-444-94994-0

Printed and bound in Great Britain by Clays Ltd, Elcograf S.p.A.

The paper and board used in this book are from wood from responsible sources.

Hodder Children's Books
An imprint of
Hachette Children's Group
Part of Hodder and Stoughton
Carmelite House
50 Victoria Embankment
London EC4Y 0DZ

An Hachette UK Company
www.hachette.co.uk
www.hachettechildrens.co.uk

Contents

Malory Towers

Fun and Games

Written by Pamela Cox

Contents

New girls at Malory Towers

'Isn't it marvellous to be going back to Malory Towers?' said Felicity Rivers excitedly, to her friend Susan Blake. 'And to think we'll be going up into the fifth form! Haven't the years just flown by?'

'Yes,' agreed Susan. 'Sometimes it seems like only yesterday that we were starting out as first formers.'

Felicity had been staying with Susan for a few days, and now Mrs Blake was driving them back to school. First, though, they had to stop to collect a new girl, who was also going to be in the fifth form, on the way.

'Mother, what did you say the new girl was called?' asked Susan.

'Millicent Moon,' answered Mrs Blake. 'I met her mother when I went out to tea the other day, and she seemed very pleasant indeed.'

'Yes, but what is Millicent like?' asked Susan impatiently.

'Well, I don't know, dear, for I didn't meet her,' said Mrs Blake. 'She wasn't there. The family have been living in France for the last year, you know, and Millicent was studying at a music academy there.'

'I wonder if she will be as eccentric as my sister

Darrell's friend, Irene?' said Felicity, with a grin. 'Remember her, Susan?'

'Yes, she was great fun,' said Susan. 'A simply brilliant musician, but completely absent-minded when it came to normal, everyday matters. I say, won't it be marvellous for us if Millicent turns out to be as mad as Irene?'

But when Mrs Blake presently stopped the car outside a neat house, the girl who stepped out didn't look at all mad or eccentric. And she didn't look as if she would be much fun either, thought Felicity and Susan, feeling a little disappointed.

Millicent Moon was tall and slim, with long, straight dark hair, intense dark eyes and a pale, serious face. Her mother and father walked to the car with her, Mr Moon bringing Millicent's trunk with him, and Mrs Blake stepped out of the car to greet them. The three grown-ups chatted for a few moments, while Millicent stood aside, an aloof expression on her face.

Inside the car, Felicity said to Susan, 'She looks awfully serious.'

'Perhaps she is just nervous,' said Susan. 'It must be hard changing schools in the fifth form, when most of the others have known one another for years, and all have their own friends.'

'Yes,' agreed Felicity. 'We must do everything we can to make Millicent feel at home.'

So, when the new girl's trunk was stowed safely in the boot, and Millicent herself slipped into the back of the car beside Felicity and Susan, she received a warm welcome.

'Hallo, Millicent,' said Susan, with a broad smile. 'Nice to meet you. I'm Susan, and this is my friend, Felicity.'

Felicity greeted the girl too, and said, 'I hope you're going to like it at Malory Towers. If there is anything you want to know, just ask Susan and me.'

Millicent gave a little smile, and, as Mrs Blake started the car, said, 'Thank you. I'm sure that I shall be happy, as long as I can play my music, and keep up with my lessons. Music is my life, you see.'

Felicity and Susan looked rather startled at this, for Millicent sounded so very dramatic, and Susan said, 'There are several girls in our form who take music lessons, but none of them are what you could call great musicians. I must say, it will be jolly nice to have someone in the form who can bash out a few tunes on the piano in the common-room, when we feel like having a dance.'

Now it was Millicent's turn to look startled, and Felicity said, 'Perhaps Millicent doesn't play the piano.'

'Oh, I do,' said Millicent coolly. 'And the violin. And the harp. And the flute. But I am used to playing classical music, and not dance tunes.'

Then Millicent turned her head to look out of the window and fell silent, while Felicity and Susan pulled wry faces at one another.

As Millicent evidently wasn't in the mood for conversation, the other two girls began to talk about their friends at Malory Towers, Susan saying, 'Sylvia won't be coming back this term. Her people are moving to Scotland, and she is going to day school there.'

'I shall miss old Sylvia,' said Felicity, with a sigh. 'I didn't much care for her at first, but she turned out to be quite a good sort.'

'I could do with a nice easy time, this term,' said Susan. 'We all worked so hard at passing School Cert in the fourth that I think we deserve a good rest.'

'Did everyone in your form pass, dear?' asked Susan's mother.

'Yes, everyone,' answered Susan. 'Even Nora and Amy, who were both quite certain that they would fail.'

'June sailed through, of course,' said Felicity, a touch of envy in her tone. 'She hardly did any studying at all, yet she still managed to get excellent marks.'

'Typical of June!' laughed Susan. 'I say, she will have to settle down a bit now that she is a fifth former, won't she?'

'Yes, I think it's going to be harder for June than for any of us,' said Felicity, thoughtfully. 'She's so fond of playing jokes and tricks, but that kind of thing is quite out of the question when one becomes a fifth former.'

Susan was about to reply to this when suddenly a low, tuneful humming filled the car. Felicity and Susan looked at one another, startled, as they wondered what it could be, then they realised that it was coming from Millicent. The girl had her eyes closed and her head back as she hummed, then, just as suddenly as it had started, the sound stopped, and Millicent opened her eyes and began rummaging in her schoolbag.

She realised that the others were staring at her, and gave a laugh.

'Sorry,' she said. 'It's just that a new tune has come to me, and I must write it down at once, while it's fresh in my mind.'

She pulled a pen and notebook from her bag, and began jotting down a series of musical notes, while Felicity and Susan watched, fascinated.

'There!' she said at last, in satisfaction. 'I shall try that out later. You did say that there was a piano in the common-room, didn't you?'

'Well, the old fifth formers had one,' said Felicity. 'So it should still be there, unless Miss Grayling has had it moved.'

'Good,' said Millicent. 'Now, do tell me more about Malory Towers.'

Now that she had written down her new tune, Millicent seemed much more amicable, and chatted pleasantly with Felicity and Susan throughout the rest of the journey.

It was a very long drive indeed, and at twelve o'clock Mrs Blake stopped the car and took the girls for lunch at a restaurant. Afterwards, the three of them all felt rather sleepy, and conversation in the car tailed off as both Millicent and Susan closed their eyes. Felicity remained awake, though, for although she felt tired, she was excited too. It was so marvellous to be going back to her beloved Malory Towers, and she simply couldn't wait to see all the others again.

Scatter-brained Nora, and her friend, the placid, good-natured Pam. Then there were Julie and Lucy, who always brought their horses, Jack and Sandy, back to school with them. Not forgetting Amy, Bonnie, Freddie – and June, of course! Who could forget June, with her bold, mischievous ways? Perhaps there would be other new girls, too, thought Felicity, as the car went on its way, getting closer and closer to Malory Towers. What fun that would be!

When they were almost there, Susan woke up, rubbing her eyes before she turned to grin at Felicity.

'Almost there!' she said excitedly.

Then Millicent stirred, and sat up, yawning.

'We're nearly there, Millicent,' said Felicity excitedly. 'Once we turn this corner you will be able to see Malory Towers. Look, there it is! Up on the cliff-top.'

'Heavens, it looks like a castle!' exclaimed Millicent, looking up at the big building, with its four towers. 'How magnificent. I feel sure that I shall be inspired to write some marvellous music in such a setting.'

Millicent had gone all intense again, and Felicity and Susan exchanged glances, trying not to laugh, while Mrs Blake frowned at them in the driving mirror.

At last the car came to a halt in the driveway, and the three girls looked out to see dozens of girls, all chattering away together, greeting friends and saying goodbye to parents.

Felicity could see Nora and Pam in the distance, and she longed to leap out of the car and run across to them.

But she was a sober, serious fifth former now, so she got out of the car in a dignified manner, and waited patiently with Susan and Millicent while Mrs Blake opened the boot and got their things out.

'Do have a good term, all of you,' said Mrs Blake, giving Susan a hug. 'And I shall see you at half-term, dear.'

Then the three girls made their way across the lawn, and found that Pam and Nora had been joined by June and Freddie.

'Hallo there! Had good hols?'

'My goodness, isn't it grand to be back?'

'I can't believe that we are fifth formers now!'

'And who's this? A new girl?'

'Oh yes, this is Millicent Moon,' said Felicity. 'Millicent, meet Pam, Nora, June and Freddie.'

The others greeted the new girl with interest, then Susan said, 'There's something different about you this term, June.'

'Is there?' said June, looking rather startled. 'I can't think what.'

'I know what it is!' cried Susan. 'You have an air of dignity about you.'

'Yes,' agreed Felicity, her eyes twinkling. 'You look far more serious and responsible than you did last term. Like a proper fifth former!'

'I was just thinking that myself,' said Nora, joining in the fun. 'I say, June, perhaps Miss James will make you head of the form now that you've gone all serious and grown-up.'

June gave a snort and said, 'Serious and grown-up? Me? What nonsense! As for Miss James making me head of the form, why, she's more likely to choose Bonnie or Amy!'

The others laughed at the thought of little Bonnie, or the haughty Amy, becoming head-girl, and Nora said, 'I wonder who she will choose? Not me, that's for sure.'

'Well, we will find out tomorrow,' said Pam. 'I say, who's that over there? Another new girl?'

The others looked, and saw a plump, fair girl, with round, grey eyes and a rather bewildered expression, standing alone.

'Poor thing,' said Freddie. 'She looks rather lost. Shall we go and say hallo?'

So the group of fifth formers went across to the new girl and Felicity said, 'Hallo there. You're new, aren't you? What form are you in?'

'I'm in the fifth form, North Tower,' answered the girl, smiling shyly. 'My name's Delia Norris. Are you all fifth formers too?'

'Yes,' answered Susan. 'And we are all in North Tower, so you had better come along with us to Matron.'

Delia bent to pick up her night case, and as she did so it flew open, her belongings spilling out everywhere.

'Oh my gosh!' said Delia, bending down to cram them in again higgledy-piggledy. 'How silly of me. My aunt is always telling me how careless and clumsy I am.'

'Well, that's not very kind of her,' said the outspoken June, and Felicity gave her a nudge, before stooping to help the new girl collect her scattered things.

'Well, my aunt isn't very kind, sometimes,' said Delia, turning red. 'She was awfully glad when my grandmother decided to pay the fees for me to come to boarding school.'

She sounded rather forlorn, and some of the others felt sorry for her.

Susan asked kindly, 'Do you live with your aunt?'

'Yes, and my two cousins,' answered Delia, closing her night case firmly. 'My father is a sailor, you see, so he is away a lot, and I have no mother. I don't think that my aunt really wanted me to live with her, and my cousins certainly didn't, for they never made me feel very welcome.'

'What a shame!' said the kind-hearted Pam, touched. 'I daresay you will be glad to be away from them.'

Delia nodded and said, 'Though I can't really blame them for being impatient with me at times. I'm such a duffer!'

The others didn't know quite what to say to this, and were relieved when Bonnie and Amy joined them.

The two newcomers were introduced to the new girls, then Felicity said, 'Well, I suppose we had better take our health certificates to Matron. Got yours, Delia? And you, Millicent? Good, well, off we go then.'

The fifth formers trooped off to Matron's room, where they found her busily ticking things off on a list. She looked up as the girls entered, and her plump face broke into a smile.

'Hallo, fifth formers,' she said. 'My goodness, how strange it feels to be saying that to you! It seems like only yesterday that you came in here as giggling, irresponsible first formers.'

'Yes, but all that is behind us now, Matron,' said June, putting on a very grave expression. 'You see before you a group of very sober, responsible individuals indeed.'

Matron laughed, and said, 'Hmm, as far as *you* are concerned, June, I will believe that when I see it. Now, do you all have your health certificates?'

One by one, the girls handed them over, apart from Delia, who opened her night case and began pulling everything out.

'Delia, what *are* you doing?' asked Susan. 'You've only just put everything back in!'

'I can't find my health certificate,' said Delia. 'I'm quite sure that it is in here somewhere.'

'Well, it had better be, my girl,' said Matron sternly. 'Or it's quarantine for you, and I am sure you don't want that.'

Delia certainly *didn't* want that, and began searching more frantically. At last the health certificate was found, tucked inside one of her slippers, and she handed it over with a sigh of relief.

Matron took it and said, 'Off you go now. You are all in the same dormitory, along with Julie and Lucy, and another new girl called Gillian Weaver.'

'Another new girl!' exclaimed Nora, as they left Matron's room and made their way to the dormitory. 'I wonder what she is like?'

The fifth formers soon found out, for when they reached their dormitory Julie and Lucy were already there, and with them was a slim girl, with narrow green eyes and long, pale auburn curls. She was very attractive indeed, and the others looked at her with interest.

'Hallo, you lot!' cried Julie. 'We've been back for ages, and we've got Jack and Sandy all settled in nicely.'

The others greeted them, then Lucy said, 'This is Gillian Weaver, who is joining our form. And I see we have two more new girls!'

There was a flurry of introductions, then Felicity said happily, 'Well, here we are, all back together again for a new term. I wonder what it will bring?'

The first day

There was just time before tea to show the new girls round a bit. The fifth formers looked in at their new common-room, before going down to the stables, to greet Jack and Sandy.

Delia and Millicent seemed rather nervous of horses and admired them from a distance, but Gillian patted their velvety muzzles and made a great fuss of them.

'Do you ride, Gillian?' asked Julie.

'A little,' said the girl. 'But I don't have much time for it, with my other interests.'

'Oh?' said Lucy. 'And what are they?'

'Well, I simply love tennis,' said Gillian. 'And I see that the courts here are super, so I'm hoping to do well at that this term. And I play the violin, too, and that takes up a lot of my time.'

Millicent's ears pricked up at this, and she said, 'I am a musician myself, and play several instruments, including the violin. Have you taken any music exams?'

'Oh, no,' said Gillian, looking quite alarmed at the thought. 'I simply play for fun.'

Millicent, who took her music very seriously indeed, looked rather disapproving at this, but the others rather liked Gillian, and Freddie took her arm, saying, 'Let's go and take a look at the swimming-pool before tea. There's just time.'

Both Gillian and Millicent went into raptures over the beautiful, natural swimming-pool, which was hollowed out of rocks and filled by the sea.

'Lovely!' exclaimed Gillian. 'I simply can't wait to go for a swim in there.'

'How beautiful,' said Millicent, in her low, dramatic voice. 'It makes me feel like composing a tune, all about the wildness and beauty of the sea.'

'Does it?' said the forthright June, sounding unimpressed. 'It makes me feel like diving in fully clothed, but as I'm a fifth former now, I suppose I shall have to restrain myself.'

Just then the bell went for tea, and Pam cried, 'Good, I'm simply starving. Come along, everyone!'

The fifth formers looked around as they entered the big dining-room, giving rather superior smiles as they saw the lower forms, who all had a mistress seated at the head of their table.

The fifth and sixth formers, however, were judged to be grown-up enough to supervise themselves at mealtimes, and ate alone.

'My word, this looks good,' said Susan, rubbing her hands together, as the girls took their seats. 'Cold ham, tomatoes, potatoes cooked in their jackets – and fruit salad with cream for afters. Scrumptious!'

As the fifth formers tucked in, the old girls pointed

out various mistresses to the new girls.

'That's Mam'zelle Rougier over there, at the second formers' table,' said Felicity. 'One of our French mistresses. She can be awfully bad-tempered, so it's best not to get on the wrong side of her.'

'And there is Mam'zelle Dupont, our other French mistress,' said Freddie. 'She's awfully good-hearted, though she has a hot temper at times. And she's a most marvellous person to play tricks on, for she is so easy to take in.'

'Not that *we* shall be playing tricks on her, of course,' said Susan, in a lofty tone. 'We shall leave that sort of thing to the lower school.'

'I can't see Miss James anywhere,' said Nora, peering round. Then she turned to the new girls, and said, 'Miss James is our form mistress. I don't know her awfully well, but she seems quite a good sort.'

'I think that she is coming back later tonight,' said Pam. 'So we will meet her properly for the first time tomorrow.'

'And where is the music master, or mistress?' asked Millicent.

'Well, not all of the girls take music lessons,' explained Felicity. 'So we have someone who comes in several times a week and gives lessons. Her name is Miss Johnston and she's supposed to be awfully good.'

'Yes, I took piano lessons with her for a while back in the second form,' said Pam. 'She's a fine teacher.'

Millicent didn't look impressed by this, and gave a

sniff. 'I daresay I shall be above the standard that she is used to teaching,' she said, rather haughtily. 'But as I have learned just about all there is to learn, perhaps it doesn't matter so very much. As long as I can get my practice in, that is the most important thing.'

The fifth formers exchanged glances, and June said smoothly, 'Perhaps you will be able to teach Miss Johnston a thing or two, Millicent.'

The others grinned, but Millicent, apparently unconscious of any sarcasm, seemed to see this as a compliment, and smiled.

'Will you be taking music lessons, Gillian?' asked Lucy.

Gillian shook her auburn curls, and said, 'No, I stopped taking lessons last year. I have brought my violin to school with me, and I love playing it, but, as I said, it is just for fun.'

Seeing that Delia looked rather left out, Felicity turned to her and said kindly, 'What about you, Delia? Do you have any amazing talents? Are you marvellous at games, or do you play an instrument, or anything?'

'No,' said Delia rather bleakly. 'I'm afraid there's nothing marvellous about me. I'm no good at games, I have no talent for music, and I'm not even very clever at my lessons. I'm just a complete duffer.'

Nora patted the girl on the back, and said, 'Cheer up! I'm jolly pleased to have you here, for it means that you may be bottom of the form once in a while, instead of me.'

The others laughed at this, even Delia herself, and

Susan murmured to Felicity, 'At least she has a sense of humour, and can take a joke. She seems quite nice, although she doesn't have much confidence in herself.'

'And Millicent has too much!' said Felicity. 'I think I like Gillian best, out of the three new girls. She seems natural, and friendly, and good fun.'

The fifth formers were allowed to go to bed when they pleased, within reason, and all of them felt very grown-up and were determined to take advantage of this.

But most of the girls had had very long journeys, and it wasn't long before some of them began to yawn.

'I think that I shall go up soon,' said Nora. 'Otherwise I shall never be able to concentrate in class tomorrow.'

Several of the others felt the same, and got to their feet, and Susan said to Millicent, 'Are you coming to bed?'

Millicent, who was engrossed in a newspaper that she had found on the table, said rather absently, 'I shall stay up a little while longer, I think.'

'What's that you're reading?' asked Pam, curiously. 'It certainly seems to have got your attention.'

Millicent looked up, and said, 'Actually it's an article about a competition to find the best school orchestra in the country. And there is an entry form here too. I was just wondering if I could persuade Miss Grayling to let me get up a Malory Towers orchestra and enter. What do you think?'

The others thought that this sounded like an extremely

exciting idea, and Felicity said, 'I should think that Miss Grayling would be very interested indeed. It's certainly worth asking her, Millicent.'

'Very well,' said Millicent, removing the page she had been reading from the newspaper and folding it carefully. 'I shall ask her tomorrow, then.'

By ten o'clock all of the fifth formers were tucked up in bed, most of them fast asleep.

Only Millicent and Delia seemed to be having trouble in settling down.

Millicent's head was full of dreams of winning the school orchestra competition, of bringing glory to Malory Towers and of having her name spoken with awe by the others.

Delia's feelings were mixed. She felt happy to be away from her mean-spirited aunt and spiteful cousins, but was anxious about whether she would fit in at Malory Towers. She liked the girls, who all seemed very friendly and jolly, and had certainly done their utmost to make her feel welcome. But she was worried that she wouldn't be able to keep up with them at lessons, or games. If only she had a special talent, like Millicent, or Gillian, she might feel like a more worthwhile person. But poor Delia was not gifted at all.

At last, though, she fell asleep, as did Millicent, and soon the only sound coming from the dormitory was Pam's gentle snoring.

After breakfast on the first morning, the new girls had to go and see Miss Grayling, the wise and kindly

Head mistress of Malory Towers. Gillian, Millicent and Delia all felt very nervous as they stood before her, thinking that she looked rather stern. But then Miss Grayling's face broke into a lovely smile, and the three girls relaxed a little as she spoke to them one by one, asking their names.

Then Miss Grayling gave the little speech that she gave to all the new girls at the beginning of term, and the three of them listened intently, feeling very stirred by her words.

At last the Head finished, saying, 'You may go to your classroom now, and please remember what I have said throughout your time at Malory Towers.'

The girls nodded solemnly, and Gillian and Delia turned towards the door. But Millicent lingered, and said rather hesitantly, 'May I ask you something, please, Miss Grayling?'

'Of course,' said the Head. 'What is it, Millicent?'

Millicent told the Head about the school orchestra competition, pleased that she seemed to be listening with as much interest as the girls had listened to her speech earlier.

At last Miss Grayling said, 'I must say that it sounds like a very good idea. We have several very talented musicians at Malory Towers, from various forms, and it would be good for them all to work together at something. Yes, Millicent, you have my permission to get an orchestra together and enter it into the competition. I suggest that you put something up on the notice-boards, then any girl who is interested can put her name down.'

'Thank you, Miss Grayling,' said Millicent, the smile that she gave making her face look much less grave than usual. 'I shall do my very best to make sure that we win.'

'I am sure that you will,' said the Head. 'But even if you don't, I hope that everyone who takes part will learn something of value from the experience.'

Millicent was rather puzzled by this. What on earth was the point of entering a competition just to learn something from it? She was going to go all out to make sure that the Malory Towers orchestra – *her* Malory Towers orchestra – won, for that was the whole point. Of course, she didn't say this to Miss Grayling, but went along to the classroom with her head full of plans.

The other girls were already seated, and Millicent took the only seat that was left, in the front row, with Gillian and Delia.

Miss James had not yet arrived, and June said, 'Did you ask the Head about the competition, Millicent?'

'Yes, and she's given permission,' said Millicent, looking and sounding more excited than the girls had yet seen her. 'Gillian, you must let me hear you play your violin, for there may be a place for you in the orchestra. And Pam, didn't you say that you could play the piano?'

'Yes,' answered Pam, looking rather doubtful. 'But I don't know that I'm good enough to play in an orchestra.'

'Well, we'll soon see,' said Millicent. 'I am going to put something up on the notice-board a little later, and I will be holding auditions for anyone who is interested.'

'To be honest, I don't know whether I *want* to be in the orchestra,' murmured Pam to Nora. 'I rather fancied a nice, easy term.'

'Well, just fluff your audition,' said Nora. 'Then Millicent won't want you.'

Just then Miss James's footsteps could be heard approaching, and the girls fell silent, while Susan got up to hold the door open for the mistress.

'Thank you, Susan,' said Miss James, with a smile. 'Please sit down, girls.'

The girls sat, and looked at Miss James curiously. She was tall and thin, with curly grey hair and hazel eyes. Delia thought that she looked kind, and felt much more comfortable.

'Well, before we get down to the business of making out time-tables, there are one or two matters I need to tell you about,' said the mistress. 'First of all, I am sure that you are all eager to know who is to be head of the form. This is something that I discussed with Miss Potts and Miss Williams, who was your form mistress last year, and I took their advice before making my decision.'

Miss James had, in fact, had a very long discussion with the two mistresses.

'Susan Blake was head of the form last term,' Miss

Williams had said. 'And very good she was too. I believe that Felicity Rivers was an excellent head-girl in the third form as well.'

'Either of them would be a good choice,' Miss Potts, the head of North Tower, had said. 'But I have a very strong feeling that Miss Grayling may make one of them Head Girl when they go up into the sixth next year. As you know, the Head Girl of the sixth will be Head Girl of the whole school. So it seems to me that someone else should have the honour this year.'

Miss James had nodded, and ran her eye over the list of names in front of her.

'Nora Woods,' she had said aloud.

'No!' Miss Potts and Miss Williams had said at once.

'Nora is a dear girl,' said Miss Williams. 'But a complete scatter-brain.'

'I think that you can also rule out Amy and Bonnie,' said Miss Potts. 'Neither of them has the makings of a leader.'

'June?' suggested Miss Williams.

'Ah, now June most definitely *is* a leader,' said Miss Potts. 'Though she is not always very kind at times. Besides, Miss Grayling and I have other plans for June.'

Miss Williams and Miss James exchanged curious glances, but Miss Potts would not be drawn, and went on to say, 'Freddie will always follow June's lead, so I don't think that she would be a good head-girl either. That leaves Pam, Julie and Lucy.'

'All nice girls, with good characters,' said Miss

Williams. 'But Julie and Lucy are so horse-mad that there is very little time for anything else in their lives, and I don't think that either of them would be very whole-hearted about being head of the form.'

'Pam was head-girl in the second form,' said Miss Potts. 'All of the girls like, trust and respect her.'

'Well, it looks like Pam will be head of the fifth form, then,' said Miss James.

Now Miss James made the announcement in class, and all of the fifth formers were delighted. Had they been in a lower form, there would have been an outbreak of cheering and clapping, but as fifth formers they were more restrained, saying, 'Well done, Pam, old girl.'

'Yes, jolly good choice.'

'You'll make a fine head-girl.'

'Oh gosh!' said Pam, feeling quite overwhelmed. 'Just as I was saying that I fancied an easy term.'

But, of course, she was as pleased as punch, and simply couldn't wait to write to her parents and tell them the good news.

Miss James smiled, and said, 'I have something else to tell you, as well. As you know, Ruth Grainger, the games captain, left Malory Towers last term. As there is no one in the sixth form who is really good enough to take her place, the new captain is going to be someone from the fifth form – June!'

For a moment June thought that she hadn't heard properly, for surely Miss James couldn't have said that she was to be games captain of the whole *school*? But the others were beaming at her, congratulating her, and Freddie was clapping her on the back, so it *must* be true!

June was both astonished and delighted, for it had never occurred to her that she would ever be given a position of responsibility at Malory Towers. It was true that she was far and away the best sportswoman in the school. But she also had a reputation for being bold, mischievous and downright wicked at times!

Miss Potts had said as much to Miss Grayling when they had talked about the matter, and Miss Grayling had said, 'Well, it is time for June to put her tricks and jokes behind her, and learn how to be a responsible young woman. There is no doubt at all that she has the drive and determination to succeed, and I feel that this could be the making of her.'

And it seemed that June was going to make the most of the opportunity offered to her, for she was already turning over various plans in her mind.

The Malory Towers teams were going to win every tennis match they went in for. She would arrange extra coaching for the lower forms, and pick out any promising youngsters. And woe betide any slackers! Even people like Bonnie and Amy, who simply loathed games, would have to toe the line.

But there was no time to think about that now, for Miss James was speaking again, saying, 'Of course, it is a very big responsibility for one person alone, so Felicity and Susan will help you.'

Felicity and Susan exchanged excited glances, both

of them wishing for a moment that they were back in the first form so that they could let out a yell! Goodness, what a term this was going to be!

A clash of wills

'Well, what a morning it's been!' exclaimed Felicity, as the fifth formers went out into the fresh air at break-time. 'Pam head of the form, June head of games for the whole school, and Millicent has been given permission to get up an orchestra.'

'Where *is* Millicent?' asked Susan, looking round.

'Oh, she's gone off to write out a notice, so that people will get to know about the auditions she is holding,' said Nora. 'I must say she's awfully keen. How about you, June? I'm surprised that you haven't started making out lists of teams yet, or putting up notices about practice times.'

June laughed, and said, 'Well, I have a lot more to think about than Millicent. All she has to do is listen to people play, and decide whether they are good enough or not. After that, it is simply a matter of rehearsing. I have to arrange matches and practices, decide on players and reserves, coach people, and do my best to bring all the slackers up to scratch!'

'Well, thank goodness you have two willing helpers,' said Julie.

'Yes, I think the three of us will work together well,'

said June, grinning at Felicity and Susan. 'Perhaps we can put our heads together in the common-room later, and decide how we are going to go about this?'

Felicity and Susan nodded eagerly, then June turned to Gillian and said, 'If you are as good at tennis as you say, you might get a place on one of the teams. It's tennis next lesson, so I shall be watching you carefully.'

Not only did June get the opportunity to watch Gillian, she actually played against her. And she soon saw that the new girl was as good as her word, for Gillian was a marvellous player and very nearly beat June. And, for once, June didn't mind, for she was absolutely thrilled to have found someone who could play tennis so well.

'You're a certainty for the team!' said June, in the changing-room afterwards. 'Just make sure that you keep your practice up.'

'Heavens, I am in demand!' said Gillian, with a laugh. 'Millicent wants me to try out for her orchestra, and now you want me to play tennis.'

'What it is to be popular!' laughed Freddie. 'What are you going to do, Gillian?'

'Well, it's quite obvious that Gillian will choose to play tennis,' said June. 'Who wants to play in a stuffy orchestra, when they can be out in the fresh air.'

Unfortunately, Millicent overheard this, and said stiffly, 'There will be nothing stuffy about the Malory Towers orchestra, June. I simply can't imagine why Gillian would want to waste her time knocking a ball back and forth, when she could be using her talent for something worthwhile.'

June opened her mouth to retort, but Bonnie interrupted to say, 'Millicent, you haven't even heard Gillian play yet. You only have her word for it that she is any good.'

This was very true, and Millicent said, 'Well, there is a little spare time before lunch. Why don't you go and fetch your violin, Gillian, and you can play for us in the common-room now?'

So Gillian sped off to get her violin from the dormitory, while the others gathered expectantly in the common-room. When the new girl came back, she had loosened her long curls from the ribbon that had been tying them back, and when Freddie asked why, Gillian said, 'I always wear my hair loose when I play the violin. It makes me feel more artistic somehow.'

Then the girl placed the violin under her chin and began to play. And what a performance she gave! The fifth formers listened, enthralled, as Gillian played, her bow darting over the strings, her enjoyment clear, as beautiful music filled the room. It was quite clear that Gillian had not exaggerated at all, and was a first-class violinist. When she finished, the girls clapped and cheered like mad.

'Simply beautiful!'

'Top-hole! Gillian, you're a marvel.'

'Millicent, you simply must put her in the orchestra.'

'I shall,' said Millicent, pleased to have found someone so talented.

Only June said nothing. She, too, had been impressed by Gillian's playing, but she badly wanted the girl to be on one of the tennis teams, and she had no intention of allowing Millicent to steal her away.

'Well, Gillian, it looks as if you must make a choice,' said Pam.

'Yes, I suppose I must,' said Gillian, with a grimace. 'If you don't mind, June and Millicent, I should like to think about it for a while.'

'Well, don't think about it for too long,' said Millicent, rather coolly. 'I need to choose my orchestra, and lick it into shape. There is no time to waste.'

June, watching Millicent closely, decided that the girl was going to be a bit of a slave-driver, and could see that she ran the risk of making herself very unpopular with her orchestra if she pushed them too hard. She herself said pleasantly, 'Of course, Gillian, you take your time. There's no hurry for you to make up your mind, and I want you to be sure that you have made the right choice.'

The rest of the fifth form stared at June hard. They knew her very well indeed, and if June wanted something badly, she didn't give up without a fight.

When the fifth formers went into the dining-room for lunch, it seemed that word had got around that June was the new games captain, for many of the younger girls nudged one another and whispered as she walked by.

Hannah, of the second form, came up to her, and said shyly, 'Congratulations, June. We second formers are simply thrilled that you are our new games captain.'

'Thanks, kid,' said June, in her usual careless way, though she was secretly delighted and rather touched by this. 'You're Hannah, aren't you? I remember watching you play last year, when you were in the first form. I hope that you are going to try out for one of the teams this term, for you were pretty good.'

Hannah, so overwhelmed that she was quite unable to speak, merely nodded, before rushing back to her table to tell the second formers that the great June had asked her to try out for one of the teams.

Millicent, meanwhile, had watched the little by-play with a sour expression, and wondered if she would be able to inspire the same devotion in her orchestra.

She had certainly stirred people's interest, for many girls, from different forms and different towers, put their names on the list that she had pinned up, and Millicent decided to hold auditions on the first Saturday of the term.

Auditions were being held in the big hall, and the rest of the fifth formers went along to watch.

'There's nothing better to do,' said June, looking at the gloomy weather outside the window, and sighing. 'I had planned to hold tennis practice for the lower forms, but it's going to pour down any minute.'

The fifth formers had to sit right at the back of the hall, for it seemed that half of the school had decided that watching the auditions would be a pleasant way to while away a rainy afternoon.

Millicent stepped on to the stage, a list of names in her

hand, and she called out, 'Pam, would you like to sit at the piano and go first?'

Pulling a face at Nora, Pam walked to the front of the hall, where the piano stood, and sat down at it. She played a simple piece of music that she knew well, and, although she had intended to play a few wrong notes and spoil her chances of getting into the orchestra, found that she couldn't, as the music took hold of her. It was a pleasant performance, and the listening girls clapped, but Millicent merely said, 'Not bad. Hannah Dixon, you play the piano, don't you? Let's see if you can do any better.'

June, sitting next to Freddie, gasped as Hannah of the second form got up, and whispered, 'Millicent is doing this on purpose! She heard me telling Hannah that I wanted her to practise hard at her tennis, and this is her way of getting back at me. I bet you anything you like that she picks Hannah to be in her precious orchestra!'

'Yes, but you can't blame Millicent entirely,' Freddie whispered back. 'Hannah must have put her name on the list in the first place.'

'Not necessarily,' said June. 'Pam didn't put her name down, but Millicent badgered her into playing anyway.'

'Can whoever is whispering please be quiet?' said Millicent sharply. 'It really is very rude when Hannah is waiting to begin.'

Millicent knew very well that it was June who was whispering, but there was an unwritten rule among the fifth formers that they did not find fault with one another in front of the younger girls.

But although Millicent hadn't named her, June was annoyed. Really, Millicent would do well to remember that she was a new girl!

Hannah played very well indeed, and Millicent gave her a word of praise when she finished her piece.

'Very good,' she said. 'I shall certainly consider you as our pianist, Hannah, though I can't say anything definite until I have heard the others.'

Several more musicians took to the stage, playing a variety of instruments. One girl played the flute, another the trumpet, and yet another the cello. There were several more pianists, too, as well as four or five violinists. Then Gillian got up, holding her violin, and Millicent said, 'There is no need for you to audition, Gillian, for I heard you play the other day.'

'I know, but I am in a musical mood today, and felt like playing my violin anyway, so I thought that I would play the tune that I played in the common-room the other day.'

To everyone's surprise, Millicent smiled and said, 'Well, that will certainly be a treat for everyone. I know that tune, so if you don't mind, I will accompany you on the piano.'

'For all her boasting about what a wonderful musician she is, I've never heard Millicent play anything,' murmured Pam to Nora. 'Now we shall see how good she really is.'

As it turned out, Millicent was very good indeed. She and Gillian held the watching girls spellbound, and several of the younger girls found tears starting to their eyes, the music was so lovely. When they finished, everyone got to their feet and clapped so hard that Felicity thought they would raise the roof!

Even June had to admit grudgingly, 'She certainly plays the piano brilliantly. In fact, she is so brilliant that I wonder she doesn't give herself the job as pianist in her orchestra. Then she can leave Hannah out of it.'

The same thought occurred to Pam, but when she suggested it to Millicent after the auditions were over, the girl said, 'I can't, for I shall be conducting, you see. I learned how to do that at the music academy, and while we have several good pianists, I doubt if there is anyone here who knows how to conduct.'

This was very true, so it seemed that one of the girls who had auditioned would have to become the orchestra pianist. Pam felt quite confident that she would not be chosen, for she had been outshone by several other girls, including young Hannah.

Seeing Millicent hunched up over a table in the common-room that evening, busily writing some kind of list, Felicity called out, 'Have you decided who is to be in the orchestra yet, Millicent?'

'I have decided on several people, but there are one or two that I haven't quite made up my mind about,' said the girl. 'I am going to decide by tomorrow, then we shall be able to call the first rehearsal. Gillian, you are in – if you want to be. But you really must let me know by tomorrow.'

'Have you decided what piece you are going to play?' asked Susan, looking up from the book she was reading.

'Yes, I am going to teach the girls a composition of my own,' answered Millicent, sounding rather smug. 'I wrote it last term at the music academy, and my teachers there thought that it was quite outstanding.'

Then Millicent spotted June looking at her with dislike, and said, 'What bad luck that you couldn't hold your tennis practice earlier, June. That's the beauty of music, you see. No matter what the weather, one can still play.'

June bit back a sharp retort, made her expression perfectly bland, and said airily, 'It doesn't matter. The weather will improve soon, and then my tennis practices will go ahead. The youngsters do so enjoy spending as much time as possible in the fresh air during the summer months.'

As it happened, the weather cleared the very next day, and the girls awoke to bright sunshine. Immediately after breakfast, June put a notice on the board to say that she would be holding tennis practice for the lower school at two o'clock. And, when the time came, she, Felicity and Susan were delighted to see that there was a good turn out.

The lower school had always looked up to June, admiring her boldness, her outspoken manner, and her reputation for playing tricks. Now that she was their games captain, many of them almost worshipped her.

Hannah was there, and June greeted her with a smile,

saying, 'I'm glad to see you here, Hannah. When I saw you playing the piano for Millicent yesterday, I was afraid that you might have decided to join the orchestra instead of playing tennis for the school.'

'Well, I put my name on Millicent's list as soon as she pinned it up, and that was before you told me that I might have a chance of getting on to the team, June.' Hannah looked up at the bigger girl and said, 'Of course, I would much rather play tennis, if you think that I am good enough, and if Millicent does want me for her orchestra I am going to say no.'

June was delighted to hear this, and she gave Hannah a clap on the shoulder.

As the second former walked away to take her place on the court, Felicity came up to June, and said, 'You look pleased with yourself.'

'I am,' said June. 'Hannah has told me that she would rather play tennis than be in Millicent's orchestra.'

'I see,' said Felicity. 'And are you pleased because you have a good player for the lower-school team, or because you have got one over on Millicent?'

June laughed, and said, 'Both. Don't worry, Felicity, I know what you're thinking, and I don't intend to let my dislike of Millicent interfere with any decisions I make as games captain. Believe it or not, I am taking my responsibilities very seriously.'

Felicity was pleased to hear this, and she and Susan felt heartened to see June taking so much trouble over the youngsters. June gave a word of praise here, and criticised there. But, Felicity noticed, whenever June made a criticism, she always told the girl she was talking to how to put matters right.

'Who would have thought it!' said Susan, as she watched June showing a little first former how to serve. 'Perhaps June is mellowing in her old age.'

'I think the fact that these kids look up to her no end helps,' said Felicity. 'They really do adore her, and June is basking in it. I just hope that she doesn't get a swollen head!'

'I don't think that she will,' said Susan. 'June is too downright to let all this hero-worship go to her head. My word, some of these kids are jolly good! Look at little Maggie there. She might be tiny, but she's jolly fierce.'

June came over to them then, a smile on her face as she said, 'Some promising players out there, don't you think?'

'That's exactly what I was just saying,' said Susan. 'We certainly have plenty of talent to choose from when it comes to the lower-school team.'

'We should do well with the upper-school team as well,' said June. 'You two will be playing, of course.'

Both girls gasped and looked at one another with shining eyes, then Felicity said, 'June, you don't have to put us in the team simply because we are helping you with your games captain's duties, you know.'

'I'm not,' said June. 'I'm choosing you because you happen to be two of the best players in the school.'

'Thanks!' said Susan, quite taken aback at this unexpected praise from June.

'I desperately want Gillian, too,' said June, her eyes narrowing. 'I shall be so disappointed if she takes up Millicent's offer of a place in the orchestra instead. I wonder if she has made her mind up yet?'

Gillian had, and she announced her decision in the common-room that very evening.

'June,' she said. 'I have decided that I would like to take up your offer of a place on the upper-school team.'

June's face lit up and she was quite unable to help shooting a look of triumph at Millicent, who looked as glum as could be.

But Gillian hadn't finished, for she went on, 'And Millicent, I should also like to play the violin in your orchestra, if I may.'

Everyone looked most surprised, and it was left to Pam, as head of the form, to say, 'But Gillian, you can't possibly do both! Why, you'll wear yourself out completely and you won't be able to concentrate on your lessons.'

'But I am being offered the chance to have fun doing the two things that I love most, so how can I possibly choose one over the other?' said Gillian. 'Don't worry about me, Pam, for I shall be perfectly fine.'

'I hope so,' said Pam, sounding extremely doubtful. 'But if it becomes too much for you, Gillian, you will simply have to give one up.'

June glanced across at Millicent, and their eyes met in a hostile look. June was thinking that if Gillian was going to give anything up it would be the violin. And Millicent was thinking that if Gillian had to eventually make a choice, she was determined that the girl was going to choose her orchestra!

An interesting rehearsal

What with one thing and another, life was very busy at Malory Towers. Millicent had chosen the girls who were to be in her orchestra, and had given them all copies of the piece of music she had written.

She had asked Hannah to be the pianist, but, feeling a little nervous, Hannah had said haltingly, 'I feel very honoured that you have asked me, Millicent, but I have decided to work hard at my tennis for June, instead.'

Millicent had looked at Hannah so coldly that the second former's knees shook, and she feared that she was about to get a scold. But Millicent merely said, 'Very well, Hannah, if that is your decision. I hope that you have made the right choice.'

Then she had gone off to find Anne, a fifth former from South Tower, and asked her if she would like to play the piano instead. Anne had been absolutely thrilled, and so grateful for the opportunity that Millicent cheered up a bit. And she was further gratified when she walked by the little music rooms that the girls used for practising in, and heard her own composition being played. All of the musicians were working very hard indeed, and Millicent really didn't see how Malory

Towers could fail to win the competition.

Delia came along the corridor as Millicent stood outside one of the music-rooms, listening to Anne rehearsing her piano solo, and she said, 'Is that the music that you wrote, Millicent? My word, you really do have a gift. How I envy you. All everyone seems to talk about at the moment is tennis, or the orchestra, but I can't contribute anything because I'm hopeless at games and no good at music. Why, when I sing at home, my aunt says it sounds like a cat yowling.'

Millicent wasn't much given to considering anyone else's feelings, but there was something so wistful in Delia's tone that she felt rather touched, and said kindly, 'Well, there are other ways you could be involved, you know, Delia. I could certainly do with someone to assist me at rehearsals, to make notes and so on.'

'Really?' said Delia, her face lighting up. 'Would you trust me to do that, Millicent?'

'Of course,' said Millicent. 'Now listen, Delia, the first rehearsal is on Tuesday, after tea, in the hall. So just you come along and I'm sure that I will find plenty for you to do.'

Delia nodded eagerly, and both girls went their separate ways, Delia thrilled to think that she was going to play a part in the orchestra's success, and Millicent feeling that she had done something very good and virtuous.

June, somewhat to her own surprise, was thoroughly enjoying coaching the youngsters at tennis. The upper school were more of a challenge, however, and in the end she abandoned her plans to make people like Amy and Bonnie attend regular practices.

'I really don't know why you bother,' said Felicity, one day, after watching a long and fruitless argument between June and Bonnie, which had ended with the latter flatly refusing to come to practice. 'You are never going to make a tennis player out of Bonnie, or Amy, for that matter, so you may as well give up.'

But June was extremely stubborn when she had set her mind to something, and continued to badger Amy and Bonnie.

'She's so persistent!' Amy complained. 'Honestly, Bonnie, sometimes I feel like giving up and going to her wretched tennis practice just so that she will leave me alone.'

But Bonnie could be stubborn too, and she shook her head, saying, 'We mustn't give in to June, or she will become even worse. I shall come up with a plan to make her leave us alone.'

In fact it was June herself who gave Bonnie an idea. She had been inspecting the white tennis dresses that the Malory Towers girls wore when they played matches against other schools, and discovered that some of them were very shabby indeed.

'Hems coming down, pockets ripped and holes in seams,' she complained in the common-room one evening. 'I can't send our teams off to play in those! We'll be a laughing stock!'

Bonnie, who had been listening intently, approached

June later, and said, 'I want to make a bargain with you. I will repair all of the tennis dresses and make them as good as new.'

June's eyes lit up, and she said, 'Would you really do that? Bonnie, you're an angel.'

'Yes, but I want something in return,' said Bonnie, before June got too carried away. 'You are to leave Amy and me alone, and not try to get us to play tennis.'

June looked down into Bonnie's sweet little face, and gave a reluctant laugh. 'You can be every bit as determined as me when you want something, can't you?' she said. 'Or when you want to get *out* of something! Well, it really would be a help to me if you would mend the dresses, Bonnie. I suppose, in your way, you will be doing your bit for the team.'

So the bargain was struck, and Bonnie, sticking to her side of it, began work on the dresses at once. Not only did she repair hems and mend seams, with her neat, tiny stitches, but she painstakingly embroidered the initials M and T, for Malory Towers, on the pocket of each dress, in deep orange.

June was thrilled, and cried, 'Bonnie, you're marvellous! Our players will look as neat as new pins now, and I shall be proud to watch them play.'

Bonnie accepted the praise graciously, but really she had thoroughly enjoyed working on the dresses, for needlework was her favourite pastime.

Millicent, who had felt extremely jealous of the smart tennis dresses that June's teams would be wearing, overheard this. All of the orchestras in the competition would be wearing their school uniforms, but Millicent had been trying to think of something that would make the Malory Towers girls stand out. Now she had a sudden brainwave, and she turned to Bonnie, saying, 'I have a project for you, Bonnie, if you're willing.'

'What is it?' asked Bonnie curiously.

'Well,' said Millicent. 'It occurred to me that it would be nice if each member of our orchestra had a pennant to hang from her music stand. Perhaps –'

'Yes,' interrupted Bonnie excitedly, her creative mind grasping the idea at once. 'I see exactly how they should look! Triangular pennants made from orange fabric, with the letters M and T embroidered in brown, so that the colours match the school uniform. How does that sound, Millicent?'

'That sounds super!' said Millicent, who hadn't got as far as thinking about the colours. 'Bonnie, would you be able to do that? If you can, I shall owe you a favour.'

Of course, Bonnie was only too pleased to help out, for she was thrilled to have a new project to work on, and she always liked being in a position where someone owed her a favour.

So Bonnie felt as if she was really doing rather a lot to help both June and Millicent. Alas for poor Delia, however; her efforts to assist Millicent did not get off to a good start.

The orchestra held their first proper rehearsal together in the big hall, and Delia made sure that all the music stands had a copy of Millicent's score there, ready and waiting.

'Thank you, Delia,' said Millicent, as she led the orchestra into the hall. 'Now, what I would like you to do is sit at the side there, and jot down any comments and suggestions I make in a notebook. Later I shall be able to read them back and make any improvements that are needed to the score. See?'

Delia nodded eagerly, and took her seat, notebook and pen at the ready.

Millicent stood in front of the orchestra, baton in hand and conducted. But, when the music stopped, she had a great many criticisms to make, for this was the first time that the orchestra had played together, and, naturally, mistakes were made. Delia was most assiduous in recording all of Millicent's remarks.

'Anne!' said Millicent sharply. 'You played two wrong notes in your solo. You really must try to do better! And Janet, you came in far too late. A mistake like that could cost us the competition. As for the violins, it was simply dreadful! Gillian was the only one of you who played perfectly. I suggest that you all spend some time rehearsing together.'

The girls knew only too well that they had made mistakes, but they rather resented Millicent's high-handed attitude.

'I don't mind having my mistakes pointed out,' muttered Janet. 'But she could be a little more polite and pleasant about it.'

Helen, one of the violinists, nodded in agreement and whispered, 'I do think she's awfully hard on us. After all, it is the first time that we have all played together. She can't expect us to be perfect!'

But it seemed that this was exactly what Millicent did expect. She made Anne play her piano solo again, and when the girl played the same two wrong notes, Millicent scolded her so harshly that she was almost reduced to tears.

'What a pity that Hannah didn't want to be pianist,' Millicent remarked scathingly. 'At least she would have taken the trouble to learn the music before turning up for rehearsal.'

Anne, who hadn't realised that Hannah had been first choice, felt very upset indeed.

For a moment she considered walking off, but she so badly wanted to be a part of the orchestra, and had already written to her parents about it. So poor Anne swallowed her pride, and stayed where she was.

But many of the others sent silent glances of sympathy Anne's way, and glared at Millicent. Unfortunately for them, Millicent, who could be very thick-skinned at times, didn't even notice.

When the orchestra played the piece for the second time, it sounded much better, to Delia's untrained ear. Quite beautiful, in fact. Millicent did not agree, and continued to criticise and suggest improvements, but Delia, who had become quite lost in the music, completely forgot to write them down. The piece that Millicent had composed was called 'Summer Serenade' and, as she listened, Delia thought that it really did capture the essence of summer perfectly, making her think of picnics, and walks along the beach.

Quite suddenly, words began to form in her head, that fitted in with the music, and, turning hastily to the back of the notebook Delia began to jot them down. Millicent, glancing across, saw the girl scribbling away, and felt satisfied that the was doing her job properly.

But Delia's sudden burst of creativity ended, and she closed the notebook as Millicent lowered her baton and spoke to the orchestra.

'Better, but not good enough!' she said, a stern expression on her face. 'I expect you all to practise until you are perfect before the next rehearsal.'

The only person who came in for unstinted praise was Gillian, and Janet remarked rather bitterly, 'Of course, the two of them are in the same form and the same tower, so Millicent is bound to favour her. I expect that the two of them are friends.'

In fact, Gillian had decided that she didn't like Millicent much at all. She thought the girl high-handed and rather humourless, and hadn't cared for some of the unkind remarks that she had made to the others.

She really doesn't know how to get the best out of people, thought Gillian, as she put her violin away. All that Millicent has done is make everyone feel terribly nervous, for now we all know that we are in for a tongue lashing if we make a mistake.

Delia, who had remained behind to collect the scores that had been left on the music stands, went across to Gillian and said a little shyly, 'You played awfully well, Gillian.'

Gillian smiled. She liked the rather sweet-natured, awkward Delia. 'Thank you,' she said. 'Though I can't help wishing that Millicent had praised some of the others as much as she praised me. I have a feeling that her sharp tongue is going to cause problems.'

'I think that she just wants everything to be perfect,' said Delia. 'She has her heart set on winning this competition, you know, and I suppose that she feels a lot rests on her shoulders, as she wrote the music as well.'

'I daresay you're right,' said Gillian. 'But I do wish that she wasn't quite so intense and serious.'

Delia was quite right about Millicent. She wanted desperately to lead Malory Towers to victory in the orchestra competition, and if they could win playing her very own composition, it would be a huge feather in her cap.

But some of the players simply weren't up to scratch, and it was up to her, Millicent, to see that they improved. She went up to Delia in the common-room that evening, and said, 'I say, Delia, do you have that notebook? I intend to go through it this evening, so that I can see where all the weak spots are.'

Delia handed over the notebook, but Millicent wasn't able to read it that evening, after all, for Matron put her head round the door and cried, 'Millicent Moon! I have a pile of your mending here, which needs to be unpicked and done again.'

Millicent, who didn't like mending at all, turned red and said, 'Sorry, Matron. I'm not very good at sewing, and I'm afraid I rushed it, rather.'

'Well, you will do it again this evening,' said Matron, sternly. 'And this time, Millicent, please do it carefully, for I shall inspect it tomorrow.'

With that, Matron handed Millicent the pile of mending, and shut the door behind her.

Millicent scowled. Blow Matron! She had so wanted to go through that notebook tonight. She wondered if Bonnie could be persuaded to do the mending for her, and glanced across at the girl. But Bonnie was busily engaged in embroidering one of the pennants for the orchestra, and Millicent decided that was far more important than her mending.

'How I hate sewing!' she said aloud, hoping that one of the girls would take pity on her and offer to do it for her. But no one did, for they had all noticed that Millicent often used the excuse of being a musical genius to get out of doing other, more mundane tasks.

Delia wondered if she should offer, though sewing wasn't one of her talents, and she opened her mouth to speak. But Pam caught her eye and gave a small shake of the head, and Delia subsided.

'Well, Millicent,' said Felicity, who was doing a jigsaw with Susan. 'It rather looks as if you are going to have to do your own mending, doesn't it?'

'We never had to do our own mending at the music academy,' said Millicent crossly, getting out her work-basket. 'It is such a waste of time, when I could be working on my piece for the competition.'

'You're getting far too wrapped up in this competition, if you ask me,' said Pam. 'And the mistresses are starting to notice it too. I overheard Miss James telling Miss Potts that she is not very pleased with you, for you don't pay attention in class.'

'Be careful, Millicent,' warned June. 'If Miss Grayling thinks that your involvement with the orchestra is affecting your class-work, she may change her mind and make you pull out.'

Millicent was quite horrified at that thought. She would have to be very careful indeed, and at least try to *look* as if she was paying attention in class.

Yet the very next second, she decided that she would take the notebook into French with her tomorrow, and slip it inside the pages of the book that the form was reading with Mam'zelle Dupont. Mam'zelle was so easy to fool that she would never spot a thing!

Millicent in trouble

Mam'zelle Dupont was in a good mood when she walked into the fifth-form classroom the following morning. She had had a good night's sleep and felt well rested, the sun was shining, and she liked these fifth formers. They were good, hard-working girls, even June, who had been such a bad girl when she was lower down the school.

Nora, one of Mam'zelle's favourites, was holding the door open for her, and the French mistress smiled, and said, '*Merci*, Nora. *Asseyez-vous, s'il vous plait.*'

The fifth formers took their seats, and Mam'zelle beamed round, saying, 'Please open your books, and we will continue reading this so-excellent story. *Ma chère* Felicity, you will begin please.'

As Felicity began reading, Millicent opened her book, into which she had already slipped the notebook. The girl was soon lost in her world of music as she began to read the notes that Delia had written, in her large, untidy handwriting, and she was able to shut out everything around her.

Gillian, who sat beside Millicent, saw what the girl was doing, and thought her very silly indeed. Millicent was going to get into serious trouble if she wasn't careful.

But Gillian couldn't very well say anything to her without attracting unwelcome attention from Mam'zelle.

So Millicent remained engrossed in her music, while the rest of the class read the French book, and no one but Gillian noticed a thing. Until Mam'zelle said, 'Millicent, you will read now, please.'

Of course, Millicent didn't even hear Mam'zelle, not even when the French mistress repeated her instruction. The rest of the fifth formers looked at one another, puzzled, and Gillian gave Millicent a nudge. Then, to her amazement, and the amazement of everyone else in the room, Millicent suddenly let out a roar.

Gillian was extremely startled, for she had barely touched the girl. But it seemed that Millicent's anger was not directed at her, for the girl stood up and yelled, 'Delia, you idiot! What on earth has happened to the notes that you were supposed to be making? You have only written down the remarks that I made after the first run-through, then there is nothing!'

The fifth formers stared at Millicent in astonishment, while poor Delia looked most taken aback. But the most surprised person in the class was Mam'zelle herself, who simply couldn't believe her ears.

Mam'zelle did not care for Millicent, for the girl paid scant attention in class, and acted as if French did not matter – as if nothing mattered, in fact, except her music. And now she dared to disrupt the class with this outburst of temper. Mam'zelle's good mood suddenly vanished, and she cried angrily, 'How dare you behave like this in my class, Millicent!'

Millicent continued to ignore Mam'zelle, who was growing redder and angrier by the second, and carried on with her tirade at Delia, whose knees were now shaking.

The fifth formers had no idea what was the matter with Millicent, whom they thought had gone quite mad, but as the girl was taking no notice at all of Mam'zelle, Pam took a hand in the affair.

She walked across to Millicent and took the girl firmly by the arm, saying sharply, 'Millicent, control yourself at once! You are behaving like a first former, and if you are not careful Mam'zelle will send you to Miss Grayling. Do behave, for heaven's sake.'

The threat of being sent to the Head seemed to snap Millicent out of her rage, for she blinked suddenly and fell silent.

Mam'zelle, taking advantage of the sudden silence, stepped towards her and said, '*Vous êtes insupportable*, Millicent! *Méchante fille!* You will be punished for this extraordinary behaviour.'

'I beg your pardon, Mam'zelle,' gasped Millicent, afraid now, and deciding that the wisest course of action was to apologise profusely to the angry French mistress. 'I simply don't know what came over me.'

Mam'zelle was moving closer, and, in horror, Millicent glanced down at the French book on her desk. If the French mistress spotted the notebook there, she would certainly be sent to the Head, and all her dreams of winning the competition would be shattered. But the notebook was gone! For quick-thinking Gillian, seeing disaster looming for Millicent, had quickly snatched the notebook away as Mam'zelle approached, and hidden it in her satchel. She had no way of informing Millicent of this, though, for Mam'zelle was scolding the girl roundly, in a mixture of French and English, and all that Millicent could do was hang her head and hope that her punishment would not be too severe.

The others watched in fascination, torn between guilty enjoyment at seeing Millicent get into a row, and embarrassment that a fifth former should have behaved in such a way. Had they been in the first or second form, this would have been a very exciting interlude in their day, but as fifth formers they felt slightly ashamed of Millicent. Only June, who saw Millicent as a rival, watched with unalloyed glee, though she would not have admitted this to the others, and made her expression perfectly grave.

At last Mam'zelle seemed to run out of steam, and came to a halt, her chest heaving as she glared angrily at Millicent.

Once again Gillian nudged her, hissing, 'Apologise again, ass! It's your only chance of staying out of trouble.'

Millicent did so, in a very meek manner, stammering slightly and with downcast eyes, and when she peeped at Mam'zelle through her eyelashes, she was relieved to see that the French mistress looked a little calmer.

But Mam'zelle still felt angry with Millicent for her extraordinary outburst, and could not let it pass.

'You will stay behind at break-time, and I shall give you a punishment,' said Mam'zelle sternly. 'And think yourself lucky, Millicent, that I do not send you to Miss Grayling!'

Millicent *did* consider herself lucky, and heaved a sigh of relief. Mam'zelle would be sure to dish out some perfectly horrid punishment, but if she had sent Millicent to the Head it might have ended with her having to pull out of the competition.

At break-time, everyone but Millicent went out into the fresh air, and the fifth formers clustered round Delia.

'What on earth was that all about?' asked Felicity, curiously. 'Millicent seemed angry with *you*, Delia, but I can't think why!'

'I was supposed to note down all her remarks during the last rehearsal,' explained Delia, rather dolefully. 'But halfway through I sort of lost myself in the music and completely forgot to write anything down.'

Delia didn't say that she had been busily jotting down her own words to set to the music, for she felt certain that the others would laugh at her. She felt hot as it suddenly occurred to her that Millicent might find the silly little rhyme written in the back of the notebook, and she made up her mind that she must get hold of it and tear the page out. Millicent had a sharp tongue, and would probably make fun of her. Of course, Delia didn't know that the notebook was now in Gillian's possession.

'Well, anyone can make a mistake,' said Susan, giving Delia a pat on the shoulder. 'Cheer up! Millicent is the one at fault, for she should not have shouted at you like that in front of everyone.'

'And she shouldn't have been reading that notebook in the French lesson,' said Pam, disapprovingly. 'I shall be having words with dear Millicent later.'

Millicent found that the fifth formers were rather cool towards her for the rest of the day, but simply couldn't understand why. The orchestra and the competition were all important to her, and, although she could have kicked herself for letting her anger getting the better of her in class, she really didn't see that there was anything wrong in her treatment of Delia. The girl had made a terrible mistake, and, in Millicent's view, she had thoroughly earned a good scolding.

Pam spoke to her in the common-room that evening, saying rather scornfully, 'Not the kind of behaviour one expects from a fifth former, Millicent. It is quite bad enough that you were working on your music, instead of concentrating on your French, but that little outburst of yours was simply disgraceful.'

Millicent turned red, and, becoming defensive, said, 'I don't see that there is any need for you to tick me off in front of the whole form, Pam.'

'Well, you yelled at Delia in front of all of us,' said Pam, quite reasonably. 'I really don't see the difference. And I think that you owe her an apology.'

'I shan't apologise!' said Millicent, growing even redder. 'Delia is an idiot.'

Bonnie, standing next to Delia, saw that the girl

looked close to tears, and pursed her lips. Suddenly she went across to her work-basket and picked up the pennants she had been working on. She had completed two, but the others were half-finished, and she walked across to Millicent, thrusting them at her.

'Here you are!' she said. 'You can finish them off yourself.'

Millicent looked simply flabbergasted, her mouth opening and closing, and she stammered, 'But, Bonnie, I can't sew! You know that I can't! You promised that you would do this for me.'

'Well, I've changed my mind,' said Bonnie, her little nose wrinkling in distaste. 'I don't like the way that you spoke to Delia, and I don't like you!'

Millicent, who had always thought of Bonnie as a rather weak, childish character, looked most taken aback, while the others watched with grins on their faces. They knew that Bonnie had a very obstinate streak in her nature, and unless Millicent made amends she would not back down.

Millicent looked at the faces around her, some of them scornful, some of them grinning at her discomfort. Gillian was looking at her as if she didn't like her very much at all, while June had a triumphant little smirk on her face. Suddenly Millicent realised that, if she refused to apologise to Delia, Gillian could decide to leave the orchestra altogether, and she would lose her best violinist. If she made the apology sound sincere enough, perhaps Bonnie would also reconsider, and finish making the pennants.

So Millicent swallowed her pride, and, trying to sound as sincere as possible, said, 'You are all absolutely right, I have been very unfair to Delia. I so badly want the orchestra to perform perfectly that I sometimes get carried away.'

Then she stepped towards Delia, holding out her hand, and said, 'Please accept my apology, Delia, old girl.'

Delia, who bore no malice and just felt relieved to be forgiven, seized Millicent's hand at once, and said, 'Of course I accept your apology, Millicent. And I hope that you will accept mine for being so stupid and forgetful during rehearsal.'

'What an ass Delia is!' whispered June to Freddie. 'It won't hurt Millicent to humble herself for once, and admit that she is in the wrong. But Delia has to go and apologise too and spoil it!'

Millicent, although she didn't feel like it at all, smiled brightly, then looked round at the others, saying contritely, 'I am sorry that my behaviour in Mam'zelle's class disgraced the form. You may be sure that it won't happen again.'

'Apology accepted,' said Pam. 'Now let's say no more about it.'

So the fifth formers went back to their various activities, and Bonnie took back the pile of sewing, which Millicent had placed on a chair.

'As you have apologised to Delia, I shall carry on making the pennants,' she said graciously. 'But my services are only on loan to you, Millicent, and a repeat of such behaviour means that I shall refuse to carry on sewing the pennants. And next time I shan't give you another chance.'

Chastened, Millicent went and sat alone in a corner, to read the French poem that Mam'zelle had given her as a punishment. She would much rather have been working at her music, but Millicent was well aware that she had had a lucky escape today, and didn't want to push Mam'zelle too far, in case she sent her to the Head.

Rather reluctantly, the girl decided that she had better start to pay attention in class, for she needed to devote all of her free time to the orchestra. And if she kept earning beastly punishments like this, she wouldn't *have* any free time.

'Gillian!' June called out suddenly. 'I'm organising a tennis practice for the fifth and sixth formers on Saturday afternoon. You'll come, won't you?'

'You bet!' answered Gillian, with enthusiasm.

The others often marvelled at Gillian's seemingly boundless energy, for she managed to fit in her orchestra rehearsals and tennis practice – not to mention lessons and prep – without feeling at all worn out.

'I don't know how you do it!' Nora said to her now. 'Honestly, Gillian, it makes me tired just to look at you sometimes.'

'That's because you're lazy,' June teased. 'But Gillian knows that good, hard practice brings rewards. Freddie, I want you there on Saturday, too, my girl. And you two, Felicity and Susan.'

Millicent looked up from her poem, a frown on her face, and said, 'Just a minute! June, Gillian can't possibly play tennis on Saturday afternoon, for I was planning to schedule another orchestra rehearsal then.'

'Hard luck,' said June, with an unsympathetic shrug. 'I got in first, so I'm afraid there's not an awful lot you can do about it.'

Millicent felt her temper rising, but, as she was already in the fifth form's bad books, she tried to speak calmly, saying, 'Gillian can play tennis at any time, but I don't have many opportunities to get the orchestra together as a whole.'

'My dear Millicent, I'm afraid that really isn't my problem,' said June coolly. 'If Gillian wishes to be on one of the teams, which she assures me she does, it is vital that she attends practice so that I can compare her standard of play with the others.'

Millicent's air of calm was fast deserting her, but at that moment Julie interrupted, to say, 'I shouldn't bother arguing about it, Millicent, for the sixth form has already booked the hall on Saturday afternoon. They are holding some sort of debate.'

'Well, that would seem to settle that, then!' said June, quite unable to keep the note of triumph out of her voice. She added kindly, 'Never mind, Millicent, perhaps you can book the hall for Sunday, instead.'

Scowling angrily at June, Millicent flung down her book, her good intentions of learning the French poem vanishing. The orchestra simply *had* to rehearse this weekend, especially after their poor showing yesterday, and all that mattered to her now was that she booked the hall for Sunday afternoon.

'Well!' said Susan, as Millicent rushed out of the room. 'It seems as if you are in for a jolly busy weekend, Gillian. What with tennis on Saturday and music on Sunday!'

'I shall have no free time at all,' Gillian realised suddenly. 'I wanted to do some shopping, for I need some new shoelaces, and I so wanted to buy some chocolate, but I shan't have time now. And I wanted to write some letters to my family and friends at home, too.'

'Well, Gillian,' said Nora. 'I can't help you with your letters, I'm afraid, but Pam and I are planning on going into the town on Saturday, so we can easily get you the things you want.'

'Thanks,' said Gillian gratefully. 'That's most awfully kind of you.'

But she had been looking forward to visiting the little shops in town herself. And it still didn't solve the problem of how she was to find the time to write her letters home. For the first time, Gillian began to wonder if she had bitten off more than she could chew!

The missing notebook

Saturday was a blisteringly hot day, and those fifth formers who were taking part in the tennis practice groaned.

'We shall all be like limp rags by the time we are finished,' complained Freddie.

But June wasn't to be deterred, and said, 'I'll ask Cook if we can have some jugs of lemonade to take down to the courts with us. That will refresh us in between games.'

So at two o'clock sharp, the girls trooped down to the tennis courts to begin their practice. Felicity and Susan played doubles against Gillian and Freddie, which June watched with a critical eye, before going off to play singles with one of the sixth formers.

Freddie wasn't quite as good a player as Felicity or Susan, for her tennis could be a little erratic. But Gillian more than made up for her faults, running all over the court and chasing every ball. Despite their best efforts, Felicity and Susan were beaten, and, afterwards, the four girls sat on the grass drinking lemonade as they watched June playing the sixth-form girl. The big sixth former was obviously suffering from the heat and tiring badly, but June looked as cool as a cucumber, her movements agile and nimble.

'June's jolly good, isn't she?' remarked Gillian. 'It's no wonder that she was made games captain, for she is so strong and determined.'

'You're not so bad yourself,' said Felicity. 'I think that you and June are pretty evenly matched.'

'I seem to tire more easily than June,' said Gillian, whose normally pale complexion had turned pink from the heat. 'I felt full of beans when we began playing, but by the end I felt as if I had been run ragged.'

'Well, I'm not surprised,' said Freddie, sipping her lemonade. 'I was off my game today, and you had to make up for me.'

'Are you sure that you aren't overdoing things, Gillian?' asked Susan, concerned. 'You've taken an awful lot on, agreeing to be part of the orchestra *and* a member of the tennis team.'

'I shall be fine,' said Gillian, putting a hand to her mouth to stifle a yawn. 'It's just that the heat has exhausted me today. I said that I could do both, and I intend to stick by my word.'

June, coming off court after running rings around the sixth-form girl, joined the others on the grass and poured herself a glass of lemonade.

'Just what I needed,' she said, after taking a long gulp. 'Gillian, you played marvellously, and I have decided that you, Elsie Horton of the sixth and me are going to be our singles players for the upper-school team against Summerfield Hall. Felicity and Susan, I would like you to play doubles. And Freddie ...'

'Don't tell me,' said Freddie, with an air of gloom. 'I'm the reserve.'

'Sorry, old thing,' said June, giving her a wry smile. 'But, as games captain, I simply must pick the best players. You don't really mind, do you?'

Freddie didn't, for although she would have loved a place on the team, she knew only too well that her play was erratic, and June would have been a poor captain if she had chosen the girl over better players, simply because she was her friend.

'Of course not,' she said. 'At least I get a day out and a ride on the team bus, if we are playing at another school.'

Satisfied that Freddie was not upset, June was in a very good mood indeed. She now had just the team she wanted, as far as the upper school was concerned, and she had a very good idea who she was going to pick for the lower-school team too. Everything was falling neatly into place!

Millicent, meanwhile, was far from happy, for she had lost her notebook. The girl still did not realise that Gillian had picked it up, and had assumed that it must have fallen into her open satchel while she was distracted by Mam'zelle. But Millicent had turned out her satchel and it was nowhere to be seen.

Millicent had searched through her desk, and looked in the common-room, too, but the book seemed to have vanished into thin air. Scratching her head, Millicent decided that she might as well give up, for she was never going to find the notebook. Perhaps it was just as well that Delia hadn't made many notes, after all, for they would have been lost. Millicent made up her mind that she would get a new notebook, and this time she would jot down her own notes, instead of trusting the job to that foolish Delia.

Someone else who wanted to get hold of the notebook was Delia, for the girl didn't want Millicent spotting her 'silly little rhyme', as she thought of it, and making fun of it, perhaps in front of the others.

So, quite unaware that the book was in Gillian's possession, Delia thought that Millicent still had it, and went in search of it.

She passed Millicent on her way to the common-room, and noticed that the girl was carrying her purse, but didn't have her satchel with her. Delia's heart leapt. Was it possible that Millicent had left her bag unattended in the common-room?

Millicent had, and, what was more, no one was about, for most of the girls were outside enjoying the fine day.

The bag was on an armchair, and Delia bent over it, looking over her shoulder every so often, as she rifled through it. The girl had no intention of stealing the book, for all that she wanted was to tear out that one page.

But her search was fruitless, and, just as she was fastening the satchel up again, Delia heard a noise behind her, and turned to see Julie and Lucy in the doorway. Both girls had just been enjoying a ride, and they were looking forward to a quiet sit-down now.

'Hello, Delia,' said Lucy. Then she frowned. 'Isn't that Millicent's bag?'

Delia wasn't noted for her quick thinking, and she flushed and stammered, as she said, 'Er – yes, that's right. I – I noticed that it had come undone, and thought that something might fall out.'

And, with that, she pushed past the two girls and made her way down the corridor, her face a fiery red.

'Well!' said Julie, astonished. 'What do you make of that?'

'Delia certainly seemed flustered, didn't she?' said Lucy. 'I say, Julie, you don't think that she was up to no good, do you?'

'Stealing, you mean?' gasped Julie. 'Surely not! Why, Delia has always seemed a very decent sort to me.'

'Yes, to me, too,' said Lucy. 'But you can't deny that her behaviour was awfully suspicious.'

'I suppose it was,' said Julie, biting her lip. 'But here comes Millicent. She will be able to tell us if anything is missing from her bag. I say, Millicent! Have a look in your bag, and tell us if anything has been taken.'

Startled, Millicent said, 'Why? What has happened?'

'Well, we caught someone messing around with it,' said Lucy. 'So you had better check it.'

'Well, if anyone was after anything in my satchel, I suppose it would be my purse,' said Millicent. 'And I had that with me, for I had just been to ask Pam and Nora if they could get me a notebook while they were in town. Still, I suppose I had better make sure nothing is missing.'

Quickly, Millicent opened the bag and went through it. At last, she said, 'No, everything is here. The only thing I can't find is my notebook, but that went missing several days ago. That's why I asked Pam and Nora to get me a new one.'

Julie and Lucy both felt very relieved, until Millicent asked, 'Who was the girl that you caught meddling with it?'

The two girls exchanged glances. Neither of them wanted to mention Delia's name, especially as it looked as if she hadn't taken anything, after all, so Julie said, 'I didn't get a good look at her, did you, Lucy? She ran out past us as soon as she knew we had spotted her.'

'That's right,' said Lucy. 'She looked as if she could have been a first or second former.'

'Well, of all the nerve!' gasped Millicent. 'The cheek of those kids! Well, I'll jolly well make sure I don't leave my satchel lying around again.'

'Phew!' said Lucy, flopping down into a chair, as Millicent went out again. 'That was close. Thank goodness we found out that Delia wasn't trying to take anything, after all.'

'Well, we can't be too sure about that, Lucy,' said Julie, looking thoughtful. 'Perhaps she was after Millicent's purse. But Millicent had the purse with her, so if Delia *is* a thief, it may be that she was just out of luck.'

Gillian was quite unaware of all the drama that was taking place surrounding the notebook. The girl had completely forgotten that she had ever picked it up, and it lay discarded now, in the bottom of her satchel. Her fingers even brushed against it when she reached in her bag for her comb, in the changing-room, after tennis. But Gillian did not notice, nor remember that the book was there, as she went into tea with the others.

Pam and Nora weren't there, as the two of them had decided to have tea in town, a privilege that the two top forms were allowed. .

'I bet they've gone to that nice little tea-shop,' said Felicity, rather enviously. 'The one that does the lovely little sandwiches, and those delicious chocolate cakes.'

'Well, we are not doing too badly,' said Susan, spreading apricot jam thickly on to a slice of bread and butter. 'This jam is super. And we've got coffee instead of tea, which makes a pleasant change.'

'I could do with a cup of coffee to keep me awake,' said Gillian, putting her hand up to her mouth to stifle a yawn. 'That game of tennis has quite worn me out.'

Millicent overheard this, and she said rather sharply, 'I do hope you're not going to be too tired to concentrate on the rehearsal tomorrow, Gillian. As you are the best violinist, you have quite a complicated solo to learn.'

'I shan't let you down,' said Gillian stiffly, nettled by Millicent's tone. 'I have been practising the solo all week.'

'That's true,' said Lucy. 'Julie and I passed one of the music-rooms yesterday afternoon, and there was old Gillian scraping away at her violin for all she was worth. I must say, it sounded jolly good. Did you really write that yourself, Millicent?'

Trying not to look too pleased at this, Millicent answered, 'Of course.'

'Well, you're very talented,' said Julie. 'Anyone would think that it had been written by a *real* composer.'

The others laughed at this, and, much to their surprise, Millicent joined in. She quite understood what Julie meant, and she was pleased at the compliment, especially as she felt that most of the fifth formers didn't really like her very much.

'The whole piece took me simply ages, and it was so difficult that I almost gave up at times,' Millicent said. 'But once I had finished, and knew that I had created something worthwhile, it was worth all the hard work. Sometimes I think that I enjoy composing more than playing.'

Felicity looked at Millicent, and thought how different she was when she was talking honestly about something that she loved. Her face looked more open, and less intense, somehow, and her rather dramatic tone of voice was lighter.

'Have you always been musical?' she asked curiously.

'Oh yes, for music is in my blood, you know,' answered Millicent. 'My mother was a concert pianist, and she taught me how to play the piano when I was quite small. I took to it at once, and it was obvious even then that I had a gift.'

Suddenly the girl gave a rather self-conscious laugh, and said, 'That sounds awfully conceited, doesn't it, but I truly don't mean it to.'

'I suppose that you were a musical genius from the moment you could walk, too, Gillian?' said Susan.

'I would hardly call myself a genius,' said Gillian, with a grin. 'I can't play a variety of instruments, as Millicent can, and if someone asked me to compose a tune I wouldn't know where to start. I do so love playing my violin though.'

That was the difference between the two girls, thought Felicity. As far as Millicent was concerned, music was the be all and end all. But she took it so very seriously that she didn't seem to get a great deal of pleasure from it. Gillian, however, took great joy in her music, and this made her performances very special, for everyone listening felt her enthusiasm and shared in it.

Pam and Nora returned to school soon after the others had left the tea-table, and joined them in the common-room.

'Hallo, everyone!' called out Pam. 'My word, we've had a super time. A spot of shopping, then a most marvellous tea.'

'Gillian, I have your shoelaces here,' said Nora, rummaging in her bag. 'And the chocolate you asked for.'

'And here is your book, Millicent,' said Pam, handing the girl a notebook identical to the one she had mislaid.

'Thanks,' said Millicent. She looked round the room to see if Delia was there, and, seeing that she was absent, said, 'I shan't trust that idiot of a Delia to make notes in it though. I shall do it myself from now on.'

'Oh, Delia's not a bad sort,' said Susan. 'She means well.'

Julie and Lucy heard this, and exchanged glances.

'I wonder what Susan would think if she knew that we had caught Delia looking in Millicent's bag earlier,' murmured Julie.

'You're not going to tell her, are you?' whispered Lucy, looking rather alarmed. 'I mean to say, we have no proof that Delia was doing anything wrong. It may have been just as she said, and she was merely fastening the bag up.'

'I shan't say anything to Susan, or anyone else, yet,' said Julie. 'But I shall be keeping an eye on Delia.'

Delia came into the common-room just then, and at once she spotted the notebook in Millicent's hand. Of course, Delia wasn't to know that it was a brand-new one, and she assumed that it was the one that contained her rhyme. Millicent slipped the book into the pocket of her school dress, and Delia's mind began to race. If only there was a way of getting hold of it for a moment. It would only take a matter of seconds to find the page with her scribbled words on and tear it out.

Delia's chance came at bedtime that evening. Millicent had changed into her pyjamas and, while she was in the bathroom brushing her teeth, Pam noticed that she had carelessly flung her dress on the bed.

'I do hope that Millicent intends to hang her dress up,' said Pam. 'She's awfully untidy, and it makes things unpleasant for the rest of us if we have to sleep in a messy room.'

'I'll hang it up for her,' offered Delia, picking the

dress up. As she smoothed it down, she could feel the notebook, still in the pocket, and her heart leapt. Delia was just about to slip her hand into the pocket, when she realised that Julie was watching her, an odd expression on her face.

Quickly, Delia moved her hand away, her face turning red, as she realised that she must look most suspicious.

'Lucy!' said Julie in a low voice. 'Did you see that?'

But Lucy, who had been deep in conversation with Freddie, hadn't seen a thing.

'Well, Delia offered to hang Millicent's dress up for her,' explained Julie. 'And she was just about to put her hand in the pocket, until she saw me watching her and stopped.'

'Heavens!' said Lucy, in dismay. 'Her behaviour is awfully strange, I must say, but no one in the form has had anything stolen, so we can't really tackle her about it. All that we can do is keep watching her.'

Delia had another opportunity to feel in the pocket of Millicent's dress the following day, when the girl left her school dress lying on the bed again. This time she was alone in the dormitory, and she seized her chance. But, to Delia's dismay, the book was no longer there. Millicent must have moved it elsewhere, for safe-keeping. How annoying! Perhaps it was in Millicent's desk? As it was Sunday, there were no lessons that day, so Delia thought that it would be a perfect opportunity to slip into the class-room unnoticed, and take a peek.

But her luck was well and truly out, for she was caught

in the act yet again – this time by Bonnie and Amy.

Cautiously, Delia lifted the lid and peered in, moving things very carefully and putting them back in exactly the same place, so that Millicent would not notice that someone had been in there. But there was no sign of the elusive notebook. Of course, Delia thought suddenly, there was a rehearsal later today, so Millicent was bound to have the notebook on her, probably in her bag. Which meant that she, Delia, had absolutely no chance of getting her hands on it until the rehearsal was over. She put the lid down, then gave a terrific start. For Amy and Bonnie had entered the class-room, and were giving her very strange looks indeed!

'W-what are you doing here?' she stammered.

'I wanted a book from my desk,' said Amy coldly. 'And what exactly are you doing, Delia?'

'I er – I thought I heard a knocking sound,' she said to the two girls, her cheeks beginning to burn. 'And it seemed to be coming from inside Millicent's desk.'

'Well, I can't hear anything,' said Bonnie, thinking Delia's explanation very lame indeed. 'Did you find anything in there?'

'No, nothing at all,' said Delia, with a nervous little laugh. 'I daresay my ears were playing tricks on me.'

'I daresay,' said Amy, with a sniff. 'But I must tell you, Delia, that it really isn't the done thing to go poking around in another girl's desk without her permission, you know.'

'Yes, I realise that,' said poor Delia, turning even

redder. 'Normally I wouldn't think of doing such a thing. It's just that …'

'You thought you heard a knocking sound,' Bonnie said, as Delia's voice tailed off.

Bonnie and Amy exchanged meaningful glances. Neither of them believed Delia's story for a moment, and thought that her manner had been very suspicious. And both of them would dearly have liked to know what she was really up to.

The term goes on

The orchestra's rehearsal that afternoon went very well indeed. There were still odd mistakes, and the occasional wrong note, but on the whole the girls played beautifully. There was only one girl who wasn't up to the standard of the others, and, strangely enough, that girl was Gillian.

Although she had spent a great deal of time rehearsing her violin solo in one of the little music-rooms, she played badly, and without her usual passion.

But Millicent, for once, held her tongue and did not scold. She noticed that Gillian looked rather pale and tired, and guessed that the girl was finding it a strain attending both the frequent tennis practices and practising her music. It was on the tip of her tongue to tell Gillian that she would have to choose between the two. But then, thought Millicent, the girl might choose tennis, and that would leave her without anyone to play the violin solo. No doubt one of the others could learn it, but Gillian was far and away the best violinist in the school, and Millicent didn't want to lose her.

But her decision to let the girl off lightly did not go down well with the rest of the orchestra.

'I was scolded for playing one wrong note,' grumbled Anne. 'And when poor Janet lost her place, I quite thought that Millicent was going to throw the baton at her!'

'Yes, but she didn't say a word to Gillian, and she played dreadfully,' said Jessie from East Tower. 'It's out-and-out favouritism.'

Millicent, quite unaware of the ill-feeling brewing, rapped sharply on her music stand with her baton, and said, 'Well, most of you played a little better today, but you are still not up to competition standard. Please spend as much time as you can practising your parts, particularly those of you with solos. I think that from now I shall hold two rehearsals a week, instead of one, otherwise we shall never be ready.'

There were groans at this, and some of the girls muttered under their breath.

'I wish that I had never joined the beastly orchestra,' said Janet, with a scowl. 'I thought that it would be fun, but this is too much like hard work.'

'It wouldn't be so bad if we got a word of praise now and again,' said Jessie. 'Millicent should take a leaf out of June's book. June works her tennis players hard, but she encourages them with plenty of praise, and knows how to get the best out of them.'

June certainly did. Helped by Felicity and Susan, she was coaching some of the first and second formers that afternoon, and it was clear that the youngsters simply adored her.

'Becoming games captain has really brought out a softer side in June,' said Felicity, watching with approval as the girl sat on the grass talking to some of the younger girls.

'I was a little afraid that the power might go to her head,' said Susan. 'But it hasn't at all, I'm pleased to say.'

Just then, June got up and came over to the two girls, and said, 'I think it's time that we decided who to put into the lower-school team.'

'Young Hannah must certainly play,' said Felicity. 'She has worked so hard, and come on in leaps and bounds.'

'I agree,' said June. 'So has little Christine. She and Dorothy play very well together, so I think that we should pick them for the doubles.'

'Barbara and Kathleen of the first form are very good too,' put in Susan. 'Perhaps we could choose one of them to play singles, and the other as reserve.'

So it was agreed that Kathleen would be in the team and Barbara would be reserve, and the fifth formers went across to the younger girls to give them the news.

There were whoops and yells from those who had been chosen, while the others cheered and clapped them on the back. Some of those who hadn't got a place on the team looked disappointed, but June noticed this and said, 'Just because you haven't been chosen this time doesn't mean that you will *never* play for the team. You have all tried your best and I feel very proud of you, and want you to keep up your practice. Don't forget that I shall be arranging some exhibition matches for half-term, and

I shall need some good players for those.'

This cheered the disappointed girls enormously. Being chosen for the half-term matches wasn't *quite* as good as playing for the school, but a tremendous honour, all the same.

The fifth formers bumped into Gillian, who had just come out of rehearsal, as they went back into the school, but the girl seemed quite preoccupied and barely noticed them, until Susan said, 'What's up, Gillian? Have you sent us all to Coventry, or something?'

Gillian blinked, then said, 'Awfully sorry, Susan. I didn't mean to ignore you, but I was in a world of my own.'

'Are you quite all right?' said Felicity, noticing how pale and strained the girl looked.

'Of course,' said Gillian, pinning a bright smile to her face. 'Just a little tired, that's all. I didn't sleep very well last night, but I'm sure that I'll make up for it tonight, and I shall be as right as rain tomorrow.'

'Why don't you go for a walk outside?' suggested June. 'That will blow the cobwebs away. It's a glorious day, and if you get some fresh air that will help you to sleep well tonight.'

'Later, perhaps,' said Gillian. 'I must go and practise my solo first, for I do so want it to be perfect.'

'She is doing far too much, and tiring herself out,' said Felicity, as the girl walked away. 'If she carries on like this, June, she won't be fit to play tennis *or* be part of the orchestra.'

'Well, it was her own decision to do both,' said June.

'I would be more than happy if she decided to leave the orchestra and concentrate on her tennis.'

But Felicity was far from happy, and she sought out Pam, the calm, sensible head of the form. Pam listened to what Felicity had to say, an unusually serious expression on her face, and, at last, she said, 'I'm going to tackle Gillian about this business. Her health and her work are both going to suffer if she carries on as she is.'

'Well, you will probably find her in one of the music-rooms,' said Felicity. 'She seems to spend most of her time in there, or on the tennis-courts.'

So Pam went off to find Gillian, and soon heard the sound of a violin coming from one of the rooms. But surely that couldn't be Gillian, for the player seemed uncertain and hesitant, with many wrong notes coming from the instrument! Quietly, Pam pushed open the door, and, much to her surprise, discovered that the violinist *was* Gillian. She hadn't heard Pam come in, and there was a frown of intense concentration on her face as she scraped the bow across the strings. Pam, watching her, thought how different she looked from the joyous, music-loving girl who had played for them in the common-room. Now Gillian looked as if she was undertaking a rather unpleasant chore.

Pam gave a little cough and stepped into the room.

Gillian immediately looked up, her bow becoming still, and said, 'Hallo, Pam. Did you want me? Only I'm rather busy, you see, for I simply must practise this solo.'

'I'd like to talk to you, Gillian,' said Pam, the serious

expression on her face so different from her usual calm, serene one that Gillian felt quite alarmed.

'I haven't done anything wrong, have I?' asked Gillian, rather anxiously.

'No, you haven't done anything wrong,' answered Pam, coming further into the room. 'But I am very worried about you, and so are some of the others.'

'Really?' said Gillian, looking most astonished. 'Well, I don't know why you should be, Pam.'

'The thing is, Gillian, that we feel you are overdoing things a bit, what with all your tennis practice and the orchestra rehearsals,' said Pam. 'You look awfully tired, and when I watched you playing just then, it seemed to me that you weren't enjoying it at all.'

'Nonsense, Pam!' said Gillian, giving a little laugh, which, to Pam's ears, sounded rather strained. 'I adore both music and tennis, so by choosing to play in the team and the orchestra, I really am having the best of both worlds. If I looked a little tense when I was playing, it's because this violin solo is awfully difficult.'

'Perhaps you are finding it difficult because you're exhausted,' suggested Pam.

'I am a little tired,' admitted Gillian.

'Well, for goodness' sake, forget about both your music and your tennis for a bit and just relax, and read a book or something.'

Gillian really didn't want to do this, for she was determined to master her solo before the next rehearsal, and couldn't afford to waste any time. But she liked the kind-hearted Pam, and could see that the girl genuinely had her best interests at heart. Besides, thought Gillian, if she went against Pam now, and insisted on carrying on with her practice, the head-girl would worry about her even more and keep a close watch on her, and perhaps even talk June or Millicent into dropping her. That would never do, for although Gillian really was finding it far more of a strain than she had anticipated to fit in both tennis and music, she was determined to stick to her word. So she smiled at Pam, began to put her violin in her case, and said, 'Perhaps you're right, and I do need a break. I'll go and sit in the sun and read my book for a while.'

So Pam went off, happy that she had talked some sense into Gillian. The head-girl wasn't to know that Gillian only stayed outside for about ten minutes, then, as soon as she was sure that the coast was clear, sneaked back up to the music-room to play her violin once more!

The other new girl, Delia, was at a bit of a loose end, meanwhile, and rather bored. She was still quite desperate to get her hands on Millicent's notebook, but the girl had it with her in the common-room and was writing something down in it. Delia had sat and watched her for a while, hoping that Millicent might go away and leave it lying around. Then she, Delia, would be able to whip out that silly rhyme she had written and destroy it, before Millicent had the chance to ridicule her.

But Millicent did not move, continuing to scribble away in the notebook, and soon she realised that Delia was watching her and became exasperated.

'Why do you keep staring at me all the time?' she snapped. 'It's most annoying. Don't you have anything better to do?'

Delia didn't answer, for the truth was that she *didn't* have anything to do. She liked the fifth formers, and most of them seemed to like her, but Delia had no particular friend of her own, so she tended to get a little left out sometimes. Millicent and Gillian didn't have special friends either, but both of them had interests and activities to occupy their time, where poor Delia had nothing.

Fortunately, Felicity and Susan came into the common-room in time to overhear Millicent's remarks. Felicity saw Delia's rather downcast expression, and said kindly, 'I say, Delia, why not come for a walk with Susan and me? We were thinking of popping over to see Bill and Clarissa.'

Delia cheered up at this, and asked curiously, 'Who are Bill and Clarissa?'

'They are two old girls who run a riding school not very far from here,' explained Susan. 'They were in the same form as Felicity's older sister, Darrell.'

'Yes, they're jolly good sorts,' said Felicity. 'Do come, Delia, for we haven't had a chance to introduce you to them yet.'

It was very pleasant to feel wanted, so Delia agreed at once, and went off happily with Felicity and Susan.

Bill and Clarissa were very pleased to see the three

girls, and made them welcome. Then they had a fine time watching some children having riding-lessons and petting all the horses. Delia was a little nervous of them at first, but once she realised they weren't going to bite her, or kick out at her, she soon relaxed. Felicity and Susan were good company, and she liked the two older girls, Bill and Clarissa, and Delia enjoyed herself very much indeed.

By the time they made their way back to Malory Towers, the girl felt in such high spirits that she began to hum cheerfully to herself. The tune that she hummed was Gillian's violin solo from 'Summer Serenade' and, almost without realising it, Delia found herself softly singing the words that she had written to accompany it.

'What is that song you're singing, Delia?' asked Felicity curiously. 'I don't think that I've heard it before.'

Delia could have kicked herself, for she hadn't realised that Felicity and Susan had stopped talking and were listening to her silly little song. Of course, Delia didn't want to admit that she had written the words herself, for the others were sure to laugh at her, so she said, 'I don't know. It must have been something that I heard on the radio and it just got stuck in my head.'

'I shall have to listen out for it,' said Felicity. 'It's awfully good.'

'Yes,' agreed Susan. 'It really captures the spirit of summer, somehow.'

Another girl might have felt proud at this, but not Delia, who hadn't come in for a great deal of praise in her life. She merely thought that the two girls were captivated by the tune, rather than the words, and that was to Millicent's credit.

'Sing a little more – louder, this time,' said Felicity, but Delia turned red and shook her head, saying, 'I can't remember any more of the words. And I'm sure that my singing voice isn't very pleasant to listen to. Let's talk instead. I say, it's coming up to half-term soon, isn't it? Won't that be fun?'

Felicity and Susan accepted the change of subject, Susan saying, 'I simply can't wait! Daddy may not be able to come, but Mother will. She has promised to take me to a restaurant for a slap-up meal.'

'My parents are both coming,' said Felicity, happily. 'I'm so looking forward to seeing them again. How about you, Delia? Will your people be coming?'

'I doubt if my aunt will bother,' said Delia. 'Not that I particularly want to see her anyway, or my cousins. My father will be on leave from his ship, though, so he is coming.'

Felicity and Susan noticed how Delia's eyes shone when she spoke of her father, and knew that she must love him very much.

'It must be awfully difficult for you,' said Felicity, earnestly. 'Having to live away from your father most of the time.'

'Yes, but he has to earn a living,' said Delia with a sigh. Then she brightened, and added, 'And it does make the times that we are together so much more special.

When he comes home on leave Father likes to spend as much time as possible with me, and we do so much together.'

'Does he know that you are unhappy at your aunt's?' asked Felicity curiously.

Delia shook her head firmly, and said, 'No, for it would only worry him if he knew, and then he wouldn't be able to concentrate on his job. Besides, there's no point in making a big fuss about it, for as long as Father is at sea there really isn't any alternative. And I suppose things could be worse. It's not as if my aunt ill-treats me, or starves me, or anything like that. It's just that I know she would rather I wasn't there, and my cousins feel the same.'

Felicity and Susan said nothing, but both of them felt rather sorry for Delia. They admired her, too, for having the strength of character to accept her situation without complaining, for the sake of the father she adored.

'I think that's jolly sensible of you, Delia,' said Felicity. 'And I don't suppose that your father will be at sea forever, so it will all be worth it in the end.'

'No, he plans to find a job on shore in a year or so,' said Delia. 'Then I shall be able to live with him all the time. In the meantime, I can't tell you how happy I am to be at Malory Towers, for it is much nicer than going to day school with my horrid cousins. The only thing I miss is not having a friend of my own.'

'Well, you're quite welcome to tag along with Felicity and me sometimes,' said Susan. 'Though I quite understand what you mean, for it is nice to have a special friend of your own.'

'Why don't you try to pal up with Gillian, or Millicent?' suggested Felicity. 'They are both on their own as well.'

'I don't think that Millicent feels very friendly towards me since I forgot to take notes at her rehearsal,' said Delia ruefully. 'And Gillian is always so busy that she doesn't seem to have time for any real friendships.'

'Well, perhaps she should make time,' said Felicity. 'I think that it would do her good to think about something besides her music and her tennis.'

'Felicity is quite right,' said Susan. 'Why don't you try and make friends with her, Delia, and take her out of herself a bit? It would do both of you the world of good.'

'All right, then, I shall!' said Delia, feeling a lot more cheerful suddenly. 'Of course, I don't know if it will work, or if Gillian will even *want* to be friends with me, but I shall certainly try.'

A new friendship

Delia was as good as her word, and, the following afternoon, when Gillian was looking for someone to practise her serve on, she seized the opportunity.

'Felicity and Susan are both helping June to coach the youngsters, and Freddie has promised to play with Helen Jones of the fourth form,' complained Gillian. 'Now what am I to do, for I do so need to practise.'

'Will I do?' asked Delia. 'I probably shan't return many of your serves, for I'm hopeless at tennis, but you are very welcome to practise on me.'

Gillian, who knew that Delia always tried to avoid playing tennis because she was afraid of showing herself up, felt very grateful indeed, and said, 'Why, thank you, Delia. Come on, let's go and get changed, and bag a court.'

In fact, Delia did manage to return a few of the other girl's serves, for Gillian was off her game a little that day.

Delia, however, had no idea of this, and began to feel that she wasn't quite as bad at tennis as she had always thought.

'Well!' she exclaimed, as she and Gillian got changed afterwards. 'Who would have thought that I could get so many of your serves back?'

Delia sounded so pleased with herself that Gillian didn't have the heart to tell her the truth. Instead, she forced a smile and said lightly, 'If you practise a little more, I daresay June will soon be giving my place on the team to you!'

Delia laughed at this, and said, 'I don't know about that. I say, Gillian, how about popping into town for a spot of tea? We can get a bus just along the road, and it would make a pleasant change from school tea.'

Gillian hesitated. She badly wanted to get in half an hour's violin practice before tea, and there wouldn't be time if they were to catch the bus.

She said as much to Delia, adding, 'Besides, I'm broke. I had to buy a birthday present for Mother last week, and I'm down to my last few pence.'

'My treat,' said Delia. 'I'm pretty well off at the moment.'

Gillian looked surprised at this, for Delia was one of the girls who had very little money. It wasn't that her father was poor, for he regularly sent money to Delia's aunt for her. But her aunt was sometimes a little forgetful about sending it on to Delia, which meant that the girl had very little to spend on herself.

'My grandmother sent me a nice, big postal order the other day,' Delia said now. 'And it's no fun going off and having tea on my own, so I'd be jolly grateful if you would come with me.'

The expression in Delia's eyes reminded Gillian of a friendly, eager-to-please puppy, and somehow she couldn't bring herself to snub the girl. Instead, she slipped her arm through Delia's, and said, 'Nonsense! I'm the one who should be grateful to you for such a treat. Thanks, Delia.'

Delia turned quite red with pleasure, and the two girls went off together to catch the bus.

Pam noticed that they were missing at tea-time, and said with a frown, 'If Gillian is missing her tea so that she can practise the violin, or play tennis, I shall be cross with her.'

'I think that she's gone out with Delia,' said Julie. 'Lucy and I saw them waiting at the bus stop along the road when we came back from our ride earlier.'

Felicity and Susan exchanged pleased glances. It seemed that Delia had taken their advice and was going out of her way to befriend Gillian.

'It will be jolly good for both of them,' said Felicity. 'I really hope that they hit it off.'

'And that will only leave Millicent without a friend of her own,' said Susan. 'Although she doesn't seem to need one, for she is so wrapped up in her music.'

'Even Millicent must have times when she needs someone to talk to, and confide in,' said Felicity. 'But really, it's quite her own fault that she doesn't have one, for she isn't the easiest of people to get on with.'

Delia and Gillian, meanwhile, were getting along like a house on fire. For the first time in weeks, Gillian's head wasn't full of music scores or tennis shots, as she and Delia chattered away together. Delia really could be very funny at times, thought Gillian, as the two girls sat in the little tea shop feasting on the most delicious crumpets, dripping with melted butter, and little scones, warm from the oven, filled with jam and cream.

'Thank you so much for inviting me, Delia,' said Gillian, as the two of them finished their tea. 'I've had a super time and it has really taken me out of myself.'

'Well, I'm jolly glad to hear it,' said Delia a little gruffly, feeling very pleased that Gillian had enjoyed herself so much.

She took a five pound note out of her purse and got up to go and pay the bill, but as she did so, she knocked Gillian's bag on to the floor, sending the contents everywhere.

'Oh, dear!' she wailed. 'I'm so clumsy.'

'Don't worry,' laughed Gillian, as the two girls crouched down to pick everything up. 'Anyone can have an accident, and there's no harm done.'

There had been a bag of sweets in the bag, and they had rolled all over the floor, and as Gillian scrabbled around picking them up, Delia spotted something that made her give a little gasp. Millicent's notebook! But what on earth was it doing in Gillian's bag? There was no time to puzzle over that just now, though. While Gillian was looking the other way, Delia grabbed it and slipped it into her pocket, giving a sigh of relief. As soon as she had a moment to herself, she would tear out the page that she needed, then she would leave the book somewhere Millicent would be sure to find it.

Delia felt horribly guilty as she and Gillian made their way back to Malory Towers, for she was an honest girl and she didn't like being in possession of something that didn't belong to her. She simply couldn't think what Gillian had been doing with Millicent's notebook, but the sooner it was back in the hands of its rightful owner, the better.

Delia slipped up to the dormitory when she and Gillian got back to the school, relieved to find that it was empty. Swiftly she ripped out the page at the back, crumpling it up and stuffing it in one of her drawers. Then she placed the notebook on Millicent's bedside cabinet. No doubt Millicent would wonder how it had got there, but that couldn't be helped!

Gillian wasn't in the common-room when Delia joined the others, and the girl guessed that she must be shut away in one of the little music-rooms, playing her violin.

There was a low hum of noise in the common-room – nothing like the hubbub that the lower forms created, for the fifth formers would certainly have considered it beneath their dignity to make such a racket. Instead it was rather a pleasant, soothing noise, thought Delia, of girls in low-voiced, friendly conversation, while the radio played soft music in the background. Little did she know that the peace was about to be rudely shattered!

'I say, Millicent!' said Nora. 'I hate to ask, but are you able to let me have that five shillings I lent you the other day? I need to buy some new stockings, for even Matron agrees that the ones I have are beyond repair!'

Millicent looked up from the music score she had been working on, and said, 'Of course. Sorry, Nora, it completely slipped my mind, but you can have it back now.'

Millicent rummaged in her bag for her purse, then she gave a little cry. 'It's gone!' she said. 'My purse is gone.'

'It can't be,' said Susan. 'Check in your pockets.'

Millicent stood up and felt in her pockets, but the missing purse wasn't there. 'Blow!' she said, frowning. 'I had a few pounds in there, too, for my mother had just sent me some money.'

'Are you sure it's not in the dormitory?' said Felicity. 'Perhaps it's in your cabinet.'

Millicent ran upstairs to take a look, and was back within minutes.

'No purse, but I did find this,' said Millicent, brandishing the notebook that Delia had left on her cabinet earlier. 'I lost it several weeks ago, and now it has suddenly turned up again.'

'How queer!' said Pam, who had begun to feel rather uneasy. How she hoped that Millicent's purse would turn up, for if it didn't that might mean that there was a thief in the fifth form.

Delia turned very red when Millicent produced the notebook, and lowered her eyes, hoping that none of the others were looking in her direction, for she felt that she must look very guilty indeed.

But some of the girls *were* looking at her. Julie and

Lucy, who had caught Delia going through Millicent's bag, and Amy and Bonnie, who had seen her looking in the girl's desk, were watching her with suspicion. When Delia turned red and looked down, Amy and Bonnie exchanged meaningful glances, while Julie nudged Lucy and murmured, 'Just look at Delia's face! The picture of guilt.'

'Millicent, when did you have your purse last?' asked Pam, taking charge of the situation. 'Think carefully.'

Millicent thought, and said, 'I had it yesterday morning, for one of the sixth formers came round to collect for Miss Potts's birthday present, and I put a shilling in.'

'That's right,' said Bonnie. 'I saw you, and I remember that you put your purse in your bag afterwards.'

'So it could have been taken any time after that,' said Felicity. 'Millicent, was your bag out of your sight at any time?'

'Only when I went to bed,' said poor Millicent, who was looking very upset now. 'I left it here, in the common-room.'

'Oh, Millicent, how silly!' said Pam. 'You should always take it up to the dormitory with you.'

'I know,' said Millicent rather sheepishly. 'I usually do, but I simply forgot last night.'

'Well, I suppose there is still a chance that it will turn up somewhere,' said Felicity, trying to sound cheery, though she didn't feel very hopeful.

'Perhaps, but in the meantime I can't pay Nora back,'

said Millicent. 'I'm awfully sorry, Nora. I shall write to Mother, of course, and explain what has happened. She will send me some more money, and I shall give it to you as soon as I can, but I'm afraid that I won't get it for a while.'

'Don't worry about that,' said Nora. 'I'm only sorry that your purse has gone missing. And I shall be sorry when Matron sees me going around in holey stockings and gives me a row!'

The others laughed at that, and Pam said, 'I will lend you the money to buy some new stockings, Nora. We can't have you disgracing the fifth by wearing ragged ones.'

The girls began to talk about other things, for no one quite liked to mention the one thing that was on all their minds in front of everyone – the possibility that there was a thief in the fifth form.

Some of the girls discussed it among themselves, though, and Amy remarked to Bonnie, 'Things look black for Delia.'

'I suppose they do,' said Bonnie. 'She doesn't strike me as dishonest, I must say, though her behaviour was most peculiar the day we caught her in Millicent's desk.'

Julie and Lucy, standing nearby, overheard this, and Julie moved closer to Bonnie, saying in a low voice, 'What was that, Bonnie? Did I hear you say that you had caught Delia in Millicent's desk?'

'Yes,' said Bonnie. 'It looked as if she was searching for something.'

Lucy gave a low whistle, and said, 'Well, Julie and I

found her looking in Millicent's bag not very long ago. She came up with some tale to explain it away, but it wasn't very convincing.'

'How beastly that this should happen now, just as we are all looking forward to half-term next weekend,' said Julie, looking worried.

'Do you think that we should tell Pam that we suspect Delia?' asked Amy. 'As head-girl, she really ought to be informed, for she is the one who will have to decide what to do.'

'I think that we should wait until after half-term,' said Bonnie. 'Otherwise it will put an awful damper on what should be a happy time.'

'I agree,' said Lucy. 'Let's just keep it between the four of us for now. And we had better keep a careful eye on Delia in the meantime, and see if anyone else's belongings disappear.'

'I say!' said Julie, suddenly. 'Didn't Delia and Gillian have tea in town together this afternoon? It would be interesting to know where Delia found the money to pay her share, for she always seems to be broke.'

'Perhaps Gillian treated her,' suggested Bonnie.

'Well, we can ask her,' said Amy. 'Here she comes.'

Just then Gillian came into the common-room, looking nothing like the happy, carefree girl who had gone to tea with Delia that afternoon.

The strained expression was back on her face, and she looked very pale. But Julie, intent on finding out what she wanted to know, didn't even notice this, and called out, 'Hi, Gillian! Come here a moment, would you?'

Bonnie, knowing that Julie wasn't the most tactful of souls, stepped forward and said, 'Are you all right, Gillian? You look awfully tired.'

'I'm fine,' Gillian assured her brightly. 'Did you want something, Julie?'

Julie opened her mouth, but, once more, Bonnie forestalled her, saying, 'Well, it's no wonder that you're tired, with all the activities that you do. Going out for tea with Delia must have been a pleasant break for you.'

Julie, who had been rather put out by Bonnie pushing herself forward, suddenly realised what the girl was doing. She was leading up to the question tactfully, rather than being blunt, and perhaps causing offence. And, by using such tactics, she was likely to get a great deal more out of Gillian, thought Julie, staring at little Bonnie with admiration.

'Oh, yes, we had a marvellous time,' Gillian was saying now. 'And a super tea! I was so grateful to Delia for inviting me.'

'She's such a thoughtful girl,' said Bonnie, smiling sweetly at Gillian. 'So generous with her time.'

'And with her money,' said Gillian. 'I've spent all of my pocket money this week, so Delia treated me. Wasn't that kind of her?'

'It certainly was,' said Bonnie. 'Especially as poor Delia never seems to have very much money.'

'Well, it was jolly lucky for me that she had just received a postal order from her grandmother,' said

Gillian. 'Otherwise I shouldn't have had such a splendid treat.'

'Well done, Bonnie,' murmured Lucy, patting the girl on the back, as Gillian moved away. 'You handled that perfectly.'

'I should say!' agreed Julie. 'Why, you didn't even have to ask Gillian who had paid for tea, for she volunteered the information.'

'It was simply a question of leading her in the right direction,' said Bonnie modestly. 'And now we know the truth. Delia received some money from her grandmother.'

But the others weren't convinced, Julie saying darkly, 'Hmm. Well, I think it's rather a coincidence that Delia happens to be in funds just as Millicent's purse goes missing.'

'I agree,' said Amy. 'I shall certainly be keeping an eye on my belongings from now on.'

'And I shall be keeping an eye on Delia,' said Lucy. 'We *all* should. I know that we have agreed not to say anything to Pam and the others until after half-term, but that doesn't mean that we can't watch Delia, and make sure that she doesn't get the chance to steal anything else.'

'Well, we don't know for certain that Delia is the culprit,' said Bonnie, looking unusually grave. 'And I, for one, would like to make absolutely sure that we have our facts right before we start making accusations.'

'You're quite right, of course,' said Lucy. 'And I would

never dream of accusing Delia, or anyone else, for that matter, without proof. All I am saying is that it won't do any harm to watch her.'

'I suppose not,' said Bonnie. 'But we must be careful that Delia doesn't realise what we are up to, for if it turns out that she *is* the person who took Millicent's purse, we don't want to put her on her guard.'

Delia, meanwhile, quite unaware that she was under suspicion, was turning over some rather disturbing and unwelcome thoughts in her own mind. She was remembering how Millicent's notebook had been in Gillian's possession, and was wondering how the girl had come by it. Had Gillian taken it from Millicent's bag? And, if so, was it possible that the girl had taken the purse as well?

Delia felt very troubled indeed, for she liked Gillian very much, and the thought that the girl might be a thief was horrible. Delia had so enjoyed the time they had spent together, and had been secretly hoping that the two of them might become close friends. But, if Gillian turned out to be dishonest, that would be quite impossible.

Just then, Gillian herself came over and sat down next to Delia, a smile of genuine friendship on her rather white face. Delia was unable to stop herself smiling back and, as she did so, she realised something. If she wanted to be a true friend to Gillian, she had to be loyal and believe in her. And, looking into the girl's open, honest face, Delia's suspicions fell away. Of course Gillian wasn't a thief! Why, she just couldn't be, for surely she, Delia, couldn't possibly like her so much if she was dishonest.

Oddly enough, Millicent herself was the person who seemed least affected by the loss of her purse. She had quickly put it out of her mind, for an idea of how she could improve Gillian's violin solo had suddenly come to her, and she was now sitting at the big table working on her score. She had been upset to discover it missing, of course, and sorry that she could not pay Nora back, for she had been brought up to believe that one should pay one's debts promptly. But she would be seeing her parents at half-term, which was only a few days away, and they would see that she was in funds again. There were far more important things in life than money, anyway, thought Millicent, feverishly scribbling down notes. Such as music. Now, if something happened to stop her working at that, it really *would* be a disaster.

Half-term

The whole school was thrilled that it was half-term, though of course the more dignified fifth and sixth formers did not show their excitement in the riotous way that the younger girls did.

Coming out of the dining-room after breakfast on Saturday morning, Felicity and Susan were almost knocked over by a noisy group of first formers, all rushing to their common-room so that they could watch for their people to arrive.

'Slow down, you kids!' said Felicity sternly. 'It might be half-term, but that is no excuse to go tearing around the corridors like mad things.'

Miss Potts, walking by in time to overhear this, smiled to herself. She could remember having to reprimand young Felicity Rivers for exactly the same rowdy behaviour when she had been a first former, eagerly awaiting the arrival of her parents.

'Sorry, Felicity,' chorused the first formers. 'Sorry, Susan.'

As the younger girls walked away at a more measured pace, Susan said rather wistfully, 'What a thing it is to be a first former. I can remember when we were just like those kids, and felt so excited about half-term that we could hardly keep still.'

'Well, I feel just as excited now as I did when I was a first former,' admitted Felicity, with a grin. 'Of course, I have to keep it inside now that I'm a fifth former, but when I think about seeing Mother and Daddy again, and the marvellous time we have ahead of us, I could dance for joy!'

'What a pity that we are too old and sensible to do just that,' laughed Susan. 'I would love to see the faces of the younger girls if they saw us fifth formers dancing a jig all the way to the common-room.'

Mam'zelle, who happened to come round the corner at that moment, caught the tail end of this remark and gave a little start.

'Ah, *non*, Susan!' she said, with a frown. 'You must remember that you are a so-sensible fifth former now, and behave with dignity at all times. If the dear Miss Grayling were to come along and catch you dancing jigs around the school she would be most displeased.'

'Yes, Mam'zelle,' said Susan meekly, though her eyes twinkled.

'Don't worry, Mam'zelle,' said Felicity solemnly, taking Susan's arm. 'I shall escort Susan to the common-room, and make sure that she behaves as a fifth former should.'

Once the little French mistress was out of earshot, the two girls burst into laughter, and Susan said, 'Dear old Mam'zelle! Trust her to get the wrong end of the stick.'

The rest of the fifth formers were in the common-room waiting for their people to arrive, all except Delia, who had been called to Miss Grayling's room.

'I say,' said Amy to Bonnie. 'You don't think that Miss Grayling has found out about Delia taking Millicent's purse, do you?'

'For heaven's sake, keep your voice down, Amy!' hissed Bonnie, looking quickly over her shoulder to make sure that no one was close enough to overhear. 'How can Miss Grayling possibly know that, for we aren't even certain of it ourselves yet. And I don't think that Millicent reported the loss to Matron, so I doubt very much that Miss Grayling even knows that it's missing.'

But Delia certainly looked very down in the dumps about something when she returned to the common-room, and Gillian went across to her, saying kindly, 'What's up, old girl? Don't tell me that Miss Grayling gave you a row?'

'No, nothing like that,' said Delia rather dolefully. 'But she did give me some disappointing news. You see, my father is still overseas, so he won't be able to come and see me for half-term. Miss Grayling had a telegram from him a short while ago.'

The fifth formers were very sorry to hear this, even Amy, Lucy and Julie, who were all more than half-convinced that Delia was a thief.

'What a shame!' said Pam. 'But perhaps your aunt and cousins will come instead.'

'I doubt it,' said Delia, with a brave attempt at a smile. 'To be quite honest, I hope that they don't, for I don't like them and they don't like me. I would rather spend half-term on my own than in their company.'

'Well, you shan't spend it on your own,' said Gillian firmly. 'You are going to come out with me and my people.'

Delia's grey eyes lit up at this, and she cried, 'Oh, Gillian, that *is* decent of you! Are you sure that your parents won't mind me tagging along?'

'Of course not,' said Gillian. 'They will be pleased to know that I have made a friend.'

A warm glow came over Delia at this. Gillian had said that she was her friend! And that made the girl more convinced than ever that Gillian couldn't have taken Millicent's purse, for if she had, then she, Delia, must be a pretty poor judge of character.

'There are some parents arriving,' said June, who was standing by the window with Freddie. 'I say, they're mine! Most unlike them to get here so early. Come on, Freddie!'

Freddie, whose own parents were unable to come, was looking forward to a lively day out with June, her parents and one of her brothers.

As the two girls went out of the common-room, Pam and Nora moved across to take their places at the window.

'There are several cars arriving now,' said Nora. 'Can't say that I recognise any of the parents. Half a minute, though! Amy, that's your mother. I didn't recognise her at first, for she has a simply enormous hat on, but then she looked up and I knew who she was at once.'

There was no mistaking Amy's mother, for she was very beautiful indeed and always wore the most exquisite clothes.

Cars arrived thick and fast after that. Julie's people turned up next, then Nora's, and then Millicent's.

The girls noticed that Millicent looked very like her mother, for Mrs Moon had the same dark eyes, long face and intense expression. Her father, however, looked rather jolly, and Pam remarked under her breath, 'I can't imagine what he has to look jolly about, though, living with Millicent and her mother. I don't suppose that it's much fun!'

But Millicent looked very pleased to see her parents, her serious face breaking into a wide smile that quite transformed it.

Soon all of the parents had arrived, and Felicity was thrilled to be with her mother and father once more.

'Well, darling,' said Mr Rivers, giving Felicity a hug, then stepping back to take a good look at her. 'Being a fifth former obviously suits you, for you look very well indeed.'

'Yes, and I do believe that you've grown a little taller since the holidays,' said Mrs Rivers, slipping her arm through Felicity's.

'I don't know about that,' laughed Felicity. 'Though I probably look a little older, what with all the responsibility of being a wise, sensible fifth former!'

Delia, too, was enjoying herself, for, although she missed her father, Gillian's parents had gone out of their way to make her feel welcome.

'I do like your mother and father so much,' said Delia to Gillian, as the two of them went off to get cups of tea for Mr and Mrs Weaver – and themselves, of course. 'Your mother is so pretty and kind. And your father reminds me very much of my own, for he has exactly the same sense of humour.'

Gillian, of course, was delighted at this praise of her parents. The girl seemed much more like her old, carefree self today, for she was looking forward to spending a happy time with her people and her friend. What was more, there would be no time for her to practise either tennis or music today, or even to think about them, and Gillian had to admit that the break was very welcome.

The morning seemed to pass in a flash, for there were mistresses to talk to, and displays of needlework and art to look at. Then, of course, the girls had to show the parents their common-room and dormitory, not to mention the grounds, which always looked very beautiful at this time of year.

Once the parents had seen and admired everything, it was time to go out for lunch. Some parents, like Amy's and Bonnie's, took their daughters out to hotels or restaurants. Others, like Julie's and Felicity's, had brought magnificent picnics with them, which they took to the beach.

Mr and Mrs Weaver took Gillian and Delia to a very nice restaurant, where they had a most delicious lunch. Over pudding, while Gillian chatted to her father, Mrs Weaver spoke to Delia, her warm, charming manner making it easy for the girl to relax. Soon Delia was confiding far more than she had intended to Mrs Weaver. Gillian's mother listened sympathetically, and laid her hand over Delia's, saying, 'Poor child! It must be terribly difficult living where you know you are not really wanted.'

'Well, I feel much happier now that I am at Malory Towers,' said Delia. 'It means that I only have to spend the holidays with my aunt and my cousins.'

Mrs Weaver looked thoughtful for a moment, then, at last, she said, 'You must come and stay with us for part of the holidays. Not if your father is home, of course, for I know that you will want to spend time with him. But if he is still at sea, then you will be most welcome, and I know that Gillian would like to have you.'

For a moment Delia was quite speechless, but at last she managed to stammer out her thanks.

Mrs Weaver smiled, and said, 'Well, my dear, there is a little something that you can do for me in return.'

'Of course,' said Delia at once, feeling quite prepared to do anything for this kind and sympathetic woman.

Mrs Weaver glanced up and, seeing that Gillian and her father were still deep in conversation, she lowered her voice, and said, 'I would like you to keep an eye on Gillian for me. She has told me all about the tennis team and the school orchestra, and I feel that she is over-working. She seems happy enough at the moment, but I know my daughter, and she has lost some of her sparkle.'

Delia nodded gravely, and said, 'Many of us fifth formers feel the same, Mrs Weaver. But Gillian simply can't be persuaded to give up one or the other. I shall do my best to try and make sure that she doesn't overdo things, though, you may be sure.'

In fact, Delia felt most honoured that Mrs Weaver had entrusted her with the task of looking after Gillian, and she meant to do her utmost to keep her word.

But there was no need to keep an eye on the girl at half-term, for Gillian seemed determined to push everything to the back of her mind and have fun. All of the fifth formers enjoyed their half-term break enormously, feeling tired but happy when it came to an end on Sunday evening.

'My word, what a super weekend,' said Pam with a contented sigh, as she settled down in an armchair.

'Wasn't it just?' agreed Freddie. 'June, your brother is an absolute scream!'

'Back to the grindstone tomorrow,' groaned Nora. 'Why does half-term always fly by so quickly?'

'You need cheering up, Nora,' said Susan, getting to her feet. 'And I know just the thing! My parents brought me a box of chocolates yesterday, from my grandmother, and I think that now is the time to open them.'

Susan went across to the big cupboard in the corner of the room and pulled open the door. Then she gave a little cry.

'What's up?' asked Felicity, alarmed.

'My chocolates!' said Susan. 'They're gone!'

Pam and Felicity went over to join her, Pam saying, 'They must be there! Chocolates don't just vanish into thin air.'

'Well, I put them on that shelf, and you can see for yourself that they are not there now, Pam,' said Susan, looking rather upset.

'I'll bet someone has moved them,' said Felicity, rummaging around in the cupboard. 'I was looking for a book in here the other day, and someone had knocked it on to the floor.'

But though she hunted high and low, the chocolates were nowhere to be found, and Pam said, 'Perhaps someone has hidden them for a joke.'

'Not a very funny one,' said Freddie. 'I was looking forward to one of those chocolates.'

'I can't think that anyone would have done that,' said June. 'Rather a first-form-ish sort of prank to play, if you ask me.'

'Yes, it is, rather,' said Julie. She glanced swiftly round the common-room, saw that Delia and Gillian were absent, and added, 'I don't think that Susan's chocolates have been hidden. I think that they have been stolen!'

The fifth formers looked rather shocked at this, and Pam said gravely, 'That's a very serious accusation, Julic. Do you have any reason for saying this?'

'Well, Millicent's purse went missing not so long ago,' said Julie. 'And it was never found.'

'I think that we should tell Pam what we know,' put

in Amy. 'After all, we said that we were going to once half-term was over anyway.'

Pam looked at Amy in surprise, and said, 'What are you talking about, Amy? Do you know something about the things that have gone missing?'

Quickly, Julie and Lucy told the others of how they had found Delia searching in Millicent's bag.

'And Bonnie and I caught her looking in Millicent's desk,' said Amy. 'Shortly before the purse disappeared.'

'It didn't disappear, it was stolen!' said June, scornfully. 'Just as Susan's chocolates have been. And it looks as if dear Delia is the thief.'

'You really should have told me all of this before, girls,' said Pam, looking very upset indeed, for she hated to think that there was a thief in the fifth form.

The others felt the same, and were disappointed in Delia, for most of them had grown to like her.

'I know that we should,' said Lucy. 'But we didn't want to put a damper on half-term, so thought that we would wait until the fun was over.'

'Well, it's certainly over now,' said Nora glumly. 'This has really brought us all down to earth with a bump.'

'What are you going to do, Pam?' asked June. 'Tackle Delia?'

'Not just yet,' said Pam, who had been looking thoughtful. 'I may have to, eventually, of course, but for now I think that we should all just watch her.'

'What's the good of that?' scoffed June. 'If Delia feels that she is being watched, she won't attempt to steal anything and we shall never catch her out.'

'Well, we will have to make sure that she doesn't know we are watching her,' said Pam firmly. 'We must all do our best to act normally when she is around, and be friendly to her. That way she won't suspect that we are on to her, and may slip up.'

'I don't agree,' said June stubbornly. 'If we speak to Delia now, she may own up and tell us where she has hidden the things she has stolen. I daresay that she has spent poor Millicent's money by now, but she can't possibly have eaten all of Susan's chocolates.'

'Well, it seems that we have a difference of opinion,' said Pam. 'So the only way to settle things is to vote. Would all those of you who are in favour of tackling Delia please raise your hands?'

Amy's hand shot up at once. Millicent, Julie, June and Lucy also raised theirs.

'That makes five of you,' said Pam. 'And who thinks that it would be better just to watch and wait?'

Of course, Pam herself put her hand up. So did Susan and Felicity, Nora and Bonnie. Freddie hesitated. June was her friend, and June wanted to get the whole thing out in the open. But Freddie couldn't quite believe that the pleasant-natured Delia was a thief. Once Freddie would have followed June's lead, but she had grown up quite a bit since those days, and now she decided that she must be true to herself and what she believed. If June took offence, then perhaps their friendship wasn't as strong as Freddie thought. So she put her hand up as well, and Pam said, 'Six. That means that we do as I suggest.'

'Gillian isn't here,' Amy pointed out. 'She hasn't had the chance to vote.'

'As Gillian is friendly with Delia, I think it's safe to assume that she would have voted with us,' said Felicity.

'Yes, and perhaps it would be best to keep Gillian in the dark,' said Susan. 'We don't want her warning Delia that she is under suspicion.'

'Quite right,' said Pam. 'June, I trust that you will abide by what has been decided?'

'Of course,' said June, looking surprised. 'Though I don't agree with it.'

'I realise that,' said Pam. 'The trouble is, June, that when you feel strongly about something, you rather have a tendency to go your own way when it comes to dealing with it.'

June flushed, for there had been several occasions in lower forms when she had confronted fellow pupils and accused them of something – sometimes wrongly. But June was older, and a little wiser, now, and didn't like being reminded of her conduct then.

'I can assure you that I have learned my lesson, Pam,' she said a little stiffly.

Pam was glad to hear it.

Just then, Delia and Gillian came in, both of them laughing and chattering happily.

Looking at the two of them, Felicity thought how much happier both of them seemed, now that they had become friends. Delia, in particular, had a sparkle in her eyes and a rosy glow to her open, honest face. For that was exactly what it was, thought Felicity, watching the girl closely, and feeling ever more certain that she couldn't be the thief.

But someone in the fifth form certainly was. And if it wasn't Delia, just who could it be?

Who is the thief?

The fifth formers stuck to their word and watched Delia carefully. When she volunteered to stay behind and tidy up the class-room for Miss James, Felicity and Susan hid themselves behind a pillar outside the class-room, and watched.

Delia was most conscientious, humming softly to herself as she wiped the blackboard, then she carefully put away the pile of books on Miss James's desk. The girl picked up a crumpled ball of paper that had fallen on the floor and dropped it in the wastepaper bin, then she went round the room making sure that all the chairs were neatly pushed under the desks. But at no time did she open any of the desks, or do anything remotely suspicious.

When her work was done, she moved towards the door, and Felicity and Susan slipped quietly away.

'Well,' said Felicity, as the two of them walked down the corridor. 'If Delia really *is* the thief, that would have been the perfect opportunity for her to go hunting in all of our desks, looking for things to steal.'

'Yet she didn't take it,' said Susan thoughtfully. 'I always found it hard to believe that old Delia was a thief, and now I find it even harder. I suppose we had better go and report to Pam.'

Pam was sitting on the grass in the sunshine, along with Nora, June and Freddie, and she looked up as Felicity and Susan approached.

'Well?' she said. 'Anything to report?'

'Not a thing,' said Felicity, sitting down next to the girl. 'Delia simply tidied up, but she didn't go in any of the desks.'

'I spied on her when she was alone in the common-room the other day,' said Freddie. 'And she didn't try to take anything then, either. The only time that she went to the cupboard was to put her knitting away.'

'Another ideal opportunity wasted,' said Susan. 'I really do think that Delia is innocent, and that we are on the wrong track.'

'Well, I don't,' said June, in her forthright way. 'I believe that she knows we are on to her, and that is why she is behaving herself at the moment. As soon as we drop our guard and stop watching her all the time, things will start to disappear again. Mark my words!'

With that, June got to her feet and said, 'Well, I'm off to tennis practice. Anyone coming?'

Freddie got up, and Felicity said, 'Susan and I will be there in a few minutes. I just want to sit and enjoy the sunshine for a little while.'

The four girls sat in comfortable, companionable silence for a few moments, enjoying the feel of the warm sun on their faces, then Susan suddenly said, 'You know, in a way I'm sorry that we didn't catch Delia trying to steal something.'

'Whatever do you mean?' asked Nora, startled. 'I thought that you liked Delia.'

'I do,' answered Susan. 'But now that it is looking as though Delia may not be the thief, it means that everyone else in the fifth form is under suspicion.'

'Exactly what I was thinking,' said Pam, sounding very troubled. 'Not a pleasant thought, is it?'

'Gosh!' exclaimed Nora, looking dismayed. 'I hadn't thought of that. How horrible!'

'It is horrible,' said Felicity. 'And it makes it even more important for us to clear this up and catch the thief as soon as possible.'

'Well, if any of you have any ideas of how we could do that, I'd be jolly glad if you would share them with me,' sighed Pam. 'For I'm stumped!'

But the others couldn't think of anything either, and at last Susan jumped up, saying, 'Come on, Felicity. Let's go and get some tennis practice in. Perhaps a little exercise will get our brains moving!'

Gillian was also at the tennis-courts, for now that half-term was over, she was working just as hard as before.

It seemed that the break had done her good, for the dark shadows beneath her eyes had lightened, and she was playing against her opponent, a West Tower girl, with renewed energy and determination.

'Good show, Gillian!' yelled June from the sidelines, as the girl sent a ball whizzing past the other girl. Then she turned to Felicity and Susan, saying, 'Ah, good, you're here. How would you like a game of doubles against Freddie and me?'

The two girls agreed to this eagerly, and took their places on the court. Felicity and Susan had played together so often that they knew one another's game very well indeed, and it stood them in good stead, for they beat their opponents comfortably.

Felicity, knowing how June hated to be beaten at anything, felt a little apprehensive as the four of them walked to the net to shake hands. But, to her surprise, June was grinning broadly.

Seeing the look of astonishment on Felicity's face, June laughed, and said, 'Are you wondering why I'm so pleased, Felicity? Well, it's because this proves that I have chosen exactly the right pair to represent us in the doubles against Summerfield Hall. I couldn't be more pleased to be beaten, for I know that you and Susan will do us proud in the tournament.'

Felicity and Susan felt pleased as well. Why, June really *was* learning the meaning of team spirit!

'Gillian is going to do well, too,' said June, looking across at the girl, who had finished her game and was sitting on the grass. 'I admit that I was a little worried about her, but now she's back on form and fighting fit.'

Gillian certainly felt fighting fit, and thought that it was marvellous what a couple of days' relaxation could do.

And it was just as well that she felt rested and

refreshed, for there was another orchestra rehearsal the following day. With that in mind, Gillian took herself off to one of the music-rooms to practise. But Delia, with Mrs Weaver's words in mind, went after her, calling, 'Where are you going, Gillian?'

'To play my violin,' answered Gillian. 'Come with me if you want. You can listen, and tell me what you think.'

Delia agreed at once, for she loved music. And she could keep an eye on Gillian, too, and make sure that she wasn't overdoing it.

There was a rapt expression on Delia's face as she perched on a stool and listened to Gillian play. Soon the girl was swaying from side to side again as she lost herself in the music, almost falling off her stool at one point!

Then Gillian began her solo, and, unable to stop herself, Delia began softly singing the words that she had written to accompany the tune. Now it was Gillian's turn to listen, and, as she did, her fingers gradually stopped moving, until the only sound that filled the room was that of Delia's sweet voice.

At first Delia didn't realise that Gillian had stopped playing, and continued to sing. Then she became aware that she was no longer being accompanied, and her voice died away.

'Sorry,' she said gruffly, looking rather self-conscious. 'I just got carried away. Don't know what came over me!'

'Heavens, don't apologise!' cried Gillian. 'Why, it sounded marvellous. I had no idea that Millicent wrote words as well.'

Delia hesitated, then decided that she didn't want to mislead Gillian, who had been a true friend to her.

So, rather reluctantly, she confessed, 'Actually, Millicent didn't write the words. I did.'

Gillian gave a gasp, and exclaimed, 'You dark horse, Delia! You've been telling us that you're such a duffer, and all the time you have been hiding this wonderful talent for song-writing.'

'I would hardly call it a talent,' said Delia, turning red at this unaccustomed praise. 'It was just a little rhyme that I jotted down at the first rehearsal.'

'Nonsense!' said Gillian. 'The words are simply beautiful, and they fit the music perfectly. And you have such a lovely singing voice.'

'Do I?' said Delia, looking most astonished.

'Yes,' said Gillian firmly. 'So sweet and pure. I know! Why don't we go down to the common-room and you can sing for the others? They will be absolutely amazed! I'll bring my violin and accompany you.'

But poor Delia was far too nervous and lacking in confidence to even think of such a thing. And she was more than half inclined to believe that Gillian was only praising her so extravagantly because she was her friend. Why, she often used to sing at her aunt's house, as she helped with the daily chores, and the reaction she got from her aunt and cousins was quite different.

Her mean-spirited cousins had told her that she sounded like a parrot squawking, while her aunt had sternly ordered her to be quiet, as the racket Delia was making was giving her a headache.

The fifth formers probably wouldn't be so unkind, for they were well brought-up, polite girls. But how dreadful it would be if they laughed at her behind her back.

'I really couldn't!' said Delia, shaking her head and looking terrified. 'My voice isn't good enough, and I would feel so nervous that it would shake terribly.'

Gillian disagreed wholeheartedly with this, but realised that if she tried to push Delia into performing for the others it would simply make her more scared. Lack of confidence was at the root of the girl's problem, she realised, and Gillian's mouth pursed as she thought that Delia's strict aunt and beastly cousins were responsible.

As Delia's friend, she really ought to do something about building the girl's confidence, but she had taken on so much herself that it would be difficult to find the time. Suddenly a thought occurred to her, and she said, 'Delia, I shan't try and persuade you to sing for the others, but if you would sing along with me sometimes when I rehearse, I really think that it would help me.'

'Really?' said Delia, surprised and pleased.

'Really,' said Gillian, solemnly. 'And who knows, perhaps you can think of some more words that you can set to the music. That would be super!'

'All right then, I shall,' agreed Delia, thinking that this was something that she would enjoy doing, and that she would feel quite comfortable singing for Gillian, and even letting her see any words she composed, for she knew that her friend would not make fun of her.

So Delia sung until she was hoarse, and when she couldn't sing any more, she sat and listened to her friend playing.

Gillian played the same few bars over and over again, for there was one note that she simply *couldn't* get right, no matter what. By the end of it, she had managed to get the note right, but she was looking pale and strained again.

Delia noticed this, and could have kicked herself. She had promised Mrs Weaver that she would look after Gillian, and make sure that she didn't tire herself out. And she had been so carried away with her singing that she had failed, and let Mrs Weaver down.

Heavens, they must have been up here in the music-room for simply ages!

In fact it was almost ten o'clock, and the others were all getting ready for bed when Delia and Gillian went to the dormitory.

'Where have you two been?' asked Felicity.

'In one of the music-rooms,' answered Gillian, with a yawn. 'Delia has been listening to me practise my violin.'

Millicent looked at the girl with approval, saying, 'That's what I like to see! A bit of dedication and hard work.'

June was less pleased, for she didn't like to see any member of the tennis team working hard for anyone other than herself. But June saw how tired and pale Gillian looked, and held her tongue.

At last everyone settled down, and Pam turned the lights out. There was no need, of course, for her to remind everyone of the no-talking rule, for as fifth formers the girls would not have dreamed of disobeying it.

One by one, the girls dropped off to sleep. Gillian was first, for she was completely exhausted. And Delia was last, for she had a lot to think about. Her feelings were mixed, for, on the one hand, she felt ridiculously pleased at the way Gillian had complimented her on her singing and the words that she had written to Millicent's tune. On the other, she couldn't help feeling that she hadn't done a very good job at getting her friend to spend more time relaxing, and less on tennis and music.

Well, tomorrow was a new day, and Delia vowed that she would work in earnest towards keeping the promise she had made to Mrs Weaver.

The thief strikes again

There was a shock in store for Amy the following morning. The girl's mother had given her a very expensive bottle of French perfume at half-term, which she had displayed proudly on her bedside cabinet. All of the fifth formers had been allowed to sniff at it, but no one had been allowed so much as a dab of the scent, for, as Amy had said, in her haughty way, 'Mummy went to a great deal of trouble to get it for me. It's very expensive, you know, and quite difficult to get hold of.'

'I should put the stopper back in, at once, Amy,' June had said gravely. 'Otherwise the scent will escape and all you will be left with is a bottle of liquid with no smell at all.'

'Rubbish!' Amy had said, though she had looked a little doubtful.

'It's perfectly true,' Freddie had said, with a completely straight face. 'My aunt once had a bottle of perfume, and she forgot to put the stopper back in, and the following day the smell had all gone! My aunt was frightfully upset, of course, for it was a birthday present from my uncle, and she had to throw it away.'

Amy was never *quite* sure when June and Freddie

were pulling her leg, but, to be on the safe side, she had put the stopper back in the scent bottle at once, and placed it carefully on her cabinet.

The others had known that June and Freddie were having a joke, and had smiled to themselves, even Bonnie unable to hide a grin at her friend's confused expression.

This morning, Amy, who always took a great deal of care over her appearance, was sitting on the edge of the bed, brushing her silky blonde hair, when her eye fell upon the cabinet, and she gave a little shriek.

There were several fifth formers in the dormitory, and they jumped, Pam saying, 'For goodness' sake, Amy, *must* you squeal like that? Whatever is the matter?'

'My perfume!' cried Amy, looking very distressed. 'It's gone!'

Everyone gathered round at once, Bonnie saying, 'Are you sure that it hasn't fallen on the floor, Amy?'

The fifth formers began to hunt for the missing perfume bottle, looking under beds and behind cabinets. But there was no sign of it.

'Where *can* it have gone!' asked Amy, who really was very upset, for expensive possessions meant a great deal to the girl.

'I should think that it has gone to the same place as Millicent's purse and Susan's chocolates,' said June, in a hard little voice. 'The thief has struck again!'

'Then we must tackle her,' said Amy. 'It's one thing to take a box of chocolates, or a purse with only a few pounds in it, but that perfume is most exclusive, and –'

'Oh, do be quiet, Amy,' said Felicity, exasperated. 'It isn't the value of the things that have been stolen that is important. It is the fact that we have a thief among us.'

'Quite right,' said Pam, well aware that, as head-girl, it was up to her to take some action. But she couldn't think quite what to do, for it really was a very tricky situation.

June, though, had very definite ideas, and she said, 'Delia must be hiding the things somewhere. Perhaps they are in her cabinet. I vote we take a look.'

But Pam said firmly, 'No. I refuse to do something so sly and underhand. Besides, we have all been watching Delia, and she hasn't taken anything, although she has had several chances.'

'Well, someone has the stolen things,' said Amy. 'And there's no denying that a bedside cabinet would make a jolly good hiding place.'

'Very well,' said Pam. 'After breakfast we shall all come to the dormitory, and I shall ask everyone to open their bedside cabinets, so that we can see what is in there. Does everyone agree that that is fair?'

The others nodded solemnly, and went to join the rest of the fifth form for breakfast. Slipping into her seat, Felicity stole a glance at Delia, sitting across the table next to Gillian.

The girl was tucking into toast and marmalade, looking relaxed and happy as she chattered to her friend, and Felicity thought that surely Delia could not look like that if she was hiding a guilty secret.

At last the meal was over, and Julie and Lucy got to their feet.

'We're off for a ride,' said Lucy. 'It's a beautiful day, and we don't want to miss a second of it.'

'Hold on a minute, please,' said Pam. 'I would like you all to come up to the dormitory for a few moments.'

Those girls who hadn't been present when it was discovered that Amy's perfume was missing exchanged puzzled glances, and Julie said, 'Why, Pam?'

'I shall tell you when we get there,' replied Pam. 'It won't take long, and I would be very grateful if you all do as I ask.'

So the fifth formers trooped back upstairs, and, once they were in the dormitory, Pam said, 'Can you all stand by your cabinets, please.'

The girls did as they were asked, Pam standing by hers as well. Then she said, 'I would like you all to open the doors so that we can see what is inside.'

'Why?' asked Gillian, looking rather bewildered.

'Well, Gillian,' said Pam. 'I hate to say this, but it appears that we have a thief in the fifth form. As you know, Millicent's purse disappeared a while ago, then Susan's chocolates, and now Amy's perfume has gone. It's possible that the thief has hidden the things in her cabinet, so we are going to check all of them. Does anyone object?'

No one did, and June, looking hard at Delia, was forced to admit to herself that if the girl was putting on an act, it was a jolly good one. She looked very shocked indeed, but not at all guilty, and was among the first to pull open her cabinet door. There was nothing in there, of course, but her own belongings, and as Pam went along looking inside all the cabinets, it soon became apparent that no one was hiding anything.

At last she said, 'Felicity, will you look in my cabinet, please, then I can put myself in the clear as well.'

Felicity did as she was asked, peering into Pam's cabinet, and moving a few things so that she could get a good look.

'Not a thing,' she said, when she had finished her search. 'Not that I expected Pam, of all people, to be hiding stolen goods.'

The girls all felt secretly rather relieved that nothing had been found in the dormitory, yet uneasy that the thief was still at large.

'A bit of a waste of time, really,' said June to Freddie afterwards. 'The thief has obviously found a safer hiding place, and we are no closer to unmasking her.'

Amy, of course, was most displeased, and she stalked up to Pam, saying crossly, 'I think that we ought to report the matter to Miss Grayling. Whoever took my perfume simply can't be allowed to get away with it. The Head must call the police, and –'

'My dear Amy, I am quite sure that the police have more important matters to deal with than your missing perfume,' said Pam coolly. 'Besides, if the police are called it will mean bad publicity for the school, and the Head won't want that if it can be avoided.'

'Then what is to be done?' demanded Amy.

'I don't know,' admitted Pam, with a sigh.

'I have an idea,' said Bonnie, coming forward.

'Then by all means let's hear it,' said Pam.

Bonnie glanced round, to make sure that no one else was in the room but the three of them. The others had all gone, and as Bonnie felt quite certain that neither Pam nor Amy was the thief, she was able to speak freely.

But first, Bonnie took something from her cabinet, and held it out to show the other two. It was a large brooch, sparkly, shiny and glittery, and Amy wrinkled her long nose in distaste, saying, 'What an awful thing! Really, Bonnie, I always thought that you had good taste.'

Bonnie laughed, and said, 'Quite hideous, isn't it? My aunt gave it to me for my birthday, and I would be most grateful if someone would steal it, for I couldn't possibly wear it.'

'What are you suggesting, Bonnie?' asked Pam, with a frown.

'Well,' said Bonnie, her eyes dancing impishly. 'If I was to leave this lying around somewhere, surely the thief won't be able to resist it. It's not particularly valuable, but it *looks* as if it might be.'

'Yes, but I don't see what good it would do,' said Pam. 'Our thief would be certain to take the brooch, but it won't help us to find out who she is.'

'Ah, but it will,' said Bonnie. 'Look!'

She held out her hand, and Pam and Amy saw that her fingers were covered with glitter.

'It comes off, see?' said Bonnie. 'And although it seems to rub off the brooch quite easily, it tends to stick to the fingers unless you wash your hands thoroughly.'

'So once the brooch has been taken, all we have to do is look at everyone's hands!' said Amy excitedly. 'My word, Bonnie, what a super idea!'

'It *is* a good idea!' said Pam, looking pleased. 'But are you sure you don't mind risking your brooch, Bonnie?'

'Not at all,' said Bonnie, with a smile. 'The thief is quite welcome to it. I shall put it on top of my bedside cabinet, where she can't help but notice it.'

'Yes, it does rather draw one's attention,' said Amy, with a shudder. 'It sparkles so much that I daresay we shall still be able to see it when the lights are out!'

Bonnie went to wash the glitter from her hands, then she and Amy went off to the common-room together, while Pam sought out Nora and bore her off for a walk along the cliffs.

As it was Sunday morning, the girls were busily engaged in their own activities. Julie and Lucy, of course, were out riding, Millicent was poring over her music, and June, helped by Freddie, was making out a list of practice times for the lower school.

Felicity and Susan were helping in the school garden, and even Gillian was enjoying a little fresh air, for Delia, mindful of her promise to the girl's mother, had insisted that she come outside for a stroll around the gardens.

Gillian had been reluctant at first, saying fretfully,

'I really should be practising my music, for there is a rehearsal this afternoon.'

'You spent most of yesterday evening practising,' Delia had pointed out, her tone of voice unusually firm. 'I think it would do you much more good to spend a little time outdoors, then you will turn up for rehearsal refreshed, and with a clear head.'

Gillian had been forced to admit that there was something in that, and said, 'It does seem a shame to be cooped up indoors on such a beautiful day. Very well, Delia, I'll come with you.'

And the two girls had whiled away a pleasant couple of hours idly strolling about the grounds, passing the time of day with Mam'zelle Dupont, admiring the beautiful blooms in the Head's garden, and simply sitting on the grass chatting about this and that.

'Well, what a nice, peaceful morning it has been!' said Gillian happily, as she and Delia made their way to the dining-room for lunch. 'I would never have guessed that simply doing nothing could be such fun.'

Delia laughed, and said, 'I do wish that I could come and watch the rehearsal this afternoon. I shall be quite at a loose end.'

'Well, come along then,' said Gillian. 'Perhaps it will help me to play better if I can see a friendly face.'

'I can't,' said Delia, with a grimace. 'You know that Millicent has banned anyone who isn't actually in the orchestra from attending rehearsals.'

'Yes, but I think that she only said that because some of

the younger girls who came to watch were fooling about, and distracting the orchestra,' said Gillian. 'She knows that no fifth former would behave like that, so I am quite sure she won't object if you want to sit and watch.'

Millicent didn't object, for she didn't want to upset Gillian, and had noticed how friendly she and Delia had become. So she smiled brightly, and said, 'Of course, Delia is most welcome to sit and watch. I know that she can be trusted not to distract anyone.'

But there were discontented mutterings from some of the orchestra members as Delia took a seat at the front of the hall.

'My friend Meg would have liked to come and watch us rehearse,' said Kathy, of the third form. 'But Millicent simply wouldn't hear of it.'

'I should have liked to bring one or two of the East Tower girls along for support, too,' said Anne, scowling. 'Millicent said no to that as well. It just isn't fair! There is one rule for Gillian, and another for the rest of us.'

'Yet Millicent expects us to play our hearts out for her,' said Janet. 'Well, I think it's about time she gave something back.'

'Yes, it really is difficult to do something whole-heartedly when we are being treated so unfairly,' said Jessie. 'I, for one, am beginning to wish that I had never put my name down to join this beastly orchestra.'

'Quiet, please, everyone!' said Millicent sharply. 'Let's begin the rehearsal. I would like you to play the whole piece through, from beginning to end.'

'What if someone makes a mistake?' called out Janet.

'If you have been practising as you should, there shouldn't be any mistakes,' said Millicent briskly. 'However, if anyone *does* play a wrong note, I want her to ignore it and carry on. What I am trying to do today is to get an idea of how the whole thing will sound.'

So the orchestra played 'Summer Serenade' all the way through, and it sounded so beautiful that even Millicent was pleased, and managed a few words of praise.

'I can hear that you *have* been practising hard,' she said, with a smile. 'Well done.'

Then she glanced at her watch, and said, 'As you have done so well, I think that you deserve a short break. We will start again in fifteen minutes.'

With that, Millicent swept from the room. Some of the orchestra followed her, keen to get a breath of fresh air, while others sat on the chairs in the hall, simply glad of a rest.

'Well, wonders will never cease!' said Jessie. 'Fancy Millicent allowing us a break!'

'And she praised us,' said Anne. '*All* of us, not just Gillian. Well, if Millicent keeps this up, I daresay it won't be so bad being in the orchestra, after all.'

But Anne had spoken too soon, for the rehearsal, which had started so promisingly, was to end in disaster.

A few minutes before the orchestra were due to take their places again, Kathy's friend Meg, along with several of her fellow third formers, peeped into the hall. Seeing that Millicent was not present, they ventured in, and the rather cheeky Meg asked, 'Where's the slave-driver?'

Kathy giggled, and answered, 'She's given us a well-earned break and gone off for a walk.'

'Yes, and I think it might be a good idea if you kids disappear before she comes back,' said Gillian. 'Unless you want one of Millicent's scolds.'

'Pooh!' scoffed Meg, forgetting for a moment that she was talking to a fifth former. 'I see that *your* friend is allowed to watch the rehearsal, Gillian.'

Gillian's eyes flashed angrily, and she said, 'How dare you speak to me like that? Apologise at once!'

Meg scowled, and hesitated for a moment, then, as she saw Gillian reach into her pocket for the punishment book that all the fifth and sixth formers carried with them, she blurted out, 'I'm sorry. I didn't mean to sound rude.'

All would have been well, and the third formers would have left quietly, but just then Millicent returned, and, on spotting the youngsters, went 'up in the air', as Kathy put it.

'Kathy, didn't I tell you that no one was allowed to watch the rehearsal without my permission?' she snapped. 'I don't take kindly to being disobeyed. You kids, clear off at once!'

Now Meg, who had just been thinking herself lucky to have escaped a punishment for cheeking Gillian, felt nettled. Why did Millicent have to be so autocratic and unpleasant all the time?

She glanced round at the rest of the third formers,

all of whom were eyeing Millicent apprehensively, and waiting to take their lead from Meg. And Meg knew that she would go up in her form's estimation no end if she stood up to the bossy Millicent.

'Why should we leave?' she asked defiantly. 'I'm sure that we have as much right to be here as Delia.'

There were murmurs of agreement from the third formers, and Millicent said, 'Delia is a fifth former, and can be relied on to behave. Unlike you youngsters. Now push off, before I dish out punishments to the lot of you!'

'Just as we were hoping that Millicent had turned over a new leaf,' murmured Janet to Anne and Jessie. 'I thought it was too good to be true.'

But Meg, with the admiring eyes of her form upon her, wasn't giving up without a fight, and began to argue with Millicent.

Thoroughly exasperated, Millicent pulled out her punishment book, quickly wrote something on one of the pages, then ripped it out and handed it to the furious Meg.

'There!' she said. 'And let it be a lesson to you to show a little respect to your elders!'

Meg was shocked when she looked at the piece of paper and saw that she had been given a hundred lines, but it was worth it when she saw the admiration on the faces of her friends.

'Never mind, Meg,' whispered Kathy, who felt quite furious with Millicent. 'I'll do half of them for you.'

'Be quiet, Kathy, and get to your place, please,' said Millicent sharply. 'And once your friends have buzzed off, you can play your part again, for I noticed several wrong notes earlier. Perhaps if you spent more time practising, and less fooling around with your friends, you would be a better musician.'

Poor Kathy's face burned, for she knew that Millicent was deliberately trying to humiliate her in front of her form. She glanced round at her friends, saw their sympathetic glances, and something inside her snapped.

'Very well,' she said coldly. 'If I am such a poor musician, Millicent, perhaps you had better find someone else to take my place.'

And, before the astonished eyes of the orchestra, Kathy picked up her trumpet and stalked towards the door. She was followed by her friends, all of them delighted that she had made a stand.

Millicent, however, was thoroughly dismayed, and called out, 'Kathy, wait! You can't just leave the orchestra like that! I shall report you to Miss Grayling.'

'You can't,' retorted Kathy in a tight little voice. 'I joined the orchestra of my own free will, and I am leaving of my own free will. Neither you, Millicent, nor Miss Grayling herself, can force me to continue.'

And Millicent was left quite speechless, for once, because she knew that Kathy was right. Blow, now what was she to do? The competition was only four weeks away, and now she, Millicent, had to find another trumpet player who could learn the music in such a short time. And Millicent had to admit that, in spite of her harsh words, she would never find another one as good as Kathy.

Mutiny in the orchestra

Millicent did find another trumpet player, but the girl was a first former who hadn't been playing for very long and wasn't up to Kathy's standard. And it seemed that Millicent had learned nothing from her mistakes, for at the next rehearsal she was so bad-tempered that Jessie also resigned from the orchestra, leaving another gap to be filled.

'These kids have no staying power,' Millicent complained to Anne, when the rehearsal was over. 'They simply can't stick at anything.'

Anne, who had been on the verge of walking out herself on more than one occasion, said nothing. Millicent was so thick-skinned that she simply couldn't see that if only she would treat her orchestra with a little more respect and kindness she would get better results.

Jessie had played the cello, and Millicent knew that there were only two other girls in the school who played that instrument – Lizzie, of the third form and Belinda of the fourth.

As Lizzie was the better player, Millicent approached her first. But, out of loyalty to her friend Kathy, Lizzie flatly refused to be part of the orchestra.

'No thanks,' she said shortly. 'I don't want to give up my free time only to be shouted at and humiliated, as poor Kathy was. And now you have driven Jessie away too. If you're not careful, Millicent, you won't have an orchestra left to conduct!'

Millicent smarted at Lizzie's words, but they sank in, and she made up her mind to be a little less hard on the players.

Belinda, who had heard about Jessie's resignation, and also knew that Millicent had asked Lizzie to replace her, wasn't at all pleased to be third choice. But, with Lizzie's words in mind, Millicent was unusually humble when she spoke to the girl, and soon Belinda found herself feeling sorry for the fifth former and agreed to take Jessie's place in the orchestra.

The fifth form knew of Millicent's troubles, of course, for word travelled fast, but few of them had much sympathy to spare for her. They thought that she only had herself to blame. Besides, they had other things to worry about, for the thief had struck again.

Poor Nora was most upset to discover that her watch, which had been a present from her parents, had gone missing. And Julie was very puzzled indeed when her purse disappeared.

'It was empty,' she told some of the others, as they sat on the lawn one sunny afternoon. 'Not so much as a penny in it, for I'm quite broke until my people send me some money next week.'

'Why on earth would someone steal an empty purse?' said Susan.

'Perhaps the thief didn't realise it was empty when she took it,' said Felicity.

'Well, that will have been one in the eye for her,' said Pam, with satisfaction. 'Gosh, wouldn't I have loved to see her face when she opened your purse, Julie, only to find nothing there!'

'Yes, but everyone in our form knew that you were broke, Julie,' said Lucy, who had been looking thoughtful. 'You were complaining about it in the common-room only the other night, remember?'

'That's right,' said June. 'And you were complaining jolly loudly, too, so we all heard you!'

'Not all of us,' said Freddie. 'Only those of us who were in the common-room that evening.'

'Let's think,' said Nora. 'It was Friday evening. Who was missing?'

'Delia and Gillian,' said Felicity. 'Gillian had gone to practise her violin, and Delia went with her.'

'Millicent was missing, too,' said June. 'I remember her saying that she had been so wrapped up in her composing and orchestra rehearsals that she was quite neglecting her practice, so she went off to one of the music-rooms as well.'

'I think we can rule out Millicent,' said Susan. 'She's hardly likely to take her own purse.'

'Unless she is trying to throw us off the scent,' said Bonnie.

'What do you mean?' asked Pam.

'Well, Millicent may have been pretending that she had her purse stolen,' answered Bonnie. 'So that we wouldn't suspect her of being the thief.'

'Well, in that case I could be the thief too,' said Amy. 'I wasn't in the common-room when Julie said that she had no money, for Matron had sent for me. So I could easily have pretended that my perfume had been stolen, then taken Julie's purse.'

But no one seriously suspected Amy. The girl had her faults, but she wasn't dishonest. Besides, Amy's parents were wealthy, and she always had as much money as she wanted, so there was no need for her to steal.

Yet the one thing that seemed to hold no attraction for the thief was Bonnie's sparkly brooch. It had lain untouched on her bedside cabinet for several days now, and, lowering her voice, Bonnie murmured to Amy, 'It's so ugly that no one even wants to steal the beastly thing!'

'Well, at least we know that our thief has good taste,' said Amy, with a laugh. 'She took my expensive perfume, yet won't touch your horrid little brooch!'

'Yes, it's a pity,' said Bonnie. 'For that would have trapped her nicely. If only we could find something a little more tasteful that we could catch her out with.'

Amy snapped her fingers suddenly. 'But we can!' she said. 'The thief has my perfume, Bonnie. And what is the use of stealing a bottle of perfume if one isn't going to wear it.'

'Of course!' said Bonnie, her eyes lighting up. 'Well

done, Amy. Perhaps all we have to do is follow our noses. We'll concentrate on Millicent, Delia and Gillian for now, as they are the three who were absent when Julie was talking about having no money.'

Millicent was extremely irritated that evening when Bonnie sat down next to her in the common-room that evening and began to sniff noisily. The girl was reading a book about great composers, and Bonnie was ruining her concentration. At last she flung she book aside, and said crossly, 'Bonnie, *must* you do that?'

'Sorry, Millicent,' said Bonnie, giving another loud sniff. 'I think I have a cold coming on.'

'Well, for heaven's sake use a handkerchief!' said Millicent. 'Or better still, go and sit somewhere else.'

Bonnie was finished with Millicent anyway, for all she had been able to smell was the faint scent of soap and talcum powder. Quite pleasant, but nothing like the strong, distinctive scent of Amy's perfume. She went across to join her friend, who had just been speaking to Delia and Gillian, and was now looking rather glum.

'Well, neither Delia nor Gillian are wearing my perfume,' Amy sighed. 'All I could smell on Gillian was shampoo, and Delia didn't seem to smell of anything at all. How about Millicent?'

'No, Millicent wasn't wearing your perfume either,' said Bonnie. 'Although, now that I come to think of it, the thief might think it was too risky to use the perfume at school. She might have decided to take it home and wear it during the hols.'

Amy didn't look at all pleased at this thought, but brightened when Bonnie said, 'Cheer up! There are still several weeks to go before we break up, which leaves plenty of time for the thief to slip up. So there is still a chance that you may get your perfume back untouched.'

But the thief didn't slip up over the next few days. Pam lost her best fountain pen, and June was simply furious when a tie-pin that she had bought for her father's birthday was taken. June always hated the thought of anyone getting one over on her, and she took the theft very hard indeed.

'I'll find out who it is, you see if I don't!' she vowed to Freddie. 'And when I do, my gosh I'll make her sorry.'

'Yes, but what on earth would a schoolgirl want with a tie-pin?' asked Freddie, puzzled. 'I mean to say, it can't be any use to her at all.'

'Perhaps the thief means to give it to *her* father as a present,' said June grimly.

'You know, June, I don't often agree with Amy, but perhaps she is right and we ought to report this to the Head,' said Freddie. 'It really is going too far now, with something vanishing almost every day.'

June heartily agreed that the thief was going too far, and getting much too sure of herself, but she still felt reluctant to report the matter to Miss Grayling. Much better, she thought, if the fifth form could have the satisfaction of catching the thief themselves, and then hauling her before the Head!

Something very surprising happened the following

day. The girls had just gone down to breakfast, but, as she reached the bottom of the stairs, Bonnie realised that she had forgotten her handkerchief, and, as she had the beginnings of a horrid summer cold, went back up to the dormitory to fetch it. And then what a shock she got! For the brooch that she had put out to catch the thief was gone!

The girl almost quivered with excitement, for she had quite given up hope of the thief falling into her trap. But now it seemed that she had. And it would be an easy matter, at the breakfast table, to take a look at everyone's hands and see whose was covered in the tell-tale glitter. Bonnie couldn't be certain whether the brooch had been there when she had woken up, for she had forgotten to look. It could have been taken overnight, or perhaps someone had sneaked it off the cabinet while the fifth formers were getting ready for breakfast. That would have been an easy matter, for there was always a lot of to-ing and fro-ing first thing in the morning, with girls in and out of the bathroom all the time.

Hastily, Bonnie stuffed her handkerchief into her pocket and made her way down to the dining-room, where she slipped into her seat, between Pam and Amy. Quickly, she whispered to both girls, telling them what had happened.

They were most astonished, and Pam said in a low voice, 'Well, it looks as if we are about to catch our thief.'

'But what if she has washed the glitter off her hands?' whispered Amy.

'It's awfully hard to get off,' said Bonnie. 'No matter how you scrub. When I handled it the other day I still had little specks stuck to my fingers the next day.'

'I say, Delia!' said Pam, raising her voice. 'Pass the marmalade, would you?'

Delia did so, and Pam took the opportunity to take a good look at her hands. They were spotless, and Pam turned to Bonnie and Amy, giving a quick shake of her head.

Over breakfast the three girls had an opportunity to inspect the hands of all of the fifth formers, even those that they were certain were quite innocent. But, by the time the meal was over, they were no further forward, for none of the fifth formers had so much as a speck of glitter on her hands.

'Well, I'm baffled!' said Pam, as she left the dining-room with Bonnie and Amy. 'Bonnie, are you absolutely certain that the brooch was in its usual place when you went to bed last night?'

'Absolutely,' said Bonnie with a firm little nod. 'But I can't be sure whether it disappeared overnight, or this morning.'

'So much for our trap!' said Amy disconsolately. 'What a let-down.'

'Not entirely,' said Bonnie with a smile. 'At least I have got rid of that dreadful brooch!'

Pam laughed at that, and said, 'Well, at least something good has come out of this awful business for you, Bonnie. But the thief is still running rings round us.

I'm afraid that, if we can't clear this matter up ourselves very soon, we really will have no choice but to report it to Miss Grayling.'

Bonnie's cold seemed to grow steadily worse during the first lesson, which was French. Mam'zelle Dupont noticed that the girl, who was one of her favourites, was sneezing rather a lot.

'Are you ill, *ma petite*?' she asked, kindly.

'Oh, it's just a little cold, Mam'zelle,' said Bonnie, smiling bravely. 'Nothing to worry about.'

Then she gave the most enormous sneeze, so loud that Freddie, sitting next to her, said afterwards that it almost blew her papers off the desk.

'*Tiens!*' cried Mam'zelle, quite alarmed. 'This is no little cold, *ma chère* Bonnie, this is a great big cold, for it makes you do a great big sneeze. You must go to Matron at once!'

Bonnie wasn't very thrilled at the thought of going to Matron, whose remedy for colds was a large dose of extremely nasty-tasting medicine. But she did so hate having a cold, for it made her nose red and her eyes water. So, looking rather brave and pathetic, she smiled wanly at Mam'zelle, and walked from the classroom.

Matron was scolding a rather sullen looking first former when Bonnie found her in the San, saying in her brisk, no-nonsense voice, 'Come now, Ruth, don't be such a baby! The sooner you take your medicine, the sooner you can get out of here and go back to your class.'

Just then, Bonnie gave another loud sneeze, and

Matron turned sharply, saying, 'Goodness me, not another one with this troublesome summer cold that's going round! Well, Bonnie, perhaps you can set an example to young Ruth here, and take a dose of medicine without complaining.'

'Of course, Matron,' said Bonnie, glancing at Ruth, who looked as if she was about to burst into tears at any second. Bonnie didn't feel very happy either, but she certainly wasn't going to let herself, or her form, down by making a fuss in front of a first former.

So Bonnie swallowed the spoonful of medicine that Matron gave her in one gulp, even managing not to grimace at the unpleasant taste.

'Not too bad at all,' she said, smiling at Ruth. 'Do you know, I think that I feel better already.'

Heartened by this, Ruth screwed up her courage and also swallowed a spoonful of the medicine, but she failed to hide her disgust as well as Bonnie had, and screwed up her face.

'Here,' said Matron, reaching into a big glass jar on her desk. 'Have a barley sugar to take the taste away.'

Ruth accepted the sweet eagerly, and went off back to her class, while Bonnie said to Matron, 'Aren't you going to offer me a barley sugar, Matron?'

'Certainly not!' cried Matron. 'I keep them for the younger girls, but certainly don't hand them out to fifth formers.'

Then her face creased into a smile, and she said, 'Oh, very well, Bonnie. As you helped me get Ruth to take her medicine, I suppose you have earned one.'

Matron handed the girl a sweet, and that was when Bonnie noticed something very strange indeed. Something that shocked her so much that she could hardly believe her eyes. For Matron's fingers were speckled with glitter!

A shock for Bonnie

Bonnie felt so stunned that, afterwards, she was quite unable to remember saying goodbye to Matron, or walking back to the classroom. But, somehow, she found herself back at her desk, suddenly aware that everyone was looking at her in concern.

'Are you all right, Bonnie?' asked Freddie anxiously. 'You look awfully pale.'

Mam'zelle, too, was worried about her favourite, and cried, 'Ah, what is Matron thinking of to send you back to your lesson in this state? You should be in bed, in the San!'

'Oh no, I am quite all right, Mam'zelle,' said Bonnie, pulling herself together. 'It's just that the medicine Matron gave me tasted so very horrid that it quite upset me.'

Mam'zelle seemed satisfied with this explanation, and Bonnie did her very best to concentrate, though it was very difficult. How on earth was she to tell the fifth form that their kindly, beloved Matron was a thief? And would they even believe her?

At break-time Bonnie dragged a very surprised Amy into a corner of the courtyard and, having looked all around to make sure that they could not be overheard, said in a low voice, 'I have something to tell you.'

'I knew that something was wrong when you came back from seeing Matron,' said Amy, with satisfaction. 'What is it?'

And then Amy listened, open-mouthed, as her friend told of her shocking discovery. Amy had no great liking for Matron, who had quickly sized her up as vain and spoilt, but even she found it almost impossible to believe that she was a thief.

'Bonnie, you simply *must* have made a mistake,' she said at last. 'Heaven knows Matron is not my favourite person, but no one could doubt her honesty.'

'Well, that's what I thought,' said Bonnie rather sadly, for she had always had a soft spot for the no-nonsense, yet kindly, Matron. 'But I saw the glitter on her hands with my own eyes.'

'Well, you will have a hard job convincing the others that Matron is a thief,' said Amy heavily. 'They all think that she is too wonderful for words.'

'I know,' sighed Bonnie. 'Even though I saw the evidence I only half believe it myself. I shall have to tell the others. I shan't accuse Matron, or say that she could be the thief. I shall simply say that she had glitter on her hands, which is the truth, and I shall leave it to the fifth formers to reach their own conclusions.'

'I suppose that is the best thing to do,' said Amy. 'When will you tell them?'

'This evening, when we are all together in the common-room,' said Bonnie. 'It's going to be jolly unpleasant, so I'd rather get it over with as soon as possible.'

So, when the fifth formers gathered in the common-room that evening, Bonnie looked round to make sure that everyone was present. There was the usual buzz of chatter, some of the girls listening to music on the radiogram, others reading and all of them looking happy and contented. Except for Bonnie, who was miserably aware that she was soon about to wipe the smiles from their faces. The girl had wracked her brains throughout the day to think of another explanation as to why Matron's fingers had been speckled with glitter, but hadn't been able to come up with anything.

She cleared her throat rather nervously now, and was just about to ask for everyone's attention when someone rapped smartly at the door. Then it was pushed open and Matron herself entered.

As the girls made to get to their feet, she said in her usual, brisk way, 'Stay where you are, girls. No need to get up, for what I have to say will only take a moment. This morning, just after you went down to breakfast, I did a quick inspection of your dormitory.'

'Heavens, Matron,' said Pam, looking alarmed. 'Don't say that someone forgot to make her bed.'

'No, I am pleased to say that everything was as neat as a new pin,' said Matron. 'Exactly as I should expect from fifth formers. There was only one thing out of place, and it was this.'

Matron reached into the big pocket of her starched, white apron and pulled something out. She stretched out her hand, and Bonnie and Amy exchanged startled glances, for in her palm lay something which sparkled and glittered.

'My brooch!' cried Bonnie.

'Ah, it *is* yours!' said Matron, handing it to Bonnie. 'I wondered if it might be, for I found it on the floor, in between your bed and Amy's.'

So that was what had happened, thought Bonnie. The brooch must have fallen on to the floor, and while the girls were making their way downstairs, Matron had done a quick dormitory inspection, and her sharp eyes had spotted it. In the time it had taken Bonnie to realise she had forgotten her handkerchief and walk back upstairs to fetch it, Matron had pocketed the brooch and made her way back to her own quarters.

'I should have asked you about the brooch when you came to my room earlier, but it went right out of my mind,' said Matron. 'Here you are, and take better care of it from now on, Bonnie.'

She handed the brooch over, then looked down at her hands, saying, 'My goodness, how the glitter comes off! I shall have to go and wash my hands now.'

Bonnie sighed with relief as the door shut behind Matron, then Pam came over and said in a low voice, 'So Matron had your brooch all along! I quite thought the thief had taken the bait, but now it seems that we are just as much in the dark as ever.'

'Yes, and I have this horrid little brooch back,' said Bonnie, sounding glum. 'I wonder if I shall ever get rid of it?'

Bonnie was unusually quiet and lost in thought for the rest of the evening, as she occupied herself with her sewing. Normally she and Amy would chatter together as she worked, but tonight Bonnie didn't seem to have much to say for herself. At last the silence grew too much for Amy, and she said, 'Whatever is the matter with you, Bonnie? I should have thought that you would have been pleased to learn that Matron isn't the thief.'

'Of course I'm pleased,' said Bonnie. 'But you know, Amy, I really don't feel awfully pleased with *myself* at the moment. You see, I knew, in my heart, that Matron would never steal anything from any of us girls. But because I had seen the evidence – or what I *thought* was evidence – I was prepared to ignore my better judgement and forget everything that I know to be true about Matron's character. It just goes to show that it's best to have faith in what you believe.'

Amy was much struck by this, and looked at her little friend with new respect, for Bonnie sounded so wise and knowledgeable.

'I really feel that I have learned something very important today,' said Bonnie, a very solemn look in her big, brown eyes. 'And it is something that I shall never forget.'

But someone who didn't seem to have learned anything in her dealings with people was Millicent.

She held another orchestra rehearsal on Saturday afternoon, and this time things went badly wrong.

Millicent was not in the best of moods, for she had planned to start the rehearsal at two o'clock, but had had to put it off until after tea.

This was thanks to June, who had already put Gillian down for tennis practice at two o'clock, and flatly refused to change it. Millicent did her best to convince Gillian that it was far more important to rehearse for the competition than play tennis, but her efforts were in vain, for Gillian said firmly, 'I can't let June down, Millicent. She put me down for tennis practice before you arranged the rehearsal, you know. But I don't want to let you down either, so if you can just hold the rehearsal later I can attend both.'

Millicent had done this, but with very bad grace indeed. Somehow the girls always seemed to feel more tired and less attentive after tea, and Millicent knew that they would not be at their best.

Her temper was not improved when she entered the hall to overhear Anne talking to Belinda.

'I think it's jolly brave of you to take Jessie's place,' Anne was saying. 'The rest of us who have been in the orchestra from the start didn't know what we were letting ourselves in for when we put our names down. But now word of Millicent's bad temper and high-handed manner has got around, so you *do* know. And you still let her talk you into it!'

Belinda gave a rather nervous laugh, and said, 'I'm not sure whether I am being brave or foolish, but no doubt I shall soon find out.'

Just then the two girls heard a loud cough behind them, and turned, startled, to see that Millicent had come in. Both of them turned red, hoping devoutly that the girl hadn't heard what they were saying.

But, as the rehearsal went on, it became clear that Millicent *had* heard.

So, Anne thought that she was bad-tempered and high-handed, and had tried to turn the new cello player against her! Well, she was in for a shock.

And, much to the surprise of the orchestra, Millicent was sweetness itself to Belinda, although the girl played a great many wrong notes.

'You have only had a few days in which to learn the music,' she said kindly. 'I am sure that you will be quite as good as Jessie was, once you have practised a little more.'

Anne, however, came in for a great deal of criticism, much of it unfair. Millicent felt very sore with Anne, for she thought it most improper of her to have spoken disrespectfully to one of the younger girls. This was very true, and Anne was regretting having done so. In fact, she had already made up her mind to go up to Millicent and apologise to her after the rehearsal. But that was before Millicent decided to humiliate her in front of the entire orchestra, and in a very short time all of Anne's good intentions had vanished.

When Millicent made her play the same passage over and over again, Anne suddenly decided that nothing, not making her parents proud, not even winning the competition for the glory of Malory Towers, was worth putting up with this for.

Deliberately, and with great relish, Anne brought her hands down hard on the keys, making a loud, discordant sound that caused the others to wince and cover their ears. Then she played the passage through for the final time, her face perfectly serious as she purposely struck all the wrong keys. The noise that Anne made was quite dreadful, but her expression and attitude were so solemn, as though she were some great concert pianist, that the others couldn't stop laughing.

Millicent listened as though she couldn't believe her ears, at first, then, when she realised that Anne was fooling, she flew into a fine rage!

'Anne, stop that at once!' she cried, quite white with anger. 'You are making a mockery of the whole thing!'

But Anne took no notice and carried on playing – and the rest of the orchestra carried on laughing!

Of course, this was really very childish behaviour from a fifth former, and Anne realised this, but there was just something about Millicent that made one *want* to behave childishly!

At last the music – if one could call it music, thought Millicent – came to an end. Anne's fingers became still on the keys, and the laughter of the rest of the orchestra ebbed away as they looked at Millicent standing before them, silent and furious.

But the girl wasn't silent for long.

'Fine behaviour for a fifth former, I must say!' she

said, her voice quivering with anger. 'And a fine example to set the younger members of the orchestra. In fact, Anne, I shall have to consider whether I can allow you back after this.'

'Oh, really?' said Anne in rather a haughty manner. 'Well, let me save you the trouble, Millicent. I wouldn't carry on playing in your beastly orchestra for the world!'

Gillian, who hadn't joined in the others' laughter at Anne's antics, stepped in to say, 'Anne, please think carefully. If you have a bone to pick with Millicent that is between the two of you, but by resigning you are letting down the orchestra and the whole school.'

'Well, you would say that, Gillian!' retorted Anne. 'Millicent never picks on you as she does on me, for you are her favourite and can do no wrong in her eyes. No, I am sorry, but my mind is made up.'

'Very well, then, go,' said Millicent, coldly.

'I shall,' said Anne, getting up from the piano and stalking towards the door. 'Do you know, I believe that I might take up tennis, instead. It will be a pleasant change to spend time with someone like June, who has the qualities that make a good leader.'

This was an unfortunate remark, for Millicent, who felt intensely jealous of June, and the way that she inspired such loyalty among the girls, bristled. And, although she did not betray it, Millicent felt extremely alarmed as Anne walked out. It had been difficult enough to replace Kathy and Jessie, but finding a good pianist at this late stage would be almost impossible.

Then Millicent suddenly remembered that Anne hadn't been her first choice. Young Hannah had, but that beastly June had got in first and nabbed her for the tennis team. Well, thought Millicent, with sudden resolve, she was going to jolly well change Hannah's mind, and get her to drop tennis and play for the orchestra instead. That would be one in the eye for June, and for Anne, too, when she saw how well the orchestra was doing without her, and how much better Hannah was.

Millicent looked round at the orchestra now. Some of them looked apprehensive, some gleeful. The girl knew that she was not going to get anything worth listening to out of them now, and decided to abandon the rehearsal for the time being. Far better, she thought, to concentrate her efforts on getting a really first-class pianist. That would give everyone's spirits a boost!

All of the girls were pleased to finish early, no one more so than Gillian. She had come straight to rehearsal from a very energetic tennis practice, and felt quite exhausted. And very soon it would be time for prep! Ah well, at least there was time for a quiet sit-down in the common-room first.

Millicent, meanwhile, was lucky enough to bump into Hannah in the corridor, and lost no time in trying to win the girl round.

'Hannah,' she said. 'I have been meaning to congratulate you on getting into the tennis team. You must be very proud.'

Hannah, who knew that Millicent had been

displeased with her for turning down a place in the orchestra, was rather taken aback by this, and stammered, 'W-why, thank you, Millicent.'

'My loss is June's gain,' said Millicent with a laugh. 'I do hope that she isn't working you too hard.'

'Oh no,' said Hannah, her eyes shining. 'June is simply marvellous, always offering help and encouragement so that somehow one wants to do one's best for her. It doesn't seem like hard work at all.'

Once again Millicent felt the familiar stab of jealousy, but she quelled it, saying brightly, 'How nice! I like to think that I have instilled the same spirit into my orchestra.'

Hannah, who, along with the rest of the school, had heard the tales of Millicent's autocratic attitude and bursts of temper, rather doubted this, but didn't dare say so.

'I may as well tell you this, Hannah,' said Millicent, leaning forward in a confidential manner. 'For you are sure to hear it sooner or later. I have had to ask Anne to resign her place in the orchestra.'

This was *almost* true, thought Millicent, for she had told Anne that she would have to consider whether she could have her back or not.

Hannah, of course, felt enormously flattered at being confided in by one of the bigger girls and, her eyes growing big, said, 'Heavens, Millicent! Whatever will you do now, without a pianist?'

'Well, between you and me, Hannah, Anne simply

wasn't up to the job,' said Millicent with a sigh. 'I decided that if I couldn't have a first-rate pianist I would rather have no one at all. Of course, it means that I am going to have to do an awful lot of rewriting, but that can't be helped.'

The girl paused for a moment, as though thinking deeply, then said, 'What a pity that you can't do as Gillian is doing, and play tennis for June, and the piano for me. Still, I suppose there aren't many girls who have Gillian's energy and commitment.'

Just then a group of Hannah's friends came along, so Millicent said goodbye and went on her way. She judged that she had said quite enough to set Hannah thinking, anyway. Millicent knew that the girl had a competitive streak, and wouldn't relish being unfavourably compared to Gillian. Really, Millicent thought, she had been quite clever in the way she had handled the situation. Hannah was sure to want to prove herself, and would soon come running to Millicent almost begging for a place in the orchestra. All she had to do was sit back and wait!

Delia makes a discovery

Millicent was quite right, for her words brought Hannah's competitive streak to the fore. The second former watched Gillian at tennis practice, a few days later, and noticed that the girl seemed to be a little off her game. She also overheard Felicity saying to June, 'Gillian really doesn't look at all well. I wouldn't be a bit surprised if she's suffering from exhaustion.'

'Oh, don't be so melodramatic!' June had scoffed. 'She's just a little tired, that's all. A good, long sleep tonight and she will be absolutely fine.'

Felicity wasn't so sure, and nor was Hannah. She began to think that it would be quite a feather in her cap if she, a mere second former, could succeed where a fifth former had failed.

So, after tea, Hannah went in search of Millicent and told her that she would be happy to play the piano for her. Millicent, of course, was thrilled and made a great fuss of Hannah, which pleased the girl enormously. So much, in fact, that she began to get a little swollen-headed and, when she returned to the second-form common-room, couldn't resist boasting a little.

'It's difficult to be so much in demand,' she said, with

a little toss of her head. 'But both June and Millicent are relying on me, so I must do my best not to let them down. Or the school, of course, for I am doing all of this for the honour of Malory Towers.'

The downright second formers, however, weren't fooled by this, and Hilda, the head-girl, said scornfully, 'Pooh! You're doing this for your own glory, my girl. You like the idea that you are "in demand", as you call it, and are enjoying setting two of the fifth formers at loggerheads.'

'What nonsense!' said Hannah, though her cheeks turned a little pink. 'Besides, June and Millicent aren't at loggerheads. How can they be, when June doesn't even know yet that I am going to be in the orchestra.'

'Oho!' cried Hilda. 'So June doesn't know yet? Well, she's going to be none too pleased when she finds out, you mark my words!'

Hilda was quite right. Millicent took great delight, that evening, in telling June that Hannah was going to play piano in the orchestra. June was very displeased, for, although she would not admit it to any of the others, she had seen the toll that being involved in both projects was taking on Gillian. She had held her tongue, for she had hoped that Gillian would see sense and resign from the orchestra. But gradually she had come to realise that Gillian was the kind of person who stuck to her word and, if she said that she would do a thing, jolly well did it! And now here was one of the younger girls – and another of her star players – trying to copy her!

June had no intention of letting Millicent see that she was annoyed, though, and said with a smile, 'I hope that she works as hard for you as she does for me, Millicent. I know that you have a talent for getting the best out of people. People like Kathy, and Jessie, and Anne . . . oh no, wait a minute! They have all resigned from the orchestra, haven't they? Well, Hannah is a sticker, just like Gillian, so at least you know that you have two players you can rely on.'

Millicent's face darkened, and June laughed softly, before saying, 'Be careful, Millicent, or your entry for the competition might just be a duet, instead of an orchestra!'

So Millicent was the one left feeling cross and uncomfortable, and she stomped away, wondering bitterly how it was that she never managed to get the better of June when they had one of their clashes.

As soon as she was out of earshot, June turned to Freddie, who was sitting beside her and had overheard the whole exchange, saying determinedly, 'She's not having Hannah. And I shall get Gillian away from her somehow, too. They are two of my best players, and I don't like to see them splitting themselves in two, so to speak.'

'But what can you do?' asked Freddie. 'You can hardly order them to resign from the orchestra. And if you make them choose, there is always the chance that they might choose Millicent.'

'I know,' said June, with a sigh. 'And I can't risk

that, for without them Malory Towers hasn't a hope of winning the tennis tournament.'

'Perhaps you and Millicent could reach a compromise,' suggested Freddie. 'You could have Gillian, and she could have Hannah, or vice-versa. At least then you both end up with someone first-rate.'

But June was far too stubborn to agree to any kind of compromise, and she was quite certain that Millicent was too.

In fact, both girls were far more alike than they cared to admit. June was firmly convinced that her tennis tournament was far more important than Millicent's little competition. And Millicent thought that tennis was just a silly game, unlike music, which was lasting and brought pleasure to so many people.

One thing the two girls did have in common was their determination to bring glory to their school. Freddie, glancing from one to the other, thought that if they had both been on the same side they would have been a formidable force indeed. What a pity that they were enemies instead!

Millicent slept well that night, for she decided that it was foolish to let June needle her. Instead, she decided to think of the good things that had happened that day. She had lost Anne, but had got Hannah – the girl she had really wanted – in her place. The youngster was going to have to put in a lot of practice to learn the music in time, but that was good too, for it meant that she would have less time to spend on tennis. And June wouldn't like that at all!

June took a little longer to get to sleep, for she was turning over various plans in her mind to get Gillian and Hannah to leave the orchestra and concentrate solely on their tennis. Hannah would be relatively easy, she decided, for the girl admired her, June, enormously. All she had to do was take an interest in one of the other youngsters, and hint that Hannah's place in the team was at risk if she spent too much time rehearsing with the orchestra. Hannah would soon fall into line, for she thought a great deal more of June's good opinion than she did of Millicent's. Once she had arrived at this decision, June felt a lot easier in her mind and soon dropped off.

Very soon all the fifth formers were asleep – apart from one. Poor Delia was feeling very troubled, for that very morning she had received a letter from Gillian's mother. Mrs Weaver had written:

I was quite concerned when I saw how ill Gillian looked at half-term. I feel so much happier now that I know that Gillian has a good friend, who will watch over her and make sure that she won't overdo things.

But although Delia had watched over Gillian, she hadn't been able to stop her from doing exactly as she pleased. Sometimes Delia would broach the subject, rather tentatively, but Gillian would always brush it aside, her manner becoming bright as she insisted that she was quite well and enjoyed having plenty to occupy her time. And Delia wasn't a strong enough character to push the matter. She sat up in bed suddenly, hugging her knees. A shaft of moonlight shone through a crack in the curtains, and she could see all of the fifth formers asleep in their beds. Delia sighed softly, wondering what the others would do in her position. If Felicity was worried about Susan, she would tell her so, straight out, thought Delia. She certainly wouldn't allow herself to be brushed off, and nor would Susan if anything was the matter with Felicity. It was the same with Pam and Nora, Julie and Lucy, and Amy and Bonnie.

None of them would be afraid of taking the bull by the horns, even if it meant the risk of causing offence, or falling out. Because they knew that their friendships would survive, and even grow stronger as a result. That was the trouble, thought Delia. She was too afraid of pushing Gillian away altogether, and losing her. But then, if she could lose her so easily, perhaps their friendship wasn't worth having.

With these thoughts churning around in her head, Delia lay down again and, at last, fell into an uneasy and fitful doze. A sound woke her, some hours later, and her eyes flew open. Blinking, she sat up and saw that the door was opening, a dark shape silhouetted there. In the middle of the night, all sorts of horrid, creepy thoughts filled Delia's mind, and she wondered if she should yell, and wake the others. Then the shape closed the door and advanced into the room, and Delia felt weak with relief as the shaft of moonlight fell on it, and she realised that it was only Gillian.

She must have been to the bathroom, thought Delia,

and whispered, 'Gillian! Are you all right?'

But Gillian had climbed back into bed and gone straight off to sleep again. Which, thought Delia, just proved how exhausted she was.

The girl mentioned the incident to Gillian the following morning, as they dressed.

Gillian laughed, and said, 'Heavens, I must have been worn out, for I don't remember getting out of bed at all! Why, I must have gone to the bathroom in my sleep.'

'You always seem worn out these days,' said Delia. 'And I can't say I'm surprised.'

Once again Gillian laughed, and brushed her friend's words aside, but this time Delia was determined not to let the matter drop so easily. She opened her mouth to speak, but before she could do so, Freddie suddenly cried, 'I say! The thief has struck again! I bought myself a new hair-slide when I went into town the other day, and it has completely vanished.'

'Are you sure it hasn't just fallen on the floor, as Bonnie's brooch did the other day?' asked Felicity. 'I know how careless you are with your things, Freddie.'

'No, for I put it in the drawer of my cabinet when I took it out last night,' said Freddie.

'That's right,' said June. 'I saw you.'

'It seems that our thief is getting desperate,' said Amy with a sniff. 'First she goes for purses, and things like watches and brooches – not to mention my expensive perfume – and now all she can find to take is a cheap hair-slide.'

'Do you mind?' said Freddie. 'It might just be a cheap hair-slide to you, Amy, but I spent the last of my pocket money on it. What's more, I don't have another one, and Miss James will probably send me out of the class for having untidy hair.'

Fortunately Felicity was able to prevent this disaster from befalling Freddie, by lending her a hair-slide of her own. But the most recent theft put everything else out of the girls' heads for the moment, and the chance for Delia to tackle Gillian was lost.

Pam was very concerned, for as head of the form she felt that it was up to her to do her utmost to catch the thief, or at least stop her, and so far her efforts had met with no success at all.

'If Freddie put her hair-slide in her drawer, that means that it must have been taken overnight, when we were all asleep,' she said. 'Right from under our very noses. And yet not one of us woke up and saw or heard a thing.'

'Perhaps it isn't someone from our form at all,' suggested Susan. 'It could be someone from another dormitory sneaking in here, and into our common-room.'

'Well, I suppose that's possible,' said Pam. 'Though I can't think who would have such a grudge against the fifth form. I have made a decision though. If the thief hasn't slipped up and been caught by the end of the week, I am going to Miss Grayling.'

No one felt very happy about this, for the girls always liked to deal with such matters themselves, if they could.

But they were forced to admit defeat on this occasion, and agree that there was nothing else they could do.

Delia, meanwhile, was very thoughtful, and very troubled. For she *had* woken up, and she had seen something. She had seen Gillian, out of her bed. But the girl had been nowhere near Freddie's cabinet. In fact, she had been coming into the dormitory from the landing. Ah yes, said a troublesome little voice in Delia's head, but suppose Gillian had already taken Freddie's hair-slide before you woke up? Suppose that she hadn't been to the bathroom at all, but had gone out to hide the hair-slide somewhere, before slipping back in? Determinedly, Delia hushed the voice. How could she even think such a thing about her best friend? And then, the little voice piped up again, there was the business of Millicent's notebook being in Gillian's bag. But Delia had never asked for an explanation. Perhaps if she had done so at the time, Gillian would have been able to clear the matter up, and these horrible doubts wouldn't keep popping up.

'Horrid, isn't it?' said a voice in her ear suddenly, making her jump. Delia turned to find Gillian standing behind her.

'I say, are you all right?' asked Gillian, frowning. 'You look awfully serious.'

'Oh, I was just thinking about all these thefts,' said Delia, turning a little red. 'That's enough to make anyone look serious!'

'Yes, that's just what I was saying,' said Gillian. 'Poor

Freddie! I know that she hasn't lost anything valuable, but it must feel horrible to think that someone has been in your drawer, and gone through all your belongings. Ugh! It quite gives me the creeps.'

Delia was cheered by this, for surely Gillian couldn't have spoken with such conviction if she really had been the thief. Smiling, she slipped her arm through the girl's, and said, 'Let's try to put it out of our minds for a while. Ah, there's the breakfast bell. I'm starving!'

'Me too,' said Gillian. 'I shall need a good breakfast, for I mean to get some extra tennis practice in this afternoon. I was quite off my game yesterday.'

'Perhaps you were off your game because you have been practising *too* hard,' suggested Delia rather timidly as they made their way downstairs.

'There's no such thing as practising too hard,' said Gillian, pulling a wry face. 'When it comes to tennis or music, it really is a case of practice makes perfect.'

'Of course,' said Delia. 'But surely even the most dedicated sportswoman or musician needs some time to relax.'

'You're absolutely right,' said Gillian, and Delia felt her heart lift. Then it sank again, as Gillian added, 'And the time to relax is when the tournament and the orchestra competition are both over. Ah, you wait, Delia, you will see a different side to me then, I promise you. I shall become so lazy that I'll make Nora look positively energetic.'

Perhaps, thought Delia, Gillian really did know best

after all. She seemed quite cheerful this morning, and the dark shadows beneath her eyes were less pronounced, although she had had a disturbed night. When June heard that she was planning to get some extra tennis practice in, she patted Gillian on the back and exclaimed, 'That's what I like to see! A bit of enthusiasm. Good for you, Gillian.'

And, in Delia's mind, that settled it. Everyone said what a marvellous games captain June was, and the whole school knew how well she looked after her players. So if June thought it was all right for Gillian to keep up the pace she had set herself, it must be.

The lower school were also having tennis practice that day, and June made a point of singling out Barbara, the reserve. She praised the girl extravagantly, applauding her every shot, so that Barbara soon began to feel quite overwhelmed. Poor Hannah, on the other hand, found herself almost ignored, though she was practising very hard indeed and really playing very well.

After her game had finished, Hannah, feeling rather hurt, went up to June and said hesitantly, 'June, have I offended you in some way?'

'Of course not,' said June brightly. 'What makes you think that, Hannah?'

'Well, it's just that I played my very hardest today, yet you didn't even seem to notice.'

'I did notice,' said June. 'And of course I am very pleased. But you see, Hannah, I have decided that I need to pay more attention to Barbara, as it is likely that she will be playing in one of the matches now. She is not as good as you, and doesn't have your confidence.'

'Barbara may be playing in one of the matches?' said Hannah, not liking the sound of this. 'I don't understand, June. I thought that she was to be reserve.'

'Yes, she is. But now that you have decided to play in Millicent's orchestra, I have to be prepared for the fact that you may find it too much,' said June.

'Oh, but I shan't!' said Hannah, dismayed. 'Really, June, I wouldn't have taken it on if I had thought it would be too much for me.'

'I'm quite sure that you wouldn't,' said June with a smile. 'But you see, Hannah, the responsibility of choosing the best players for the team doesn't lie with you. It lies with me. And if I think that your commitment to the orchestra is interfering with your tennis, then I may have no choice but to replace you.'

Poor Hannah felt so upset that she could barely speak. Why, she had written to her parents and grandparents to tell them that she was playing in the tournament, and they had written back, all of them telling her how proud they were. If June were to drop her now it would be too bad!

'Cheer up, Hannah,' said June. 'I haven't dropped you yet. And even if I do, why, you will still have the honour of playing in the orchestra. Of course, you will just be one of many, and the real glory – if you win – will be Millicent's. Now, if you were to win your tennis match, it would be your victory, and yours alone.'

Clever June gave Hannah a few moments to digest this, then she called out, 'Oh, jolly well played, Barbara! Hannah, do excuse me, while I go and speak to Barbara.'

Hannah was left alone, and she thought hard. June's words had hit home, as the girl had known they would. The honour of the school was very important, but how marvellous it would be to have a slice of the glory all to herself, thought Hannah. And, if she won her singles match, that is what she would have. She glanced across at Barbara, who was hanging on June's every word, staring up at her with an adoring expression. Oh, she simply couldn't bear it if the girl took her place on the team, and got what she so badly wanted herself! Hannah's mind was made up. Now came the difficult bit – informing Millicent of her decision!

A most peculiar night

The atmosphere in the fifth-form class-room was not at all pleasant during prep that evening. As Lucy remarked to Julie, 'You could cut the air with a knife.'

The reason, of course, was that Hannah had told Millicent of her decision not to play piano in the orchestra after all. Millicent had been simply furious, and had been very cold indeed to Hannah.

June, on the other hand, was delighted when Hannah sought her out and told her that she had decided to devote herself to tennis.

'I'm very pleased to hear it,' June had said with a wide smile. 'I didn't relish the idea of losing one of my best players to Millicent. I feel sure that you have made the right decision, Hannah. But then, I always knew that you would, for you're a very bright kid.'

These words of praise were very pleasant to hear, and Hannah felt more convinced than ever that she had been right to leave the orchestra, though she still felt a little upset at letting Millicent down.

The next person to seek June out was Millicent. She found her down by the tennis courts, along with Felicity, Susan, Freddie and Gillian, and all five girls knew from the expression on Millicent's face that she was in a temper.

The girl wasted no time in getting to the point, saying angrily, 'You mean beast, June! How dare you lure Hannah away from me?'

'Lure?' repeated June, with a soft laugh. 'Let me assure you, my dear Millicent, there was no luring necessary. Hannah is quite capable of reaching her own decision, and that is exactly what she did.'

'Yes, with a little help from you, no doubt,' snapped Millicent. 'You are determined to sabotage my efforts to win the orchestra competition.'

'Oh, don't talk nonsense,' said June, beginning to lose patience now. 'I hope that you do win the competition, but not at the cost of my tennis tournament.'

'Well, I'm hardly likely to win without a pianist,' said Millicent bitterly. 'In fact, we might as well pull out.'

'Come now, Millicent,' said Felicity, beginning to feel a little sorry for the girl. 'There are several girls in the school who can play piano, and I'm sure that there is still time for someone to learn the music. You'll find someone.'

'Yes, someone third-rate,' said Millicent bitterly. 'Hannah and Anne were by far the best players in the school.'

'And you've lost them both,' said June, in a light drawl that made Millicent long to shake her.

Just then Pam came up, and seeing Millicent's angry expression and June's mocking one, her heart sank.

'What's up?' she asked, dreading the answer.

But Millicent's eyes suddenly lit up, and she almost pounced on Pam, seizing her arm.

'Hey!' shouted Pam. 'Steady on, Millicent!'

'Sorry,' said Millicent, slackening her grip. 'Pam, I've just remembered that you play the piano. How would you like to be in the orchestra?'

'Good idea,' said June, with a grin. 'Pam, Millicent was just saying that she was looking for a third-rate pianist!'

'June, do be quiet!' said Felicity, seeing that Millicent looked as if she was about to explode again. But the girl calmed herself and said evenly, 'Actually, I said that I feared I might have to make do with a third-rate pianist. Then I remembered you, Pam. Do say that you will do it.'

Pam looked into Millicent's intense, earnest face and saw at once how much the competition meant to her.

'Very well,' she said at last. 'I will do it, for the sake of the school. But please understand this, Millicent. I will not be bullied or humiliated by you. Any of that kind of thing, and I shall resign at once. Is that clear?'

'Absolutely,' said Millicent, feeling very relieved indeed. Pam wasn't the best pianist in the school, but she was better than no one. And perhaps Millicent could re-write things a little, so that she didn't have quite such a complicated solo to learn.

'Well, all has ended happily,' said June, smiling. 'Millicent has found her third-rate pianist, and Pam has the satisfaction of knowing that she was only third choice.'

Millicent shot June a poisonous glare and stalked off,

while Pam said amiably, 'You know, June, if we weren't in the fifth form I would scrag you.'

June laughed at this, while Susan said, 'I hope you know what you've let yourself in for, Pam.'

The easygoing Pam shrugged, and said, 'Well, it's as I said to Millicent. Any nonsense and I shall clear off. How do you find her, Gillian?'

'Well, I know that she can be very harsh to some of the others,' said Gillian. 'But she's never been unpleasant to me.'

'No, because she is afraid that you will leave her high and dry,' said June. 'And she can't afford to lose anyone else.'

'Yes, as it is she's scraping the bottom of the barrel, having to suffer me as pianist,' said Pam drily.

'Ah well, never mind,' said June, a wicked sparkle in her eyes. 'I daresay she will tell the others to play more loudly so that they drown out all your wrong notes. Ouch, you beast! That hurt!'

The others laughed, as Pam playfully punched June in the shoulder. She really was very good-natured, thought Gillian, joining in the laughter. Then, all of a sudden, a great wave of tiredness seemed to wash over her, as it often did these days, and she put a hand over her mouth to stifle a yawn.

'An early night for me tonight, I think,' she said.

'I should think so,' said Pam. 'I went past one of the music-rooms last night and heard you practising until almost ten o'clock. You were singing, too. I must say, you have the most beautiful voice.'

Gillian looked puzzled for a moment. She hadn't been singing, and she certainly didn't have a beautiful voice – far from it! Then she remembered that Delia had been with her, and had sung along to the music. The girl had added some more words to the little song she had written and had wanted to see how they sounded. And they had sounded fine, sung in Delia's melodic, lilting voice. But Delia still firmly refused to believe that she had any talent at all, and Gillian knew that she would not want the others to know that it was she who had been singing.

So she said, quite truthfully, 'Oh, my voice is nothing special, Pam.'

'You're too modest,' said Pam. 'You really must sing for the girls in the common-room one evening.'

'Perhaps,' said Gillian, making up her mind to develop a sore throat at the earliest opportunity.

Gillian really did feel quite exhausted, and she surprised the others by going to bed at eight o'clock that evening.

'Heavens!' said Bonnie. 'Fancy going up to bed early when you don't have to.'

'I'll come with you,' said Delia.

'You don't have to,' said Gillian. 'Stay up and chat with the others if you want to.'

But Delia insisted that she felt tired as well, so the two girls said goodnight to the others and made their way up to the dormitory.

In fact, Delia had made a plan. She intended to get to sleep early, and wake up a few hours later, just to see if anyone did come into the dormitory and try to steal anything.

Gillian fell asleep as soon as her head touched the pillow, and as soon as she had dropped off, Delia set her little alarm clock for one in the morning and placed it under her own pillow. Of course, it might be that the thief would not strike tonight, in which case Delia was in for a long, lonely and very boring night. But that was a chance she would have to take, and if the thief did come in it would all be worth it.

Very soon Delia was asleep too, and the rest of the fifth formers were careful to make as little noise as possible when they came up a couple of hours later, so as not to disturb the sleeping girls.

Soon all was quiet, and remained so until one o'clock, when Delia's alarm clock went off. She woke at once and slipped her hand under the pillow to stop the muffled ringing. Then the girl sat up and looked round, relieved to see that no one else had heard it, for everyone was fast asleep.

Half an hour crept by very slowly indeed, and Delia wished that she had a torch, so that she might have read under the covers. At last, more for something to do than because she really wanted it, she went to the bathroom to get a glass of water. And while she was in there, she heard the unmistakable sound of footsteps on the landing. Delia waited until she heard them going downstairs, then, very softly, she opened the bathroom door and peeped out.

Yes, someone was walking down the stairs. Someone wearing spotted pyjamas, and with a very distinctive head of red hair. Gillian!

Delia's heart sank. Surely she hadn't woken up in the hope of catching the thief only for it to turn out to be her best friend? But she could think of no other reason for Gillian to be wandering around in the middle of the night. She waited for the girl to reach the bottom of the stairs, then padded soundlessly after her, keeping her distance and staying in the shadows.

Delia watched as Gillian went into the common-room, her heart thumping so loudly that she was sure the girl must be able to hear it! But Gillian was intent on whatever she was doing, and didn't so much as glance round.

Delia hid herself in an alcove just along the corridor and waited and listened. Gillian was muttering something to herself, and Delia strained to hear what it was. It sounded as if she was saying, 'Where is it? Where is it?' over and over again. How odd! What on earth could she be looking for? A few moments later Gillian emerged. She was carrying something, Delia saw, and the girl had to stop herself from gasping out loud when she saw what it was. A delicate little embroidered spectacle case that Bonnie had made for her aunt's birthday. Bonnie had only finished it last night, and had put it in her needlework box, which she kept in the common-room cupboard. But what on earth did Gillian want with it? She didn't even wear spectacles. Delia shook herself. What did that matter? What was more important, and deeply shocking, was the discovery that Gillian, her dearest friend, was the thief. Oh dear, now what was she to do?

Someone else had woken up in the fifth-form dormitory. Felicity, disturbed by a sudden, loud snore from Susan, in the next bed, had woken with a start and, after trying unsuccessfully to get back to sleep again, sat up and rubbed her eyes. That was when she noticed that two of the beds were empty. One was Delia's, but whose was the other? Oh yes, Gillian's, of course. But where on earth could the pair of them be?

Surely Gillian hadn't been so foolish as to go and practise her music at this hour, and had persuaded Delia to go with her? If one of the mistresses caught them they would be in big trouble, and it would reflect badly on the whole form.

Felicity glanced across at Pam, and debated whether to wake her. But the head-girl was sleeping so soundly that she didn't have the heart. Instead, Felicity climbed out of bed, put on her slippers and decided to try and track down the absentees herself.

Fortunately she didn't have far to go, for when she got downstairs she could see Gillian quite clearly. But what on earth was she doing?

Under the stairs was a big cupboard, which was used for storing all sorts of odds and ends. Gillian had opened the door, and appeared to be putting something in there, Felicity saw, feeling completely bewildered. What very peculiar behaviour!

Delia suddenly appeared behind Gillian, so intent on what her friend was doing that she didn't even notice Felicity standing in the shadows.

Delia moved closer to Gillian, and peered into the cupboard, giving a gasp as she saw what else was in there. Nora's watch, Susan's chocolates, Amy's perfume – all the things that had been taken from the girls recently.

Poor Delia felt quite sick. How could she have been so mistaken in her reading of Gillian's character? She would have to tell the others, of course. It was only fair. Then they would all get their things back, and the form as a whole would decide what was to happen to Gillian.

'Gillian!' she hissed, standing right behind the girl. But Gillian didn't turn round. In fact, she didn't even seem to know that Delia was there at all. Instead, she was inside the cupboard, arranging all of the stolen things into a neat pile.

Felicity had been watching all this with a puzzled frown on her face, and she stepped out of the shadows, making Delia jump.

'Felicity!' she gasped. 'Oh, you did give me a fright.'

'Never mind that,' said Felicity. 'Delia, what on earth is going on here?'

'See for yourself,' said Delia sadly, indicating the pile of stolen belongings in the cupboard.

Now it was Felicity's turn to gasp, but before she could ask for an explanation, Gillian turned round, a strange smile on her face.

'I've found it,' she said. 'I just hope that I remember where I put it tomorrow.'

There was a queer, glassy look in her eyes, and she seemed to be staring straight through the two girls. It sent shivers up and down Delia's spine, and she said, 'Stop it, Gillian! You're talking nonsense.'

'Wait a minute!' said Felicity, realisation dawning on her. 'Delia, she's sleepwalking! I don't believe that Gillian knows we are here! I remember when I was in the first form, there was a girl in the dorm next door who used to do it. She came into our dorm a few times, and it was jolly frightening at first, until we realised what she was doing.'

'Oh!' said Delia, her brow clearing. 'We had better wake her up, then.'

'No, don't do that,' said Felicity quickly. 'I remember Matron telling us that you should never wake sleepwalkers. The shock can do them terrible harm.'

'Then what do we do?' asked Delia.

'We simply guide her back to bed,' said Felicity. 'You take one arm, Delia, and I will take the other.'

Gillian proved quite unresisting, and the two girls got her out of the big cupboard, then shut the door. Then they led her back upstairs and to her own bed, watching in astonishment as she climbed in, and went straight off to sleep as though nothing had happened.

'Well!' whispered Delia. 'What a very strange night this has been.'

'Very strange,' agreed Felicity in a low voice. 'And it's not over yet. Come with me, Delia.'

179

'Where are we going?' asked the girl.

'To the bathroom,' said Felicity. 'We need to discuss this, and I don't want to disturb the others.'

Things are cleared up

The two girls tiptoed to the bathroom and shut the door softly behind them. Then Felicity turned to Delia, and said, 'Am I to understand that Gillian took those things?'

'It looks like it, I'm afraid,' said Delia, and explained how Gillian had come out of the common-room with Bonnie's spectacle case.

'She was muttering to herself all the time she was in there,' Delia said. 'Something that sounded like, "Where is it?", over and over.'

'This is a strange business,' said Felicity. 'But there is one good thing that has come out of it.'

'Oh?' said Delia, quite unable to think what it could be.

'Of course,' said Felicity. 'Gillian must have been taking those things while she was sleepwalking. So although she is the thief, she's not *really* a thief, because she didn't know that she was stealing.'

'Yes!' said Delia, looking much happier suddenly. 'I say, Felicity, the others will see it that way too, won't they? I mean to say, they won't want to haul poor Gillian up before the Head, will they?'

'I am quite certain that they won't,' said Felicity. 'Once they know the whole story they will see that

Gillian wasn't to blame. And they will be jolly glad to get their things back, too.'

Delia seemed reassured by this, and lapsed into thoughtful silence for a few moments. At last, she said, 'Sleepwalking isn't a good thing, is it, Felicity?'

'No, it's not,' said Felicity, looking very grave. 'I believe that it usually means the sufferer is troubled about something, or is overdoing things.'

'Well, poor old Gillian has been doing far too much,' said Delia, feeling very guilty indeed. 'I just wish that I had been firmer with her, and tried harder to get her to relax. But I'm afraid I'm not very good at being firm with people.'

The girl looked so forlorn that Felicity felt touched, and she gave her a pat on the shoulder, saying, 'Well, Gillian is one of those people who sticks to a decision once she has made her mind up. You mustn't blame yourself, Delia, for people like that are very hard to move. I know that Pam tried speaking to her too, and she failed to make any impression on her.'

Felicity paused for a moment, then went on, 'But I am afraid that the sleepwalking puts a different complexion on things. Gillian must be *made* to listen to reason, and I think that we will have to call in someone in a position of authority to talk to her.'

'Miss Grayling?' said Delia, looking rather scared.

'I was actually thinking of Matron,' said Felicity. 'She has had experience in these matters, you know. I remember how well she took care of Jenny, the girl who started sleepwalking when we were in the first form.'

'Of course!' said Delia, brightening. 'Matron is just the person.'

'Well, you and I will go to her tomorrow, Delia,' said Felicity decidedly. 'She will know what to do for the best, you may be sure.'

Now that they had decided on a course of action, the two girls suddenly felt tired, and Felicity gave a yawn.

'Heavens, what a night!' she said. 'Come along, Delia, we'd better get some sleep, for it will be time to get up before we know it.'

So the two girls crept back into their dormitory, and, as Gillian had earlier, fell asleep at once.

After breakfast the following morning, there was half an hour before the first lesson began. Felicity and Delia had put their heads together in the dormitory that morning and made a plan. As soon as breakfast was over, Delia said to Gillian, 'How about a quick walk in the grounds before Maths?'

Gillian had agreed to this, and, once the two girls were out of the way, Felicity said, 'I would like you all to come with me, please. I have something to show you.'

The fifth formers were rather startled at this, and Nora said, 'What is it, Felicity? A surprise?'

'In a manner of speaking, yes,' said Felicity. 'Do come along, everyone, and you'll see.'

Felicity led the curious fifth formers to the big cupboard where Gillian had hidden their things, and she pulled open the door. There was a moment's astonished silence, then the astonished cries of the girls filled the air.

'My purse!'

'And mine! And Nora, there is your watch.'

'My perfume is here,' said Amy in delight. 'And it looks as if it hasn't been used at all.'

'Felicity, how did you discover this?' asked Pam, looking bewildered. 'Do you know how they came to be here, and who the thief is?'

'Yes, I do,' answered Felicity and, as quickly as possible, she told the others the story of how she and Delia had discovered Gillian sleepwalking last night.

As she had expected, the fifth formers were most sympathetic, and didn't blame Gillian at all for her actions.

'I just feel relieved that there is a simple explanation, and that we know there isn't a thief in the fifth form,' said Nora.

'Yes, it's a weight off all our minds,' said Freddie. 'It really was horrible feeling that there might be a thief in our midst.'

'Poor Gillian,' said Susan. 'I should think she will be absolutely mortified when she discovers that it was she who took our things – even though she did it in her sleep!'

'Well, I don't want her to find out just yet,' said Felicity. 'At break-time Delia and I are going to tell Matron about Gillian's sleepwalking, for I really feel that this is something we can't deal with ourselves.'

'Yes, you're quite right,' said Pam. 'Very well, we

shan't say a word to Gillian, and we shall all have to try and behave quite normally towards her until Matron has seen her.'

This wasn't easy, of course, for the girls felt so sorry for Gillian that they went out of their way to be extra nice to her. So much so, that the girl began to wonder what she had done to deserve it! And the two who were nicest of all were June and Millicent, for both of them felt a little guilty, knowing that it was largely their fault that Gillian was so overworked that she had begun sleepwalking.

Pam too felt a little guilty, for she had known that Gillian was tired, and doing far too much. True, she had tried to speak to Gillian about it, but when the girl brushed her concerns aside, perhaps she, Pam, as head-girl, should have gone to Matron or Miss James and let them deal with it.

At break-time Felicity and Delia went off to tell Matron the extraordinary story of Gillian's sleepwalking, though they left out the part about her taking their things. Matron listened, her expression becoming more serious as the tale went on, and when the girls had finished she said gravely, 'You did the right thing in coming to me, girls. This is a very serious matter, and must be dealt with before Gillian exhausts herself completely.'

Delia looked rather anxious, and said, 'I'm afraid that she will be angry with Felicity and me for going behind her back like this.'

'Now, don't you worry your head about that,' said Matron, kindly. 'I daresay she may feel annoyed with you at first, but once she has had a good rest and feels better, she will soon realise that you did it for her own good.' Matron got to her feet. 'Now I had better go and find Gillian, and break the news to her that she has been sleepwalking. Then I'm going to tuck her up in bed in the San.'

'She won't like that, Matron,' said Felicity.

'She won't have any say in the matter!' said Matron with a grim smile. 'I had better tell Miss Grayling all about it, as well, for it won't do to keep her in the dark.'

Indeed it wouldn't, for the Head took a keen interest in the welfare of all the girls, and would certainly want to be kept informed of Gillian's progress.

Gillian was very surprised when Matron approached her in the courtyard and said, 'Gillian, may I have a word with you in my room, please?'

'Of course, Matron,' said Gillian, looking rather puzzled. 'Is something the matter?'

'No, but we need to have a little talk,' Matron said, laying a firm but gentle hand on Gillian's shoulder and leading her away.

The others felt very subdued when they went into their French lesson, and Mam'zelle Dupont, noticing how listless they seemed, felt quite concerned about them, and gave the fifth formers a very easy time indeed.

Gillian did not return to class that day and, after tea, an anxious Delia went to Matron's room in search of news.

'She is sleeping now,' said Matron. 'And I'm hoping that she will go right through until morning.'

'When will she be able to come back to class, Matron?' asked Delia.

'Not for a few days, I'm afraid,' said Matron. 'And when she does, she must give up this nonsense of being in the tennis team and the school orchestra. Oh yes, I know all about that,' said Matron, smiling a little at Delia's surprised expression. 'Gillian and I had a very long talk earlier. She has known for some time that she has been overdoing things, but didn't know how to get out of it without letting either June or Millicent down. Well, the outcome is that she will have to let the pair of them down, for she is in no fit state to take on any extra activities.'

'Oh dear,' said Delia, looking very unhappy. 'I do feel that I am partly to blame for this, Matron, for I promised Gillian's mother that I would keep an eye on her. I'm afraid that I haven't done a very good job.'

'Well, I've no doubt you did your best,' said Matron, kindly. 'But you could hardly force Gillian to give up one of her commitments.'

'No, but it's jolly lucky that *you* managed to talk some sense into her,' said Delia. 'I can't think how you got her to listen to you.'

Matron laughed at this, and said drily, 'Well, Delia, I have a great many years' experience in dealing with stubborn, strong-willed girls. Gillian soon realised that she had met her match in me! Now, off you go and you may come and visit Gillian tomorrow. Tell the others that they may come too, but no more than two at a time.'

Delia went off to relay this news to the fifth formers. They were all pleased to learn that Gillian would be able to return to class in a few days, but June and Millicent were dismayed to learn that they had both lost their star player.

'But Gillian *must* play in the orchestra!' cried Millicent, a look of horror on her face. 'I simply can't manage without her. We have already had so many set-backs, and now this.'

'If that isn't just like you, Millicent,' said Felicity scornfully. 'Poor Gillian is ill, and all that you can think about is your precious orchestra.'

Millicent flushed, and said, 'Of course I'm concerned about Gillian, and I want her to get well as much as any of you. I can't help worrying about my orchestra, though.'

'And what about you, June?' said Susan. 'I suppose you're fretting about who is going to take Gillian's place in the tennis tournament.'

'Nothing of the sort,' said June, coolly. In fact, she was just as bitterly disappointed as Millicent, but was clever enough not to betray it to the others. 'Freddie is reserve, so she will take Gillian's place.'

A cheer went up at this, for everyone liked the cheerful, good-natured Freddie, and all were pleased that her chance had come to shine. Freddie herself turned quite pink with pleasure, and said, 'Now don't make me practise too hard, June, or *I* shall exhaust myself too, and end up in the San with Gillian.'

Delia, armed with a large bar of chocolate and the good wishes of the others, went off to visit Gillian the following morning. She felt a little apprehensive at first, for she was afraid that Gillian might be angry with her for going to Matron.

But, much to her relief, the girl greeted her with a warm smile, saying, 'Delia, how lovely to see you! My word, is that enormous bar of chocolate for me? How super!'

As she sat down on the edge of the bed, Delia was relieved to see that her friend looked much better after a good, long sleep, the colour beginning to return to her cheeks and the dark shadows beneath her eyes much less pronounced.

The two girls chatted about this and that for a while, then Delia said, rather hesitantly, 'Gillian, I do hope that you aren't annoyed with me for speaking to Matron about you. But I really was awfully worried, and didn't know what else to do.'

'Well, I was a bit cross with you at first,' admitted Gillian. 'But now that I feel well rested I am seeing things more clearly, and realise that you have done me a favour. I had begun to see that I was overdoing things, but I've always been a sticker, and couldn't bring myself to say to either June or Millicent that I wanted to pull out. I thought that everyone would think I was weak, and couldn't keep to my word. But then you and Felicity caught me sleepwalking, and once Matron told me what I had been doing, I knew that I simply couldn't go on like this without making myself really ill. You're a jolly good friend, Delia.'

'Thanks,' said Delia, rather gruffly. 'I only wish that I had been firmer with you earlier on. Your mother asked me to keep an eye on you, you know, at half-term. I feel as if I've let her down a bit.'

'Nothing of the sort,' said Gillian, putting her hand over Delia's. 'It was all my own stupid fault for not taking any notice of you. I knew what you were trying to do, in your own gentle way, but I was so sure that I knew what was best for me, I just brushed your worries aside. And you are so lacking in confidence that you let me.'

This was certainly true, and Delia nodded.

'Well,' said Gillian, 'from now on, if you have anything to say to me I want you to tell me straight. Even shout at me, if need be, and, even if I don't agree with what you say, I shall take notice of you!'

'I don't know if I shall shout,' laughed Delia. 'But I shall certainly tell you what's on my mind. Which reminds me, we have cleared up that business of the fifth-form thief.'

'Really?' said Gillian, her eyes growing wide. 'Who was it?'

'Well, the thing is, Gillian,' said Delia, 'it was you.'

Gillian, of course, looked completely taken aback, and, quickly, Delia rushed on, 'You didn't take things intentionally. We all know that you would never do that.

But you were doing it while you were sleepwalking. Felicity and I caught you in the act.'

And Delia explained everything to an astonished Gillian, who listened open-mouthed.

'Well!' she said, once the girl had finished. 'How very peculiar. My goodness, the others must be furious with me.'

'Of course they aren't, silly,' said Delia. 'They all know quite well that you couldn't help it. It really was queer, Gillian, when you were rummaging about in the common-room in your sleep. You kept saying, "Where is it?", as though you were looking for something.'

'Did I?' said Gillian, looking very surprised. 'I wonder what it could have been. I have absolutely no recollection at all of sleepwalking, or of taking anyone's things, or of looking for anything! I am glad that the others don't hold it against me. I bet that June and Millicent aren't too pleased that I'm going to be out of action, though.'

'Millicent certainly isn't,' said Delia, pulling a face. 'June seemed to take it quite well, though. She is putting Freddie in your place.'

'Good old Freddie!' said Gillian, pleased. 'Delia, wouldn't it be fun if we could get a place on the coach and go along to cheer the team on? I might not be able to play, but it would be nice to go and watch.'

Delia thought that this was a very good idea indeed, and just the thing to speed up Gillian's recovery. She went straight to June, and put the idea to her.

'Yes, it will be nice if we can take some of the Malory Towers girls along to cheer us on,' said June. 'I have already booked a coach for the team, so I shall see if we can get another one to take the girls who want to come and watch.'

The second half of the term was passing very quickly, and there was only a week left until the tennis tournament, and two weeks until the orchestra competition.

Freddie, determined to do her very best for the school, was working hard at her tennis, and, although Gillian's illness had been a blow, June felt certain that her team would make her proud.

But Millicent was not so confident in her orchestra. She gave Gillian's solo to Fay, one of the second violins, and, although the girl played every note correctly, she lacked Gillian's fire and passion. The same could be said of Pam, who rarely made a mistake, but wasn't a natural musician, as some of the others were.

'Neither of them do my music justice,' thought Millicent, who was beginning to think seriously about pulling out of the competition altogether. The dream that she had had of bringing glory to Malory Towers by winning the competition with a first-class orchestra was beginning to slip away. Many of the top musicians had left, and Millicent was forced to admit that it had been largely her fault. She had driven away Anne, Jessie and Kathy. And if only she had been a little more sensitive and understanding with Gillian, and noticed that the girl wasn't well, she might not have become ill either.

Yes, Millicent was learning some hard lessons in the last few weeks of term. If only she had learned them earlier, how much easier her time at Malory Towers might have been!

A big chance for Delia

The day before the tennis tournament, the heavens opened. Walks and horse-rides were cancelled, tennis and swimming were out of the question, and the girls grew very bored indeed cooped up indoors.

June got permission from Miss Grayling to use the telephone in her study, so that she could speak to the games captain of Summerfield Hall, and, reluctantly, both girls agreed that the tournament must be postponed until the following Saturday.

'The same day as the orchestra competition,' said Gillian, when June made her announcement. 'It's just as well that I'm not playing in either, otherwise I would have to split myself in half.'

Millicent was not at all pleased about this, and felt as if June was trying to steal her thunder. She could just picture the tennis team returning home triumphant next weekend, while the orchestra came home dispirited and empty-handed.

June, seeing the girl's sour expression, and correctly guessing her thoughts, laughed and said, 'Don't blame me, Millicent. You can hardly hold me responsible for the rain, you know!'

Fortunately the rain cleared a couple of days later, and the girls were able to resume the outdoor activities they loved so much. Gillian, although she was no longer involved, went along to watch some of the tennis practices, and was pleased to see that Freddie was on top form.

'It makes me feel better about letting you down,' she said to June.

'You didn't let me down,' said June, with her usual frankness. 'I let *you* down, Gillian, for I knew that you were working too hard, yet I let you carry on pushing yourself because I so badly wanted you for the team.'

'Well, I'm enjoying taking things easy now,' said Gillian. 'Delia is making sure that I don't overdo it.'

Delia was, though she raised no objection when Gillian asked Millicent if she could sit in on the rehearsal the following day.

'Of course,' said Millicent. 'I only wish that you were playing, for Fay is nowhere near as good as you.' Then she added hastily, 'Not that I am trying to persuade you to take her place, for I know that you have been ordered to rest. And I don't want Matron after me.'

Listening to Fay play her solo, Gillian had to agree with Millicent. Somehow the whole orchestra seemed listless and lacklustre, the girl thought. They needed something to lift and inspire them.

Evidently Millicent thought so too, for, as the orchestra took a break, she sat down beside Gillian and said despondently, 'We don't have a hope of winning at this rate.'

A sudden thought struck Gillian, and she clutched Millicent's arm, saying excitedly, 'Millicent! Is there anything in the competition rules that says you can't have a singer in your orchestra?'

'I don't think so,' said Millicent. 'Why?'

'I have an idea,' said Gillian, leaping to her feet. 'I'll be back in a minute.'

And, leaving a puzzled Millicent to stare after her, Gillian went off in search of Delia.

She found the girl in the common-room, and cried, 'Delia, come with me, at once!'

'Come where?' asked Delia, looking a little alarmed.

'To the hall,' answered Gillian, taking her arm. 'You are going to save Millicent's orchestra.'

'Me?' squeaked Delia. 'How?'

'You are going to sing with them,' said Gillian, pulling Delia out of the door.

But Delia came to a dead stop at this, saying, 'No! Gillian, I couldn't possibly. Why, I would be simply terrified!'

'You can,' Gillian told her firmly. 'Think of the honour of the school. Think how proud your father will be. And think how sick your aunt and cousins are going to look when they find out that you *do* have a talent, after all.'

Delia laughed at that, but said, 'It's one thing to sing along when you're playing your violin, Gillian, but quite another to sing in front of a hall full of people. My voice isn't good enough.'

'It is,' insisted Gillian. 'You have a beautiful voice,

but, as I have told you before, no confidence. Well, my girl, now is the time to look inside yourself and *find* some confidence. Millicent needs you!'

Millicent looked very surprised when Gillian returned with Delia, and she wasn't very impressed on being told that the girl was going to sing along to the violin solo. Delia was a complete duffer, everyone knew that. And she herself admitted that she had no talent for anything. Still, the rehearsal couldn't get much worse, so Millicent allowed Gillian to have her way, and a very scared Delia took to the stage.

She was so nervous that her knees shook as she took her place beside Fay. But then the opening bars of the violin solo started, and something strange happened. The music seemed to take her over completely, so that Delia forgot about Millicent, Gillian and the rest of the orchestra. And as she opened her mouth and began to sing, Millicent gave a gasp.

Delia most certainly *did* have a talent! A marvellous talent. The rest of the orchestra listened, spellbound, as Delia's voice filled the room, pure and clear. As for Fay, she seemed inspired, and played as she had never played before. When the song ended, there was silence for a few moments, then thunderous applause broke out, everyone getting to their feet to clap, and those girls who were closest to Delia patting her on the back.

'My word!' cried Millicent. 'You are a dark horse, Delia. That was simply beautiful. Fay, you played superbly as well.'

'That's because Delia's song somehow brought the music to life for me,' said Fay, grinning with pleasure.

'That settles it, then,' said Millicent, firmly. 'Delia, you must sing with us at the competition.'

The orchestra, along with Gillian, agreed vociferously with this and Delia, overwhelmed and delighted at being the centre of attention, found herself agreeing. Certainly her sweet, simple song seemed to have breathed new life into the orchestra, for the rest of the rehearsal went swimmingly.

Afterwards, in the common-room, Gillian couldn't wait to tell everyone the news, and Delia was persuaded to sing her song again for the fifth formers. They listened, enthralled, then, for the second time that day, Delia was on the receiving end of a round of rapturous applause.

'Absolutely marvellous!'

'You'll bring the house down at the competition!'

'My goodness, Delia, have you any other hidden talents we ought to know about?'

'That's the song I heard you sing once before,' said Felicity. 'You told me that you had heard it on the radio.'

'Well, that wasn't quite true,' said Delia, flushing a little. 'I wrote the words myself, and set them to Millicent's music.' The girl turned to Millicent. 'In fact, I began writing them at that first rehearsal, when I was supposed to be making notes for you.'

'And I was so angry with you,' said Millicent, with a groan. 'Heavens, if only I had known the way things were going to turn out, I would have encouraged you, instead of ticking you off. I always wondered why there was a page missing from the back of my old notebook, and now I know why!'

Delia gave a self-conscious little laugh, and said, 'You'll never know the trouble I went to, to get hold of that notebook, Millicent. I was so afraid that you would read my words and make fun of them.'

Millicent turned red at this, feeling a little ashamed, for she probably *would* have made fun of Delia. Heavens, what a lot of mistakes she had made this term, and all of them in her dealings with people. Well, she was going to make an effort to be a lot more kind and considerate in future.

'Aha!' cried Julie suddenly. 'That's what you were doing the day Lucy and I caught you looking in Millicent's bag! You were trying to find the notebook!'

'And you must have been looking for it when Amy and I found you going through Millicent's desk,' said Bonnie. 'Well, what a relief to have that cleared up! Of course, I never really thought that you were the thief.'

The fifth formers fell silent all of a sudden, everyone looking at Delia, who had turned rather pale. 'You thought that I was the thief?' she said, in a low voice.

'We did suspect you, yes,' said Pam, deciding that it was best to be honest.

'You must understand how it looked,' said Lucy. 'Things suddenly started going missing around the same time as you started going through Millicent's things.'

'Yes, it did look most suspicious,' put in Amy.

'I suppose it must have,' said Delia. 'I never had the slightest idea that you thought I might be the thief. And all because I didn't want Millicent to find the words that I had written!'

'Well, I forgive you for going through my things,' said Millicent, clapping Delia on the back. 'Everything turned out all right in the end. There was no thief, and I have gained a beautiful song and a marvellous singer for the orchestra. Just out of curiosity, though, where *did* you find that notebook? I had been hunting high and low for it for simply ages, then as soon as I bought a new one it simply appeared on my cabinet.'

'Gillian had it in her bag,' said Delia.

'Did I?' said Gillian, looking most surprised.

'Yes, it fell out that day we were in the tea-shop,' said Delia. 'I suppose you must have taken it one night when you were sleepwalking, and for some reason you hid it in your bag, instead of the cupboard.'

'Wait, I remember now!' exclaimed Gillian, clapping a hand to her brow. 'I slipped it into my bag in French, Millicent, the day you got into a row with Mam'zelle. I thought that if she spotted it on your desk you would have got into even more trouble, so I hid it, meaning to give it back to you later. Then I simply forgot that I had it!'

'I thought I was supposed to be the scatterbrain of the fifth form!' laughed Nora.

'Well, we certainly seem to be clearing up a few mysteries lately,' said June. 'The thief that never was, the disappearing notebook and Delia's hidden talent!'

Everyone laughed at that, and Millicent said, 'I, for one, am very glad that Delia's hidden talent has been discovered. She has certainly given the orchestra a new lease of life.'

June looked slyly at Millicent, then she turned to Delia and said smoothly, 'I say, Delia, I don't suppose you're secretly a marvellous tennis player, are you? Now that Freddie's on the team I could do with another reserve.'

Outraged, Millicent glared at June. Then she saw the twinkle in the girl's eyes and burst out laughing.

June laughed too, then she held out her hand and said, 'You and I have had our differences this term, Millicent, but I wish you the best of luck in the competition on Saturday. It will be too marvellous for words if you win it for Malory Towers.'

'And I hope that your team wins the tennis tournament,' said Millicent warmly, taking June's hand. 'My goodness, wouldn't it be wonderful if we both came back to school victorious?'

But when Saturday came, Millicent's victory looked in doubt. In fact, it seemed as if she and her orchestra would not be able to enter the competition at all!

The tennis team were standing in the driveway, waiting for the coaches that would take them and the spectators to Summerfield Hall. The players looked very smart indeed in their spotless white dresses, and when the orchestra came out, wearing their summer uniforms, June exclaimed, 'Gosh, I wish Miss Grayling could see us now! Don't we all look neat and tidy!'

Miss Grayling did see the girls, for she came out to offer a few words of encouragement, accompanied by Miss James and Mam'zelle Dupont.

'I shall be very proud of you all if you win,' she said, with her lovely smile. 'But I shall still be proud of you if you lose, for I know that you will do your very best, and that is what is important.'

'Ah, yes,' said Mam'zelle, beaming at the assembled girls. 'And how smart you all look, is it not so, Miss James?'

'Yes, indeed,' said Miss James, with a smile. 'And now I see that your coaches are coming, so we will leave you to it. Good luck, everyone!'

As the three mistresses made their way back inside, Millicent suddenly gave a groan and cried, 'Oh my gosh!'

'What is it?' said Gillian, looking at her in alarm, for the girl was as white as a sheet.

'Oh, Millicent, don't say that you are ill! How is the orchestra to manage without a conductor?'

'I'm not ill,' said Millicent in a queer, tight little voice. 'I've just realised that I have forgotten to book a coach for the orchestra.'

'Millicent, please tell me that you are joking,' said Pam, dismayed. 'How on earth could you have forgotten something as important as that?'

'I was so wrapped up in rehearsing, and getting the music right, that it went completely out of my head,' said the girl in a hollow tone. 'Well, that's it, I'm afraid. We can't enter the competition and that's all there is to it.'

Millicent could almost feel the wave of disappointment that washed over the girls. She felt bitterly disappointed too, and very angry with herself. How *could* she have been so stupid?

But June, who had overheard, said, 'Wait a minute! Millicent, we have two coaches – one for the team and one for the girls who were coming to watch. It means that we will have to leave the spectators behind, but why don't you take our second coach?'

'June, would you really do that for us?' said Millicent, hardly daring to believe that she had heard the girl correctly.

'Yes,' said June. 'Your competition is in the next town to our tennis tournament, so the driver will only have to go a little farther. Now buck up, and get your instruments on board.'

The girls who had been hoping to watch the tennis were disappointed at having their day out spoiled, of course, but they took it well, and stood aside to let the orchestra get on. Gillian was going with them, for Delia felt quite sick with nerves and had insisted that she would not be able to perform unless her friend came along too.

'I felt quite relieved when Millicent said that she hadn't booked the coach,' Delia confided to Gillian, as they took their seats. 'For it meant that I wouldn't have to sing. Now I feel sick again.'

'You'll be fine,' said Gillian, giving her arm a squeeze. 'I mean to try and get a seat in the front row when the competition starts, so if your nerves get the better of you, you can look at me, and pretend that you are singing just for me.'

But the big town hall where the competition was taking place was packed, and Gillian had to settle for a seat near the back.

'Oh dear,' she thought. 'I do hope that Delia will be all right.'

Of course, Delia wasn't the only member of the orchestra who felt nervous, for several of them could almost hear their knees knocking as they waited backstage for their turn to come. Millicent too was very anxious, but she hid it well, knowing that it was her job to try and have a calming influence on the others.

The competition began, and Gillian, in the audience, watched as one orchestra after another performed. Some of them were very good indeed, some not so good. But none of them had a singer, and Gillian felt sure that, if her friend could only hold her nerve, her voice would win the competition for Malory Towers.

At last it was their turn, and Gillian felt her heart beat a little faster as Millicent led the girls on to the stage. Each girl carried one of the colourful little pennants that Bonnie had made, and as they took their places they hung them from the music stands.

Then the performance began, and it went very well indeed, the audience enjoying it enormously. Then came the violin solo and Delia, who had been standing in the shadows, walked to the front of the stage. She glanced swiftly along the front row for a glimpse of Gillian, but, of course, she couldn't see her. As luck would have it, though, there was a man in the front row who looked very like her own, dear father, and Delia decided that, if her nerves overcame her, she would pretend to be singing for him.

But, once again, as soon as she began to sing, the sick, fluttery feeling in her stomach vanished, and Delia gave a marvellous performance. When she had finished, the audience clapped for so long that it was several minutes before the rest of the orchestra could continue playing the rest of the piece. But Millicent didn't mind the hold-up at all, for the spontaneous burst of applause proved just how well Delia had done.

And the whole orchestra received a standing ovation, once they had stopped playing. Gillian, of course, clapped louder than anyone, feeling absolutely delighted, for none of the other orchestras had got one. Malory Towers had won, she was certain of it!

A wonderful end to the term

Meanwhile, things were also going well for the tennis team.

The juniors had only lost one of their matches, while Felicity and Susan had scored a comfortable victory over their opponents in the doubles.

Freddie, too, had played her heart out, and the others had cheered until they were hoarse when she narrowly beat her opponent.

'Well done, Freddie!' yelled June, clapping her on the back as she came off the court. 'I doubt if Gillian herself could have played better.'

And now it was the final match, with June playing the captain of Summerfield Hall.

The two were very evenly matched, for although the Summerfield girl was much bigger than June and had a very powerful serve, she was less agile.

The opposing captain won the first set, and June the second. The two girls were equal in the third set, when disaster struck. June, running forward to return her opponent's service, stumbled and fell heavily, twisting her ankle. The Summerfield games mistress dashed on to the court as June gave a little cry of pain, and administered first aid.

'Well, it's certainly not broken,' she said, after gently feeling the ankle. 'Probably just a bad sprain. Hard luck on you, though. I'm afraid that the match will have to be abandoned.'

But June wasn't standing for that!

'No,' she said firmly, getting gingerly to her feet. 'I intend to play on.'

'Well, you've plenty of pluck, I'll say that for you,' said the games mistress. 'Very well, but if that ankle is causing you too much pain, for heaven's sake say so, before you do any more damage!'

June's ankle was very painful indeed, but she was determined to see the match through. And she did, with gritted teeth, but as she could only hobble it was quite impossible for her to return some of her opponent's shots, and she lost.

'Never mind, old thing,' said Felicity, in the changing-room afterwards. 'Miss Grayling will still be proud of you, for you played your very best.'

'The funny thing is that I *don't* mind,' said June, sounding most surprised. 'It really is queer, for you know how I hate to lose at anything. You, Susan and Freddie all played splendidly, and so did the lower school. So in spite of my wretched ankle, we have won the tournament and that seems to be all that matters.'

'June, I do believe that you've found that team spirit we knew was hiding inside you somewhere!' said Susan.

'Do you know, I think you're right!' said June, much struck. 'Fancy that! Although I suppose, as I'm games captain, team spirit is quite a good thing to have.'

'I would say it was essential,' said Felicity. 'Now come along, for we have to be presented with the cup, then we had better get you back to Malory Towers so that Matron can take a look at your ankle and bandage it up.'

The kitchen staff at Malory Towers, aware that today was a very special occasion, had prepared an extra-delicious tea. Julie and Lucy, walking past the dining-room, glanced in, their eyes lighting up as they saw all the good things being laid out by the staff.

'Fruit cake, chocolate cake, sandwiches of every kind – and my goodness, those scones look delicious,' said Julie.

'Well, I daresay that both the tennis team and the orchestra will be jolly hungry when they arrive back,' said Lucy. 'I do hope that they have good news and this turns out to be a celebration tea.'

The tennis team arrived back first, June and Freddie holding the cup aloft between them, and a rousing cheer went up as they entered the common-room.

'Jolly good show!' cried Nora. 'Do sit down and tell us all about it.'

The two girls were glad to put the big cup down on the table, for it was very heavy, and June hobbled towards the nearest armchair.

'What on earth has happened to you, June?' asked Bonnie.

'Sprained my ankle,' said June, with a grimace. 'I suppose I should go and see Matron, but let us tell you all about the tennis tournament first.'

Matron, however, had other ideas, and a few minutes later she appeared in the doorway of the common-room, saying in her brisk way, 'June, I hear that you've hurt your ankle. Come with me at once, please.'

'Bad news travels fast,' said Felicity. 'How did you hear about it, Matron?'

'The games mistress at Summerfield telephoned to tell Miss Grayling about it,' answered Matron. 'She thought you might need a bandage, and from the looks of it she was right, for your ankle is swelling already.'

'But, Matron, I was just about to tell the girls about our marvellous victory,' protested June.

'Ah yes, I heard that you had won the tournament as well,' said Matron, her face creasing into a smile as she looked at the big cup standing on the table. 'Congratulations!'

'Thank you,' said June. 'Matron, I'll be along in ten minutes or so, when I've had a chat with the others.'

'You will come now,' said Matron, in a tone that warned June she would be unwise to argue. 'You might be a fifth former, but when it comes to your health I still know best.'

Grumbling a little, June limped along behind Matron, leaving Felicity, Susan and Freddie to tell the fifth formers all about the tennis tournament. Matron did her work very thoroughly indeed, and by the time June got back to the common-room, the orchestra had returned.

Another cup stood next to the one that the tennis team had won, and the beaming smiles on the faces of

Millicent, Gillian, Delia and Pam told their own story.

'Everyone played splendidly,' Millicent was saying, as June walked in. 'And as for Delia, she sang magnificently.'

'A double celebration!' said June, patting Millicent on the back. 'How marvellous!'

Just then the bell went for tea, and, as the girls made their way downstairs, Gillian said to Delia, 'I'm awfully proud of you, you know.'

'Thanks,' said Delia, turning pink. 'I'm rather proud of you, too.'

'Me?' said Gillian, with a laugh. 'But I haven't done anything!'

'Oh yes, you have,' said Delia. 'For one thing, you gave me the confidence to sing in front of people. And I really think that you have been an absolute brick today. You should have been taking part in the tennis *and* the competition, and you ended up doing neither. But you haven't complained once.'

'Well, I'm not all that sorry, to be honest,' said Gillian. 'I was thinking the other day, you see, about my sleepwalking. Do you remember telling me that I was saying, "Where is it?"'

Delia nodded, and Gillian went on, 'Well, I think that what I was searching for was my sense of fun. As soon as I started practising in earnest, all of the fun went out of tennis and music for me, and they became a chore. I shall never let that happen again.'

And Gillian never did. As the term drew to a close,

she occasionally partnered one of the others at tennis, or played a dance tune on her violin in the common-room, but only for amusement.

Millicent, too, seemed like a different person now that the competition was over. The girl was much less intense, and joined in the others' fun and conversations without looking as if her mind was elsewhere.

'My music will always be important to me,' she said one day, when Nora commented on this. 'But I'm going to make time for other things too. I'm going to try and have a break from it until I go back to the academy next term.'

'Oh, are you leaving us?' said Felicity, surprised.

'Yes, I only found out myself this morning,' said Millicent. 'My father is going back to work in France, so Mother and I are going with him, and I shall be going back to the academy.'

'We shall miss you,' said Pam, who liked this new, carefree Millicent much better than the old one.

'Well, I shall miss all of you,' said Millicent, genuine regret in her tone. 'And dear old Malory Towers. I have learned a lot here, mostly about myself.'

'Yes, not all of the lessons Malory Towers has to teach can be learned in the classroom,' said Susan.

'My goodness, you do sound wise and learned,' said June. 'Just as a fifth former should. Though I must say, it's about time.'

Unfortunately, Susan then ruined the effect by throwing a cushion at June, who promptly threw it back, only to hit Bonnie instead. She retaliated at once, and soon most of the form was involved in a very undignified cushion fight.

No one heard the door open, or saw Miss James peep in. The mistress retreated at once, extremely startled. Well, really! The fifth formers were always so good and well-behaved in class, and always set such a good example to the younger ones. Who would have guessed that they chose to spend their free time in such an unseemly manner?

But Miss James's lips twitched as she walked away. They might be near the top of the school, but they were still young girls after all, and entitled to let off a little steam.

At last it was the last day of term, and as the fifth formers packed, Delia was called to Miss Grayling's office.

The others were a little concerned, Gillian in particular looking very anxious and pacing up and down the dormitory.

'I say, Gillian, you'll wear the carpet out if you keep doing that,' said Freddie. 'Do calm down. I'm sure it can't be bad news for Delia.'

It wasn't, for the girl looked the picture of happiness when she returned to the dormitory.

'Guess what?' she said excitedly. 'My father is coming home on leave today, for a whole month! He is on his way here now to collect me.'

'That's simply wonderful,' said Pam. 'I'm so pleased for you, Delia.'

'Yes, you won't have to spend all of your hols with

your horrid aunt and cousins now,' said Nora.

'She won't have to spend *any* time with them,' said Gillian happily, giving her friend a hug. 'Delia is coming to stay with us for the rest of the hols.'

'Delia, promise me that you will keep up with your singing when I am gone,' said Millicent, who was busily going round writing down everyone's names and addresses, and making promises to keep in touch.

'I shall,' said Delia. 'It gives me such pleasure.'

'And it gives everyone else pleasure too,' said Felicity. 'What a marvellous gift to have.'

At last the fifth formers were all packed, and they made their way down to the big hall, with their night cases.

'What a racket!' said Bonnie, screwing up her face as they reached the bottom of the stairs.

Indeed it was! Girls yelled, mistresses shouted as they tried to keep order, the parents who had arrived early looked bewildered, and *everyone* kept tripping over the bags and cases that were lying around everywhere.

Mam'zelle Dupont was much in evidence, for she always liked to say goodbye to all the girls, and she beamed when she saw two of her favourites, Nora and Bonnie, coming down the stairs.

'Ah, *mes petites*!' she cried, putting an arm around each of them. 'You have come to say goodbye to your old Mam'zelle. Soon you will be gone from Malory Towers. Soon you will be at home with your loving parents. Soon you will have forgotten all about your school, and the mistresses. Soon –'

'Mam'zelle, we will be back before you know it,' said Nora, a little alarmed. Dear old Mam'zelle took these farewells so very seriously, and at the moment she looked as if she might burst into tears.

Bonnie, noticing that the mistress's eyes looked suspiciously moist, pulled her handkerchief from her pocket, and something else flew out at the same time, landing at Mam'zelle's feet. That wretched brooch!

Mam'zelle, who had a great liking for ornate jewellery, spotted it at once and stooped to pick it up.

'Ah, how exquisite!' she said, holding it in her hand. 'Bonnie, you must take great care of it, for I am sure that it must be a family heirloom.'

'Oh no, just a piece of costume jewellery,' said Bonnie. 'As a matter of fact, I've never worn it, for I don't care for it very much.'

'But it is so pretty!' said Mam'zelle, looking at Bonnie as if she was quite mad. 'How can you dislike it?'

'Just bad taste on my part, I expect,' said Bonnie, her eyes dancing. 'I know, Mam'zelle! Since you like it so much, why don't you keep it? You can wear it in the holidays and it will remind you of us girls.'

Mam'zelle cheered up enormously at this, thanking Bonnie profusely. Then she gave each girl a hug, in turn, before pinning the brooch to her blouse and going off to display it proudly to the other mistresses.

'Well done, Bonnie,' said Nora. 'You managed to stop Mam'zelle from becoming too sentimental.'

'And I got rid of that ugly brooch,' said Bonnie

happily. 'Two birds with one stone.'

Soon most of the girls who were being collected by their parents had gone, and the big hall became emptier, as only the train girls were left.

And at last the big coaches arrived to take them to the station, Felicity and Susan walking down the steps of the school together.

'Another term over,' said Susan. 'And what an eventful term it's been.'

'Hasn't it just!' said Felicity. 'You know, Susan, now I always feel a little more sad at the end of each term than I used to when we were lower down the school. I suppose it's because I know that it won't be so very long before we say goodbye to Malory Towers forever.'

'Well, we still have one more term in the fifth,' said Susan. 'Then a whole year in the sixth, so really we still have quite a time to go. And I intend to make the most of every minute!'

'Yes,' said Felicity, sounding a little more cheerful. 'That's what we'll do, Susan, when we come back. Make the most of every minute.'

Malory Towers

Secrets

Written by Pamela Cox

Contents

On the train

'Well, Felicity,' said Susan Blake. 'How does it feel to be going back to Malory Towers as Head Girl?'

Head Girl! No matter how often she heard the words, Felicity Rivers still felt a little thrill of pleasure at them.

She had been astonished, disbelieving, delighted and – above all – honoured, when Miss Grayling, the Head mistress of Malory Towers, had announced at the end of last term that she was to be Head Girl. And Susan had felt exactly the same when the Head had told her that she was to be Felicity's deputy, assisting her friend with her duties. The two girls had been best friends since they were first formers, and were very close indeed. Miss Grayling knew that they would make an excellent team, for both girls were responsible, trustworthy and kind-hearted. She could certainly rely on them to do their best for Malory Towers and its pupils.

Of course, Felicity's parents had been proud and delighted too, and so had her sister Darrell, who had once been Head Girl of Malory Towers herself. Darrell had hugged her younger sister excitedly when Felicity arrived home for the holidays, crying, 'Congratulations! Miss Grayling has made a splendid choice. I wonder if you feel as thrilled as I did when she told me that I was to be Head Girl?'

'I should rather think I do!' laughed Felicity, hugging Darrell back. 'Thrilled and overwhelmed, for it is a tremendous responsibility.'

'I'm sure that you will do a splendid job,' the girls' father had said, overhearing this. 'Just as Darrell did, when she was Head Girl.'

'And you will have Susan to back you up,' Mrs Rivers had added. 'My goodness, it's becoming quite a family tradition, isn't it? Perhaps one day, my dears, your daughters will be Head Girls of Malory Towers too.'

This was a very pleasant thought indeed, and Felicity had beamed at her parents and sister, seeing the love and pride in their faces and feeling a warm glow inside. It was a feeling that had lasted all through the holidays and still lingered.

'It's going to be a very testing term for both of us,' said Felicity now. 'What with our new responsibilities *and* studying for Higher Cert.'

The two girls were sitting in the little café at the railway station, waiting for the train that was to take them back to Malory Towers, and Susan gave a groan, saying, 'Higher Cert! That's the only thing that has spoiled what has been an otherwise marvellous holiday for me – having to spend some time studying.'

'Well, it will all be worth it when we pass,' said Felicity sensibly. 'Though in some ways I can't help envying those who aren't going in for it, for they will have a nice, carefree term, while the rest of us are slaving away like mad.'

'Yes,' said Susan with a rueful grin. 'Sometimes it pays to be a duffer! Nora and Delia aren't going in for it, and nor is Amy.'

'Bonnie is, though,' said Felicity with a grin. 'She didn't intend to, then June said that she thought Bonnie was very wise, for she would never pass in a million years.'

'And, of course, Bonnie saw that as a challenge, and at once changed her mind,' laughed Susan. 'Jolly clever of June, for Bonnie has a good brain, if she chooses to use it.'

'Well, June is the one person in our form who won't have to worry about studying,' said Felicity rather enviously. 'She only has to read a page once to memorise it. Darrell says that her cousin, Alicia, was exactly the same.'

'Yes, it's so unfair,' said Susan. 'June will get top marks without even trying, while the rest of us will be burning the midnight oil and worrying whether we will manage to scrape through.'

'June won't get off completely scot-free, though,' said Felicity. 'She is still games captain, and will have to work hard at that.'

Just then the door of the little café opened, and a girl wearing the Malory Towers uniform entered.

She was thin, and rather plain, with straight, mousy-brown hair, and her eyes looked very scared behind the big glasses she wore.

Felicity and Susan guessed that she must be a new girl, and felt rather sorry for her, as she looked so nervous. As Head Girl, it was Felicity's duty to make her feel at ease, so she called out, 'Hallo there! You must be waiting for the train to Malory Towers.'

The girl looked at Felicity, then at Susan, her expression becoming even more scared, then she advanced rather timidly, and said in a very quiet voice, 'That's right. I'm starting in the sixth form.'

'Well, we are in the sixth form too,' said Susan. 'Do sit down and join us. This is Felicity Rivers, Head Girl of Malory Towers, and I am Susan Blake, her best friend and deputy.'

This information seemed to startle the girl a little, for she blinked rapidly, before sitting down and saying, 'I'm Alice Johnson. My goodness, what luck to bump into the two most important girls in the school.'

'Well, I don't know that I would go that far,' laughed Felicity. 'Miss Grayling, our Head mistress, would most certainly say that each girl at Malory Towers is as important as the next, and she is quite right.'

'And a lot of the lower school would argue that our fellow sixth former, June, is the most important person in the school,' said Susan. 'She is games captain, you see, and most of the youngsters simply adore her.'

Alice smiled rather nervously at this, and, quite suddenly, it struck Felicity that there was something oddly familiar about her. Then the smile disappeared, and so did Felicity's feeling that she had seen the girl somewhere before. It really was most strange!

Susan glanced at the big clock that hung on the wall, saying, 'I would offer you a cup of tea, Alice, but the train will be here any minute. We really should go.'

So the three girls left the café, weaving their way through groups of Malory Towers girls, mistresses and parents, until they reached the platform from which their train would leave.

Miss Potts, the house-mistress of North Tower, was there, with a small group of excited, chattering first formers, and she greeted Felicity and Susan with a smile.

'Well, girls,' she said. 'It is nice to see you back. I never got the opportunity at the end of last term to congratulate you both. Felicity, I am sure that you will make a fine Head Girl, and Susan, I know that you will do everything that you can to help.'

The two girls thanked Miss Potts, and, nodding towards the unruly first formers, Felicity said, 'It seems strange to think that one of these youngsters will one day be Head Girl.'

'At the moment, it seems quite impossible to believe!' said Miss Potts drily. 'Daphne, *is* there any need to yell like that? Katie is standing right next to you and she isn't deaf, though she may well end up that way if you keep shouting in her ear like that.'

'Sorry, Miss Potts,' said Daphne, a slim, pretty girl with short dark curls and merry brown eyes.

'Why, it's Daffy Hope!' said Felicity. 'Hello, Daffy. Sally told me that you were starting at Malory Towers this term, and asked me to look out for you.'

'Is that Sally's young sister?' asked Susan as she, Felicity and Alice boarded the train. 'She seems a bit of a handful.'

'Oh no, I've met her heaps of times and she's a very nice, well-behaved kid,' said Felicity. 'I daresay she's just excited at going off to boarding school for the first time.'

Sally Hope was Darrell's best friend, and the two families had become very close over the years, so when Sally had asked Felicity to keep an eye on her young sister, she had agreed at once. It wouldn't be a very difficult task, she thought, for Daphne – or Daffy, as most people called her – was such a good kid, and not the kind of girl to get into mischief.

The three sixth formers quickly found an empty carriage, and, as they took their seats, Susan looked out of the window and said, 'I can see June and Freddie coming along the platform. We must save a couple of seats for them.'

But June and Freddie did not get on the train immediately, for they were distracted by a little by-play on the platform. While the two girls stopped to greet Miss Potts, a latecomer arrived, accompanied by her mother, and it soon became evident that she wasn't in the best of moods.

'I don't see why the chauffeur couldn't have driven me to school,' she complained loudly. 'It's simply beastly having to rough it on the train.'

'Now, Violet dear,' said her mother rather nervously.

'You know very well that Benson had to drive Daddy to an important meeting today.'

'He could quite easily have taken a taxi,' said Violet, looking sullen. 'Then I shouldn't have had to get up so early. You know how I hate getting up early, Mummy.'

'Yes, darling, but you know that you will have to get used to it when you are at school,' her mother said. 'You will get into awful trouble if you sleep in and are late for breakfast, you know.'

'It's too bad!' said Violet, looking as if she were about to burst into tears. 'There will be all sorts of beastly rules that I shall have to keep, and I shan't be able to have my own way at all.'

And Violet was used to getting her own way, thought June, watching the little scene in amusement. A little *too* used to it, by the look of things.

Violet was a short, plump girl, with carefully curled golden hair, rather small grey eyes and a turned-up nose.

'As though she has a bad smell under it,' murmured Daffy Hope to the little group of first formers, giving a sniff and imitating Violet's high and mighty expression.

The first formers giggled at this, and June, overhearing, had to hide a grin as she glanced at Daffy. She didn't know who this cheeky little first former was, but she had certainly hit the nail on the head!

The spoilt Violet, meanwhile, was just complaining to her mother about how ugly the school uniform was, and as she stamped her foot angrily, Miss Potts decided to take a hand in the matter.

'Good morning,' she said, going across and holding out her hand to Violet's mother. 'You must be Mrs Forsyth, and this, I presume, is Violet. I am Miss Potts, house-mistress of North Tower.'

Mrs Forsyth shook Miss Potts's hand and said, 'I'm pleased to meet you, Miss Potts. I'm afraid that Violet is feeling a little under the weather today. You see, she has always had a governess before, and has never been to school. You must understand that she is rather nervous.'

Miss Potts had met Violet's type before, and quickly sized her up as a spoilt mother's girl. The child wasn't nervous at all, merely furious that she was being sent away to school, where she would have to do as the others did, and wouldn't be able to get her own way by throwing tantrums. Well, perhaps Malory Towers would do her good, and Violet would learn to settle down and be sensible. Miss Potts, glancing round at the other first formers, who were looking at Violet with a mixture of contempt and amusement, certainly hoped so, or things would be very difficult for the girl.

The mistress had also sized up Mrs Forsyth – a pleasant enough woman, but rather weak and silly. Her lips were beginning to tremble now, and Miss Potts knew that, if she was not firm, there would be a long and emotional farewell, which would not do either Violet or her mother any good at all.

So she laid a firm hand on Violet's shoulder and said briskly, 'Come along then, Violet. Say goodbye to your mother quickly, please, then pick up your night case and get on the train.'

Both Violet and her mother looked rather affronted at being robbed of their dramatic farewell, but neither of them dared flout the stern Miss Potts, so they had to content themselves with a brief hug and promises to write.

Then the first formers, along with June and Freddie, moved towards the train, Daffy Hope managing to position herself behind Violet, and sticking her tongue out behind her back.

Once again, June's lips twitched. What a naughty little monkey that girl was, yet there was something rather likeable about her.

Violet, however, thought differently, for she turned round just in time to see Daffy with her tongue out, and scowled at her. Before she could say anything to Daffy, though, June said firmly, 'Get on the train at once, please. You're holding everyone up.'

Violet turned her scowl on June, but one look at the sixth former's face warned her that it would be most unwise to argue! Quickly lowering her eyes from June's, Violet turned away and clambered aboard the train.

Miss Potts remained on the platform, waiting for any stragglers, while June and Freddie, joining the other three sixth formers, were greeted warmly.

The two newcomers looked at Alice curiously, and Felicity said, 'This is Alice Johnson, our new girl. Alice, this is June, our school games captain, and her friend, Freddie Holmes.'

Alice gave her nervous smile, and greeted the two girls in her quiet voice, while June's sharp eyes narrowed.

'Have I met you somewhere before?' she asked.

'Oh, no,' said Alice, shaking her head. 'We have never met before.'

'That's odd,' said June. 'For there's something familiar about you. Perhaps you remind me of someone, though I can't for the life of me think who it is at the moment. Never mind, I'm sure it will come to me.'

Alice looked quite terrified at this thought, and Felicity said, 'That's funny, because earlier on I thought that I recognised you too, though I'm quite sure we have never met. Have you ever had a sister at Malory Towers?'

'No, I'm an only child,' answered Alice.

She had turned rather red, and Freddie, guessing that the girl didn't like being the centre of attention, quickly changed the subject and began telling the girls about Violet Forsyth.

'My goodness, she sounds a perfect little beast,' said Susan.

'Well, Miss Potts won't stand any nonsense from her,' said Felicity.

'I don't think the first-form kids will, either,' said June with a smile. 'One of them in particular seems an imp, and she soon let Violet know what she thought of her. I don't know the kid's name, but she was a pretty little thing – dark, curly hair and laughing brown eyes.'

'Why, that sounds like Daffy Hope,' said Felicity. 'Sally's sister.'

'Really?' said June, raising her dark brows in surprise and saying rather mockingly, 'I would never have guessed, for she is the opposite of solid, sensible Sally.'

'Nonsense,' said Felicity. 'I can't think why you believe that she's an imp, June. And Susan, you said that she looked like a handful, but you're both quite wrong, for she is every bit as sensible and responsible as Sally.'

'Is she?' said June, with a quizzical look at Felicity. 'Or are you sure that *you* aren't mistaken, Felicity?'

In the first-form carriage, meanwhile, Daffy Hope was quickly establishing herself as leader of the first form, the others liking her mischievous nature and sense of fun. For June and Susan were quite right. There were two sides to Daffy Hope. The sweet, well-behaved girl that her family was so proud of was very different from the Daffy her school friends knew.

Indeed, Mrs Hope had been most upset when the form mistress at Daffy's prep school had spoken to her about the girl's naughty behaviour.

Daffy had talked her way out of it easily, convincing her mother that the mistress had got her confused with another girl called Daphne, and for the rest of the term she had not dared misbehave. But now that she was away from home, and her parents, it was quite another matter.

Daffy was at a slight advantage to the others, for while they were alone, and feeling rather shy and nervous, she had her best friend from prep school with her.

Katie was Daffy's partner in mischief, and ably seconded her friend as she kept the first form in stitches.

One person who was not impressed with Daffy, however, was Violet. The only thing that had made her agree to come to school was the thought that she would be able to lord it over the others. She had pictured them vying for her friendship, but instead they were all over that silly Daffy. It simply wouldn't do!

So Violet raised her voice, and said to the carriage at large, 'It was my birthday last week.'

No one quite knew what to say to this, so there was an awkward silence, then the girl went on, 'Mummy and Daddy bought me a kitten, for a present. But it's not just an ordinary kitten, you know, it's a pedigree Siamese, and worth an absolute fortune. It would make you stare if I told you how much Daddy had paid for it.'

The girls *were* staring – in disbelief. But Violet decided that their silence meant that they were very impressed indeed, and went on boastfully, 'She sleeps in her own special bed, lined with velvet, you know, and has her own toys, and she is fed on chicken and fish, not shop-bought cat food, like ordinary cats. Her name is Princess Willow, but I just call her Willow, for short.'

'Why not call her Princess, instead?' asked one of the first formers, Maggie, who felt a little uncomfortable that no one was responding to Violet.

'Oh, it's so silly,' said Violet, putting her hand up to her mouth and giving a little giggle. 'You see, Princess is Daddy's nickname for me. So we couldn't give my kitten the same name.'

'What a lovely nickname,' said Daffy very sweetly.

'You know, Violet, I think we should give you a nickname too. Don't you agree, girls?'

The others, ready to agree to anything Daffy said, nodded eagerly, while Violet smiled at this. She had read several school stories, and knew that only the most popular girls were given nicknames. She really *had* made a good impression.

Daffy smiled at her, and said, 'Yes, I've come up with a very good nickname for you, Violet. Your Highness!'

'Oh!' said Violet, rather surprised at this odd choice of nickname. 'Is that because you think I look like a princess?'

'No,' answered Daffy. 'It's because you're *high* and mighty, you're always on your *high* horse and you've always got your nose stuck *high* in the air!'

The others roared, while Violet turned red with rage, and gave an infuriated squeal. 'Even her voice is high!' laughed Katie.

Violet simmered with rage. How dare that horrid Daffy make fun of her? Oh, she was going to hate it at Malory Towers, she just knew it, with no one to spoil her and pet her, or take her side against these beastly girls. If only she could persuade her parents to take her away!

Back at Malory Towers

It was a very long journey to Malory Towers, but most of the older girls were used to this, and had brought books with them to while away the time if the conversation flagged. The youngsters, however, hadn't, so they soon became either very bored and restless, or very tired, and fell asleep.

In the sixth-form carriage, only Alice had fallen asleep, while Felicity and Susan read their books, and June and Freddie pored over a crossword puzzle together.

Looking up from her book, Susan happened to glance across at the sleeping Alice, whose glasses had slid sideways across her face, giving her rather a comical look. Susan smiled, then she stared harder at Alice, and whispered, 'You're right!'

'Who's right?' said June. 'And, more importantly, what is she right about?'

'Alice,' answered Susan, leaning forward and keeping her voice low, so as not to disturb the sleeping girl. 'You and Felicity said that she looked familiar, and I couldn't see it myself, but now I do.'

Alice suddenly shifted position, so that her hair fell over her face, and Freddie said, 'Blow! I wanted to have a good look, though I really can't say that I recognised her on first sight.'

'She seems awfully nervous and timid,' whispered Susan.

'Yes, but she's pleasant enough,' said Felicity. 'I expect that Alice will open up a bit when she knows us better.'

'I wonder if she's any good at lacrosse?' said June, ever the games captain. 'I doubt it somehow. She doesn't look the sporting type.'

Just then Alice stirred, stretched and sat up, blinking as she pushed her glasses back on to her nose.

The others immediately felt guilty, and hoped that she hadn't overheard them talking about her, although they hadn't said anything bad.

But it seemed that Alice hadn't heard a thing, for she said in her soft voice, 'Oh dear! Did I fall asleep? How rude of me.'

'Don't give it a thought,' said June airily. 'We old hands usually bring something to keep us occupied on the journey, so that we don't drop off.'

'Well, I shall remember that next term,' said Alice.

'At least the worst of the journey is over now,' said Felicity. 'We shall be at the station very soon, then we go the rest of the way by coach.'

The first formers were all wide awake when the train stopped at the station, and thoroughly over-excited. But Miss Potts had joined them now, and Daffy Hope, realising that she was a force to be reckoned with, was on her best behaviour, she and Katie walking sedately beside the mistress as they made their way to the big coaches.

Felicity spotted her, noting her sweet expression, and the respectful way in which she looked up at Miss Potts when the mistress addressed her. How on earth could Susan and June, both of them normally so shrewd, have misread her character so badly?

She might have changed her opinion had she been on the same coach as the first formers, and seen Daffy pulling faces behind Miss Potts's back, and making the others laugh by pushing the tip of her nose up to imitate Violet's snooty expression each time the girl looked at her.

But the sixth formers were on a different coach, so Felicity remained in blissful ignorance.

Alice seemed very interested as the others pointed out various landmarks to her on the way to Malory Towers, her eyes lighting up as she saw the sea in the distance.

'We aren't allowed to swim in it, though,' Felicity warned her. 'There was a terrible accident a few years ago, when one of the old sixth formers tried swimming in the sea. The current caught her and pulled her on to some rocks, and she was badly hurt. It was only thanks to June that she didn't drown. So stick to the school swimming-pool, if you fancy a dip. It's quite beautiful, you know, for it's hollowed out of rocks and filled by the sea.'

'Yes, I remember,' said Alice, and Felicity stared at her. How on earth could Alice remember the swimming-pool, when she had never been to Malory Towers – unless she was lying?

At once the girl turned red, and said hastily, 'I mean,

I remember my mother telling me about the pool. She saw it, you see, when she came down to see Miss Grayling about me coming here.'

Well, that was perfectly possible, thought Felicity, for Miss Grayling often showed parents who were thinking of sending their girls to Malory Towers around the school, and she always took them to the swimming-pool. And Alice was certainly very nervous and timid, which explained why her manner was rather strange sometimes. So Felicity dismissed her doubts, and turned her attention instead to the first glimpse of Malory Towers, which thrilled her just as much now as it had when she was a first former.

Alice gave a gasp as she saw the beautiful old building perched on the cliff-top. Each of its four towers – North, South, East and West – was a separate house, with its own dormitories, dining-room and common-rooms.

'Impressive, isn't it?' said June, smiling at Alice's look of wonder.

'I'll say,' breathed Alice. 'I feel so lucky to be here.'

Moments later, the coaches drew to a stop at the top of the long driveway, and the girls retrieved their night cases from the luggage rack, before getting out.

As always on the first day of term, the grounds were very busy indeed, as girls greeted one another noisily and said goodbye to parents.

June's sharp eyes spotted some of their fellow sixth formers, and she said, 'Let's go and say hallo. Come along, Alice.'

Alice followed meekly in the wake of the others as they made their way across the lawn, and soon she was being introduced to yet more sixth formers. There was the calm, good-tempered Pam and her scatterbrained friend Nora, and the rather snobbish Amy, with her little friend Bonnie.

All four girls greeted Alice, and Pam said, 'Let's go and give our health certificates in to Matron. Got yours, Alice?'

The girl nodded, and the sixth formers made their way towards North Tower. They passed several younger girls on the way, and Felicity was amused, and rather touched, to hear the awe in their voices as they greeted her.

Correctly reading her expression, June clapped her on the back and said, 'You'll have to get used to it, you know, now that you are Head Girl. The younger ones are bound to look up to you no end.'

'Of course, you've already had experience of it, haven't you?' said Felicity, for June had been games captain of the school since she was in the fifth form. 'I don't know that I shall *ever* get used to it, though.'

Matron greeted the sixth formers with a cheery smile, and said, 'Well, well, it seems hard to believe that you are all top formers now. And fancy you being Head Girl, Felicity! Why, I can remember you coming in here as a shy, rather scared first former. And you too, Susan.'

'What about me, Matron?' asked June.

'You were never shy and scared in your life, June!' laughed Matron. 'But I remember you, all right. Now, let me have your health certificates, then I will allocate you your studies.'

The girls listened to this with mingled excitement and sadness.

It would be marvellous to have their own studies, of course, but they would miss the happy times they had shared together in their big common-room.

As Matron handed out study keys, Felicity noticed that Alice was looking rather forlorn, and realised that it was going to be especially hard on the new girl having a study to herself. It would have been much easier for her to get to know the others if they had had a common-room. The sixth formers would have to coax her out of her shell a little, decided Felicity, then she would feel quite comfortable about popping into the others' studies whenever she felt like a chat.

So Felicity was pleased when Matron said, 'Felicity, as Alice is the new girl, I have given her the study next door to yours, then you are on hand if she feels a bit lost and lonely.'

'Good idea, Matron,' said Felicity, giving the new girl's arm a friendly squeeze. 'Don't worry, Alice, if you need some company in the evenings you can always pop into my study. I'm sure that goes for the others too.'

Everyone agreed at once, though Amy was rather half-hearted. She always chose her friends very carefully indeed, and didn't think that she would have anything in common with this rather plain, dull girl.

The sixth formers were simply dying to see their

studies, and unpacked as quickly as possible. There were four more sixth formers in the dormitory, already putting their things away, when the girls arrived – Gillian, Delia, Julie and Lucy, and the others greeted them happily.

'Hallo! Had good hols?'

'Have you been to Matron yet and got your study keys?'

'My word, Gillian, just look at all your freckles! You must have spent all summer out in the sun.'

'Julie, I suppose you've brought Jack with you, as usual. And Lucy, how is Sandy?'

Julie and Lucy were both horse-mad, and brought their horses, Jack and Sandy, to school with them each term. The two girls were great friends, and, over the years, their horses had become great friends too, Lucy swearing that Sandy pined during the holidays when he couldn't be with Jack.

'Do hurry up and unpack, everyone,' said Gillian, who was busy tying back her mane of auburn hair. 'We're simply dying to see our studies. Matron has put Delia and I next to one another, so we are both very pleased.'

Felicity looked at Gillian's friend Delia, who was beaming all over her face, and thought how much the girl had changed since starting at Malory Towers.

Delia had been rather diffident and lacking in confidence as a new girl, but then, almost by accident, she had discovered that she possessed a wonderful talent for singing and writing songs. That, along with the friendship she had forged with Gillian, had done wonders for her confidence, and Delia had blossomed. She was still – as she said herself – a complete duffer at lessons, and would never be top of the class, but she was a pleasant, kind-hearted girl, popular with everyone.

The sixth-form studies were on the floor below the dormitory, and each girl opened the door of her own little room with a feeling of anticipation. They were furnished with a desk and chair, as well as a comfortable armchair, and had a bookcase on which the girls could put personal belongings, such as photographs, as well as their books.

Felicity wasted no time in getting out a framed photograph of her parents and sister, Darrell, but instead of placing it on a shelf, she put it on her desk, so that she would be able to see it every time she looked up from her work.

There was a great deal of to-ing and fro-ing as the girls went up and downstairs to fetch things to make their studies look more 'homely', as Nora put it. Then, of course, they had to visit everyone else's rooms and give their opinions.

'I say, Felicity's is bigger than ours, and she has *two* armchairs. Most unfair!'

'Well, the Head Girl always gets the biggest study.'

'Ours are much cosier, anyway, though I can't say I'm awfully keen on the curtains in mine.'

Most of the girls had added a photograph of their parents, or a beloved pet, or some other little touch to show who the study belonged to. Bonnie had spent the holidays embroidering a beautiful cushion, which she had placed proudly on the armchair. And Nora's mother had given her a little vase, while Susan's had donated a small table-lamp.

But one little study remained curiously bereft of all personal belongings, and that was Alice's.

'Haven't you brought a photograph of your family?' asked Pam.

'I meant to, but I must have forgotten to pack it,' said the girl rather dolefully. 'I must say, my poor little study looks awfully plain next to yours. I shall have to write to Mother and get her to send me something to brighten it up.'

'If you like, Alice, I can make you a cushion,' offered Bonnie, taking pity on the girl. 'Just like mine, but in different colours.'

Alice's face lit up at this, but before she could accept, June said, 'Oh no, you can't, my girl. Not if you're studying for Higher Cert. You'll have no time for sewing or embroidery.'

Bonnie's face fell, and June went on wickedly, 'Unless, of course, you've changed your mind and decided that it's too much like hard work.'

'Nothing of the sort!' declared Bonnie, a firm set to her delicate little chin. 'I'm going in for Higher Cert, all right, and I jolly well intend to pass with flying colours!'

'That's the spirit, Bonnie!' said Lucy, patting the girl on the back.

'Oh well, it looks as if you'll have to send for something from home after all, Alice,' said Delia.

'I shall make you a cushion once the exams are over, Alice,' said Bonnie. 'That's a promise.'

Just then the bell went for tea, which everyone was very glad of, for they were all extremely hungry.

As they made their way down to the big dining-room, the sixth formers were overtaken by a noisy horde of first formers, Daffy Hope among them, and Felicity called out, 'Less noise, please, kids! I know you're all excited, but do try to calm down a little.'

'Sorry, Felicity,' said Daffy, at her most demure, and Felicity grinned to herself as the youngsters went on their way, slightly more quietly. Little monkeys! Even sweet, angelic Daffy was getting caught up in the first-day excitement. And who could blame her, for surely there wasn't a better place to be than Malory Towers.

Who is Alice?

After breakfast the following morning, all of the new girls had to go and see Miss Grayling, the Head mistress.

Almost all of the first formers were new, and there were quite a lot of them, so they went in first. Then it was the turn of the other new girls, including Alice. As Head Girl, Felicity escorted them all to the Head's room, then she sat outside on a chair, waiting for Alice, so that she could show her the way to the sixth-form classroom.

Miss Grayling was a serene, calm-faced woman, with startlingly blue eyes, which could look very cold when she was angry, or twinkle brightly if she was amused. She was also extremely shrewd, and had an extra-ordinary ability to read the characters of the girls who stood before her. As she addressed each girl, asking her name and her form, her eyes seemed to linger on Alice, for she knew a great deal about the girl. The sixth formers would have been very surprised indeed if they had known all that Miss Grayling knew!

Then Miss Grayling gave the little speech that she always made at the beginning of each term, and Alice listened intently, taking in every word. Really, she felt as if the Head might have been speaking to her, and her alone!

'One day,' began Miss Grayling, 'you will leave Malory Towers and go out into the world as young women. You should take with you eager minds, kind hearts and a will to help. You should take with you a good understanding of many things, and a willingness to accept responsibility, and show yourselves as women to be loved and trusted.'

The Head paused for a moment, her eyes moving from one girl to the other, then she went on in her low, clear voice, 'All of these things you are able to learn at Malory Towers – if you *will*. I do not count as our successes those who have won scholarships, or passed exams, though these are good things to do. I count as our successes those who learn to be good-hearted and kind, sensible and trustworthy, good, sound women the world can lean on. Our failures are those who do not learn those things in the time they are here.'

Again Miss Grayling paused, and Alice vowed there and then that she was going to be a success, whatever it took.

The Head spoke again, saying, 'Some of you will find it easy to learn these things, others will find it hard. But they must be learned, one way or the other, if you are to be happy after you have left here, and if you are to bring happiness to others.'

She was about to say more, but suddenly the telephone on her desk rang.

'I think that this is an important telephone call that I

have been expecting,' said Miss Grayling. 'You may go to your class-rooms, girls, but please take my words with you, and think about them.'

The Head's clear voice had carried to Felicity, waiting outside. The girl remembered listening to the very same words when she had first come to Malory Towers, and she knew what Miss Grayling had been about to say next – *'You will all get a tremendous lot out of your time at Malory Towers. See that you give a lot back.'*

The words had made a great impression on Felicity, and had stayed with her throughout her time at the school. She hoped that she had succeeded in giving something back to the school that had taught her so much, and would continue to do so in her last year.

The door of Miss Grayling's study opened, and the new girls emerged. One look at their rapt faces was enough to tell Felicity that the Head had made a great impression on them too.

Alice's eyes were shining behind her big glasses, and she said to Felicity in her rather high, nervous voice, 'What a marvellous person Miss Grayling is! I really feel that I want to do my best, for myself and for the school.'

'Well, I'm very pleased to hear it,' said Felicity with a smile. 'We'd better get along to our class-room now, for Miss Oakes will be there soon and she won't appreciate it if we are late.'

'Is that our form-mistress?' asked Alice. 'What is she like?'

'I don't know her very well,' said Felicity. 'But

according to last year's sixth formers she can be rather stern, though she is always fair. And she doesn't have much of a sense of humour, which is a shame.'

Miss Oakes *didn't* have a great sense of humour, but she was a fine teacher and, although she didn't suffer fools gladly, took a keen interest in the welfare of her girls.

There was a low hum of chatter in the sixth-form class-room as the girls waited for their mistress, but no ragging or fooling about. As top formers, that kind of thing was quite beneath the girls' dignity.

In the first-form class-room, however, it was a very different story, and the girls were making a terrific racket as they waited for their mistress, Miss Potts.

The head-girl of the first form was a quiet, rather colourless girl named Faith, and she had been chosen because she had already been at Malory Towers for one term.

'Faith is not a natural leader in any way,' Miss Potts had said to Miss Grayling, when they were discussing who should be head of the first form. 'But it would be quite unfair to make one of the new girls head-girl over her.'

'Very true,' Miss Grayling had agreed. 'Besides, we don't yet know the characters of the new girls, and what qualities they have. So it would be quite impossible to predict which of them might make good head-girls.'

'Quite,' Miss Potts had said. 'And who knows, this might be the making of Faith, and bring out some hidden depths in her.'

So Faith, rather to her alarm, suddenly found herself

head-girl of a very unruly first form. But, although Faith might be head-girl, Daffy Hope was emerging as the true leader of the form. Naughty, lively and mischievous, every girl wanted to be her friend, whereas poor Faith was too quiet and shy to be very popular.

Someone who was decidedly *un*popular was Violet, and the first formers had soon grown heartily tired of her conceit, her boasting and her stuck-up ways. Violet had also taken an intense dislike to Daffy. Not only was she extremely jealous of the girl's popularity, but the horrid nickname that Daffy had given her – *Your Highness* – had stuck, and how she hated it!

Daffy was telling an amusing story about something that had happened in the holidays, keeping the others in fits, while Violet watched, her little snub nose in the air and an expression of disdain on her round face.

Katie spotted her, and said, 'What's the matter, Your Highness?'

'I know what it is,' said Daffy, giggling. 'We forgot to curtsey when Violet came into the class-room.'

And, with that, the naughty girl got to her feet and curtsied dantily, while the others roared with laughter, so loudly that they didn't hear Miss Potts approaching.

Violet, turning red, jumped to her feet and began giving Daffy a tremendous scold. Unfortunately for her, however, she had her back to the class-room door, and didn't see the form-mistress come in. But wicked Daffy did, and at once she put on a very hurt, scared expression, saying to Violet in a soft, trembling voice, 'Oh, how cruel and hurtful of you! I can't think what I've done to make you dislike me so.'

Miss Potts, accustomed to the utmost respect from her classes, was not at all pleased. The girls hadn't stood up when she came in, and no one had held the door open for her. Her sharp eyes took in the scene at a glance, looking from Daffy's innocent face to Violet's red, angry one.

'Would someone care to explain to me what is going on here?' she asked, her tone icy.

No one did, a scared hush falling over the first form now, and Miss Potts turned to Faith, saying, 'Well, Faith? The other girls might be new, but you have already been in my form for a term, and know the standard of behaviour I expect. That is why you are head-girl. And, as head-girl, it is your duty to keep the others in order.'

'Sorry, Miss Potts,' mumbled a very red-faced Faith, getting to her feet. The others hastily stood up too, and Daffy, feeling a little sorry for Faith, came to her rescue.

'I'm terribly sorry, Miss Potts,' she said, at her most charming. 'Violet and I were having a – a little disagreement, and that is why we didn't hear you come in. It won't happen again, I promise.'

'I should hope not,' said Miss Potts sternly, looking hard at Daffy. 'You are Daphne Hope, aren't you?'

'Yes, Miss Potts,' answered Daffy. 'My older sister, Sally, was in your form many years ago.'

'Yes, I remember Sally well,' said the mistress, her stern features relaxing a little. Sally had been a model pupil – reliable, hard-working, honest and trustworthy –

and Miss Potts hoped that her younger sister would take after her.

'Well,' she said at last. 'As this is the first full day of term, we will say no more about it. But be warned, all of you, that any further incidents like this will be punished most severely. Now, please sit down.'

The girls did as they were told, but not before Daffy and Violet exchanged angry glares, while Faith looked from one to the other uneasily. Her first day as head-girl, and she was already in hot water with Miss Potts. How on earth was she going to win the respect of her unruly fellow first formers and keep order? Oh dear, it looked as if her first term as head-girl could also be her last!

Things were going much more smoothly for the sixth formers, though those taking Higher Certificate grimaced when they received their timetables, and realised how much extra work they would have to do.

Felicity felt quite envious when she overheard Delia whispering to Nora, 'I say, we have quite a lot of free time each week, as we don't have to study for Higher Cert. I think that I'm going to enjoy this term!'

Alice wasn't studying for Higher Certificate either, and she intended to make good use of her free time by making herself as helpful as she could to the others, as well as to the mistresses. Her brains weren't of the highest order, and she was no good at sports, yet she desperately wanted to become one of Malory Towers' successes. And she meant to do her best to become a good and trustworthy person, the kind of girl who would make Miss Grayling proud.

So, when Miss Oakes asked for a volunteer to hand out books, Alice leapt to her feet so quickly that she almost knocked over her chair.

'I'll do that, Miss Oakes,' she said eagerly.

And another opportunity to be of assistance arose later, when Miss Oakes, who had to dash off to a meeting, asked if someone would be good enough to stay behind and clean the blackboard at break-time.

Alice's hand was in the air before anyone else had a chance to raise theirs, and she remained behind in the class-room while the others went outside to get some fresh air.

'Dear me,' drawled June, a touch of malice in her tone. 'It seems that Alice is going to be a teacher's pet.'

'Don't be unkind, June!' said Felicity. 'She's probably just keen to make a good impression.'

'Yes, give her a chance,' said Susan. 'Perhaps this is Alice's way of trying to fit in.'

'Well, if she wants to make a good impression, she would be far better off running errands for us girls,' laughed Nora. 'Now, if Alice offered to do my darning that would certainly impress me!'

The others laughed at this, but they soon discovered that Alice's good deeds weren't confined to the mistresses.

At lunch, Freddie dropped her fork on the floor, and before she could bend to pick it up, Alice had retrieved it, before announcing that she would go to the kitchen and fetch her a clean one.

Then, when Delia half-jokingly said that she would love a second helping of pudding, Alice offered to give hers up.

'Oh, I couldn't possibly take your pudding, Alice,' said Delia, quite flustered. 'I eat far too many sweet things, anyway, and I'm sure that it won't hurt me to go without.'

'Oh, please take it, Delia,' said Alice, pushing her pudding plate towards the girl. 'Really, I feel full up and don't think that I can eat it.'

'Well, if you're quite sure,' Delia had said, a little reluctantly.

And Alice had insisted, a beaming smile spreading over her face as Delia began to eat. And, watching her, Felicity once again had the sensation that she had met Alice before.

Pam, sitting next to Felicity, said in a low voice, 'How very odd!'

'What is odd, Pam?' asked Felicity, turning to look at the girl.

'Well,' said Pam. 'When Alice smiled just then, I had the strangest feeling that I knew her.'

'That really *is* strange,' said Felicity. 'Because I had exactly the same feeling. And I felt it when we were on the train together, too. So did Susan, and June.'

'Really?' said Pam. 'How very peculiar! Perhaps she has a sister . . .'

'She *doesn't* have a sister who came to Malory Towers,' Felicity interrupted. 'She told us that she is an only child.'

'Oh,' said Pam, crestfallen. 'But the funniest thing of all is that when I look at Alice now, I feel quite certain that I have never seen her before.'

'Yes!' said Felicity. 'It seems to be only when she wears certain expressions that I think she seems familiar. It's very queer indeed.'

'Nonsense!' scoffed June, who had overheard all of this. 'There's nothing strange or queer about it. Alice simply reminds us of someone, and one day it will come to one of us, when we are least expecting it. We'll say, "Oh yes, she looks like that girl so-and-so, who used to be in South Tower." You'll see!'

June's explanation was so reasonable and so matter-of-fact that Pam and Felicity felt sure that she was right, and even felt a little ashamed of themselves for allowing their imaginations to run away with them.

Alice found another opportunity to help that evening. Susan had come to Felicity's study, and the two girls were talking about the work they would have to do for Higher Cert.

'I intend to knuckle down right away,' said Susan, a determined look on her face. 'I want to get a head start.'

'Good idea,' said Felicity. 'I shall do the same, though it will seem awfully queer studying alone. I'm used to doing it in the common-room, with everyone groaning and sighing. I don't know that I shall be able to concentrate without it!'

'Well, I expect we shall soon get used to the peace and quiet,' said Susan, getting up. 'I'm off to get a couple of hours reading in now, before bed-time.'

Shortly after Susan had departed, someone tapped softly at Felicity's door, and she called out, 'Come in!'

The door was pushed open, and Alice peered round, a rather nervous smile on her face.

'Can I help you, Alice?' asked Felicity.

The girl ventured further into the room, saying rather hesitantly, 'Actually, I was hoping that *I* might be able to help *you*. You see, Felicity, I overheard you talking to Susan earlier. Not that I was eavesdropping, but your door was open and I happened to be walking past. And I thought that perhaps I could help you with your studying.'

'It's very kind of you to offer, Alice,' said Felicity, looking rather puzzled. 'But I really don't see how you *can* help.'

'Well, when I was studying for School Cert a couple of years ago, my father used to test me on how much I had learned by asking me questions,' explained Alice. 'I found that it helped me tremendously.'

'That's not a bad idea,' said Felicity, smiling. 'Sit down, Alice, and grab that history book.'

Delighted that her offer of help had been accepted, Alice sat in one of the armchairs and opened the book.

Then she began to test Felicity by asking questions, feeling very impressed indeed when the girl answered most of them correctly.

'My goodness, you're clever!' said Alice when they had finished. 'I should think that you will pass with flying colours.'

'I'm not particularly clever really,' laughed Felicity. 'Though it's very nice of you to say so. It's just that I spent a lot of time in the holidays studying. Now, June, on the other hand, is really clever – and very lucky! She has the most amazing memory, and facts just seem to stick in her head. She hardly needs to study at all.'

'Yes,' said Alice, with a laugh. 'I remember –'

Then she stopped suddenly, turning rather red, before continuing hastily, 'I remember when I was at my last school, there was a girl like June. She could read a poem once, and then recite it perfectly. How we all envied her.'

Then Alice glanced at her watch, and, jumping to her feet, said, 'Heavens, is that the time? I must go and finish my Maths prep before bedtime. I'll see you later, Felicity.'

And she dashed from the study before Felicity even had time to thank her for her help. Felicity had a feeling that Alice had been about to say something else when she had started talking about the girl at her old school, and just stopped herself in time. And, now that she came to think about it, Miss Oakes hadn't given them any Maths prep today!

How odd. And what a strange girl Alice was.

At the pool

The first week of term flew by, and soon the old girls felt as if they had never been away. Of course, it took longer for the new girls to settle in, especially the first formers.

Violet continued to irritate everyone with her boastful, conceited ways. It was quite obvious, from her expensive clothes and wonderful belongings – many of which she had brought to school with her – that the girl came from a wealthy family. And, as Daffy said, she never missed an opportunity to rub people's noses in it.

'My parents wanted to send me to a much more exclusive school,' Violet said in the dormitory one evening, looking at her surroundings with an air of disdain. 'The dormitories were so much nicer than the ones here, and even the lower school had studies of their own instead of common-rooms.'

'Well, why didn't they?' asked an outspoken girl called Ivy. 'I'm sure that you would have fitted in much better at one of those snobbish places than here, at Malory Towers.'

'Perhaps the school was a little *too* exclusive for Violet,' said Daffy slyly. 'And the Head refused to take her.'

'Nothing of the sort,' said Violet, with a haughty toss

of the head. 'If you must know, my grandmother insisted that I should be sent here. You see, she was a schoolgirl here, many, many years ago. And, when I was born, she made Daddy promise that he would send me here too. He tried to make her change her mind, so that I could go to a more superior school, but Grandmother wouldn't hear of it and held him to his word.'

'Well, at least there's one sensible person in your family,' said Katie. 'And I, for one, think that Malory Towers is a jolly fine school, although I haven't been here very long.'

The others agreed heartily, and Violet pouted crossly, turning away to pick up a silver-backed hairbrush from her bedside cabinet.

All of the first formers had personal belongings on top of their little cabinets – a photograph, a mirror, or some little trinket that they had brought from home. But Violet's cabinet was absolutely crammed with things. There was the silver-backed hairbrush and a matching mirror, a little jewellery box and various perfumes and lotions. Then there were two photographs, both in very ornate frames. One was of her beautiful Siamese cat, Willow, and the other was of Violet and her parents.

The girls had been most amused to see the family photograph, for, although Mrs Forsyth was quite a pretty woman, it was clear that Violet had inherited her looks from her father, for he had the same small eyes and snub nose.

Violet had also brought a number of dresses to school

with her and, as she hung her school uniform in her wardrobe, Daffy caught a glimpse of one hanging up. It was a pale pink party dress, festooned with frills and ribbons, and the girl couldn't think why Violet had brought it to school with her. And suddenly a wicked idea came to her.

As soon as Violet went to the bathroom, she gathered the others round and explained it to them.

'Oh, I say!' chuckled Ivy. 'What a super idea, Daffy!'

'Marvellous!' said Katie, clapping her hands together in glee. 'You are naughty, Daffy, but so funny.'

Even Faith, the quiet head-girl, giggled, though all the girls made themselves look perfectly serious when Violet returned.

'Our first Saturday at Malory Towers tomorrow night,' said Daffy, climbing into bed. 'I must say, I'm looking forward to tomorrow evening.'

'Why, what's happening tomorrow evening?' asked Violet, a puzzled look on her face.

'Don't you know?' said Katie. 'On Saturday evenings, everyone dresses up for supper. I'm going to wear the yellow dress with the satin bows that Mother made for me in the holidays. What about you, Daffy?'

'I shall wear my blue one, with the lace collar,' Daffy said. 'It really is beautiful. Violet, you simply *must* wear your pink party dress. I bet that you'll look lovely in it.'

Violet, quite unaccustomed to compliments from Daffy, looked at her a little suspiciously, but, as the others launched into descriptions of the imaginary dresses they intended to wear, her suspicions vanished and she became caught up in the excitement.

The first formers talked until long after lights out, and poor Faith simply didn't know how to stop them. At one point she ventured to say, 'No more talking, please, girls.' But her voice was so quiet that the laughter and chatter of the others quite drowned it out. In fact, they were making so much noise that no one heard footsteps approaching, or the door open. It wasn't until the light was suddenly switched on, making everyone blink, that the first formers realised Mam'zelle Dupont, who was on duty that night, had entered.

'Ah, *méchantes filles*!' she cried. 'You are very bad, to be talking after the lights have gone out. See how you disturb the poor little Daphne?'

Daffy, who had swiftly become one of Mam'zelle's favourites, was blinking and rubbing her eyes, a very disgruntled look on her face. No one would have guessed that she was the one who had been making most noise!

Mam'zelle certainly didn't, and she turned to Faith now, saying sternly, 'Faith, it is not right that you allow these bad girls to disobey the rules! As head-girl, it is your duty to see that they behave properly, and you have failed.'

'Sorry, Mam'zelle,' mumbled Faith, looking very downcast indeed.

The others began to feel a little uncomfortable. They had quickly realised that Faith was too weak to be a good leader, and had taken advantage of this. But no one wanted to get the girl into trouble.

Ivy spoke up, saying, 'We are all sorry, Mam'zelle. It wasn't Faith's fault, truly it wasn't.'

'No, she did tell us to be quiet,' said Maggie, who slept in the bed next to Faith and had heard her half-hearted attempt to remonstrate with them. 'But we took no notice.'

'Ah, you are all wicked girls, except for the dear Daphne, who has been trying to sleep,' said Mam'zelle, wagging her finger.

Faith felt that it was little unfair that Daffy, who had talked more than all the others put together, was the only one not to be scolded, but she would not dream of sneaking on the girl. Why, that was quite unthinkable!

'I do not want another sound from this dormitory tonight,' said Mam'zelle. 'I shall be back later, and if there is any noise you will all get extra French prep next week.'

No one wanted that, so as soon as the door closed behind Mam'zelle, everyone snuggled down under the bedclothes, and, as they were really very tired, it wasn't long before everyone dropped off.

Saturday dawned bright and sunny, and it was unusually warm for the time of year.

'I might go for a dip in the pool,' said June, at the breakfast table. 'Anyone care to join me?'

'I'd love to come,' said Felicity with a sigh. 'But I suppose I had better do some studying.'

Miss Oakes happened to walk by the sixth formers' table at that moment, and overhead this.

'Felicity,' she said. 'I insist that you go for a swim. In fact, I insist that *all* of you Higher Certificate girls take some time off today, for I know how hard you have been working. I positively forbid you to study!'

The girls were very pleased to hear this, for they really did feel in need of relaxation, and, as Pam said, 'We can't possibly disobey our form-mistress. I'll join you for that swim, June.'

In the end, most of the sixth formers went to the pool. Amy and Bonnie, who hated any kind of exercise, went off to Amy's study for a good gossip, while Julie and Lucy went horse-riding. Alice refused to get changed and get into the pool, saying that she wasn't a very good swimmer, but she went along with the others and sat at the side, watching them.

The girls had a very pleasant time indeed, the strong swimmers like Felicity, Susan and June doing as many lengths as they could, while others, like Delia and Nora, preferred to paddle around in the shallow end.

But their peace was rudely shattered when they were joined by a group of first formers.

'Hallo, Felicity,' said Daffy. 'Do you mind if we join you? Miss Potts said that we might swim today, as the weather is so lovely.'

The sixth formers could hardly say no, as Miss Potts had given her permission, but the pool suddenly seemed rather overcrowded with a dozen or so giggling, excited first formers splashing around.

Violet Forsyth, who looked most ungainly in her

swimming costume, stood uncertainly on the edge. She couldn't swim and was afraid of the water. The girl would much rather be indoors, but unfortunately she had made the mistake of boasting about her swimming-pool at home. Somehow the boasting had got out of hand and turned into downright lies.

The first formers had come down to see the pool on their first day and, while the others had been in raptures over it, Violet had merely shrugged, and said in a bored manner, 'I suppose it's all right, but it's nowhere near as nice as our pool at home.'

'Oh, do you have your own swimming-pool?' Katie had asked, pretending to sound most impressed. 'How marvellous!'

Encouraged by this, Violet had gone on to tell the listening girls about the marvellous garden parties her parents held in the summer, where all the guests swam in the pool.

'I'll bet you're a wonderful swimmer, Violet,' Daffy had said admiringly.

And foolish Violet, who loved nothing more than being the centre of attention, had got quite carried away, and told the first formers of how she swam several lengths in the pool every day, when the weather was warm enough.

But Daffy noticed now that the girl hung back and didn't venture too close to the edge – hardly the behaviour of someone who felt quite at home in the water. Besides, if Violet swam every day, as she claimed, surely she wouldn't be so plump, thought Daffy.

It was quite true that Violet had a swimming-pool at her home, but the girl never used it. And now she was regretting her boasting, for she had been quite unable to get out of going down to the pool with the others, and soon her lie would be exposed in front of them all.

'Come on, Violet!' Daffy called out. 'Jump in!'

Violet had no intention of jumping in, but she realised that she couldn't stand shivering on the edge forever. So she walked gingerly down the steps, fervently hoping that, amongst such a crowd, no one would notice that she wasn't actually swimming.

But Daffy's sharp eyes were watching, and she smiled to herself as she saw Violet clinging to the side in the shallow end.

Some of the sixth formers didn't care to share the pool with the boisterous youngsters and got out. Soon only Felicity, Susan and June were left, and they had to call the first formers to order on several occasions.

Violet, who had been barged into by Maggie and splashed by Ivy, had had quite enough of the pool, and decided to slip away and get dressed. No one seemed to have noticed that she wasn't joining in with the swimming, and, with luck, the weather would turn cold soon, so she wouldn't have to come down to the pool again. She had got away with it!

But Violet was quite mistaken, for Daffy spotted her getting out of the pool, and followed her.

'Not going in already, are you?' she asked. 'You haven't even been in the deep end yet.'

'I think I'm getting a cold,' said Violet, turning red. 'It's probably best if I don't swim any more today.'

Daffy grinned to herself, knowing that the girl hadn't swum at all. But she looked most concerned, and said, 'I daresay you're right. Listen, Violet, when you have changed, would you mind coming back to the pool and throwing some pennies into the water, so that I can dive for them?'

Since she had nothing better to do, and didn't really feel like sitting in the common-room on her own, Violet agreed.

The girl was soon back at the pool, fully dressed, and she stood at the side, close to Alice, calling out, 'Daffy, I have some pennies in my pocket when you are ready.'

Daffy climbed out of the pool and up on to the lowest diving board. Standing poised on the edge, she shouted, 'Throw one in now, Violet!'

Violet obliged, and Daffy did a beautiful dive into the water, causing June to say to Susan, 'That kid dives jolly well! I shall have to bear her in mind for the swimming competition next summer.'

'Yes, she's a strong swimmer, too,' said Susan, as Daffy swam to the side of the pool and stretched her arm up so that Violet could take the penny back from her.

Violet bent forward to take the coin from Daffy, feeling rather nervous, for she didn't like being so close to the edge.

And suddenly, the girl felt Daffy's hand close round her wrist in a firm grip, there was a tug on her arm, and Violet felt herself being pulled towards the deep water. Instinctively, she flailed about with her free hand, trying to find something to hold on to. Alas, the only thing was poor Alice! Somehow, Violet managed to seize her ankle as she was falling into the water, and the whole thing was like some terrible chain reaction, as, with a squeal of terror, Violet fell into the pool, and Alice fell in right behind her.

Violet sank like a stone, and although Alice could swim a little, she didn't like the deep end, and the weight of her clothes was dragging her down.

June and Susan, taking in all that had happened in a glance, went to the aid of the two girls at once. Felicity, at the other end of the pool, didn't realise what was happening at first, but as soon as she heard the commotion she swam down to the deep end and helped Susan get the shocked Alice to the surface and out of the pool.

'Are you all right, Alice?' asked Felicity, as the girl sat down on the ground, gasping for air.

Quite unable to speak, Alice could only nod, and Susan said, 'Let her get her breath back, then we had better get her to Matron. Violet, too.'

'Here are your glasses, Alice,' said Felicity, who had found them at the edge of the pool. 'They must have slipped off when you fell in.'

Alice took them from her, and, in the split second before she put them on, Felicity felt that little stirring of recognition again. Then, once Alice's glasses were on her nose again, it vanished. Felicity gave herself a little shake, telling herself sternly that she was making far too much out of it, and it was as June had said – Alice merely reminded her of someone. There were far more important things to think about now, anyway.

It had taken all of June's strength to pull Violet to the surface, for the girl was plump and heavy. Felicity helped June to get her out of the pool, and they laid her on the ground.

Violet was still, her eyes closed, and, for a moment, Daffy thought that her heart would stop in fright. It had only been a prank, she had just meant to scare Violet, not do her any harm.

Then, to Daffy's tremendous relief, the girl opened her eyes and began to sob noisily.

'Well, there can't be much wrong with her if she can cry so loudly,' said June drily. Then she turned to Daffy and said sternly, 'That was a very dangerous prank, which could have had serious consequences if we sixth formers hadn't been around.'

Daffy's knees trembled, for she was a little in awe of the games captain.

'Whatever do you mean, June?' asked Felicity, quite astonished. 'Surely you aren't suggesting that Daffy pushed Violet and Alice in.'

'She didn't push Violet, she pulled her,' said June grimly. 'I saw her. Poor Alice just happened to get in the way.'

'It's true, Felicity,' said Susan, seeing her friend's look of disbelief. 'I saw Daffy deliberately pull Violet into the water as well.'

Felicity was quite speechless, so June said, 'Whatever were you thinking about, Daffy, to pull a girl who can't swim into the deep end? You must have known how dangerous it was.'

'We didn't know that Violet couldn't swim,' piped up Katie, in defence of her friend. 'She is always bragging to us about her swimming-pool at home, and telling us what a marvellous swimmer she is.'

Daffy said nothing, for she had realised that Violet couldn't swim, yet she had plunged her into the deep end anyway. June was quite right – she *hadn't* stopped to think how grave the consequences could have been.

Fortunately for Daffy, however, June had now turned her attention to the still-sobbing Violet, who was sitting up now. June said firmly, 'Do stop crying! Violet, is this true? Did you lead the girls to believe that you could swim?'

With the eyes of the first form upon her, Violet turned red and kept her eyes down, as she muttered, 'Yes.'

'Well, what a foolish thing to do!' said Felicity scornfully. 'I hope that you see now, Violet, what trouble lies can lead to.'

'How was I to know that that mean beast Daffy would pull me in?' cried Violet, feeling that it was rather too bad that she was getting a share of the blame as well.

'Daffy will be punished, you may be sure of that,' said Felicity. Then she glanced at June, saying, 'But I think that a few extra swimming lessons for Violet may be in order?'

'Exactly what I was thinking,' said June with a grim

smile. 'Violet, please come to my study this afternoon and we will make out a time-table.'

Poor Violet groaned inwardly, but she did not dare disobey June. She would find a way of paying Daffy Hope back for this.

'And you, Daffy, will come to *my* study this afternoon,' said Felicity, sounding unusually annoyed, for she felt very disappointed in Daffy. 'Where I shall give you a suitable punishment.'

'Yes, Felicity,' said Daffy, looking and sounding very subdued indeed.

But, now that she knew that Violet was going to be all right, Daffy felt quite unworried. She felt certain that Felicity, who had known her family for years, would not come down on her too hard.

In fact, Violet had come off very much worse, for, as well as her unexpected dip in the pool, she now had to face the prospect of extra swimming lessons with June!

As Felicity, Susan and June bore the two dripping wet girls off to Matron's room, Daffy smiled to herself.

Everything was going her way! She was ruling the roost in the first form, and had convinced most of the mistresses that she was a good, sweet girl. Pulling the wool over Felicity's eyes would be too easy for words!

Daffy in trouble

'Good heavens!' exclaimed Matron, getting up from her chair as the little group entered her room. 'Whatever has happened?'

'An accident at the swimming-pool, Matron,' said Felicity. 'Alice and Violet fell in.'

Violet seethed, for it had been no accident and she opened her mouth to say so. Then June gave her a nudge, and a stern look of warning. Violet knew at once what June was trying to tell her – that it wasn't done to sneak.

And Violet didn't really want to be sent to Coventry by the rest of her form, for it was pleasant to have people to boast to, even though the others never seemed very impressed. So she said nothing, and decided that she would find some other way of getting even with Daffy Hope.

Matron was bustling about now, putting the kettle on and giving the two girls blankets.

'Go into the little bathroom there and get out of those wet things at once,' she said briskly. 'Then wrap those blankets around yourselves while I make some nice, hot tea. When you have both warmed up a little I shall check that you have suffered no ill effects.'

Clutching their blankets, Alice and Violet trooped off

to the bathroom, and Matron turned to the others.

'An accident, you say?' she said, sounding most suspicious. 'Well, I expect the first formers to fool around by the swimming-pool, but I am most surprised to find a sixth former involved.'

'Alice really did get knocked in by accident, Matron,' said Susan. 'She wasn't fooling around.'

'Well, I'm pleased to hear it,' said Matron. 'Now, don't stand there dripping all over my floor! Off you go, and get changed.'

The three girls were still in their swimming costumes, for they had wanted to get Alice and Violet to Matron's room as quickly as possible.

Now they were beginning to feel a little chilly themselves, so they sped off back to the changing-rooms.

'I could do with a nice, hot cup of tea myself,' said Felicity as they dressed. 'Let's all go back to my study and I'll put the kettle on.'

This was a very welcome suggestion indeed, and the three girls made their way to Felicity's study. They passed Bonnie's study on the way, and, as her door was open, they could see the girl hard at work inside, her curly head bent over a book as she scribbled down notes.

'My word, Bonnie really is taking this seriously,' said Susan. 'I say, Bonnie! Didn't you hear what Miss Oakes said? We are supposed to take today off.'

'You can overdo it, you know,' said June. 'I thought that you and Amy were going to spend some time together?'

'Well, we had a lovely chat while you were down at the pool,' said Bonnie. 'Then I thought that I could get a head start on you others by studying today while you are all enjoying yourselves.'

'Well, not only has Miss Oakes forbidden it, but *I* forbid it, too,' said Felicity with mock-sternness. 'We really do need to relax every now and then, you know, Bonnie, then we can go back to our studying feeling refreshed.'

'Yes, come along to Felicity's study with us, and have a cup of tea,' said June, taking Bonnie's arm and pulling her up from her chair.

Amy, who was feeling very bored and lost without her little friend, came along then, and Felicity cried, 'Amy! We are trying to persuade Bonnie not to work so hard, and would be very grateful if you would add your word to ours.'

'I already have,' said Amy, sounding rather disgruntled. 'Really, Bonnie, I don't see that taking one day off from your studies would do any harm. We could go into town after lunch and spend our pocket money. Then we could have tea in the little tea-shop. My treat.'

Bonnie's eyes lit up at this, and she said, 'That *would* be fun, I must say.'

'Well, that's settled, then,' said June cheerfully, leading Bonnie from the room. 'We are *all* having a day off, even you, Bonnie.'

'Yes, come on, let's get that kettle on, Felicity,' said Susan. 'I'm simply dying for a cup of tea.'

In the end there was quite a crowd in Felicity's study, for Amy came along too, and they were also joined by Alice, who had been given a clean bill of health by Matron. Felicity had to perch on the window-sill, but she didn't mind at all, for it was nice to be with her friends, and to laugh and joke with them.

Alice was the first to leave, saying that she had to write a letter to her parents, and, as the door closed behind her, Susan said, 'Alice never says much about her parents, or her home life, does she?'

'Well, she's rather shy,' said Felicity. 'Perhaps we should ask her, and try to draw her out a little.'

'It's obvious that her parents are very wealthy,' said Amy unexpectedly.

'Is it?' said June, surprised. 'Not to me it isn't. I mean to say, she doesn't have any marvellous possessions, or boast about how rich her family are. Unlike some people.'

Amy, who knew that this was aimed at her, flushed. Her parents were very wealthy indeed, and she liked to make sure that people knew it.

'Her clothes are very expensive,' said Amy, rather stiffly. 'I can tell, for some of them come from the same shops I get mine from. And she has a handbag in her wardrobe exactly like one I have at home. Mother bought it for my birthday last year, and it cost an awful lot of money.'

Amy knew about such things, so the others believed her words, and it made them even more curious about the new girl.

At last the others drifted away and only Felicity and Susan remained in the study.

'What punishment are you going to give young Daffy Hope?' asked Susan curiously. 'I suppose that it's difficult for you, what with your family and hers being such close friends.'

'I have made up my mind that I will treat Daffy exactly as I would any of the other kids,' said Felicity firmly. 'It certainly wouldn't be just or fair to show her any favouritism. She must apologise to both Violet and Alice, of course, and I shall forbid her to leave the school grounds next Saturday.'

'If you ask me, she's getting off quite lightly,' said Susan.

'Ah, but you see, the first formers are planning a picnic on the beach next Saturday, if the weather is fine,' said Felicity, with a smile. 'Imagine how young Daffy will feel, watching the others go off to enjoy themselves, while she has to remain at school alone.'

'All right, I take that back,' said Susan. 'Daffy isn't getting off lightly at all! Let's just hope it makes her think twice before playing such a dangerous trick again.'

Daffy knocked on the door of Felicity's study at three o'clock, and, on being told to come in, was surprised to see Alice and Violet there. And she didn't like the malicious, slightly triumphant look that Violet gave her at all!

Felicity had asked the two girls along, for she wanted to be sure that Daffy apologised to them both. Alice had been a little reluctant, saying, 'Oh, but Daffy didn't cause me to fall into the water deliberately, Felicity. I should feel most uncomfortable if you made her apologise to me.'

But Felicity had stood firm. 'The kid needs to learn to think about the consequences of her actions. You falling in was one of those consequences, and I insist that she says sorry to you,' she had said.

Violet, of course, had needed no persuading, quite delighted to think that her arch-enemy would have to apologise to her under the stern eye of the Head Girl.

'Daffy,' said Felicity coolly. 'I trust that you have now had time to think about your behaviour?'

Daffy, at her most demure, nodded and said meekly, 'Yes, Felicity. It was very bad of me, and I shall never, ever do such a thing again.'

'I am pleased to hear it,' said Felicity. 'Now, before I give you your punishment, I think that you have something to say to Alice and Violet.'

Daffy, realising at once what Felicity wanted her to do, wasn't at all pleased! She didn't mind saying sorry to Alice – indeed, she had intended to do so before Felicity had prompted her. But apologising to that hateful Violet, who was certain to gloat, was quite another matter.

But, glancing at Felicity's determined expression, Daffy realised that she really didn't have any choice in the matter.

'Alice, I'm most awfully sorry,' she said sincerely, looking up at the bigger girl. 'I really didn't mean for you to fall into the pool as well. I had no idea that Violet would grab hold of you like that.'

Alice accepted the apology graciously, then Daffy turned to Violet.

'*Dear* Violet,' she said, making her tone sickly-sweet. 'I simply don't know what came over me, and I hope that you, too, will accept my most sincere apologies. But some good has come out of it, for June is going to teach you to swim, and I know how much you will enjoy that.'

Of course, Daffy knew quite well that the girl was dreading the swimming lessons, and Violet, realising this, scowled at her. Felicity, however, noticed nothing amiss, and felt pleased that Daffy had apologised so sincerely and so readily.

'Violet?' she said.

Violet would have liked nothing better than to refuse Daffy's apology, but she knew that it would earn her a scold from Felicity, so she accepted it rather stiffly, a sullen expression on her face.

'Well,' said Alice, looking rather relieved as she edged towards the door, 'I shall go back to my study now.'

'You can go too, Violet,' said Felicity.

Violet, who had hoped that she would be able to stay and hear what Daffy's punishment was to be, looked rather put out, but followed Alice from the room.

As the door closed behind the two girls, Felicity turned to Daffy, staring hard at the girl. Looking at the first former's sweet face and innocent expression, it was hard to believe that she was capable of any mischief whatsoever. As far as Felicity was concerned, Daffy's behaviour at the pool that morning was completely out of character, and hopefully the punishment she was about to dish out would ensure that it was not repeated.

Felicity got out the little punishment book that all the top formers carried with them, and wrote something on one of the slips in her neat handwriting. Then she tore it out and handed it to the first former.

Daffy took it, thinking what a bore it was that she would have to give up some of her free time to write out lines, or learn a poem or something. Then her face fell as she looked at the punishment slip.

'But we first formers are going for a picnic next Saturday!' wailed Daffy, looking at Felicity in dismay. 'If I'm confined to school, that means I shall miss it.'

Felicity couldn't help feeling a little sorry for the girl, but she was determined to stick to her word, and said crisply, 'Well, perhaps you should have thought about that before pulling Violet into the swimming-pool! I am sorry, Daffy, but the punishment stands. You may go now.'

Scowling every bit as darkly as Violet had a few minutes earlier, Daffy left the study. She would have liked to slam the door behind her, but didn't dare. Felicity might call her back and give her another punishment!

Halfway down the corridor, she stopped and looked at the punishment slip again, her mind racing. It wasn't just the severity of the punishment that bothered her, but the fact that she had boasted to the others about how Felicity was a friend of the family, and would be sure to let her off lightly. Now she would lose face in front of the first form, and that silly Violet would crow over her like anything! Then a thought came to Daffy. There was no need to tell the others about her punishment, for if she went on the picnic Felicity would never know!

So when she joined the others in the first-form common-room, and they crowded round to ask what her punishment had been, Daffy laughed and said cheerfully, 'Felicity let me off scot-free. Didn't I tell you that she wouldn't come down hard on me?'

'That's hardly fair,' protested Ivy, frowning. 'I'm sure if it had been one of us others we would have been punished.'

'Well, I did have a small punishment,' admitted Daffy. 'I had to apologise to Her Highness. And to Alice, of course, but I didn't mind that.'

'It must have been dreadful saying sorry to Her Highness, though,' said Katie, sympathetically. 'No wonder she has been looking so smug!'

Violet, who was sitting in an armchair reading a book, overheard this and glared at Katie, who promptly stuck out her tongue at the girl.

Daffy pulled Katie aside, saying in a low voice, 'Listen, Katie, I'm going to tell you something, but you mustn't let any of the others know. Promise?'

'Of course,' said Katie at once. 'You can count on me.'

Quickly Daffy told Katie that Felicity had forbidden her to go on the picnic, and Katie gasped, 'Oh, no! I didn't think that Felicity would be so harsh.'

'Nor did I,' said Daffy with a grimace. 'But it doesn't

matter, for I'm going anyway. Felicity will never find out.'

'I certainly hope not, for your sake,' said Katie, torn between shock that Daffy was going to disobey the Head Girl and ignore her punishment, and admiration at her daring. 'If she does, you'll be for the high jump all right!'

'Pooh!' said Daffy, tossing her dark curls. 'Who cares for Felicity and the rest of those stuffy sixth formers? I came to Malory Towers to have some fun, and that's exactly what I intend to do!'

Trouble in the first form

There was more trouble for Violet at supper that evening. The first formers watched, trying hard to hide their smiles, as Violet got out her beautiful pink dress and laid it carefully on the bed.

The girl saw the others staring, and said, 'Aren't you going to get changed?'

'There's plenty of time,' said Daffy. 'I'm going to have a bath first.'

'And I need to wash my hands,' said Katie. 'I don't want to get dirty marks on my lovely party dress.'

'I wonder if I have time to wash my hair?' said Maggie.

The others had planned this carefully, for they wanted to make sure that Violet was the last to use the bathroom.

'She always spends ages titivating herself,' Daffy had said. 'If we can time it so that she is in the bathroom when the bell goes for tea, the rest of us can be gone by the time she comes out, and she won't realise that she is the only one who is dressed up like a dog's dinner!'

Violet was rather disgruntled to be the last one in the bathroom, but there was little she could do about it.

'Don't take too long, Violet,' called Ivy, as the girl, at

last, made her way to the bathroom. 'The rest of us are about to get into all our finery.'

But, of course, the first formers didn't get into their finery at all! As it was a Saturday, they were allowed to wear their own clothes, but no one dressed for supper at all. All of the girls wore quite plain dresses, or jumpers with skirts or trousers.

'Her Highness is going to stick out like a sore thumb,' chuckled Katie, rubbing her hands together in glee.

'Let's make our way to the dining-room now,' said Daffy. 'We want to make absolutely certain that we are out of the way when Violet comes back in, or the whole trick will be ruined.'

So, when Violet entered the dormitory, just after the bell had sounded for supper, she was very surprised indeed to find it empty.

'Mean beasts!' she thought, slipping the flounced, frilly dress over her head. 'They might have waited for me.'

But, as she admired herself in the mirror, Violet came to realise that, perhaps, it was a good thing the others had gone in to tea without her. She would be able to make a grand entrance, and every eye would be upon her.

And Violet was quite right, for every eye *was* upon her – but not for the reason she had hoped!

Miss Potts, sitting at the mistresses' table, was the first to spot the girl, and her jaw dropped.

The mistress had very little time for what she termed fripperies, and she frowned heavily. Really, what a silly girl Violet was, dressing up as if she were attending some grand party! Did she really think that by doing so she would make people admire her? Instead, she had made herself look quite ridiculous.

Then the sixth formers spotted her, and Freddie, taking a sip of tea, choked.

'My word!' gasped Gillian. 'What a sight!'

A peal of laughter came from the first-form table, and June cast a sidelong glance at Daffy Hope. The girl's eyes were brimming with mischief, a broad grin on her face as she gazed at Violet, before whispering something to Katie.

At once, June realised what had happened. Those wicked first formers had tricked Violet into making herself look silly. And if Daffy wasn't at the back of it, she would be very surprised indeed!

Of course, the sixth formers no longer played such childish tricks, but, as June saw the dawning horror on Violet's face, she couldn't help wishing that she had thought of this one when she was younger, for it was really very funny.

Unsurprisingly, poor Violet didn't think it was at all funny! She had walked into the dining-room with her head held high, looking very pleased with herself indeed. But it hadn't take her long to realise that she was the only girl wearing a party dress, or to see the grins of amusement on the faces around her. The girl turned as red as a beetroot, wishing that the floor would open up and swallow her.

The shrewd Miss Potts, seeing the girl's look of dismay and confusion, and the mirth of the first formers, also realised that Violet had somehow been tricked. She got to her feet.

'Come along, Violet,' she said, taking the girl's arm and leading her across to the first-form table. 'It is nice to see that *one* of my form has taken the trouble to make herself look nice. Ivy, you don't appear to have brushed your hair at all! And Daphne, I see that you have already managed to spill tea over your skirt.'

This was said loudly enough for several people nearby to overhear, and June grinned to herself as Daffy turned red. Ah, the first former might be able to fool silly little Violet, but she would never get one over on Miss Potts!

Daffy had, indeed, turned red and, as Violet slipped into an empty seat beside Faith, and Miss Potts went back to her own table, she muttered to Katie, 'Potty didn't really mean that about Violet looking nice, you know, for she has no time for people who fuss over their appearance. She only said it to try and make the rest of us feel small.'

'You must admit that she's jolly sharp, though,' said Katie, looking at the mistress in awe. 'She obviously realises that we were behind the whole thing.'

Violet, of course, was delighted that Daffy had found herself on the receiving end of Miss Potts's sharp tongue. Her feelings were soothed still further when Faith, who felt a little guilty about the trick, said softly, 'You really do look nice, Violet. Personally, I think it's a pity that we *don't* all get dressed up on a Saturday evening.'

Mam'zelle Dupont, at the head of the first-form table, also thoroughly approved of Violet's appearance.

'The good Miss Potts is quite right,' she declared. 'It is nice to see young people looking their best. Now, when I return to *la belle* France, and have dinner with my so-dear family, my nieces and nephews always wear their finest clothes. That is how it should be.'

And at once Mam'zelle launched into a string of anecdotes about her beloved nieces and nephews, which bored most of the first formers heartily, but which they were forced to listen to politely.

Violet, however, began to feel that the whole episode hadn't been such a disaster after all. She was in the good books of both Mam'zelle and Miss Potts, and that horrid Daffy had been scolded as well. So Violet ate her supper quite happily, listening with the appearance of interest to Mam'zelle's tales, and enjoying the disgruntled expressions on the faces of the others.

'Well, that didn't go quite as well as I had hoped,' said Daffy glumly as the first formers left the hall. 'And, worst of all, I feel as if Violet has somehow come out on top.'

'Cheer up!' said Katie, clapping her on the back. 'It was jolly funny at first, when it suddenly dawned on Violet that she was the only one who looked as if she was going to a party. If only Miss Potts hadn't interfered, all would have been well.'

But worse was to come. On Monday morning, Miss Potts sent Violet to take a message to Miss Parker, of the second form, and as the door closed behind the girl, she got to her feet, looking at her class very sternly indeed.

'Please listen, everyone,' said the mistress, her tone so

crisp and authoritative that there wasn't a girl in the room who didn't pay attention. Even Daffy sat up straight in her chair, her gaze fixed on the mistress.

'That was a marvellous trick you played on Violet the other day,' she began. 'Even though it was rather a mean one, in my opinion. It has also come to my attention that there was an incident at the swimming-pool on the same morning, which involved Violet and one of the sixth formers falling into the pool and having to be rescued.'

Miss Potts's eyes rested on Daffy for a moment, and the girl tried to stop herself from turning red.

'However,' Miss Potts continued, 'I understand that the culprit has already been punished by Felicity Rivers, so I will say no more about the dangers of such horseplay. What I *will* say, however, is that I will not stand for any more nonsense. I understand that not all of you like Violet, but as you go through life you will meet all sorts of people, and will find that it is not possible to like each and every one of them. But, for the sake of harmony, it is necessary that you learn to get along with them. I trust that there will be no more tricks played on Violet, for if I hear about it I will dish out a very severe punishment. Is that quite clear?'

'Yes, Miss Potts,' chorused the girls in very subdued tones.

Violet came back then, so Miss Potts let the matter drop, but the girls discussed it at break-time.

'You will have to stop playing tricks on Violet now, Daffy,' said Faith, with what authority she could muster.

But Daffy merely said scornfully, 'No such thing. I shall just have to be more careful, that's all. Her Highness is such a marvellous victim!'

'Absolutely!' said Katie, backing her friend up, as always. 'Besides, Violet deserves another trick because of the way she spoke to Daffy on Saturday night.'

When the first formers had gathered in the common-room after supper on the fateful night, the others had quite expected Violet to go and change out of her party dress, but she had sat in one of the big armchairs, a vision in pink frills, and picked up a book.

'Aren't you going to change, Violet?' Ivy had asked.

'Why should I?' Violet had said, a stubborn look coming over her round face. 'I am perfectly satisfied with the way I look. So were Miss Potts and Mam'zelle. Why, even Faith said that I looked very nice.'

At once, everyone turned accusing eyes on Faith, who turned red. Though, she thought, there was no reason at all for her to feel guilty. She had only been trying to make Violet feel a little less uncomfortable.

'I must say, the colour does suit you,' Daffy had drawled. 'When you're angry your cheeks go all pink, and the dress matches them perfectly!'

Then Violet had flung down her book and got to her feet, saying angrily, 'Well, you look like a – a mop, with those silly, untidy curls all over the place! You think you're so wonderful, don't you, Daffy Hope? Just because your sister used to come here, and you know the Head Girl! Well, just you remember that pride comes before a fall, and I promise you, I shall get back at you for trying to trick me tonight!'

'*Trying* to trick you?' laughed Daffy, quite unmoved by the girl's anger. 'I would say that I succeeded very nicely. Wouldn't you, girls?'

Of course, the others agreed with Daffy at once, apart from Faith, who said nothing at all.

The row had ended with Violet flouncing off to bed, but the only person she upset by doing that was herself, for she was far too angry to sleep, and soon became very bored indeed!

Faith thought of this now, as she watched the others crowding round Daffy, all of them most impressed by her boldness and daring.

Faith herself, however, was beginning to find Daffy a little tiresome. She didn't resent the girl's popularity, for lively, amusing people like Daffy always *were* popular. But she disliked the way that the girl dismissed everything that she said, and didn't seem to recognise that she was head of the form. And the others, eager to copy Daffy in everything, were following suit.

Well, it was her own fault, she supposed, for being a weak character. The first form needed a strong leader, and, as it didn't have one, it was inevitable that someone would step into the breach. Not for the first time, Faith wondered if the honourable thing to do would be to go to Miss Potts and resign, for there was no denying that she wasn't making a very good job of things.

But just then, Daffy glanced round and spotted Faith

standing on the edge of things as always, a rather forlorn expression on her face. And since, despite her mischievous ways, she was a kind-hearted girl, she moved across to her, taking her arm in a friendly way, and saying, 'Come on, Faith, old girl! There's just time for a quick ball game before Geography. You'll play, won't you?'

Katie and one or two others added their voices to Daffy's, and suddenly Faith felt a warm glow spread over her, her gloomy feelings dropping away. The first formers weren't a bad lot, at heart. She would just have to find her own way of dealing with them, and of carrying out her responsibilities as head-girl.

'Yes, you come along with us, Faith,' cried Katie, taking her other arm. 'Let's go and have some fun!'

Alice's puzzling behaviour

The first formers might be having fun, but those sixth formers who were studying for Higher Certificate were working very hard indeed.

Alice, as always, was eager to help, but not everyone appreciated her well-meaning efforts.

Pam was most grateful when the girl offered to post a letter for her, so that she could carry on with her studying. June, however, was extremely displeased to enter her study one afternoon, only to discover that someone had tidied it.

'I say!' she cried. 'What on earth has happened here? Someone has tidied all my papers away.'

'Well, you must admit that it did *need* tidying,' said Freddie, coming in behind her and looking at the neatly arranged desk. 'Why, there was so much stuff on there before, you couldn't even *see* the desk.'

'Yes, but although it might have looked a mess to everyone else, *I* knew exactly where everything was!' said June, sounding very dismayed. 'My lists of teams for sports were in that corner, my English work was there, and my Maths there. I like working in a jumble. Now how am I supposed to find anything?'

It didn't take long for June to discover that Alice was the culprit, and she wasted no time in setting the girl straight.

'Look here, Alice,' she said. 'I don't appreciate you coming into my study without my permission and messing about with my things.'

'I – I'm sorry, June,' said Alice meekly. 'I was only trying to help.'

'Well, I have had to waste precious time in finding everything that you tidied away and putting it back where it was,' said June shortly. 'So you haven't helped me at all. Run round after the others if you want to, but leave me alone!'

Felicity, who overheard this, took June to task, saying, 'You were a little hard on Alice, June. She meant well.'

'I daresay,' said June. 'But I can't bear people trying to organise me! To be honest, Felicity, she gives me the creeps, always hovering around.'

Felicity protested at this, but she knew what June meant. There was an unwritten rule that if a study door was open, it meant that the occupant was 'at home' – as Susan put it – to visitors. If the door was closed, it meant that whoever was in there didn't want to be disturbed. Most of the girls kept their doors open, for it made them feel more united, and created a friendly atmosphere. But Alice had a disconcerting habit of suddenly appearing in people's doorways.

On one occasion she had quite startled Felicity, who had been completely engrossed in her work. Then she had looked up and seen Alice standing there, and almost jumped out of her skin.

'Alice!' she had gasped. 'Goodness, you gave me quite a fright!'

'I'm so sorry, Felicity,' Alice had said. 'I just came to see if there was any way that I could help you.'

Felicity, who was getting on very well on her own, didn't quite know what to say. She didn't want to spurn Alice, for the girl was so very eager to please. On the other hand, she badly wanted to pass Higher Certificate, and she couldn't allow Alice to interfere with that.

In the end she compromised by asking Alice to copy out some notes that she had scribbled down in class, for they really were difficult to read and Alice's handwriting was very neat.

But the incident quite destroyed her concentration, and when the good-natured Pam complained that she was tired of Alice constantly interrupting her studies, Felicity decided that something must be done.

'I don't quite like to push her off altogether,' said Pam. 'For I was very grateful when she cleaned my shoes the other day. It seems mean to make use of her when it suits us, then tell her to go away when we don't want her.'

'Yes, it's tricky,' said Felicity. 'I suppose the poor girl feels at a bit of a loose end, for we are all so busy studying that none of us has really got the time to get to know her.'

'We're not *all* studying,' Pam pointed out. 'Nora isn't going in for Higher Cert, and nor are Amy and Delia.'

'Why didn't I think of that?' exclaimed Felicity. 'We can ask those three to take Alice under their wing a bit.'

Pam laughed, and said, 'Nora and Delia might agree, but I can't see you having much joy with Amy. Apart from Bonnie, she looks down on everyone, and I can't see why she would treat Alice any differently.'

'I'm not so sure,' said Felicity thoughtfully. 'Amy seems to think that Alice's family are wealthy, so she may consider her worthy of her friendship.'

And it seemed that Felicity was right. She and Pam spoke to Nora, Delia and Amy later that day about Alice, and all three of them agreed that they would do what they could to befriend the new girl. But, to the astonishment of the sixth formers, it seemed to be Amy who was making the most effort, for Alice was constantly in and out of the girl's study over the next few days.

'Well, it seems that you were right, Felicity,' said Pam. 'I'm not sure that I approve of Amy's reasons for becoming Alice's friend, if she is only doing it because of her supposed wealth. But at least Alice seems happy.'

'I don't care what Amy's reason is,' said June, overhearing this. 'As long as she is keeping Alice occupied and out of our way!'

But none of the girls guessed what was behind Amy's kindness to the new girl, until Felicity peeped into the girl's study one evening, and was astonished to see her doing a pile of mending.

'Heavens, Alice!' she cried. 'There's enough mending

there to keep you busy for a week! Whatever have you been doing?'

'Oh, it's not all mine,' said Alice. 'Some of it is Amy's. She so dislikes doing it, and I am only too pleased to be able to help.'

Felicity frowned at this, for it was the rule at Malory Towers that the girls did their own mending.

She said as much, and Alice flushed, saying, 'Well, I couldn't bear to see poor Amy struggling with her mending, knowing that I could do it more quickly and so much better.'

Felicity, who knew that Amy was very good indeed at getting out of the little jobs she didn't want to do, frowned, and, noticing this, Alice said, 'Oh, please don't say that I mustn't do it, Felicity! Amy was so grateful to me, and I should feel that I was letting her down.'

'Well, as you're so keen, I shan't try to stop you,' said Felicity. 'But don't let Amy make a slave of you, Alice.'

'I shan't,' promised Alice.

Over the next few days, though, it became clear that Amy *was* taking advantage of Alice.

It was Amy's turn to do the flowers in the classroom that week, and Gillian, who came in to get a book from her desk, was most surprised to see Alice doing them instead.

'Amy is busy with something,' Alice had explained, when Gillian questioned her. But, a few minutes later, Gillian had seen Amy, strolling arm in arm through the grounds with Bonnie, not looking at all busy!

Julie, going into the dormitory after prep one evening, was taken aback to find Alice going through Amy's bedside cabinet.

'It's quite all right,' said Alice, turning red as she saw the suspicious look on Julie's face. 'Amy sent me to fetch her face cream.'

'Well, I don't see why Amy can't fetch it herself,' said Julie in her blunt way. 'Spoilt, lazy creature.'

Then Bonnie popped into Amy's study one evening, and was surprised to find Alice tidying up in there.

'Thank you so much, Alice,' said Amy with a dazzling smile when the girl had finished.

'Dear Alice,' she murmured to Bonnie, as the girl left the room. 'How she loves making herself useful.'

'And how you love making use of her,' said Bonnie drily.

'I think it's rather decent of me,' said Amy with a righteous air. 'I'm stopping her from getting on everyone else's nerves, and making her feel needed.'

'I suppose that's true,' said Bonnie, amused at her friend's reasoning. 'Make the most of her while you have her, though, for I know that Felicity doesn't approve of you taking advantage of Alice. Once Higher Cert is over, she is sure to step in and put a stop to it.'

Felicity didn't approve of Amy's behaviour at all, but with her responsibilities as Head Girl, and all her extra studying, she scarcely had time to think about the problem, let alone solve it.

June was also very busy for, as games captain, she

had to coach the younger girls, pick lacrosse teams and arrange matches with other schools. There had also been her swimming lessons with Violet. Fortunately, June didn't need to spend as much time studying as the others, for she was blessed with an amazing memory and got very good results with the minimum of effort.

Daffy Hope, who was small and very agile, had a natural talent for lacrosse, and June would have liked to choose her for one of the teams. But the girl played the fool too much, and June decided that, until she settled down a bit, she could not pick her.

'Gather round, everyone!' called June, at the end of a practice session with the first and second formers. 'And I will tell you who I have chosen to be in the lower-school team for the match against Marlowe Hall.'

The girls gathered round eagerly, their faces shining in anticipation, and June began to read out a list of names. The lucky girls whose names were called turned red with delight, as they were cheered and thumped on the back by their friends. Ivy and Katie, of the first form, were simply thrilled when June told them that they were in the team, and Katie murmured to Daffy, 'You're certain to be in, old girl, for you are a much better player than Ivy or me.'

But Daffy's name wasn't mentioned at all, even when June told the girls who the reserves were.

And, rather to her own surprise, the girl felt very hurt, and rather humiliated, for she knew that she was far better at lacrosse than at least half of the girls who had been chosen. She simply couldn't understand why June had overlooked her, and wondered if she should ask the games captain. But then, June might think that she was awfully conceited. Besides, she didn't want the games captain to know how much she cared!

Daffy hung back as the others went to get changed, all of them chattering excitedly, and June called her over.

'Daffy, you are wondering why you weren't chosen for the team, aren't you?' said June, getting straight to the point. She was extremely shrewd, and had seen the hurt and confusion on the girl's face when her name hadn't been called out. 'Well, I will tell you. It is because you fool around too much. Now, I was much the same at your age, so I am not criticising you for it. But the thing is, it's my responsibility to choose the best team to represent Malory Towers, and that means I can't have anyone on there who is going to act the goat at a crucial moment.'

Daffy felt very downcast at this, but she wasn't about to let June know, so she shrugged, and said with her usual cheery smile, 'Oh well, never mind. I daresay it would have been an awful bore having to attend all those extra practices anyway.'

June stared after Daffy as the girl walked away, whistling a cheerful little tune. Daffy *did* mind, she thought. She minded a lot. June knew this, because the first former reminded her very much of herself when she had been in the lower school.

Daffy had a lot of hard lessons to learn before she became a responsible, trustworthy person, and Malory

Towers was certainly the right place to learn them! June sincerely hoped that it wouldn't be too long before the girl found a sense of pride in her school, and a little team spirit.

But it wasn't in Daffy's nature to be downhearted for long. On the whole, she was having a marvellous time at Malory Towers, and there was still so much to look forward to. There was Mam'zelle to play tricks on, Violet to annoy, birthdays coming up – and, of course, the picnic on the beach tomorrow. Daffy was anticipating this eagerly, for the fact that she was disobeying Felicity made it all the more thrilling, and gave an edge to her excitement.

Violet, who had a great deal of pocket money, had ordered a simply enormous chocolate cake for the picnic, which she was going to collect from the baker's shop the following morning. She couldn't resist boasting to the others about it as they came out of the changing-rooms.

'It's simply magnificent,' she said. 'And cost an absolute fortune. But Daddy said that I am to spend as much as I like, and if I run short of money he will send me more.'

The others rolled their eyes, and Ivy said, 'But how will you ever learn to manage your money responsibly if you always go to your father every time it runs out?'

Violet gave a little laugh, and said, 'My family is so wealthy that I don't need to worry about things like that. All I need to think about is how to spend it.'

Alice happened to be walking by at this moment, and she stopped dead on hearing Violet's words.

'Violet!' she said in an unusually sharp tone. 'May I have a word with you, please?'

Violet looked rather surprised, but went over to Alice at once, while the rest of the first formers walked off.

Alice looked at the girl, noticing her small, spiteful-looking eyes, her smug expression, and general air of being very pleased with herself indeed. Here was someone who badly needed taking down a peg or two!

'Violet,' she began. 'I couldn't help overhearing what you were saying to the others just now. And let me tell you, you won't win any friends by boasting about your wealth.'

Violet turned red, and said rather stiffly, 'I can't help it if my father has lots of money.'

'No, but you can stop yourself ramming it down the others' throats,' said Alice. 'I can't make you stop boasting, of course, I can only advise you. If you want to be happy at Malory Towers, give the girls your warmth and your friendship, don't try and win them over with your wealth.'

Violet had nothing to say to this and, as she walked away, Alice sighed to herself. She doubted very much that the girl would change overnight, but hoped that she would listen to her words, and act on them. Suddenly a voice right behind her called her name, making her jump, and Alice turned sharply to see Felicity standing there.

'Sorry, I didn't mean to frighten you,' said Felicity. 'The thing is, Alice, I heard what you said to young Violet just then. I had no intention of listening in, but I was just coming round the corner, so I couldn't help it.'

'Oh!' said Alice, looking rather alarmed. 'Do you think that I shouldn't have said anything?'

'Not at all,' said Felicity emphatically. 'As top formers, it is our job to guide and advise the young ones, and what you said was fine. I couldn't have put it better myself.'

Alice felt so thrilled that she was quite speechless for a moment, and Felicity went on, 'You sounded as though you were speaking from experience.'

'Violet reminds me of – of someone I used to know,' said Alice. 'This girl made herself very unpopular indeed, and I shouldn't like to see Violet going the same way.'

'Well, you've certainly done all you can to put her on the right track,' said Felicity, taking the girl's arm as the two of them began to walk towards the school. She felt pleased to have discovered that Alice had another side to her personality, and there was more to her than the timid, eager-to-please girl the sixth formers knew. But there was still such a lot about her that they had yet to discover, and Felicity decided to ask the girl a question that had been on her mind.

'Alice,' she said, pulling the girl to a halt suddenly. 'Why is it that you are so determined to go out of your way to run errands for others, and make a slave of yourself for someone like Amy?'

The ready colour rushed to Alice's cheeks again, her tone a little breathless as she said, 'It's quite simple. I just like to help people. I know that I am privileged in some ways, and this is my way of giving back. It's as Miss

Grayling said in her speech, on the first day of term – *You will all get a lot out of your time at Malory Towers. See that you put a lot back.'*

'Yes, I see,' said Felicity, thinking that Amy had been right, and that Alice must come from a very wealthy family indeed, if she felt the need to give so much back. But something about the girl's words troubled her, something that she couldn't quite put her finger on.

It was as Felicity was dropping off to sleep that night that she realised what it was, and the thought made her wide awake.

Alice had quoted words to her that Miss Grayling was supposed to have said in her speech. But Felicity had been outside the door, listening, and the Head *hadn't* said those words, although she usually included them. But this time, the telephone had rung before she was able to say the words. So where had Alice heard them?

Daffy is deceitful

There was a slight chill in the air on the morning of the first formers' picnic, but it was bright and sunny, with no wind, and nothing could mar their high spirits.

'We're setting off shortly before noon, aren't we?' said Katie. 'It should be a bit warmer by then.'

'We're to go to the kitchen later, to help Cook cut sandwiches to take with us,' said Daffy.

'And I must pop to the baker's, to collect my cake,' said Violet, with a great air of self-importance.

'Well, you can't go alone,' said Faith. 'Only the fifth and sixth formers are allowed out on their own. Someone must go with you.'

Unsurprisingly, no one was keen on the idea of walking to the baker's shop with Violet and, in the end, Faith, as head-girl, decided that she had better volunteer herself.

'Don't be long!' Daffy called after them. 'We shall need everyone to pitch in and help with the sandwiches.'

'Yes, Daffy,' said Faith meekly and, casting a sidelong glance at her, Violet wondered how the quiet, timid head-girl felt about Daffy usurping her authority and taking over as leader of the first form. Faith had no special friend of her own, and never confided in anyone, and Violet thought that she might be glad of someone to talk to. Why, for all she knew, the head-girl might feel just as bitter towards Daffy as she, Violet, did, and it would be good to have someone on her side.

So, as the two girls walked, Violet was at her sweetest, taking great pains to encourage Faith to talk.

Used to being overlooked by the others, Faith wasn't accustomed to talking about herself and was a little reticent at first. But she soon blossomed under Violet's interest, and began telling the girl all about her parents, and her two young brothers. Of course, all of this was very boring to the self-centred Violet, but she put up with it patiently, just waiting for a chance to drop Daffy's name into the conversation.

And Violet's patience was rewarded, for as they left the baker's shop with the chocolate cake, all neatly wrapped in a cardboard box, done up with string, they bumped into Gillian and Delia.

'Hallo, kids!' said Gillian. 'That's a most interesting-looking box you have there, young Violet.'

'It's a chocolate cake, Gillian,' said Violet. 'For our picnic later.'

'Oh yes, you first formers are all going to the beach, aren't you?' said Delia. 'Well, not quite all of you, for, of course, Daffy Hope will be left behind.'

'Serves her right, if you ask me,' said Gillian. 'She's not a bad kid, but that was a very dangerous trick she played on you the other day, Violet. I think that Felicity's punishment of not allowing her to go to the picnic was very just.'

Of course, this was news to the two first formers, who both looked quite astonished. Violet recovered quickly, however, and said graciously, 'Well, I was very upset and frightened, but I do feel sorry for Daffy, being left behind. I shall have to save her a piece of my chocolate cake.'

Faith, not quite as quick-brained or as cunning as Violet, listened to all this with a puzzled frown on her face, and, seeing that she was about to seek enlightenment from the two sixth formers, Violet seized her arm, saying, 'Well, I suppose that we had better hurry back to school, or the others will think that we have got lost. Goodbye, Gillian. Goodbye, Delia.'

And, carrying the cake-box between them, the two first formers began to make their way back to school. Once they were out of earshot of the sixth formers, Faith stopped, and said, 'Well, what do you make of that, Violet? I could have sworn that Daffy told us Felicity had let her off without a punishment.'

'She did tell us that,' said Violet with a snort. 'Because she wanted us to think that she is well in with the Head Girl. But now we know the truth – Felicity forbade Daffy to take part in the picnic, and Daffy intends to disobey her.'

'Oh dear!' wailed Faith. 'It really is terribly wrong of Daffy, and I know that it's my place to tell her that she is in the wrong, and shouldn't come on the picnic. But Daffy is a strong character, and I am not! Violet, how on earth am I to get her to listen to me?'

Violet's mind had been working quickly, and she said, 'Well, I don't see how you can be held responsible if Daffy chooses to be naughty and disobedient. I think that you should tell her that you know the truth, and what she decides to do after that is really a matter for her and her conscience.'

'I suppose that you are right,' sighed Faith. 'I only hope that Felicity doesn't find out, or Daffy *will* be in hot water.'

Violet smiled to herself at this. Felicity *was* going to find out – she would make sure of that!

'I do admire your patience, Faith,' said Violet sweetly. 'It must be so irritating for you when Daffy tries to take the lead all the time, when it should be you who does so.'

'I'm not cut out to be head-girl, I know that, for I am not a leader,' said Faith, sounding unhappy. 'Miss Potts only allowed me to be because I had already been in the first form for one term.'

'Well, it's early days yet,' said Violet. 'There is plenty of time for you to learn how to become a good head-girl. And how to put that dreadful Daffy in her place!'

Faith looked so alarmed at the thought of putting Daffy in her place that Violet decided she had better change the subject. She chatted amicably to the girl as they walked back to school, telling Faith all about her doting parents, her beautiful home and her beloved Siamese cat, Willow.

Faith, like the rest of her form, thought that Violet was boastful and rather snobbish, but found herself warming to the girl. So few of the first formers took the trouble to talk to her, that it was rather pleasant to enjoy a gossip like this – even though Violet was doing most of the talking!

As they reached the school gates, Violet said, 'You know, Faith, I really have enjoyed your company this morning. Now, I know that you don't have a particular friend, and nor do I, so what do you say to the two of us palling up?'

Faith didn't know quite *what* to say. This was the first time that anyone had asked to be her friend, and her heart was warmed. But the other girls wouldn't like it at all, and might shun her as they shunned Violet.

Violet wasn't particularly clever, but she could be quite sly and cunning when she set her mind to something, and she guessed at the thoughts that were running through Faith's head.

'Of course, I shall quite understand if you don't want to be friends,' she said, sounding rather forlorn. 'I know that the others don't like me very much. But then, they don't seem to have an awful lot of time for you either, probably because you are so quiet. It just seems a shame that we should both be on our own, when we could have so much fun together.'

Violet's words tipped the scales and, from somewhere inside herself, Faith found a spark of courage. Why should she let Daffy, Katie and the rest of them stop her from making a friend, when none of them wanted to befriend her themselves? Let them think what they wanted to!

'You're quite right,' she said, smiling shyly at Violet. 'I should like to be friends with you very much.'

So when the two girls joined the others in the kitchen to help cut sandwiches, the rest of the first formers were astonished to see them giggling and chattering away together as they worked.

'I'm surprised at you, Faith,' said Daffy, finding herself next to the head-girl as the two of them washed up afterwards. 'I thought you had more sense than to make friends with Her Highness.'

Faith was needled by this and, though her voice trembled a little at her own daring, she managed to retort, 'And *I'm* surprised at *you*, Daffy. For I know that Felicity told you you were not to join us on the picnic. It really is very deceitful of you to disobey her, you know.'

Daffy was so taken aback at these harsh words from the timid Faith that she completely forgot to ask the girl how she knew all this. And – most unusually for Daffy – she was quite speechless for a moment.

She soon found her tongue, however, and said, 'You're not going to sneak on me, are you?'

'Of course not!' said Faith indignantly. 'Why, I would never do such a thing! Though I should think more of you, Daffy, if you showed a little respect for Felicity and did as she told you.'

But Daffy didn't care very much for Faith's opinion of her, and was determined to go on the picnic with the others.

Meanwhile, Violet, busy packing one of the picnic baskets that the first formers were taking with them, was thinking hard. How could she make sure that Daffy was found out by Felicity? Sneaking was quite out of the question, for Felicity would be so disgusted with Violet that she might even refuse to listen to her. Besides, Violet didn't want to come out into the open, or Felicity might let Daffy know who was responsible for her disgrace. What about an anonymous letter, slipped under the door of the Head Girl's study?

No, that was no good either, for it could easily be dismissed as a piece of spite, or an attempt at stirring up trouble. What Violet needed was something that would prove, beyond doubt, that Daffy had been to the picnic.

Suddenly an idea came to her, and she darted towards the kitchen door, Ivy calling after her, 'I say, Violet, where are you going? We shall be leaving in a few minutes!'

'I just need to fetch something from the dormitory,' Violet called back. 'I shall be back in two ticks.'

So she was. Most of the others had gone on ahead, but Faith had hung back, waiting for Violet.

'What's that?' she asked, noticing that Violet had a small bag slung over her shoulder.

'My camera,' said Violet. 'It was a birthday gift from my uncle, and it's a really good one. I thought that it might be nice to take some photographs at the picnic, and put them in an album.'

'What a super idea,' said Faith. 'It will be something nice to look back on when we are top formers.'

Violet agreed to this with a smile. Little did Faith realise that she had quite different plans for the photographs! She badly wanted to get her own back on Daffy, for it was all her fault that she now had to take swimming lessons from June. How she hated having to bathe in that beastly, cold water! And how she hated June and her sharp tongue, though she would never dare say so to the girl's face! Violet was the only girl in the school who was hoping that the spell of unseasonably mild weather would break, for once it did she would be safe from swimming lessons until the spring.

Felicity and Susan, meanwhile, had popped down to the stables with Julie and Lucy.

'I've hardly seen anything of Jack and Sandy this term,' said Felicity. 'And I've been saving some sugar lumps for them both. Hallo, who's this?'

A little tabby cat was sitting outside Jack's stable, and as the four girls approached she padded towards them, mewing in greeting.

'This is Queenie,' said Lucy with a grin. 'She belongs to one of the gardeners, and Miss Grayling has given permission for her to live in the stables.'

'She's awfully sweet,' said Susan, bending to stroke the little cat, who purred in appreciation. 'Reminds me a bit of our cat at home.'

'Jack and Sandy simply adore her,' said Lucy. 'Just watch this.'

Lucy opened the door of Sandy's stable, and the cat darted in, going straight up to the horse and weaving in and out of his legs, purring ever more loudly. Sandy wasn't at all alarmed, but whinnied softly, as if he were greeting his little friend, before bending his head and nudging Queenie gently with his big muzzle.

'Well, Sandy, it looks as if you have another admirer,' said Felicity, patting the horse's sleek neck. 'It's a wonder that you and Jack don't get quite big-headed, with all the fuss that is made of you both.'

In the end, Felicity and Susan decided to accompany the other two girls over to Five Oaks, the local riding stables. Five Oaks was run by two old Malory Towers girls, Bill and Clarissa, and the sixth formers often popped in to visit them.

Julie and Lucy went on horseback, of course, while Felicity and Susan had to walk, and the girls were most amused when Queenie attempted to follow them out of the stable yard.

'No, Queenie, I'm afraid that you can't come with us,' said Susan with a laugh. 'You might wander off and get lost.'

Fortunately, the gardener who owned Queenie appeared then, with her dinner, so the cat was distracted and the girls made their escape.

The four spent a pleasant afternoon at Five Oaks, Julie and Lucy enjoying a canter round the paddock, while Felicity and Susan petted the horses and strolled about the grounds. Then they sat in Bill and Clarissa's cosy kitchen, chatting with the two girls as they ate slices of Clarissa's delicious home-made fruit cake, washed down with big cups of tea. Bill was just about to refill their cups when a distant, ominous rumble could be heard, and Lucy said in dismay, 'Oh dear, surely that can't be thunder?'

'I'm afraid that it is,' said Clarissa, who had got up to peer out of the window. 'The sky has suddenly gone awfully grey.'

'We had better get the horses back to school, in that case,' said Julie. 'Poor Jack doesn't like storms at all, and I'd like to stable him before it breaks.'

Fortunately it was only a five-minute ride from Five Oaks to Malory Towers, but it took Felicity and Susan, on foot, a little longer. By the time that they reached the school gates, Julie and Lucy were already stabling their horses, and big drops of rain had just started to fall.

'Phew!' said Susan. 'It looks as if we got back just in time.'

'We are not the only ones,' said Felicity, nodding towards a group of girls who were approaching the gates from the other direction. 'It's the first formers coming back from their picnic.'

The first formers had had a simply marvellous time, making sandcastles, taking their shoes and socks off and paddling at the water's edge, and, of course, eating the delicious picnic.

Violet cut everyone an enormous slice of her chocolate cake, which everyone agreed was simply scrumptious.

'The best cake I've ever tasted.'

'Heavenly! It just melts in the mouth.'

'Delicious! Thanks very much, Violet.'

Daffy and one or two others waited for Violet to boast about how much the cake had cost, but, to their surprise, she accepted everyone's thanks and compliments with a smile. The girl really was on her best behaviour, Daffy realised, when she got out her camera and said cheerily, 'Let's take some photographs so that we can all remember this happy time.'

'Ooh, yes, let's!' cried Katie, clapping her hands together. 'Violet, will you take one of Daffy and me, please?'

Of course, Violet was only too happy to do this, and it didn't occur to Daffy for a second that allowing herself to be photographed at the picnic was rather foolish. The girls posed happily, pulling silly faces at the camera, and Daffy was silliest of all, getting herself into almost every photograph. At last, Violet said, 'That's it, I'm afraid. The film is all used up now. Faith, if you will come into town with me on Monday I can take it in to be developed.'

'Of course,' said Faith at once. 'I can't wait to see them.'

And that was when the sky had turned dark, and the same rumble of thunder that the girls at Five Oaks had heard sounded. Some of the girls were scared of thunder, and they began packing everything away rapidly.

'We had better get back to school before the heavens open,' said Ivy with a shiver. 'Come along, everyone!'

The girls trooped happily back to school, and it was as they were almost at the gates that they saw Felicity and Susan coming towards them.

Daffy was at the back of the little group, and she cast a horrified glance at Katie, who acted quickly.

'Get behind that tree,' she hissed, giving her friend a shove. 'And don't move until you're certain Felicity and Susan have gone.'

The two sixth formers greeted the first formers as they turned in at the gates together, Felicity swiftly running an eye over the group to make sure that Daffy wasn't there. She felt pleased when she realised that the girl had obeyed her orders, and hoped that she wouldn't have reason to punish the first former again.

There was no time to ask the youngsters how they had enjoyed their picnic, for just then the heavens *did* open, and the first formers ran squealing towards the school.

Felicity and Susan followed in a more orderly fashion, and soon only Daffy was left outside in the rain. The girl waited for a few moments before stepping out from the shelter of the tree, then she moved stealthily up to the gates, slipping through them when she realised that the others were out of sight. Walking up the long drive, the girl grinned to herself. She had got away with it!

A marvellous trick

'My word, won't I be glad when Higher Cert is behind us and we can relax a little,' said Felicity to Susan as the two girls slipped into their seats in the class-room. 'Thank heavens we don't have Maths this morning, for I spent all of last night studying it and I simply couldn't face it today.'

'Well, it won't be long now,' said Susan. 'Only a couple of weeks until half-term, and the exams start immediately afterwards.'

'And once the exams have finished, we have our lacrosse matches against Marlowe Hall,' said June. 'It's a pity that you two are so busy studying that you haven't had much time to practice, otherwise I should certainly have put you in the upper-school team. As it is, I have had to fall back on the fourth and fifth formers.'

'You will be in the team though, won't you, June?' said Felicity. 'We must have *someone* from the sixth on there.'

'Oh yes, I shall be playing all right,' said June, who didn't seem to be feeling the pressure of the forthcoming exams as the others did.

'Lucky you,' said Susan enviously. 'I wish that I

had your marvellous memory and didn't need to study so hard.'

'Yes, it's awfully unfair,' said Freddie, joining in. 'While I'm sighing and groaning over my books for hours, June has memorised everything in a matter of minutes and is off to lacrosse practice.'

'I'm just lucky, I suppose,' said June. 'It must run in the family, for my cousin, Alicia, was just the same.'

'I wish it ran in my family,' sighed Felicity. 'But I know that Darrell had to study just as hard as me to get good results.'

'Well, I'm just as busy as you are, in my own way,' said June. 'What with arranging practice times and coaching. Thank goodness the weather has turned too cold for swimming now, and I don't have to give Violet swimming lessons any more. I don't know who found them more trying, her or me!'

Then the girls fell silent, getting to their feet as they heard Miss Oakes approaching, and soon the English lesson was under way, the sixth formers silent as they concentrated hard on their work.

Miss Oakes, looking at all the heads bent over books, felt very pleased with her form, for the majority of them were good, hard-working girls. The mistress knew very well that, if she were to leave the room now, they could be trusted to get on with their work and not play the fool. Even June, who had been such a scamp when she was lower down in the school!

The first formers, however, in the class-room next to

the sixth form's, could *not* be trusted alone, and they were very pleased that Mam'zelle Dupont was late, for they were planning a little surprise for her!

The first form had an extra member that morning – in the form of Queenie, the stable cat. The girls had taken her from the stables after breakfast, and had been playing with her non-stop, so that now the little creature was ready for a nap.

'Which is just what we want,' said Daffy happily, stroking Queenie as she lay peacefully on her lap. 'We don't want the cat getting out of the bag too soon!'

'We had better hide her quickly,' said Katie. 'Mam'zelle could arrive at any second.'

Daffy gently lifted the cat up, and gave her to a girl called Jenny, who sat at the front of the class.

'You know what you have to do, Jenny,' said Daffy.

Jenny, her eyes alight with amusement, nodded eagerly as she took Queenie, placing the sleeping cat on the floor between her desk and Violet's.

'Move your satchel, Violet,' said Jenny. 'And I'll put mine just here, so that Mam'zelle won't be able to see Queenie from her desk.'

Violet obliged, for she was looking forward to the trick as much as the others. She was very poor at French, and had come in for a great many scoldings from Mam'zelle, so anything that wasted time in the class was fine by her.

She didn't care for Queenie, however, and said with a sniff, 'How very ordinary she looks, compared to my own beautiful Willow. Willow has the most wonderful blue eyes, and she wears a collar set with tiny little jewels, and –'

'And she eats fresh salmon every day, out of a dish made from the finest bone china,' said Daffy, making the others laugh.

Violet scowled, but there was no time to retort, for the sound of Mam'zelle Dupont's high heels could be heard coming along the corridor, and Daffy rushed to hold the door open for her.

Mam'zelle looked flustered, for she hated being late for any class, but Daffy had quickly become one of her favourites, and the sight of the girl's sweet smile soothed her a little.

'*Merci*, Daphne,' she said, patting the girl's dark curls, before walking to the big desk at the front of the class. '*Bonjour, mes enfants*. Sit down, please, and get out the French grammar prep that I set you on Monday.'

The girls got their books from their desks, and Daffy put up her hand, saying, 'Please, Mam'zelle, I have done my very best, but I'm afraid that I didn't understand some of the grammar rules that you explained to us. Would you mind awfully explaining to me again, for I do so want to do well at French?'

Of course, Mam'zelle was delighted to hear this, and only too happy to help her favourite, and she went to Daffy's side at once. The girl's desk was at the back of the classroom and, as soon as the French mistress's back was turned, Jenny moved swiftly.

Mam'zelle Dupont had a very large handbag, which she took everywhere with her, and it sat unattended under her desk now. Quickly, Jenny scooped up Queenie, carried her to the mistress's desk, and deposited her in the handbag. The cat, annoyed at having her nap disturbed, opened her eyes and gave a little mew of protest, but fortunately Ivy happened to sneeze loudly at the same time, so Mam'zelle heard nothing. Once she was in the bag, which was warm and comfortable, Queenie soon settled down again and, with one eye on Mam'zelle, Jenny fastened the top of the bag, leaving a little gap so that the cat could breathe.

Then she darted back to her seat, winking at the others, who were all doing their utmost to stifle their giggles.

At last Mam'zelle finished with Daffy, then she went round the class collecting everyone's prep, before returning to her own desk. The lesson progressed smoothly, until Queenie, refreshed by her long nap, awoke, feeling in need of a little exercise.

Mam'zelle was writing something on the blackboard when she became aware of a strange noise coming from under her desk, and she turned sharply.

'*Tiens!*' cried the French mistress, looking most alarmed. 'What is this strange noise that comes from under my desk?'

'A strange noise, Mam'zelle?' said Jenny, looking puzzled. 'I can't hear anything. Can you, Violet?'

Violet shook her head solemnly, and just then the noise started again, more loudly this time. It really was a most peculiar sound, thought Mam'zelle, a strange hissing and spitting and yowling, as though some wild beast was under her desk, but there was nothing to be seen.

Of course, all of the girls could hear the noise, and all of them were struggling to contain their laughter now. Katie had stuffed a handkerchief into her mouth, while Ivy lifted the lid of her desk to hide her mirth from the French mistress.

Then Mam'zelle gave a little shriek, tottering backwards on the high-heeled shoes she always wore, and Daffy said, 'Why, Mam'zelle, whatever is the matter?'

'My bag, he moved!' wailed poor Mam'zelle, as white as a sheet. 'He wobbled from side to side, then jumped up and down.'

'But that's impossible!' said Daffy, making a tremendous effort to keep her face straight.

'Ah, Daphne, it is not impossible, for it is happening!' cried Mam'zelle. 'Come and see for yourself, then you shall believe me.'

Mam'zelle meant for Daffy to come and see, but the whole class surged forward, crowding around Mam'zelle's desk.

'I can hear something!' said Katie. 'And it seems to be coming from your handbag, Mam'zelle.'

'I hear it too,' said Daffy gravely. 'It sounds like – like a soul in torment!'

'Nonsense!' said Mam'zelle stoutly, though she looked a little alarmed. 'I have no tormented souls in my handbag.'

This was too much for Ivy, who went off into a peal of laughter, so contagious that several of the others joined in. Katie was holding her sides, while tears poured down Faith's cheeks.

'Ah, *méchantes filles*!' cried Mam'zelle. 'I do not see anything at all amusing about this.'

'Mam'zelle, I really think that you should open your handbag, so that you can see exactly what is going on in there,' said Jenny.

Mam'zelle gave a little moan and seemed rooted to the spot. It was quite plain that she was far too afraid to open the bag, and Daffy stepped forward, saying nobly, 'Mam'zelle, with your permission, *I* shall open the bag. Please stand back, everyone.'

Mam'zelle jumped back at once, almost treading on Violet's toes, and the girls, giggling, followed suit.

Cautiously, her expression very grave indeed, Daffy moved towards the handbag and unfastened it, making it look as though her hands were shaking uncontrollably, so that the others started to laugh again. Then she pulled the handbag open, springing to her feet and giving a squeal as Queenie shot out. Mam'zelle was no great lover of cats, and she, too, squealed as Queenie made straight for her, while the first formers roared with laughter.

In the class-room next door, Miss Oakes and the sixth formers wondered what on earth was going on.

The first formers had been noisy all morning, and Miss Oakes had cast a great many irritated glares at the wall that separated the two class-rooms. Now, though, it sounded as though a perfect riot was going on, making it quite impossible for the sixth formers to concentrate. Miss Oakes gave an angry exclamation as she stalked to the door. It seemed that Mam'zelle must have left the room, and those irresponsible first formers had taken advantage of her absence to act the goat. Well, Miss Oakes would soon set them straight!

The mistress got the shock of her life when she pushed open the door of the first-form class-room and a little tabby cat shot out straight past her, then ran away down the corridor as if her life depended on it.

And, far from being away from the class, Mam'zelle Dupont was in the thick of the disturbance. She sat in her chair now, as white as a sheet, while Daffy fanned her with a book and the rest of the first form stood around, chattering excitedly.

'Mam'zelle!' said the mistress sharply. 'What on earth is going on here? My girls can hardly hear themselves think!'

Miss Oakes's stern tone quelled the first formers, who all slunk away to their seats, and Mam'zelle sat up straight in her chair and said excitably, 'Ah, Miss Oakes, it was dreadful. The cat was in my bag, and then she got out of the bag and attacked me!'

Of course, poor Queenie hadn't attacked Mam'zelle at all. The little cat was very affectionate, and had simply rubbed herself against Mam'zelle's legs. Mam'zelle, however, had not appreciated this gesture at all, and, for one moment, the girls had thought she was about to faint.

'A cat in your bag, Mam'zelle?' repeated the astonished Miss Oakes. 'How did a cat come to be in your bag, may I ask?'

Mam'zelle Dupont had been so bewildered by the morning's happenings that she hadn't had leisure to consider this. Now, though, a doubtful look came across her face and she looked suspiciously at the first formers. Each and every one of them, though, looked a picture of innocence, and Mam'zelle dismissed her unworthy suspicions at once.

'It is a mystery,' she said to Miss Oakes. 'It must have climbed in and gone to sleep while my bag was open.'

'Hmm,' said the sixth-form mistress, also looking at the innocent faces of the first formers. Miss Oakes was not so easily fooled as Mam'zelle, and she wasn't taken in for one moment.

'Well, I shall leave you to it, Mam'zelle,' she said. 'And I trust that I shan't have cause to come in and complain again!'

Mam'zelle felt rather put out at being spoken to in such a way. Ah, how hard and unfeeling these English mistresses could be at times, to those of a more sensitive disposition. Miss Oakes had seen how distressed she, Mam'zelle, was, yet had not spoken one word of comfort.

But the girls could see that Mam'zelle was 'in a paddy', as Daffy put it, and were at their sweetest, sympathising warmly with the French mistress as she speculated on how Queenie could have come to be in her bag, and talked at length about her dislike of cats. In fact, Mam'zelle talked so much that she wasted the rest of the lesson, just as the naughty first formers had hoped! But the first formers had gone up in her estimation, for they were dear, good-hearted girls and their concern for her had warmed her heart.

'Dear old Mam'zelle,' chuckled Ivy, as the class followed the French mistress along the corridor. 'She doesn't so much as suspect that we were the ones who put Queenie in her bag.'

'My big sister, Sally, told me that she was a most marvellous person to play tricks on,' said Daffy with satisfaction. 'And it seems that she was right.'

'Was Sally as naughty and daring as you are, Daffy?' asked Jenny curiously.

'Heavens, no!' said Daffy, with a giggle. 'She was as good as gold. I mean to say, she enjoyed a joke and a trick, but she was more of a watcher than a doer.'

'And you are most definitely a doer, Daffy!' giggled Katie. 'I say, did Sally give you any useful information on the other mistresses?'

'A little,' answered Daffy. 'She warned me to beware of Mam'zelle Rougier's temper, and not to get on the wrong side of Miss Potts.'

'She's quite right,' said Faith seriously. 'Don't forget that I have already been in her form for one term, and I know how stern she can be at times.'

'She's not a bad sort,' said Ivy. 'Although I certainly

wouldn't like to be in her bad books.'

'Yes, you had better watch out, Daffy,' said Maggie. 'Potty looked at you most suspiciously the other day, when she was talking about the tricks that had been played on Violet.'

But Daffy only laughed, saying with a careless shrug, 'I'm not afraid of old Potty. She might be sharp, but I've never met a mistress who can get the better of me!'

Puzzles and plots

As it was the largest, Felicity's study soon became a meeting place for the North Tower sixth formers. At a pinch, they could all squeeze in, though it meant girls sitting on the desk and window-sill, or even on the floor!

Felicity was quite happy for her study to be used as a common-room some of the time, provided that the others understood that there were times when she needed to study and must not be disturbed.

But, although the sixth formers knew this, the younger girls didn't, and Felicity often *was* disturbed, by a timid tapping on the door, as one member or other of the lower forms asked her advice on a problem. However busy she was, Felicity never turned anyone away, for it was her duty to help and guide the youngsters, and one she was determined not to shirk.

June also had a devoted following of youngsters, and one person who looked up to her enormously was Daffy Hope.

Daffy had heard all about June from her sister, Sally, long before she had started at Malory Towers. June, according to Sally, was the wickedest, boldest girl that the school had ever had, famed for her ready wit, sharp tongue and – above all – her jokes and tricks. Daffy longed to be just like her and, although June had not put her in the lacrosse team, the girl looked up to her no end.

She was delighted when, the day after the trick on Mam'zelle, June had stopped her in the corridor, and said, in a low voice, 'What's all this I hear about the stable cat getting into Mam'zelle Dupont's handbag?'

For a moment Daffy had wondered if she was in for a scold, then she saw the twinkle in June's eyes and grinned, saying innocently, 'That was quite a mystery, June. I simply can't imagine how the poor creature came to be trapped in there.'

June laughed out loud at this, and said, 'You're a monkey, Daffy Hope! Well, it's good to know that there is someone who will keep the tradition of playing tricks going at Malory Towers once I have left. Keep up the good work!'

Daffy, of course, had seen this as praise of the highest order, and walked off with her head in such a whirl that she almost bumped into Mam'zelle Rougier.

'Oops, sorry, Mam'zelle!' she said. 'I didn't see you there.'

The thin, rather severe-looking French mistress glared at Daffy, and shook her head sternly, but the first former didn't even notice. What did anything matter, when she was basking in the glow of June's praise? And it was much more pleasant to be praised for jokes and tricks than for her skill at games, Daffy thought. After all, there were many good lacrosse players at Malory Towers, but there was no one who could plan a successful trick like she, Daffy, could.

June, meanwhile, went off to join a little gathering in Felicity's study. Susan was there, of course, along with Bonnie, Amy, Delia and Gillian, all of them drinking cups of tea and happily munching on biscuits.

'Room for one more?' asked June, sidling in.

'Yes, but I'm afraid you'll have to sit on the floor,' said Felicity. 'Do help yourself to tea and biscuits.'

June did so, then found herself a comfortable spot on the floor, her back resting against the wall.

The sixth formers chattered amicably about anything and everything – except the forthcoming exams. It had been agreed that, when they all got together like this, the subject was out of bounds, and was only ever mentioned in passing. If anyone ever tried to discuss the exams in any depth, they were immediately shouted down and threatened with being sent from the room!

'Yes, it's bad enough that we have to do all this studying,' Gillian had said. 'When we get the chance to meet up in what little free time we have, we need to put them out of our minds completely.'

'Half-term soon,' said Susan, taking a bite of a ginger biscuit. 'Goodness, haven't the weeks just flown!'

'I'll say,' said Delia. 'I simply can't tell you how much I'm looking forward to seeing my father.'

All of the girls were looking forward to seeing their people again, and Felicity said, 'No matter how far up the school you get, the excitement of half-term never fades.'

Alice put her head round the door just then, and, seeing that the room was so crowded, she said, 'Oh! Sorry, Felicity, I didn't realise that so many of the girls were in here. I'll come back another time.'

'No, come in, Alice,' called Susan in a cheery voice. 'Felicity doesn't mind her study being used as a meeting place at all!'

So Alice squeezed in, poured herself a cup of tea and sat down next to June.

'We were just talking about half-term, Alice,' said June. 'Will your parents be coming?'

'Oh, no!' said Alice, looking quite horrified at the thought.

This puzzled the others and, seeing their expressions, Alice said hastily, 'They will be on holiday, you see. It was all arranged ages ago, so they can't cancel now.'

'What a shame,' said Felicity, feeling sorry for the girl. 'Well, you're very welcome to come out with me and my people, you know. I'm not sure whether they'll be bringing a picnic, or taking me to a restaurant, but it's sure to be good fun.'

'Why, thank you, Felicity,' said Alice, her face lighting up. 'I would like that very much.'

Delia and Gillian got up to leave, and June moved over to sit in the empty chair beside Felicity, murmuring, 'Rather you than me.'

'Oh, June, that's a little unkind!' protested Felicity. 'Alice might be a little odd, but she's not a bad sort.'

As she spoke, a memory of something that Alice

had said to her the other day came back to Felicity. She had meant to question Alice about it, but had been so busy that it had slipped to the back of her mind. She mentioned it now to June, saying in a low voice, 'June, you know on the first day of term I took the new girls to see Miss Grayling?'

June nodded, and Felicity went on, 'Well, Alice said to me the other day that the Head had said to them, *You will all get a lot out of your time at Malory Towers. Make sure that you put a lot back.*'

June shrugged, and said, 'Miss Grayling always says that to the new girls on their first day. I can remember her saying it to us.'

'But that's just it,' said Felicity. 'She *didn't* say it this time! The telephone in her study rang just as she was about to get to that bit. I was outside and heard everything quite clearly.'

'That *is* peculiar,' said June. 'Have you tackled Alice about it?'

'No, I meant to, but with one thing and another it sort of slipped my mind,' said Felicity.

'Do it now,' said June.

'No, not with so many people around,' said Felicity firmly. 'I shall speak to her about it when we are alone.'

Both girls glanced across at Alice, who had taken her glasses off and was rubbing at her eyes.

'It's very strange,' said June. 'But it's only at certain times I get that feeling of familiarity about Alice. And this is one of those times.'

'It's because she's taken her glasses off,' said Felicity. 'I always get it then as well. And when she smiles.'

June made no reply, for she was staring at Alice hard. Felicity gave her a nudge, saying, 'What's up with you? I thought you said that the only reason Alice seems familiar is because she reminds us of someone.'

'I did,' said June, bringing her gaze back to Felicity. 'But now I'm having second thoughts. After what you have just told me, I'm beginning to think that there is a decided mystery about our Alice. And did you notice how she reacted when I asked if her people were coming at half-term?'

'Yes,' said Felicity. 'Almost as if she was ashamed of them.'

'Or terrified of us meeting them,' said June. 'I think that once the exams are over, we might do a little investigating.'

'Yes,' said Felicity, nodding. 'My word, I was hoping for an easy time after the exams, but what with trying to find out what's up with Alice – not to mention stopping her running round after Amy – I'm going to have my hands full!'

Soon after that, the group began to break up, until only Felicity, June and Bonnie were left.

'I suppose I had better leave, too,' said Bonnie, getting up and moving to the door.

'Stop a minute, Bonnie!' Felicity called out, suddenly spotting something. 'Alice has left her glasses on the floor, and you almost stepped on them.'

Bonnie glanced down at the floor, picking up a pair of glasses that lay near her feet.

'How careless of her!' she exclaimed. 'I say, shall I try them on?'

And, without waiting for an answer, Bonnie slipped the glasses on to her nose, much to the amusement of the other two.

'My goodness, you do look different, Bonnie!' laughed June. 'Very sober and studious!'

'Yes,' said Felicity, grinning. 'It's amazing the difference that a pair of glasses can make to a face. But you'd better take them back to Alice, Bonnie. I bet she's as blind as a bat without them.'

'And I'll bet she isn't,' said Bonnie in rather an odd voice, taking the glasses off and looking at them with a puzzled expression.

'Why do you say that?' asked June, frowning.

'Because the lenses are made from plain glass,' said Bonnie.

'Are you quite sure?' asked June, astonished.

'See for yourself,' said Bonnie, handing the glasses to June.

The girl put them on, exclaiming, 'Bonnie is right! But why on earth would Alice wear glasses made from plain glass?'

'It makes no sense at all,' said Felicity, completely bewildered.

'There are quite a few things about Alice that don't make sense,' said June, giving the glasses back to Bonnie.

'She is hiding something, I'm sure of it, and it must be something bad.'

'You can't be certain of that, June,' protested Felicity, who didn't see things in quite such a black and white way as the other girl.

'I can,' replied June. 'Otherwise why would she bother to hide it at all?'

Felicity couldn't think of an answer to this, except that she felt, instinctively, that Alice wasn't a bad person.

'What do you think, Bonnie?' she asked.

'I don't know *what* to think,' said Bonnie. 'But I can tell you one thing.'

'What?' chorused Felicity and June.

'She hasn't been wearing glasses for long,' said Bonnie. 'You see, people who have been wearing glasses for a long time get little dents either side of the bridge of their nose. My aunts have them, and so does my cousin. Alice doesn't. I noticed that the other night, when she took them off to go to bed.'

'Yes, you're right!' exclaimed June. 'My father and grandparents have them too.'

'Well, I'll take them across to Alice now,' said Bonnie. 'Do you want me to say anything to her?'

June and Felicity exchanged glances, then Felicity said, 'No, not yet. I think that Alice has something to hide, just as you do, June, though I don't necessarily think it's something bad. But until we are certain, and have time to get to the bottom of things properly, I would rather not put her on her guard.'

As Bonnie left, June said to Felicity, 'I bet you regret asking her out with you and your people at half-term now.'

'No,' said Felicity, after considering this for a moment. 'If she is having a happy time and feeling relaxed, she may let something slip.'

'Yes, you may be right,' said June. Then she looked at her watch, saying, 'Heavens, I've got lacrosse practice with the lower school in five minutes! I'll just go and round up Freddie. Would you like to come along with us, Felicity, and give your expert opinion?'

'I don't know about my opinion being *expert* exactly!' laughed Felicity. 'And I really should get down to some studying. But it's awfully tempting to play truant for an hour or two, and see how the kids are doing.'

'Marvellous!' said June, grinning as she hauled Felicity to her feet. 'Come along then, let's go and find old Freddie!'

The weather was a little chilly that afternoon, and the three sixth formers wrapped up warmly in coats, hats and scarves as they stood watching the first and second formers play lacrosse.

'Well played, Hilda!' yelled June. 'Maggie, stick closer to Elizabeth – yes, that's it!'

'Young Daffy Hope plays jolly well,' said Felicity, watching the girl as she ran down the field like a streak of lightning. 'Yet I notice that you haven't put her in the team, June.'

'She's marvellous,' agreed June. 'When she wants to

be. But, at any second, she could lose interest in the game and start playing the fool to amuse her friends.'

'Can't afford to have anyone with that attitude on the team,' said Freddie. 'Imagine if she did that in a match!'

But, for once, Daffy *didn't* play the fool. She wanted to show June that she had made a big mistake in leaving her out of the team, so the girl put every ounce of effort into the game and played superbly.

June noticed, and was impressed. As the game ended, she murmured to Felicity and Freddie, 'Well, it looks as though I may have to eat my words. Daffy, come here!'

Daffy walked across to June, and the games captain took her to one side, saying, 'Look here, Daffy, you did jolly well today. Turning over a new leaf?'

'I am as far as lacrosse is concerned,' answered Daffy.

'Well, what a pity that it's too late to put you in the team now,' said June. 'Now that the players have been announced, it really wouldn't be fair of me to drop one of the others to make room for you.'

'No, I quite see that,' said Daphne, putting on a brave face, though she felt a little miserable. She had *so* hoped that June would think that she was too brilliant to leave out.

'Cheer up!' said June, giving the girl a little pat. 'There's always next term, and if you go on at this rate, you're an absolute certainty for the team then. In fact, I shouldn't be surprised if you didn't turn out to be the star player!'

This *did* cheer up Daffy enormously, though the girl

might not have felt quite so happy if she had known what Violet had in store for her.

Violet, accompanied by Faith, had been into town to collect the photographs of the first-form picnic, and the two girls now sat side by side on a sofa in the common-room, poring over them. They were alone, for the others were at lacrosse practice, or horse-riding, or walking in the fresh air. Neither Violet nor Faith, however, cared for fresh air, especially when it was cold, and much preferred being indoors, huddled up by the fire.

'This one that Katie took of the two of us is awfully good,' said Faith. 'Do you think that I might have a copy to send home to my people?'

'Of course,' said Violet. 'I say, Faith, this is a nice one of the whole form. Except for me, of course, for I was taking the photograph.'

It was a very nice photograph, the first formers sitting in a row in the sand, their happy smiles showing what a marvellous time they were having. And Daffy Hope was right in the centre of it. At once, Violet decided that Felicity simply had to see that photograph – though how she was going to achieve that was something she hadn't thought out yet.

The girl threw a sidelong glance at Faith, whose head was still bent over the photograph. She hadn't meant to say anything to her about her plan to get Daffy into hot water, but suddenly it occurred to her that two heads might be better than one. Besides, the temptation to boast was becoming too hard for Violet to resist.

She put her head close to Faith's, and said in a confiding tone, 'Shall I tell you a secret?'

Faith nodded eagerly, and Violet went on, 'I mean to make sure that this photograph falls into Felicity Rivers's hands.'

'Why?' asked Faith, puzzled.

'Don't you remember?' said Violet. 'Felicity told Daffy that she wasn't to take part in our picnic, but Daffy disobeyed her. And if Felicity sees this photograph she will know it, and come down hard on Daffy.'

Violet sat back and waited for Faith to congratulate her on this clever plan. But she was disappointed, for Faith was quite horrified.

'Violet, you simply can't do such a thing!' exclaimed Faith. 'Why, sneaking is just about the lowest thing that you can do, and if any of the others were to find out, they would never forgive you.'

Violet frowned at this, and said rather sullenly, 'Well, I think Daffy deserves it. She has been horrible to me, and shown no respect at all towards you, as head-girl.'

Faith couldn't deny this, and said, 'I agree that Daffy needs a lesson, but I'm not sure that this is the way to go about it. Look here, Violet, let's think about it for a bit. Wait until after half-term, and if you are still determined to go ahead with your plan then, I will back you up.'

Violet wasn't entirely happy with this, but she agreed, saying, 'I suppose I can afford to wait another week. In the meantime, I shall have to think of a way of getting that photograph to Felicity, without her knowing that it is me who is behind it.'

Violet knew Felicity's views on sneaks only too well, for she had overheard the Head Girl scolding a second former only a few days ago. Hilda, the second former, had gone to Felicity to report that another member of her form had played a mean trick on her, and Felicity had said rather scornfully, 'Really, Hilda, if you are going to come running to me, or to Miss Parker, every time someone plays a childish trick on you, I'm afraid that you are going to make yourself very unpopular with the rest of your form. Sneaks are considered the lowest of the low at Malory Towers – and at every other decent school, for that matter.'

Seeing that Hilda had turned rather red, Felicity had said in a kinder tone, 'You know that if anyone is deliberately setting out to make you unhappy you can tell me, and I will step in. But tricks like the one you have told me about are just part and parcel of school life, and you must learn to grow a thicker skin.'

No, Felicity would certainly not look favourably on Violet if she simply went and handed her the photograph. She would have to think of a much more cunning way of doing it.

In the meantime, though, there was half-term to look forward to, and the whole school, from the youngest member of the first form to the oldest member of the sixth, got caught up in the excitement.

The beginning of the week seemed to go very slowly,

then there were only three days left, then two, and suddenly it was the day before half-term.

Mistresses and top formers became used to the sight of the younger girls skipping along the corridors, laughing and chattering noisily, but they were lenient with them, for they knew that the girls were just giddy with excitement at the thought of seeing their people again.

The sixth formers, of course, behaved with more restraint, but inwardly they were just as thrilled as the youngsters. Several of them found it hard to get to sleep on the night before half-term, but none of them was tempted to talk or whisper after lights out, for such things simply weren't done when one was in the top form.

It was otherwise in the first-form dormitory, where the girls made so much noise that it brought Matron in on them.

'My goodness, what a dreadful racket there is in here!' cried Matron, snapping on the light and making the first formers blink. 'Off to sleep at once, all of you, or you'll be fit for nothing tomorrow.'

'But, Matron, we're so excited it's simply impossible to sleep!' protested Katie. 'Can't we talk for just ten more minutes?'

'Not even ten more seconds!' said Matron sternly. 'If I hear another sound from this dormitory, I shall personally telephone each and every one of your parents in the morning and tell them that half-term is cancelled!'

Of course, the first formers knew that Matron had no intention of carrying out her threat, but not one of them, not even Daffy, dared to flout her orders. And after she left, there wasn't a sound from the dormitory, as the girls fell asleep, one by one.

They were woken by the sound of the dressing-bell, and in every dormitory in the school the cry went up, 'Wake up, everybody! It's half-term!'

A super half-term

Felicity was delighted that her parents were among the first to arrive, for it meant that she was able to spend a little time alone with them.

'I hope you don't mind, Mother and Daddy,' she said, 'but I have asked someone to join us for lunch. Her name is Alice, and her parents aren't able to come today.'

'Poor girl,' said Mrs Rivers, her ready sympathy stirred. 'Of course we don't mind. Daddy and I thought that we would take you to a restaurant today, as it's a little cold and windy for a picnic.'

Felicity was quite happy about this, and she felt thrilled when Miss Grayling made a point of coming over to speak to her parents, saying, 'Felicity is doing a simply marvellous job as Head Girl. Not that I ever doubted she would, of course.'

'We are very proud of her indeed,' said Mr Rivers, his face glowing with pride.

'And rightly so,' said Miss Grayling with a smile. 'Of course, she has also been working very hard at studying for her exams – as have most of the sixth formers. I hope that all of the girls will put them out of their minds this weekend, and concentrate on enjoying themselves instead.'

The sixth formers were determined to do just that, and Felicity saw many of her friends as she looked around.

There was Bonnie, with her doting parents, and Amy with hers. Lucy strolled arm in arm with her pretty mother, and June shared a joke with one of her brothers. It really was a very happy scene indeed.

The first formers were also having a grand time, though there had been bad news for Faith. Her parents had telephoned Miss Grayling at the last moment to say that they would not be able to come because one of Faith's young brothers was ill. The others had been very sympathetic, for it was very hard to have to stand and watch on a day like this, while everyone went off with parents, grandparents, brothers and sisters to have a jolly time. Daffy felt very sorry for Faith, and decided that she would ask her parents if Faith might come along with them, but Violet spoke up first, laying a hand on Faith's shoulder, and saying, 'Never mind, old girl! You can come along with my people and we will be very pleased to have you.'

This was said in an extremely loud voice, so that the whole of the form would overhear and think what a kind, generous person Violet was. In fact, the only person who was fooled was Faith herself, who was very grateful indeed and thanked Violet profusely.

The others rolled their eyes, Katie muttering to Ivy, 'Her Highness just wants to make Faith feel grateful to her, for then she will have an even greater hold on her.'

'Yes,' agreed Ivy. 'And it will provide Violet with a

marvellous opportunity to boast to Faith, and show off, and prove what adoring parents she has.'

Violet's parents might have been adoring, but they quite failed to impress the first formers.

The girls giggled when they set eyes on Mr Forsyth, who was short and round, and it was quite clear to see where Violet had inherited her turned-up nose and small eyes from. He also seemed rather short-tempered, his expression habitually irritable, except when he was talking to his darling Violet.

'Gosh, I'm glad *my* father isn't like that,' whispered Daffy to Katie. 'And Violet's mother is simply awful!'

This was rather unfair, because Mrs Forsyth wasn't really awful at all, just a rather weak and silly woman, always pandering to the whims of her overbearing husband and spoilt daughter.

Violet squealed when she saw her parents' big, expensive car pull up in the drive, glancing round quickly to make sure that the others were watching before she ran to greet her people.

'My little princess!' cried Mr Forsyth, his discontented look replaced by a fat smile, as he held his arms out to Violet. She ran into them at once, enveloped in a big hug, before turning to Mrs Forsyth, who bent to kiss her cheek.

'We've brought someone else to see you, as well,' said Mr Forsyth with a laugh. 'Here you are, Princess!'

He reached into the back seat of the car, emerging a few moments later with the most beautiful cat the first

formers had ever seen. She was very sleek and aristocratic-
looking, cream-coloured with chocolate tipped ears and
tail, and with brilliant blue eyes.

'She's been pining for you,' Mr Forsyth was saying.
'So I thought to myself, why shouldn't Willow join in
the fun of half-term and come to see her mistress.'

Violet was absolutely delighted to see her pet, of
course, taking the cat from her father and crying,
'Willow! Oh, how marvellous! Look, everyone!'

The first formers crowded round, for most of them
were very fond of animals and were keen to take a closer
look at Willow. Violet was very gratified indeed at their
exclamations.

'How lovely she is!'

'What marvellous eyes!'

'May I stroke her, Violet?'

'Fancy bringing a cat to visit at half-term. I say, Violet,
you're going to have to be awfully careful that she
doesn't leap out of your arms while you're carrying her
around. She might run off and get lost.'

'Oh, I shan't need to carry her,' said Violet with
rather a smug smile. 'Daddy, did you bring the lead?'

'Of course, Princess,' said Mr Forsyth, reaching back
into the car to bring out a lead, which exactly matched
the cat's blue velvet collar.

'You can't put a cat on a lead!' cried Daffy. 'I never
heard of such a thing!'

'Just watch,' said Violet, thoroughly enjoying being
the centre of attention. Deftly she clipped the lead on to

Willow's collar, then set the cat down on the ground. She walked a few yards, and the girls were both amused and astonished to see that Willow padded along beside her as obediently as any dog.

'Well, I never!' said Ivy. 'How super!'

Daffy, who was not at all pleased at the attention Violet was getting, suddenly grinned and nudged Katie, whispering, 'Watch out for fireworks! Here comes Potty. I'll bet that *she* won't think it's at all *super* to have a cat wandering round and getting under everyone's feet at half-term!'

Indeed, Miss Potts looked a little disapproving when she first spotted Willow, nor did she care for Mr Forsyth, who, on seeing her frown, said rather pompously, 'Ah, you're Violet's form mistress, aren't you? Now, Violet told me your name – I shall remember it in a second. Ah yes, Miss Potty! Look here, Miss Potty, my wife was none too keen on me bringing Violet's pet along, for she thought that there might be some objection. But as you can see for yourself, Willow is very well-bred and well-behaved, and so she should be, for I paid a pretty penny for her, I can tell you!'

Miss Potts's frown deepened, as Violet turned red and the rest of the first form giggled.

'My name is Miss Potts,' said the mistress rather pointedly, adding stiffly, 'And as for the cat, I really don't think . . .'

But her words tailed off, for Willow decided that she rather liked this tall, stern-looking woman, and rubbed herself against Miss Potts's ankles, purring loudly. Miss Potts, who was secretly quite fond of cats, bent to stroke the pretty little creature, and, somewhat to her own surprise, found herself saying, 'Well, as long as she is kept on a lead, I am sure that it will be all right, just this once.'

Then, as though to make up for this moment of weakness, she snapped, 'Katie! Your parents have just arrived, and as they have come a long way, I suggest that you go and greet them, instead of standing there with an idiotic grin on your face.'

The Rivers were nearby when Daffy Hope's people arrived, the two sets of parents greeting one another happily, for they were old friends.

'Well, Felicity!' said Mrs Hope, once she had hugged an excited Daffy. 'It seems like only yesterday that you were starting out as a first former at Malory Towers, and now here you are, Head Girl!'

'And speaking of first formers, how is young Daffy settling in?' asked Mr Hope, a big, good-humoured man. 'I'll bet she's as good as gold, just like her older sister was.'

Felicity looked at Mr and Mrs Hope, their faces shining with pride in their younger daughter. Then Daffy caught her eye, a pleading expression on her face, and Felicity's lips twitched. She certainly didn't want to upset the Hopes, today of all days. Besides, it really wasn't her place to report Daffy's bad behaviour to them. That was up to Miss Potts, or Miss Grayling herself. So Felicity said, 'I think I can safely say that Daffy is going to leave her mark on Malory Towers,' and received a grateful smile from the younger girl.

Mr and Mrs Hope seemed satisfied with her reply too and, as she watched the family walk away, Felicity found herself hoping that Daffy would not let them down.

All of the girls spent a very happy morning with their parents, proudly showing them round the school, introducing them to their friends and talking to mistresses. Then it was time for lunch, and everyone went off with their people to different restaurants.

Violet's parents, of course, had chosen a very expensive restaurant, and Faith, who had never been to such a place before, was quite overawed as she followed the family inside. The girl felt very nervous of Mr Forsyth, and his loud, rather pompous manner, though fortunately he took little notice of Faith, devoting himself to Violet instead.

Mrs Forsyth, however, rather liked the quiet, shy girl, and thought how pleasant it was to be with someone so softly spoken and undemanding for a change. So the two of them enjoyed a nice chat over lunch, and Faith soon lost her nerves and began to think that Violet's mother was really rather sweet.

Willow, of course, was unable to come into the restaurant, and had been left in her basket in the car, and Faith didn't know whether to be shocked or amused when Mr Forsyth ordered an extra portion of chicken and instructed the waitress to wrap it up, so that the cat might share in the treat!

The restaurant that Felicity's parents had chosen was

less expensive, but very nice indeed, and Alice thanked Mr and Mrs Rivers for inviting her along.

'That's quite all right, my dear,' said Mrs Rivers with a smile. 'I am just sorry that your own parents couldn't come.'

She thought that Alice was rather a strange girl, so nervous and eager to please, but she seemed pleasant enough, and Mrs Rivers was glad that Felicity had taken her under her wing.

They enjoyed a most delicious lunch, and it was as they were having pudding that Mr Rivers said, 'Well, exams next week for you two girls. I expect that you will be glad when they are behind you and you can relax a bit.'

'I certainly will,' said Felicity with feeling. 'Alice isn't going in for Higher Cert though, lucky thing!'

'No, I'm not clever enough,' said Alice with her nervous little laugh. 'And even if I was, I'm not very good at settling down to study. I lose concentration too easily.'

Mr Rivers looked surprised at this, and said, 'Well, I don't know anything about how good your brains are, but I should have thought that after all your years at Malory Towers you would have learned how to knuckle down and study.'

'Yes, but Alice hasn't *been* at Malory Towers for years, dear,' said Mrs Rivers. 'Remember, Felicity told us that she only joined the school at the beginning of this term.'

'But I've seen you before, I'm certain of it,' said Mr Rivers, staring hard at Alice from beneath his dark eyebrows. 'Are you quite sure that you only started this term?'

Felicity looked up sharply, glancing first at her father, then at Alice, who had turned bright red, and was blinking rapidly behind her glasses.

Seeing that she was quite tongue-tied, Mrs Rivers came to the rescue, saying, 'Really, Alice ought to know when she started at Malory Towers.'

'I think I must have one of those commonplace faces,' said Alice at last, finding her tongue. 'Several of the girls say that I look familiar to them, isn't that so, Felicity?'

Felicity nodded, but her mind was working rapidly. So her father recognised Alice, too! The whole thing just got more and more peculiar!

Felicity got the opportunity to have a word alone with her parents before they left to go to the hotel they were staying at, and she said, 'I just wanted to thank you both for such a marvellous treat, and for letting Alice share in it, for it has been the most marvellous day! And there's still tomorrow as well, before we have to get back to the grindstone.'

Mrs Rivers was about to say something when her husband suddenly clicked his fingers, and exclaimed, 'Got it!'

'Got what?' asked Felicity and Mrs Rivers, completely puzzled.

'Now it's gone!' said Mr Rivers, looking most annoyed. Then he saw that his wife and daughter were watching him in bewilderment, and gave a laugh.

'Just for a moment, I had a sudden flash of memory,' he said. 'Something to do with Alice, but then it vanished before I could grasp it.'

'Oh, Daddy!' cried Felicity. 'Well, if it comes back to you, do let me know. Quite a few of us girls feel that there is something familiar about her, and we are sure that she is keeping some secret from us.'

'Well, when someone is guarding a secret, it is often because they are ashamed of something,' said Mrs Rivers, sounding very wise. 'But secrets usually come out, sooner or later. And when Alice's is revealed, I hope that you and your friends will be kind, Felicity, and not judge her harshly.'

'Of course not,' said Felicity. 'I just wish that I could get Alice to confide in me, for it would be far better if she told someone the truth rather than it just coming out.'

'Well, perhaps between us we can try to coax her out of her shell a little tomorrow,' said Mrs Rivers.

But the following morning, after breakfast, Alice came up to Felicity, and said, 'I'm awfully sorry, but I don't think that I will be able to come out with you and your people today. I feel rather sick, so I'm going to go and see Matron.'

'What a shame!' said Felicity. 'Well, if you feel better later, do come and join us.'

But, as Alice went off to find Matron, Felicity couldn't help wondering if she was just making an excuse, for the girl didn't look ill, and her appetite had seemed good at breakfast.

'Blow!' thought Felicity. 'I think Daddy scared her a little yesterday, and now it means that Mother and I won't have the chance to talk to her today. Oh well, at least it will be nice to have my parents to myself!'

Violet's parents came over again on Sunday, and, once again, they brought Willow with them, the little cat attracting lots of attention from the girls as Violet paraded her around on her lead.

Even the sixth formers and the parents were amused, Nora saying to her mother, 'My goodness, just look at that! I wonder what our old moggy at home would do if I tried to walk him on a lead.'

'I should think that he would run away and we would never see him again,' laughed Nora's mother.

Two people who weren't amused, however, were Mam'zelle Rougier and Mam'zelle Dupont, and both of them united in their belief that Malory Towers was no place for cats.

'It is bad enough that we have that creature in the stable,' said Mam'zelle Dupont, shaking her head. 'The one that tried to attack me. Now we must have cats at half-term too!'

'What next?' said Mam'zelle Rougier, her thin, stern face set in lines of disapproval. 'Are we to allow pet dogs, and rabbits and mice at Malory Towers?'

Mam'zelle Dupont gave a faint shriek at this, for the thought of mice always filled her with terror, and she and Mam'zelle Rougier linked arms and went indoors, where no cats lurked to disturb their peace.

Faith was very taken with Willow, and rather envious of Violet for being mistress of such a beautiful pet.

'How I wish that she could stay at Malory Towers with us,' the girl sighed as she stroked and petted the cat. 'My word, wouldn't it make the others sit up and take notice!'

'Yes,' said Violet, staring hard at her friend. 'Yes, it jolly well would! Faith, what a marvellous idea. I shall keep Willow here at school with me.'

'But, Violet, you can't!' cried Faith, quite aghast. 'I was only joking, you know. Why, Miss Grayling would never allow it!'

'Ah, but I'm not going to ask Miss Grayling,' said Violet, a smile spreading over her face. 'I shall smuggle Willow into school, and we shall keep her there in secret. None of the mistresses will know that she is there.'

The first formers would be simply thrilled, thought Violet, and wouldn't that be one in the eye for Daffy Hope! Even she did not have enough daring to smuggle a pet into the school.

Once again Faith tried to protest, but it was too late. Violet was running across the lawn to her parents, who were sitting on one of the benches, and putting her idea to them.

Faith, leading Willow, followed more slowly, and reached the bench in time to hear Mrs Forsyth say, 'Violet, you can't! Why, you would be expelled if any of the mistresses discovered Willow. Think of the disgrace! Besides, Willow is a very valuable cat, what if she runs away?'

But Mr Forsyth brushed his wife's protestations aside, saying testily, 'Nonsense! Now, my dear, you know very well that you and I were thinking of going on a little holiday shortly. I am quite sure that Willow would be much happier here with her mistress while we are away, than at home with only the gardener and housekeeper for company. And I'm sure that my princess is quite clever enough to keep her away from the prying eyes of the teachers.'

'Of course I am,' said Violet happily, knowing that her father would overrule her mother, and she would get her way. 'There is a little box-room just above our dormitory, where no one ever goes, and Willow will be quite safe in there.'

'But that won't be good for her!' said Mrs Forsyth. 'She needs to be taken out every day and given exercise.'

'She will be,' said Violet. 'I shall put her inside my coat and take her out every day, when there's no one around. And if I'm not able to do it, there will be no shortage of willing helpers.'

'Oh, dear!' wailed Mrs Forsyth. 'Faith, what do you think of this idea?'

Faith hesitated. She badly wanted to back up Mrs Forsyth, but Violet was her friend, and she would have to endure days of sulks and tantrums if she went against the girl. So Faith swallowed, and said, 'I'm sure that, between us, we first formers can make sure that Willow is looked after, and that no one discovers her. It would be such fun to have her at school.'

'That settles it then,' said Mr Forsyth, clapping his hands together. 'Willow stays at Malory Towers!'

Shocks and surprises

The girls were all pleasantly worn out after their busy half-term, but the first formers were reluctant to go to bed, each and every one of them determined to stay up until the bell went. They were in the common-room when Violet and Faith, having just said goodbye to Mr and Mrs Forsyth, came in, carrying a large wicker hamper between them.

'Oho, what's this?' said Ivy, sitting up straight. 'Goodies?'

'Not exactly,' said Violet as she and Faith set the hamper down on the floor. 'It is something very nice though.'

'Well, don't keep us in suspense,' said Daffy. 'Let's have a look.'

Violet lifted the lid of the hamper and reached in. There were gasps of amazement as she lifted out Willow, and Jenny said, 'Violet, have you gone quite mad? You can't possibly have Willow here at school with you! Miss Potts will soon discover her, then she will be sent home.'

'Oh no, she won't,' said Violet coolly. 'I intend to keep Willow in the little box-room upstairs.'

Then she looked round at the first formers, and said with a smile, 'I hope that some of you will help me to feed her, and take her for walks.'

Of course, almost everyone wanted to help look after Willow, apart from one girl – and that was Daffy.

'It's cruel,' she said. 'Willow is used to roaming around in your big house. You can't possibly keep her cooped up in a box-room.'

'You didn't think it was cruel when you put Queenie into Mam'zelle Dupont's handbag,' said Violet. 'In fact, you thought that it was rather a good joke.'

For once, the ready-witted Daffy was lost for words, and could only glare at Violet.

'Let's take her up to the box-room now,' said Maggie. 'We shall have time to settle her in before bedtime.'

'We had better not all go,' said Faith. 'If Matron or Miss Potts comes along and see us all trooping upstairs they will smell a rat.'

'That's true,' said Violet. 'You and I must go, of course, Faith. Then Maggie and Ivy, you follow in a few minutes, but make sure the coast is clear first.'

The four girls had great fun making Willow feel at home, fussing her and petting her.

'She has had plenty to eat today,' said Violet. 'And she had a walk just before we brought her in, so she should be fine overnight.'

'If we turn the hamper on to its side, and put this old blanket in there, it will do for a bed,' said Faith. 'It's probably not what Willow is used to at home, but it will do.'

'Yes, and someone had better go to the shop tomorrow and buy her some food,' said Ivy, tickling the cat under the chin. 'She can't be fed on scraps all the time, for that won't be good for her.'

The four returned to the common-room just before the bell for bed-time went, and Violet was besieged by a crowd of eager girls, all offering to help look after her pet.

'I can help to feed her, Violet!'

'Oh, do let me take her for a walk! I'll be very careful that no one sees us.'

'I would so love to play with her, for she will need company at times.'

'There will be plenty for everyone to do,' said Violet, casting a sly glance at Daffy, who hadn't said a word.

The girl had been thinking hard, though. Everyone wanted to be Violet's friend now. But it wasn't because they liked her, it was simply because they wanted to share in the fun of looking after the cat. And, knowing Violet, thought Daffy, it wouldn't be very long before the novelty of being popular went to her head, and she began queening it over everyone. When that happened, her brief spell of popularity would soon be over.

Daffy also realised that if she stood out against the others, and refused to take an interest in Willow, it would look like sour grapes on her part.

So she returned Violet's sly look with a sweet smile, saying, 'Count me in, too, Violet. I have always wanted a cat of my own, and helping to look after Willow will be the next best thing.'

Violet looked rather surprised at this, but as the bell went for bed-time then, she said nothing.

As she snuggled down in bed, though, her thoughts were pleasant ones. Everyone wanted to be friends with her now, and soon she would win the whole form over. Why, even that horrid Daffy Hope had asked if she could help care for Willow. Violet smiled to herself in the darkness as she thought of Daffy, for the girl had a shock coming to her. Somehow, Violet was going to make sure that Felicity found out that the girl had been at the picnic, then Daffy would really be in hot water!

'I simply must think of a way for Felicity to see that photograph, without her knowing that it is me who is behind it,' said Violet to Faith, the next morning.

'But, Violet, you can't possibly go ahead with your plan now!' said Faith.

'I don't see why not,' said Violet, frowning. 'You agreed with me that Daffy needs to be taught a lesson.'

'Yes, but don't you see?' said Faith. 'You are not in a position to stir up trouble for *anyone* now. If you sneak on Daffy, and she so much as suspects that you are behind it, she will retaliate by letting it slip that you have smuggled Willow into the school. Then you will be in as much trouble as she is – probably more!'

Violet bit her lip, for this had not occurred to her.

'Blow! Yes, I suppose that you are right, Faith. Well, I shall just have to think of some other way of getting back at Daffy.'

As it happened, though, Felicity *did* find out about Daffy's disobedience, and it was Faith – quite unwittingly – who was responsible.

Violet and Faith had been putting the photographs of the picnic into an album one Saturday afternoon, and, as they finished, Violet said, 'Faith, would you be a dear and put the album on my cabinet in the dorm? I must go up to the box-room and feed Willow, for she will be starving.'

As Violet ran up the back stairs leading to the little box-room, Faith made her way to the dormitory, but as she turned a corner, she walked smack into a third former, and the album flew from her grasp.

'Hey, watch where you're going!' said the third former, glaring at Faith before going on her way.

'Well!' thought Faith. 'Of all the nerve! It was as much her fault as mine.'

The girl quickly picked up the album, but – in her haste – didn't notice that one of the photographs had fallen out. And Felicity, walking down the same corridor a few minutes later, found it.

She picked it up, smiling at the happy faces that grinned up at her. Why, it was a photograph of the first-form picnic! Then, quite suddenly, Felicity's smile vanished, replaced by a grim expression. For there, in the centre of the photo, looking as if she was having a marvellous time, was Daffy Hope!

So, Daffy had disobeyed her, and gone to the picnic after all! Well, she would be punished for it, that much was certain.

Susan was in her study as Felicity walked by, a stern look on her face, and she called out to her friend.

'Whatever has happened?' she asked. 'You've got a face like thunder!'

Felicity dropped the photograph on Susan's desk, saying, 'Just take a look at that!'

Susan studied the photograph, then looked up at Felicity, a puzzled frown on her face.

'It's the kids at their picnic,' she said. 'But I don't see what there is in that to put you in a temper.'

'Look again,' said Felicity. 'And you will see that there is someone there who shouldn't be.'

Susan did look again, and gave a gasp. 'Daffy! The sly, deceitful little beast! I must say, she is as different from her sister Sally as can be!'

'Yes, Sally is absolutely straight and honest,' said Felicity. 'And Daffy isn't. It's one thing to be naughty and mischievous, but outright deceit and disobedience is something I will not tolerate.'

'I should jolly well think not!' said Susan indignantly. 'What a shame that you should have to deal with it now, though, right in the middle of exams.'

'Well, I'm not going to deal with it now,' said Felicity. 'I shall send for Daffy, and tell her that I know what she has done, but I won't punish her until after the exams are over. Then I shall have leisure to come up with a really fitting punishment!'

'And Daffy will have a week or so in which to ponder her fate, and think about what is going to happen to her,' said Susan, with a grim smile. 'That is quite a punishment in itself.'

'Well, it's no more than she deserves!' said Felicity crossly, going across to the door.

'Hi, Eileen!' she called out, to a passing second former. 'Run along to the first-form class-room, would you, and tell Daffy Hope to come to my study at once.'

'Yes, Felicity,' said the second former obediently, and ran off.

Daffy was surprised, but not alarmed, when Felicity's message was delivered, for it did not occur to her for a second that she could be in trouble. It didn't do to keep the Head Girl waiting, so Daffy obeyed the summons at once.

She was rather surprised by Felicity's stern expression, then she remembered that the sixth formers were taking Higher Cert at the moment, and all of them were feeling the strain.

'Hallo, Felicity,' she said brightly. 'Eileen said that you wanted me.'

'I do,' said Felicity, getting straight to the point. 'Daffy, it has come to my notice that you attended the first-form picnic, after I expressly forbade you to do so. What do you have to say?'

For a moment, Daffy was unable to say anything at all, for she was quite lost for words!

The girl could only stare at Felicity in horror as she wondered how on earth the Head Girl had found her out.

At last, she said, 'Yes, I did go to the picnic, Felicity. I'm sorry that I disobeyed you.'

'Are you?' said Felicity. 'Or are you sorry that you have been caught out?'

'Both,' said Daffy truthfully. She had enjoyed every moment of the picnic, but now that she was about to get some perfectly horrid punishment, she wondered if it had been worth it!

Daffy felt very uncomfortable as Felicity stared hard at her, and wished that the Head Girl would just get it over with and reveal what her punishment was to be.

She was quite astonished, therefore, when Felicity said, 'Very well, you may go now.'

'But – but aren't you going to punish me?' stammered Daffy.

'Oh, yes,' said Felicity coolly. 'But not today. Please come and see me at the same time next Saturday, when I shall have decided what to do with you.'

Daffy's heart sank. She might have known that she wouldn't get off that lightly! The girl walked towards the door, then a thought occurred to her, and she turned, saying, 'Felicity! How did you find out that I had disobeyed you?'

'That is none of your business, Daffy,' said Felicity. 'But I hope it will be a lesson to you that lies and deceit are usually found out eventually.'

Daffy was thoughtful as she made her way back to the common-room. Who had known that she had been ordered not to go on the picnic? Katie, of course, but Katie was her best friend and would never sneak on her. Who else could it be? Of course! Faith had known, for she had spoken to Daffy about it just before the picnic, and been most disapproving. The girl had sworn that she wouldn't sneak, but she must have, for how else could Felicity have found out?

Everyone but Violet was in the common-room when Daffy entered, a scowl on her face as she slammed the door behind her.

'What's up?' asked Katie, looking alarmed. 'Don't say that Felicity gave you a scold.'

'It's worse than that,' said Daffy, flinging herself down into an armchair. 'I'm to be punished, because someone has split on me.'

At once the first formers crowded round Daffy.

'Split on you? Why, what have you done?'

'Did Felicity find out about that trick you were going to play on Mr Young?'

'Don't say that someone told her you sneaked into the second form's dormitory the other night!'

'No,' said Daffy. 'She found out that I disobeyed her by going to the picnic, after she had forbidden me to.'

A gasp went up for, of course, most of the first formers didn't know that Daffy had been banned from joining the picnic.

'Well, I have to admire your nerve,' said Ivy, after the whole story had been told. 'No wonder Felicity was furious!'

'But who could have split on you?' said Katie, who had been puzzling over this. 'I was the only person who was in on the secret, and you surely can't think it was me!'

'I know that it wasn't you, Katie,' said Daffy. 'But

someone else did know, and that person must have told Felicity.'

The first formers followed the direction of Daffy's hard stare, and they realised that she was looking at Faith.

'Faith, is this true?' said Jenny, looking shocked. 'Did you sneak to Felicity?'

'Of course she did,' said Daffy scornfully. 'Faith didn't approve of me disobeying our Head Girl at all, did you, Faith?'

'No, I didn't,' answered Faith, stung by Daffy's unjust accusation. 'As a matter of fact, I don't approve of a lot of things that you do, Daffy. But that doesn't mean that I would sneak on you.'

Into this tense atmosphere walked Violet, and she realised at once that something was wrong.

'Did you know that your friend was a cowardly little sneak, Violet?' asked Katie.

'What on earth are you talking about?' asked Violet, quite astonished.

'Faith knew that Felicity had said I wasn't to go on the first-form picnic,' said Daffy. 'And Felicity has found out that I disobeyed her, so Faith must have split on me.'

Violet listened to this with mixed feelings. She was delighted that Daffy was in trouble with Felicity. But she felt sorry for Faith, and as she knew that her friend had strong feelings about sneaks, she felt quite certain that she wasn't the culprit.

Of course, she, Violet, had also known about Felicity's punishment, but she couldn't very well say so, or the others might suspect her of being the sneak!

But, to her credit, she spoke up for Faith, saying scornfully, 'What nonsense! As if Faith would think of doing such a thing!'

'Well, you would stick up for her,' said Jenny. 'The two of you have been as thick as thieves lately.'

'I vote we send her to Coventry!' shouted Katie.

Some of the others murmured agreement, and poor Faith looked ready to faint.

'I shall do nothing of the sort,' said Violet, going across to Faith and taking her arm.

'Then you will be sent to Coventry, too,' said Daffy, in a hard voice.

'That isn't for you to decide, Daffy Hope!' said Violet. 'The others will decide whether they want to send Faith and me to Coventry. But anyone who does won't be allowed to help look after Willow, or play with her.'

This, however, was a mistake. The first formers didn't care for Violet's ultimatum, much as they loved Willow. And Daffy was still unofficial leader of the first form, and a very strong character. So when Katie cried, 'Very well, let's have a show of hands! All those in favour of sending Faith – *and Violet* – to Coventry, please put your hands up now,' every hand went up.

'Well,' said Daffy with satisfaction. 'That's that. Come on, girls, who's for a game of something before tea?'

Daffy is punished

At last exams were over, and the relief among the sixth formers was almost tangible.

'I feel like doing something completely mad!' said June at breakfast one morning. 'Like diving fully clothed from the topmost diving board, or running down the corridor yelling at the top of my voice.'

'Go on, then!' said Freddie promptly. 'I dare you!'

A few years ago, June would have taken Freddie up on this instantly. Now, though, she gave a regretful sigh, and said, 'If only I could! But Miss Grayling would probably expel me for setting a bad example to the kids.'

'Talking of kids,' said Susan to Felicity in a low voice, 'have you decided how you are going to punish Daffy Hope yet?'

'No,' said Felicity. 'I've scarcely had time to think about it. But she is coming to see me this afternoon, so I had better put my thinking cap on.'

'There seems to be some sort of rift within the first form,' said Susan. 'Just look at them now.'

Felicity glanced over at the first-form table, and noticed that Faith and Violet seemed to be seated a little apart from the others. And, although Violet kept up a determinedly bright flow of conversation, Faith looked the picture of misery. What on earth was going on there? Felicity wondered.

She found out later on that day, when she spotted Faith walking down the corridor near the sixth-form studies, a defeated slump to her shoulders and a rather woebegone expression on her face.

Feeling sorry for the girl, Felicity went up to her and said, 'Is everything all right, Faith, old girl?'

The kindness in Felicity's tone and the concerned expression on her face were too much for Faith and, quite suddenly, tears started to her eyes. Seeing them, Felicity quickly laid a hand on the girl's shoulder, guiding her into her study.

There, she shut the door and sat Faith down, saying, 'Well, now, whatever is all this about?'

Faith began sobbing in earnest, and it was a while before she could speak, but at last she dried her tears, and said, 'Oh, Felicity, Daffy and the others have sent Violet and me to Coventry, and it is so unjust of them!'

At the mention of Daffy's name, Felicity's lips tightened, and she said, 'Why have they sent you to Coventry, Faith?'

Faith hesitated for a moment, then she looked at Felicity's warm, open expression, and blurted out, 'Well, actually, Felicity, it's because of you.'

'Me?' said Felicity, astonished. 'You will have to explain more clearly, Faith, for I don't have the slightest idea what you are talking about.'

'Well, someone sneaked to you about Daffy going on the first-form picnic,' said Faith. 'And Daffy has decided that it was me. Of course, Violet stuck up for me, because she is my friend, so the first formers aren't speaking to either of us.'

A sudden thought struck Faith, and she went on, 'Oh, Felicity, if you were to tell Daffy that it wasn't me who sneaked, she and the others would believe you and they would start talking to Violet and me again.'

Felicity was silent as she contemplated all sorts of dire punishments for Daffy. Really, the girl's behaviour went from bad to worse! Not content with being naughty and disobedient, she had made a false accusation against Faith, causing great unhappiness for the girl.

The expression on Felicity's face was so stern that, for a moment, Faith feared that she had said something wrong.

Then the girl smiled, and said, 'Don't worry, Faith. I will be seeing Daffy later, and I will have a great deal to say to her. One thing you may be sure of, though, is that your spell in Coventry will end today.'

Felicity sounded so determined that Faith felt quite reassured, and went off to find Violet in a much happier frame of mind.

Daffy, meanwhile, had decided that her best hope of getting off lightly was to act contritely in front of Felicity, and perhaps even squeeze out a few tears. Only the hardest-hearted people could bring themselves to be unkind to Daffy when she cried, and no one could accuse Felicity of being hard-hearted.

The girl rubbed hard at her eyes as she walked to Felicity's study that afternoon, so that they would look red, and the Head Girl would think that Daffy had been sobbing her heart out as she waited in terror to hear what her punishment would be.

Alas for Daffy, Felicity was not taken in at all!

She steadfastly ignored Daffy's red eyes, and her occasional doleful sniffs, and proceeded to give the girl a scolding which almost reduced her to genuine tears!

'I am very disappointed in you, Daffy,' said Felicity. 'Because you have such a lot of good in you, and could become a worthwhile person, if only you wanted to be. But it seems to me that all you want to do at Malory Towers is play around and make trouble for others with your spiteful ways.'

Daffy reeled at this, for although it was certainly true that she enjoyed playing around, she didn't consider herself a spiteful person at all. Felicity was quite wrong! Just look at how popular she was with the others, and spiteful people were never popular.

'That's not fair, Felicity!' she cried, hurt. 'I'm not spiteful, truly I'm not!'

'No?' said Felicity. 'You have been very spiteful to poor Faith, and to Violet.'

Daffy turned red. How on earth did Felicity know about that?

'Faith has been sent to Coventry because she is a sneak,' said Daffy rather stiffly. 'And Violet stuck up for her, so we are not speaking to her either.'

'Faith is NOT a sneak!' said Felicity firmly. 'And if you are going to set out to judge people, Daffy, it would be a very good idea if you checked the facts first.'

Felicity sounded so very sure that, for the first time a doubt began to creep into Daffy's mind, her heart sinking as she wondered if she had made a very big mistake!

'I didn't find out about your deceit from Faith,' went on Felicity. 'This is what tripped you up, Daffy.'

And Felicity pulled open the drawer of her desk, getting out the incriminating photograph, which she placed in front of Daffy.

The first former gasped, and said, 'Where did you get this from?'

'I found it in the corridor, not far from your common-room,' said Felicity. 'Someone must have dropped it. So, now you see, Daffy, no one sneaked on you. Not Faith, and not any of the others.'

Daffy was horrified. She had accused Faith wrongly, and had encouraged the others to send her – and Violet – to Coventry.

'It was very wrong of me,' she said, sounding most subdued. And, for once, Daffy was not merely pretending to be contrite, she really meant it. And Felicity could tell from the girl's manner that she was sincere. She didn't need to tell Daffy that she owed the two girls an apology either, for the first former went on, 'I shall tell them both that I am sorry, of course, and I shall do it in front of the others.'

'I am very glad to hear it,' said Felicity. 'You know,

Daffy, you seem to have spent rather a lot of time this term apologising to people. If only you would learn from your mistakes, you might not have to say sorry quite so often!'

Daffy nodded solemnly, and Felicity said, 'Now we come to your punishments. Since you avoided the last one, I'm sure you will agree that it is only fair that you receive two.'

Daffy groaned inwardly, but did not protest, for she knew that Felicity was being quite fair and just.

'You are to go to bed one hour early next Saturday night,' said Felicity. 'I know that the first and second formers have been given permission by Miss Grayling to hold a dance in the hall, but I am afraid that you will miss it. And this time, Daffy, I shall be checking personally to make sure that you have obeyed me.'

This was a bitter blow, for the whole form had been looking forward to the dance, but Daffy swallowed hard and said meekly, 'Yes, Felicity.'

'In addition,' Felicity went on, 'as you are so fond of sending people to Coventry, you will send yourself to Coventry for one day. This punishment will also take place on Saturday, and you are not to talk to anyone from the second you get up on Saturday morning until Sunday morning. Nor must any of the others talk to you, and I shall be asking Faith to report to me if anyone breaks the rules. Is that quite clear?'

'Quite clear,' said Daffy faintly. This punishment was even worse than the first, for Daffy loved to chatter, and it would be very difficult for her to keep quiet for a whole day! But she had well and truly earned her punishment, and this time she was determined to face it.

It was with a heavy heart that the girl went back to the first-form common-room. Most of the others were there, and Daffy didn't shirk what she had to do, but went over to Violet and Faith, saying in a clear voice, 'I owe you both an apology.'

The others immediately stopped their chatter, and came round to listen.

'I have just been to see Felicity,' said Daffy, 'and I know now that it wasn't Faith who sneaked on me. I should have made sure before I accused you, and I'm very sorry. Please will you forgive me?'

Faith was a good-natured girl, and she took the hand that Daffy held out to her at once, saying, 'Of course. I'm just glad that it is all over now.'

'Well, we should never have sent you to Coventry, or you either, Violet, and I am sorry about that, too,' said Daffy.

Violet was less gracious, refusing to take Daffy's hand, and merely inclining her head rather coldly.

Some of the others, who had been quick to follow Daffy's lead and only too ready to believe her accusations, murmured apologies too. The outspoken Ivy said roundly, 'You idiot, Daffy! You made us all believe that Faith was a sneak, and we have been quite beastly to her because of it, and to Violet.'

Daffy turned red, and said, 'Well, you may be sure

that I will think twice before I accuse anyone of anything ever again.'

'I'm very glad to hear it,' said Violet with a disdainful sniff.

'You will be pleased to hear that I am being punished,' said Daffy, looking directly at Violet. 'None of you are to speak to me at all next Saturday, and I am not allowed to go to the dance.'

Some of Daffy's friends cried out at this, feeling that it was a very harsh punishment, but Ivy said, 'Well, it jolly well serves you right! And this time, Daffy, I hope that you won't try to get out of your punishment.'

'I won't,' said Daffy ruefully. 'That is another lesson I have learned.'

'If Faith wasn't the sneak, how did Felicity find out that you had been at the picnic?' asked Katie curiously.

'She found one of the photographs,' said Daffy. 'Someone must have dropped it.'

'Heavens, that must have been me!' gasped Faith. 'Violet and I were putting them in an album the other week, and I dropped it when I was taking it up to the dorm. One must have fallen out. So it was my fault that you got into trouble with Felicity after all!'

'Yes, but you didn't get me into trouble deliberately,' said Daffy, patting the girl on the shoulder. 'And that makes a huge difference!'

Felicity, meanwhile, was in her study, telling Susan all that had happened.

'I think that you handled it very well,' said Susan.

'I really do. The thing is, with people like Daffy, you have to come down hard on them or they just take advantage of you.'

'Don't I know it!' said Felicity. 'I say, Susan, what about a walk in the grounds before tea? I could do with some fresh air.'

Susan agreed at once, and as the two girls walked to the door, her sharp eyes suddenly spotted something lying on the floor.

'Here, what's this?' she said, stooping to pick it up. 'Why, it's a silver locket. Rather a nice one, too.'

Felicity took the locket from Susan and inspected it, saying, 'The chain has snapped. I wonder if it belongs to Daffy? She could have dropped it when she was in here earlier.'

'No, for there are some initials engraved on the back,' Susan pointed out. 'And they aren't Daffy's. It says JJ. I don't think I know anyone with those initials, do you?'

Felicity thought hard for a moment, and said, 'There's a girl in the fourth form called Julia Jenks, but she certainly hasn't been in my study, so I don't know how she could have dropped it here.'

'How odd!' said Susan. Then a thought occurred to her, and she said, 'I say, Felicity, you don't suppose that this could have been stolen from Julia, do you? Perhaps the thief dropped it.'

'It's a possibility, I suppose,' said Felicity. 'Though rather a horrible one. And, for all her faults, I don't think that Daffy is a thief.'

'Well, who else has been in your study today?' asked Susan.

'June and Freddie popped in this morning,' said Felicity. 'So did Delia. Oh, and Alice came in to give me back a book that she had borrowed.'

'Well, we can certainly rule out June, Freddie and Delia,' said Susan. 'Though it's true that we don't know much about Alice.'

The two girls looked at one another rather uneasily for a moment, then Felicity said firmly, 'I've just been telling young Daffy off for jumping to conclusions and accusing people wrongly, so I don't intend to fall into the same trap myself. I think that the best thing to do would be to hand it in to Matron, then she can put a notice up.'

As luck would have it, the two girls bumped into Julia Jenks on their way to Matron's room, and Felicity said, 'Julia, have you lost a locket just lately? We have found one with your initials on it.'

Felicity took the locket from her pocket, and Julia said, 'No, it's not mine, Felicity. I only wish it was, for I don't own anything half as pretty as that.'

'Well, what a mystery!' said Susan, as she and Felicity went on their way. 'There is no other girl in the school with the initials JJ, so who on earth can it belong to?'

Getting to know Alice

Felicity soon put the mystery of the locket to the back of her mind, as she had plenty of other things to think about.

Now that exams were over, Amy and Bonnie were spending a lot more time together. But Felicity knew that Alice was still a frequent visitor in Amy's study, and that Amy hadn't invited her there simply for the pleasure of her company.

She sent for Amy one day, and wasted no time in getting to the point.

'You are taking advantage of Alice,' she said bluntly. 'I know that she does all the little jobs that you want to get out of, and it simply isn't fair.'

Amy turned red, and said rather haughtily, 'If Alice chooses to do my jobs for me, I don't see what business it is of yours, Felicity.'

'It's my business because I am Head Girl,' Felicity told her. 'And it seems to me that it is all very one-sided, for Alice isn't getting anything in return.'

'She has my company,' said Amy with a shrug. 'And that is what she really wants, you know – company and friendship. Besides, I don't see any of you others rushing to make friends with her.'

'That's not fair, Amy,' said Felicity. 'You know very well that we have all been busy studying. And now that the exams are over, all that is going to change. I want every sixth former to make an effort with Alice, and try to bring her out of her shell. That includes you, Amy. But I *don't* want to see you using her as a slave, however willing she is, and I would be grateful if you would respect my wishes.'

Rather sullenly, Amy agreed, and when she had left, Felicity went to Alice's study and tapped on the door.

'Come in!' called out Alice, in her high, rather nervous voice. 'Oh, hallo, Felicity. Do sit down.'

Felicity sat, noticing as she did so that Alice had a small photograph album on the desk in front of her. The girl hastily shut it, and Felicity said, 'Are those photographs of your people? May I have a look?'

But Alice quickly slid the album into a drawer, saying hastily, 'It's empty. I bought it the other day, because Mother said that she was going to send me some photographs from home. I'm still waiting for them to arrive, though.'

Felicity knew that this was untrue, for she had seen quite clearly that there were photographs in the album, just before Alice shut it. But if the girl wished to keep them private, Felicity could hardly insist on seeing them.

So she changed the subject, saying, 'You never talk much about your home, or your people, Alice.'

'Well, there's not much to say,' said Alice, blinking

rapidly behind her glasses. 'My parents are quite ordinary, and so is my home.'

Yet Amy was convinced that Alice came from a wealthy family, because of her expensive clothes. Well, perhaps she didn't want to boast about it, thought Felicity, and that was very much to her credit.

'Do you have any brothers or sisters?' she asked.

'Oh no,' said Alice. 'It's just my parents and me. You have a sister, though, don't you? I've heard the others talk about her, and she sounds marvellous.'

So it went on. Each time Felicity tried to draw Alice out, the girl responded with the briefest of answers, before asking a question of her own. So when Felicity left Alice's study a little while later, she knew no more about the girl than she had before. She was standing in the corridor puzzling over this, when a small voice behind her said, 'What are you doing standing there, Felicity?'

Felicity turned, to see that Bonnie had come up behind her, and she was struck by a sudden brainwave.

'Bonnie!' she said, taking the girl's arm. 'Do come into my study for a moment. I want to ask you a favour.'

'What is it, Felicity?' asked Bonnie, sitting down in an armchair.

Felicity looked at little Bonnie for a moment. The girl was very small and dainty, with a childish, lisping voice. In many ways she appeared more like a first former than a sixth former. But Bonnie was very shrewd indeed, and extremely good at sizing people up. She also had a knack of getting people to open up and confide in her, and Felicity had decided that she might come in very useful now.

'Bonnie, I would like you to have a chat with Alice,' she said. 'See if you can get her to talk about herself a bit.'

'Find out what her secret is, you mean,' said Bonnie, with a smile. 'All right, I'll do my best. It won't be easy, for as soon as anyone tries to get her to talk about herself, she clams up, or changes the subject.'

'Some of us feel that she is familiar, as if we have met her before,' said Felicity.

'Yes, I heard some of the others talking about it,' said Bonnie. 'Though I am quite certain that I don't know her. Nor does Amy, and Freddie is sure that she has never met her before. Lucy, Gillian and Delia don't recognise her either.'

Felicity frowned over this, then said slowly, 'You, Freddie and Amy joined Malory Towers in the third form, didn't you? And Lucy came when we were in the fourth.'

'That's right,' said Bonnie. 'And Gillian and Delia didn't join us until the fifth form. What are you getting at, Felicity?'

'Well, as none of you seem to recognise Alice, perhaps she was someone we knew when we were in the first or second form.'

'I suppose that makes sense,' said Bonnie. 'Well, Felicity, leave it to me and I'll see if I can get anything out of her.'

While the sixth formers puzzled over Alice, Daffy was

not having an easy time of it in the first form. Some of the others had been very annoyed with her for falsely accusing Faith of sneaking, and, when her day of being sent to Coventry arrived, found it all too easy to ignore her.

Violet's popularity, on the other hand, had gone up, for the girls were missing Willow and all of them begged to be allowed to help care for her again. Violet had been a little stiff with them at first, but, at last, knowing that it would annoy Daffy, she had graciously forgiven them.

Daffy deeply resented seeing Ivy, or Jenny, or one of the others sneaking off to the box-room with Violet, and it was even harder to bear because she only had herself to blame.

Only Katie remained steadfast and loyal, but Daffy knew that she would have to work hard to win back favour with the others.

Inspiration came to her when she received a letter from her grandmother one breakfast-time, and she opened it to find that it contained a substantial postal order.

She slipped it into her pocket without saying anything to the others, but an idea had taken root in her mind, and she thought about it all day.

That evening, in the common-room, she stood up and clapped her hands together loudly, to get everyone's attention.

'Listen!' she cried. 'It seems to me that it has been a little dull around here lately, and I think that it's time we livened things up.'

'What are you going to do?' called out Violet. 'Start a

big row by flinging wild accusations around?'

Daffy swallowed the retort that sprang to her lips, put on a contrite expression, and said, 'Actually, I was hoping to make amends to you all for that.' She pulled the envelope from her pocket and waved it in the air, saying, 'My grandmother sent me a postal order today, with instructions to spend it on anything I please. And what would please me more than anything would be to throw a midnight feast for you all!'

Of course, this caused a perfect hubbub, the eyes of the first formers lighting up. Even Violet couldn't help looking pleased at the prospect of a feast.

'My word, that's awfully generous of you, Daffy!'

'I should say. A feast – what fun!'

'Of course, we others will contribute something as well.'

'When shall we have it?'

'What about next Wednesday evening?' suggested Katie. 'Potty is away that evening, for I overheard her telling Matron so.'

'Next Wednesday evening it is, then,' said Daffy, beaming round. 'We can have it in the dormitory, and use that big cupboard on the landing to store our goodies in.'

There were 'oohs' and aaahs' at this, and Ivy said, 'Jenny, shall you and I pop into town before tea tomorrow, and buy some biscuits or something?'

'I shall buy another of those big chocolate cakes, like the one I got for our picnic,' said Violet. 'I say, wouldn't it be super if Willow could come, too?'

Many of the girls thought that this was a splendid idea, but Daffy said, 'Of course Willow can't come! You would have to trail all the way up to the box-room to fetch her, and then go and put her back again once the feast was over. And the more we wander about, the more chance there is of us being caught.'

The others reluctantly agreed with this, and Daffy muttered under her breath to Katie, 'I don't want that pampered little beast at my party.'

'Which pampered little beast are you talking about?' asked Katie, her eyes alight with mischief. 'Violet or Willow?'

Daffy laughed at this, her spirits lifting as she looked round at the happy, excited faces of the others. The thought of a feast had brightened everyone up, and put her back in their good books. And Daffy intended to see that she stayed there!

Bonnie, true to her word, asked Alice to go into town with her the next afternoon.

'Amy is busy, and I do so hate going on my own,' said Bonnie. 'I really would like your company, Alice, and you can help me carry my shopping.'

Of course, the idea of helping Bonnie appealed to Alice enormously, and she agreed at once.

Now that exams were over, Bonnie was happy to have leisure to pursue her favourite hobby of needlework and, as they reached the little town, she said to Alice, 'I can set to work making that cushion cover I promised you now. Let's go into the haberdashery shop, and you can choose the fabric and embroidery silks.'

'Oh, Bonnie, that would be marvellous!' cried Alice, thrilled. 'Of course, I shall pay for all the materials. But are you sure you wouldn't prefer to make something for yourself?'

'No, for there is nothing I need at the moment,' said Bonnie. 'I am just happy to have something to work on. Besides, I promised you a cushion cover, and that is what you shall have.'

The two girls spent a pleasant half hour in the haberdashers, and Bonnie was surprised to find that, for someone so diffident and timid, Alice had very definite ideas on what she wanted. Although, in Bonnie's opinion, her taste wasn't very good.

The girl chose a deep, purple fabric, and a variety of brightly coloured silks for the embroidery. When Bonnie ventured to suggest that perhaps fewer colours might look more effective, Alice brushed this aside, saying, 'I like colourful things. And my father sends me as much money as I wish, so I can afford to buy a few extra skeins of silk.'

Unseen by Alice, Bonnie raised her eyebrows at this, for it was the first time that the girl had referred to her family's wealth. Though she had said it quite matter-of-factly, and not in a boastful way, as Amy, or that conceited little first former Violet, might.

'Well, that was fun!' said Bonnie, as the two of them left the little shop, Alice carrying her purchases in a large brown paper bag.

'Yes, it was,' said Alice, smiling. 'I say, Bonnie, there's

a little tea-shop across the road. Let's go in and have a cup of tea and some cake – my treat, as a thank you for being kind enough to make me one of your lovely cushion covers.'

Bonnie accepted gratefully, and soon the two girls were comfortably seated at a little table by the window, chatting happily together as they tucked into delicious jammy buns, washed down with big cups of tea.

A harassed-looking woman with twin daughters, aged about eight, came in and sat at a table near theirs, the two little girls talking at the tops of their voices as they vied for their mother's attention.

'Heavens, what a din!' said Bonnie, grimacing. 'I must say, I'm awfully glad that I'm an only child, for I should hate to have to share my parents' affection, wouldn't you, Alice?'

Alice, who found Bonnie's company very pleasant and relaxing, considered this for a moment, her head on one side. 'I used to feel like that,' she said at last. 'But now I think that it might have made me a better person if I had had a brother or sister.'

Bonnie was careful not to show any surprise at this remark, for she knew that Alice would clam up. Instead, she laughed, and said jokingly, 'I'd rather be a spoilt brat than a good person.'

'But you are a good person, Bonnie,' said Alice earnestly. 'I know that your parents adore you, for I saw you with them at half-term. But I'll bet they don't give you everything you ask for.'

'No, for they can't afford to,' said Bonnie honestly. 'They aren't fabulously wealthy, as Amy's parents are. They give me their love unstintingly, though. Sometimes too much.'

'*Can* you give someone too much love?' asked Alice, surprised.

'Sometimes you can give them too much of the wrong kind of love,' said Bonnie. 'You see, Alice, when I was small I was quite ill, and had to be taken great care of. And, even when I got better, Mother would insist on wrapping me up in cotton wool.'

'Oh!' said Alice, who had had no idea of this. 'Well, I suppose it is understandable, for she must have been very worried about you.'

'Of course,' said Bonnie. 'And I quite see that now. But when I was younger, I often found it quite annoying and wanted to rebel against it and stand on my own two feet. And yet, I always find it comforting to know that my parents are there, ready to help me if I am in trouble, or comfort me if I am sad, just as they were when I was a small child.'

Alice was very struck by this, and said, 'Yes, that is how I feel about my mother and father.' Then she went quiet, and Bonnie, sensing that she was building up to something, said nothing, but nibbled at her cake and appeared quite unconcerned. At last her patience was rewarded, and Alice blurted out, 'I wish that I didn't feel ashamed of them, but Father does embarrass me so, at times!'

'Really?' said Bonnie, sounding as nonchalant as possible. 'How?'

But Alice seemed to realise that she had said too much, and retreated right back into her shell. All Bonnie could get from her after that was polite chit-chat. But the girl was not dismayed, for Alice had given away a lot more than she knew.

Pam, Nora, June, Freddie and Susan were in Felicity's study that evening when Bonnie went to report to her. Quickly, she told them what had happened and, in disgust, Nora said, 'Well, what a waste of time, Bonnie! As far as I can see, all that you did was went shopping and had tea and cakes! Very nice for you, but it doesn't really get us any further!'

'My dear Nora,' said Bonnie, shaking her head. 'It is precisely because of that attitude that Felicity chose *me* to talk to Alice, and not *you*!'

Nora looked rather put out, while June, who had a great deal of respect for Bonnie, laughed, and said, 'Come along, Bonnie! Tell us what you *really* learned about Alice.'

'Very well,' said Bonnie. 'I learned that she has been spoilt, and used to having her own way, but that she has tried hard to change. I learned that she loves her parents, but is ashamed of them. And, perhaps more importantly than anything else, I learned that she is ashamed of herself – or, at any rate, of something that she did in the past, which she would now like to make amends for.'

Freddie gaped at Bonnie, open-mouthed, and

said, 'How on earth can you know all that?'

'Bonnie listens to people,' said Felicity, getting up and giving the girl a pat on the shoulder. 'And there is no one quite as good as her at reading between the lines. Well done, Bonnie.'

'Yes, I take my hat off to you,' said Pam. 'I don't think that any of us others would have been quite as successful as you at getting Alice to open up.'

'I agree,' said Susan. 'But, despite Bonnie's efforts, we are really no further forward, for we still don't know why Alice is so familiar to us. Well, to most of us, anyway.'

'Yes, we are,' said June, a very thoughtful look on her face. 'It's as if we have a jigsaw, and must put the pieces together. Bonnie has given us a few of the pieces, but there are still some missing. All we have to do is find them.'

Several of the first formers had been into town that day, too, to buy food for their midnight feast.

The big cupboard outside the first-form dormitory gradually filled up with goodies over the next few days, and as Daffy and Katie opened it one morning, to put in a tin of biscuits that Ivy had just given them, their eyes lit up.

'Scrumptious!' sighed Katie happily. 'Tinned sardines and pineapple, chocolate, gingerbread cake – ooh, and an enormous pork pie! How marvellous!'

'It's going to be the best feast ever,' said Daffy, placing the tin of biscuits on a shelf.

And it would clinch her place as leader of the first form,

thought the girl, though she did not say this to Katie.

As the day of the feast dawned, the first formers grew increasingly excitable and giggly, almost driving Miss Potts and Mam'zelle Dupont to distraction.

'Really, I don't know what is the matter with this class today,' said Miss Potts in Maths on Wednesday morning. 'I have already had to tell Maggie off for daydreaming, and Ivy for chattering. And it is quite obvious to me that none of you have your minds on your work. Well, if you don't knuckle down and give me your full attention, I'm afraid that you will have to make up for it by doing an hour's extra prep tonight.'

Of course, none of the first formers wanted that, so they decided that they had better settle down and behave.

Mam'zelle, who took the first form for the last lesson of the day, grew very vexed at their restlessness and threatened all kinds of dire punishments. Even the quiet Faith chattered animatedly to Violet, bringing the French mistress's wrath upon her head.

'Ah, even you, Faith, who are normally so good and so obedient – even you plague me today. I shall send you to bed one – no, two – hours early tonight. I shall send the whole *class* to bed two hours early!'

As the whole form was simply dying for bedtime to come, this amused them greatly, and Faith thought that Mam'zelle was going to explode with anger when they all started giggling.

Fortunately, Daffy saved the situation, by keeping a

straight face and saying piously, 'Come, now, girls, you are all taking advantage of Mam'zelle's good nature, and it won't do!'

Then she smiled sweetly at the French mistress, and said, 'The thing is, Mam'zelle, we are going on a lovely, long nature walk tomorrow afternoon, and we are all looking forward to it so much that I am afraid everyone has become a little over-excited.'

Mam'zelle accepted this explanation readily, for she knew how these English girls adored their country walks, even when the weather was bad. Though it seemed very odd indeed to her! But Daffy's contrition, coupled with her pretty smile, soothed her a little, and she said more calmly, 'Well, you will all please forget about your walk for the moment, and concentrate on your French. Anyone who displeases me will miss the walk, and come to me tomorrow afternoon for extra coaching instead!'

Violet, who did not care to be outside in the cold weather, didn't know which was worse – a nature walk, or extra French coaching! But as the others had no intention of missing out on their walk and settled down, the girl decided that she had better do the same.

Shortly before tea that day, Miss Potts came up to Felicity, and said, 'I am sorry to ask you this at such short notice, Felicity, but I wonder if you would mind looking in on the first formers before you go to bed tonight? I am going to the theatre with a friend, you see, and shall be staying the night with her. Miss Parker had agreed to look in on them for me, but she has been taken ill with flu and is in bed.'

'Yes, of course I will do it, Miss Potts,' said Felicity at once. 'You can rely on me.'

Jenny of the first form, who happened to be walking by, overheard this, and dashed off to tell the others the news.

'Jolly good!' said Ivy. 'I daresay Felicity will want to get off to bed, so she will probably just pop her head in at the door on her way up and not trouble us again.'

'Yes, and she's a jolly good sport anyway,' said Maggie. 'I bet that even if she did catch us having a feast she wouldn't split.'

Daffy, who knew only too well just how stern Felicity could be on occasion, wasn't so certain of this. But, as the Head Girl would be safely tucked up in bed by the time the feast began, she wasn't terribly worried about it.

There was a great deal of laughing and chattering after lights out that evening in the first-form dormitory. Daffy, of course, was in the thick of it, and Faith, who had just about given up trying to control the unruly first formers, lay silently in her bed and said nothing. But, as time went on, she nerved herself to raise her voice, saying, 'I say! Hadn't we better settle down before Felicity does her rounds?'

Many of the others ignored this, and carried on talking, but when Daffy backed Faith up and said, 'Faith is quite right. Besides, we had better get some sleep or we shall never be able to wake at midnight,' there was immediate silence.

Faith did not mind this at all, but Violet felt resentful on her behalf, and, in the darkness, her lips tightened. She made no comment, though, for the girl had something else up her sleeve, and, when the feast began, Daffy would soon see who was the most popular girl in the first form.

At last, one by one, the first formers dropped off to sleep, and when Felicity gently pushed open the door, shortly before eleven o'clock, there wasn't a sound to be heard. Felicity smiled to herself as she pulled the door softly to behind her. The first formers were such little monkeys this term that she had half-expected to be called upon to break up a pillow fight, or some such thing. Thank heavens that they were all fast asleep, for she was longing for her own bed.

An hour after Felicity had looked in, the little alarm clock that Daffy had placed under her pillow went off, startling her into wakefulness. For a moment she couldn't think why the clock had gone off when it was still pitch dark, then she remembered, and sat up excitedly in bed, hugging her knees and smiling to herself. It was time for the midnight feast – *her* midnight feast!

Midnight feast

Quickly, Daffy padded round the dormitory, waking all the sleeping girls. Silently, they climbed out of bed, putting on dressing-gowns and slippers.

'Katie and I will fetch the things from the cupboard,' whispered Daffy. 'Ivy, there are some plates under my bed that I managed to borrow from the kitchen. Jenny and Maggie, you fetch tooth mugs, so that we have something to drink out of. Faith, you and Violet . . . I say, where *is* Violet?'

'She can't have gone far,' said Faith. 'For she was here a minute ago. Perhaps she has gone to the bathroom.'

But Violet hadn't gone to the bathroom. The girl was quite determined that Willow would be at the feast, and she was tiptoeing upstairs to the box-room to fetch her pet.

The little cat was very pleased to see her mistress, for she was feeling rather bored and restless, and she mewed as Violet stooped to pick her up. It sounded very loud in the still of the night, and Violet whispered, 'Shush now, Willow, or you will get me into the most awful trouble. Come along, let's go and join the feast.'

Then Violet tucked the cat into the front of her

dressing-gown and made her way back to the dormitory.

The others were busy setting all the food out on plates in the middle of the floor when she returned, and everyone looked up in alarm as the door opened.

'Oh, it's you, Violet!' said Katie. 'My goodness, what a start you gave me. Where have you been?'

'Never mind that,' said Daffy crossly. 'For heaven's sake, shut the door behind you, quickly, Violet. And someone had better put a couple of pillows along the bottom, where the gap is, then we can put the light on.'

Ivy quickly pulled the pillows from her own bed, arranging them along the bottom of the door, before switching on the light. Then she gave a gasp, as she saw Willow's head poking out from Violet's dressing-gown.

'Willow!' she cried. 'Oh, Violet, you brought her after all. How marvellous!'

'For goodness sake, keep your voice down!' hissed Daffy, before turning to Violet and saying angrily, 'I told you that you weren't to bring Willow to the feast.'

'Why should I do what you say?' said Violet, tossing her golden curls. 'You aren't head of the form, though you sometimes behave as if you are.'

'No, but it's my feast,' said Daffy. 'And I have the right to say who comes and who doesn't. I've a good mind not to let you share in it, Violet!'

Violet was about to make a sharp retort when Jenny said, 'We can hardly throw Violet out of her own dormitory while we enjoy the feast. Besides, she has provided us with that lovely tin of sweets, as well as that delicious-looking chocolate cake, so it wouldn't be fair not to let her share.'

'Very well,' said Daffy with bad grace. 'But that cat had better not cause any trouble.'

'She will be as good as gold,' said Violet, removing Willow, who was beginning to wriggle, from her dressing-gown and placing her on the bed.

Then the first formers sat on the floor, in a big circle, and settled down to enjoy their feast.

'Scrumptious!' sighed Maggie, taking a bite of pork pie. 'Simply scrumptious.'

'You know, I normally hate sardines,' said Ivy. 'But for some reason I can eat no end of them at a midnight feast.'

'Well, save some for the rest of us!' laughed Ivy. 'I say, Faith, pass the ginger beer, would you?'

The girls ate hungrily, until all that was left was the chocolate cake, sweets and biscuits.

'Shall I cut the cake?' asked Violet.

'Yes, do,' said Jenny. 'I feel awfully full, but I daresay I shall find room for a slice.'

But it was as Violet finished cutting the cake that Willow, who had behaved very well throughout the feast, sitting on the bed, being fed the occasional tit-bit and watching the proceedings with interest, decided to take a little exercise.

The cat suddenly leapt from the bed, landing right in the middle of the cake and showering Daffy, who had just leaned forward to take a slice, with crumbs, chocolate and cream.

There was a horrified silence, and everyone waited for Violet to throw a tantrum and scold the cat. But, to everyone's astonishment, she threw back her head and laughed until the tears poured down her cheeks. One by one, the others started to laugh too, for Daffy really did look comical with cream all over her face and crumbs everywhere.

Daffy, however, was not at all amused. That beastly cat had ruined her feast, and made her a laughing stock! Had it been one of the other girls who had been covered in cake, Daffy would have joined in the laughter with everyone else, but although the girl liked to play jokes, she didn't care to be on the receiving end of them, and felt extremely humiliated.

'It's all very well for you to laugh,' she hissed. 'But just look at the state of my dressing-gown! I shall get into a dreadful row with Matron, and it's all your fault, Violet, for bringing that cat in here.'

'I'm sure that we can get the worst of it out, without Matron knowing anything about it,' said Katie soothingly, seeing that Daffy's feathers were seriously ruffled. 'Come on, let's go along to the bathroom and see what we can do.'

The two girls went out quietly, the muffled laughter of the others ringing in Daffy's ears and making her feel simply furious.

'That horrid cat!' she said to Katie, once the two of

them were in the bathroom. 'I wouldn't be a bit surprised if Violet had trained her to do that, just as I was leaning over.'

'I don't think that one *can* train cats,' said Katie doubtfully, thinking of her own cat at home. 'They seem to do pretty well as they please.'

'Well, it's all her fault, anyway,' said Daffy. 'I ordered her not to bring it to the feast and she went against my wishes. I'll pay her back for this, somehow, Katie, you see if I don't!'

'What are you going to do?' asked Katie, her eyes wide.

'I don't quite know,' answered Daffy. 'But I'll think of something, you may be sure.'

Then the two girls set to work sponging Daffy's dirty dressing-gown. Fortunately, it was as Katie had said, and they managed to get most of the sticky mess that the cake had made off it. Then Daffy washed her face and rinsed her hair, thinking that she should be sitting with the others, enjoying the biscuits and sweets, instead of wasting time like this – and at her own feast, too!

The others had cleared away the ruined cake when Daffy and Katie returned to the dormitory, and Violet, glancing at Daffy's wet hair, couldn't resist saying, 'My word, Daffy, you do look a drip.'

The others laughed at this, and it was just too much for Daffy, who gave the girl a shove. It wasn't a particularly hard or violent shove, but the unexpectedness of it caught Violet off balance, and she fell against one of the bedside cabinets. Unfortunately, two large, heavy bottles of ginger beer were perched precariously there, and they fell to the floor with a resounding crash.

The first formers stood rooted to the spot, gazing at one another in horror and, at last, Maggie whispered, 'Do you think anyone heard that?'

'I should jolly well think they did!' said Faith, beginning to collect the plates up. As head of the form, she would be held responsible if they were caught out. 'Come on, everybody, don't just stand there! There's a very good chance that one of the mistresses will be upon us in a minute.'

That thought made the first formers spring into action, and they scurried round, pushing bottles, empty tins and all other evidence of the feast under beds and into cabinets.

Violet, meanwhile, scooped up Willow, and said, 'I must get her back to the box-room quickly.'

'There isn't time,' said Faith. 'If one of the mistresses comes along and finds your bed empty, you will really be in hot water! You'll just have to take Willow into bed with you, and do your best to keep her quiet.'

'This is all your fault, Violet,' said Daffy with a scowl. 'If you hadn't brought Willow to the feast –'

But Faith, for once, wasn't taking any nonsense from Daffy, and she interrupted to say sternly, 'This is no time to argue over who is to blame. Get into bed at once, Daffy – all of you, in fact – and settle down.'

For a moment it looked as if Daffy was going to argue

with Faith, too, but then the girls heard the unmistakable sound of footsteps approaching, so she quickly scrambled into bed and snuggled down under the covers, closing her eyes tight. The others did the same, Violet putting Willow right down under the bedclothes, and praying that the cat wouldn't give herself away by mewing.

Everyone held their breath as the footsteps got closer, the landing light clicked on and, at last, the door opened. The first formers wondered which mistress had heard them. Stern Mam'zelle Rougier, perhaps? Or the hot-tempered Mam'zelle Dupont? Worse still, what if the noise had roused Miss Grayling herself?

But, as the light from the landing showed, it was none of these feared mistresses who stood in the doorway. It was Felicity!

In fact, the crash the bottles had made hadn't been quite as loud as the girls had feared, and hadn't woken anyone. Felicity, however, had been unable to get to sleep, for, although she was tired, something was playing on her mind. At last she remembered that she hadn't gone back to her study before going to bed, and had left the light on in there. Inwardly groaning with annoyance, the girl had got out of bed and gone to her study, which was directly below the first formers' dormitory. That was when she had heard the crash, and, as Miss Potts was away, had gone to investigate.

All of the girls were in their beds, apparently sound asleep, as she opened the door, and Felicity began to wonder if the noise had come from somewhere else. But, just as she was about to leave, a nervous, smothered giggle came from Maggie's bed. Instantly suspicious, Felicity snapped the light on, and a few of the girls sat up slowly, blinking.

'Felicity!' said Daffy, with a very convincing yawn. 'Is something wrong?'

'I heard a noise from this dormitory,' said Felicity, staring hard at the girl. 'A very loud noise.'

'Well, we didn't hear anything,' said Katie, rubbing her eyes. 'Perhaps you were mistaken, Felicity.'

Felicity's instincts told her that she hadn't been mistaken at all, and that the first formers had been up to something. Then, glancing down, she saw a pile of biscuit crumbs in the middle of the floor, and she knew. The little monkeys had been having a midnight feast! Felicity's lips twitched, as she instantly made up her mind not to report the girls to Miss Potts. It would have been quite another matter if they had broken a very serious rule, such as leaving their own tower, but a feast was just a bit of fun, and something that most schoolgirls enjoyed at some time. Felicity had certainly enjoyed them when she was lower down the school.

'Perhaps I was mistaken,' said Felicity, her eyes twinkling. 'Faith, you are head of the dormitory, aren't you? Well, perhaps you will see to it that it is thoroughly tidied before Matron does her rounds tomorrow. I am sure that you don't want to get an order mark, for that really would – er – take the biscuit!'

Those girls who were sitting up stared at their Head

Girl in astonishment, while the ones who were pretending to be asleep could hardly believe their ears. Then Felicity went, shutting the door softly behind her. As soon as the sound of her footsteps died away, a flurry of whispering broke out.

'Well, isn't Felicity decent?'

'Golly, what a sport!'

'I always knew that old Felicity was a good sort!'

'I say, Violet, thank heavens Willow didn't mew and give herself away!'

'Yes, she's fallen asleep, thank goodness,' said Violet. 'Perhaps I had better take her back to the box-room now.'

But Faith, taking a stand, said firmly, 'No, we'll have no more wandering around tonight, for we have been jolly lucky so far. Violet, she will have to stay here tonight, and you must take her back in the morning, before we go down to breakfast.'

'All right, Faith,' said Violet, pleased at the thought that she would have her beloved pet with her all night.

Some of the girls began to whisper again, and Faith said, 'We'll have no more talking, either. You never know, Felicity might take it into her head to come back, and I don't think she would be so lenient with us a second time.'

And, much to her surprise and pleasure, the first formers fell silent immediately, and in a very short time, all of them were fast asleep, worn out by their late night.

Everyone found it very difficult to get out of bed the next morning, and again Faith took charge.

'Violet, do get up!' she begged, shaking the girl. 'You must get Willow back to the box-room at once! And you others, we need to sweep these crumbs up and clear all the rubbish from under the beds. There is no time to waste!'

Groaning, the girls reluctantly got out of their warm, cosy beds.

'I feel sick!' groaned Maggie, clutching her stomach. 'I can't possibly eat any breakfast.'

'You must eat a little,' said Katie. 'Or the mistresses will guess that something is up. Though, I must say, I don't feel terribly hungry myself.'

'I don't suppose any of us do,' said Faith. 'Ivy, run along and see if you can find a dustpan and brush, would you? And Jenny, do you mind taking the plates back to the kitchen? The rest of us will clear this rubbish away.'

But one person still remained in bed, the covers over her head, and that was Daffy. Faith frowned, for she didn't see why the girl should get out of the cleaning up. She walked across to Daffy's bed, and said, 'Come on, Daffy, there's work to be done.'

'Just five more minutes,' mumbled Daffy sleepily.

'No, Daffy!' said Faith sharply. 'We need everyone to pitch in if we are to have the dormitory tidy before we go to breakfast.'

Slowly, Daffy sat up and looked round the room, at the first formers all busily tidying up, and she said, 'I don't see dear Her Highness pitching in! It's too bad, especially as she was responsible for spoiling the feast.'

'You know very well that Violet is hiding Willow away,' said Faith. 'And as for her spoiling the feast – well, Daffy, you were the one who pushed her, and that is what caused the bottles to crash to the ground.'

'She had already spoiled it before that,' said Daffy, getting out of bed. 'By allowing that cat of hers to jump on the cake.'

'Oh, I don't know,' said Ivy, returning with the dustpan and brush in time to hear this remark. 'Personally, I thought it was jolly funny.'

'It was,' agreed Maggie with a grin. 'What a pity Violet didn't have her camera ready. She could have taken a marvellous photograph of you, Daffy, all covered in chocolate cake!'

Daffy was most displeased, especially when Ivy handed her the dustpan and brush, saying, 'Make yourself useful, Daffy!'

The girl toyed with the idea of flatly refusing, but she sensed that many of her form were still feeling cool towards her, partly because she hadn't made Willow welcome at the feast, and partly because she had pushed Violet and brought things to an abrupt end. It really was most unfair, thought Daffy. She had suggested the feast so that she could get back into the good books of the first formers, but the opposite had happened – and all thanks to that silly Violet!

All in all, it wasn't a good morning for the first formers. Maggie felt so sick after breakfast that she was sent to Matron, and given a large dose of extremely nasty-tasting medicine. And the whole class was so tired and inattentive that both Mam'zelle Rougier and Miss Potts gave them extra prep as a punishment.

Most of them agreed that it had been worth it though, for they really had enjoyed the feast. And Violet had enjoyed it most of all, for not only had she annoyed Daffy by bringing Willow to the feast, but she had had the pleasure of seeing her enemy humiliated. She really would have to buy Willow a special treat for that!

Daffy, however, was extremely subdued and downcast – until tea-time, when she was struck by a simply marvellous idea for getting back at Violet.

'Katie,' she whispered to her friend. 'Come to one of the little music-rooms after prep tonight. There is something I simply have to tell you.'

So, after prep, the two girls sneaked away to one of the little music-rooms, and Katie, looking at Daffy's mischievously sparkling eyes, said eagerly, 'What is it? You're up to something, I can tell.'

Daffy grinned, and said, 'I have worked out how I am going to teach Her Highness a lesson.'

'How?' asked Katie at once.

'By taking away something that she values,' said Daffy. 'Listen carefully, Katie. This is what we are going to do.'

A shock for Violet

An outbreak of flu ran through the school over the next week, and it seemed that half of the girls and several of the mistresses went down with it.

June was in despair, for several of her best lacrosse players were taken ill, and she groaned to Freddie, 'We shan't have a hope of winning our matches at this rate! Even some of the reserves have gone down with this beastly flu, so I am going to have to make up completely new teams.'

Poor Matron was run off her feet for, as she complained to Miss Potts, 'No sooner do I get one sick girl back on her feet and out of the San, than someone else goes down with it.'

'Well, let's just hope that you don't catch this wretched flu, Matron,' Miss Potts had replied. 'I don't know what we should do without you to care for all these sick girls.'

Violet and Maggie were both confined to the San for several days, and although Maggie was pleased to be under Matron's expert care, Violet fretted terribly about Willow.

'Don't worry,' Faith assured her when she came to visit one day. 'The rest of us are taking great care of her.'

But there was a dreadful shock in store for Violet on the day that she returned to class. Of course, she wanted to satisfy herself that Willow hadn't pined away without her, and before the first lesson started, she and Faith made their way up to the box-room.

'Willow!' Violet called softly, as she pushed open the door. 'Willow, I'm back.'

She waited for the cat to pad across the floor to her, purring loudly, but Willow did not appear.

'How odd!' said Faith. 'She usually comes running as soon as someone opens the door.'

Violet looked rather worried, then she heard a purring sound coming from the cat's basket, and she walked across and peered in. Then she gave a little shriek, which startled Faith and made her rush to Violet's side, saying, 'Violet, do be quiet! No one must know that we are here.'

'Yes, but look, Faith!' said Violet, lowering her voice a little. 'Willow is gone, and this – this *creature* – is in her place.'

Faith looked down at the basket – and gasped. For there, instead of the sleek, well-fed Willow, was Queenie, the stable cat!

As though sensing Violet's disapproval, Queenie suddenly leapt out of the basket and fled through the open door. She knew where she wasn't wanted!

'I thought you said that Willow was fine,' said the distressed Violet, rounding on Faith. 'You told me that you and the others were caring for her.'

'We were,' said Faith, feeling quite shaken. 'Why, I fed her myself just before breakfast. And Ivy took her out on the lead immediately afterwards.'

'Ivy must have left the door open then,' said Violet. 'And Willow has got out. Why, she could be anywhere!'

'Of course Ivy didn't leave the door open,' said Faith. 'For it was firmly closed when we got here.'

'Someone has stolen her then,' said Violet, a look of horror crossing her face. 'It's the only explanation.'

'But who would steal her?' asked Faith in astonishment.

'You'd be surprised,' said Violet solemnly. 'She is very valuable, and anyone who knows anything about cats would be able to tell that at once. Someone could have been passing and looked in through the fence when we were exercising her, and made up their mind to take her.'

'Yes, but how on earth would they have got in to the school?' asked Faith, not quite convinced.

'It wouldn't be too difficult,' said Violet. 'Why, there are often strangers here, if you think about it. Only yesterday a man came to mend the piano. And there are always butchers and bakers and so on delivering food to the kitchen.'

'I suppose that's true,' said Faith. 'Or perhaps one of the maids could have discovered her. I don't think that they earn an awful lot of money, you know.'

'I never even thought of that,' said Violet, looking quite horrified. 'Faith, we must get Miss Grayling to telephone the police at once!'

'We can't,' said Faith. 'If you tell Miss Grayling that you have been keeping your pet cat here all these weeks she'll be simply furious. Why, she might even expel you. No, Violet, we must solve this ourselves.'

'Yes, I suppose that we must,' said Violet, close to tears. 'Poor, dear Willow, I do hope that she hasn't come to any harm.'

In fact, Willow was very comfortable indeed. Daffy and Katie – for it was they who had taken her – had found her a home in an old shed behind North Tower that was no longer used. The two girls had lined a cardboard box with a blanket, and had made sure that the cat had plenty of food and water.

'We'll have to exercise her, too,' said Daffy as they watched the cat settle in. 'But we must be jolly careful that no one spots us.'

Katie said nothing, for although she had gone along with Daffy's plan, she didn't feel at all happy about it, and said so.

'I don't like it, Daffy. It's stealing!'

'Of course it's not, silly,' laughed Daffy, brushing this aside. 'We are going to give Willow back to Violet, in a few days, so how can it possibly be stealing? I'm just teaching her a lesson, that's all.'

'Well, I wish you had thought of another way,' said Katie miserably. 'I think it's rather a cruel thing to do, to both Violet and Willow. And I don't see why you had to put Queenie in Willow's place!'

'Oh, that was just for a joke,' said Daffy. 'Dear Violet

is such a little snob I just wanted to picture her expression when she found a common moggy like Queenie in her precious Willow's place.'

But Katie was not in the mood to be amused, saying worriedly, 'I expect that Violet will have discovered Willow is missing by now.'

Katie was not at all reassured when she saw Violet's pale, stricken face in the Maths lesson a short while later. As for Miss Potts, she was so alarmed by the girl's appearance that she wanted to send her straight back to Matron.

'It's quite all right, Miss Potts,' said Violet, struggling to speak normally. 'I would rather be in class.'

Miss Potts, who had dismissed Violet as spoilt and lazy, was encouraged that she was showing some strength of character, and said kindly, 'Very well, but you are not to overdo things. Just sit quietly and read your book, Violet, while I go through some sums on the blackboard with the others.'

'Are you quite sure that you are all right, Violet?' asked Jenny, in the common-room that evening. 'You've been awfully quiet all day.'

Violet exchanged a glance with Faith, who said, 'I think that you should tell the others what has happened. After all, the more people who are looking out for Willow, the more chance you have of finding her.'

So, her voice almost breaking, Violet told the others what had happened to Willow. Of course, there was a perfect outcry.

'Who on earth would do such a mean thing?'

'Don't worry, Violet, old girl. I feel quite certain that no harm will come to Willow.'

'Yes, do try not to worry, Violet, though it must be awfully difficult not to.'

Daffy did not add her voice to the others. She had hoped to let Ivy and one or two others in on the joke, and suddenly realised that they would not think it was funny. For the first time, the enormity of what she had done was beginning to dawn on her, and she was regretting her actions. What was more, she felt a pang of conscience as she looked at Violet's pale, unhappy face, and very uncomfortable it was too!

'Well, the whole of the first form is behind you, Violet,' said Ivy. 'If there is anything we can do to help find Willow, we will do it.'

There were murmurs of agreement from everyone, even Daffy and Katie, who thought that they had better say something, or it would look very suspicious! But both girls felt sick with guilt.

Meanwhile, there had been drama in the sixth form, too. It had happened in Miss Oakes's English class when Alice, who, Felicity noticed, had been looking rather peaky, stood up to go to the mistress's desk. The girl swayed on her feet, gave a moan, and then crumpled to the floor.

'Good heavens!' cried Miss Oakes. 'June, go and fetch Matron at once, please.'

June sped from the room, returning a few moments

later with Matron. Alice had revived a little by this time, and was sitting up, while Miss Oakes bent over the girl, holding her hand.

'Well, now, what have we here?' said Matron in her brisk but kindly way as she bustled in. 'My goodness, Alice, you do look pale.'

She stooped and placed a cool hand on Alice's hot forehead, saying, 'Just as I thought, you've caught a dose of this nasty flu that's going around. A few days' rest in the San, and you will be as right as rain. Miss Oakes, do you think you could help me get Alice to her feet?'

'Of course,' said the mistress, taking one of the girl's arms. Matron took the other and, between them, they helped Alice to stand up, though the girl looked as if she might have collapsed again, if it hadn't been for the support of Matron's strong arm around her waist.

Matron helped Alice from the room, and Felicity said, 'Poor old Alice! She looked awfully white.'

'Well, she is in good hands with Matron,' said Miss Oakes. 'I only hope that none of you others have caught the flu.'

Lucy and Gillian had already gone down with it, but were now back in class, feeling 'as good as new', as Lucy put it. The others, however, had escaped the illness and, over the next few days, didn't let the fear of catching it put them off visiting Alice.

Matron would not allow any visitors on the day that she had been taken ill, but the following afternoon she announced that Alice was feeling a little better and might have two visitors. So, shortly before tea, Susan and Pam went along to the San, and were pleased to see Alice sitting up in bed, with a little more colour in her cheeks. She had been given a little room of her own, just off the main San, Matron explaining, 'I have two second formers and one first former recovering rapidly in the main San, and as Alice needs peace and quiet, I thought that she would be better off in here on her own.'

'Poor old thing!' said Pam, handing the girl a bottle of barley sugar.

'The others all send their love,' said Susan. 'I shall be able to tell them that you are looking a little better.'

'I feel a little better, too,' said Alice with a weak smile. 'Matron has taken such good care of me. It's awfully dull, though, sitting here in bed, with nothing to do.'

'Well, Felicity is coming to see you tomorrow,' said Pam. 'I shall ask her to bring you a book.'

The three girls chatted amiably, until Matron came to shoo Susan and Pam out, saying, 'Alice is going to have some tea now, and then I hope that she will get a good night's sleep.'

Matron escorted them out, and, once they were back in the main San, Susan suddenly remembered something.

'Matron!' she said. 'Did anyone ever claim that locket that Felicity and I handed in to you? The one with the initials JJ on it?'

'Yes, someone did, as a matter of fact,' answered Matron.

'Who was it?' asked Susan curiously. 'Apart from Julia

Jenks, Felicity and I simply couldn't think of anyone with those initials.'

But, before Matron could answer, one of the second formers yelled out and demanded her attention.

'I'm coming, Jane!' called Matron. 'And I'm not deaf! There really is no need to shout *quite* so loudly!' Then she turned back to the sixth formers, shaking her head. 'Honestly, girls, these youngsters are running me ragged. Tell Felicity that she may come and see Alice tomorrow.'

'Blow!' said Susan, as she and Pam stepped out into the corridor. 'I never did find out who the mysterious locket belonged to.'

'Mysterious locket?' said Pam, raising her eyebrows. 'Do tell.'

Susan told the girl all about the locket that she and Felicity had found, and Pam laughed, saying, 'Didn't it occur to you that the locket might have been handed down to one of the girls by her mother or grandmother? The initials on it could have belonged to them, and not to whoever owns it now.'

'Of course!' said Susan, her brow clearing. 'I never thought of that. What a shame, I thought that we had stumbled on a good mystery.'

In the first-form dormitory that evening, Katie took Daffy aside as the girls got ready for bed.

'Daffy, even you must realise that we can't keep Willow away from Violet any longer. We must put her back in the box-room.'

'I know,' said Daffy, looking slightly shamefaced. 'I

only meant it as a joke, to pay Violet back for spoiling the feast, but I realise now that I shouldn't have done it. Don't worry, though, Katie, we will simply sneak Willow back into the room when no one is around. And nobody will ever guess that we had anything to do with it.'

Alas for the two girls, sneaking Willow back into the room proved more difficult than either of them had anticipated. The following morning, they discovered that one of the maids had taken it into her head to sweep the landing just outside the box-room, and they had to retreat hastily down the stairs before Willow, wriggling violently inside Katie's coat, escaped.

'I'm sure that landing hasn't been swept for weeks,' said Daffy crossly as they took the cat back to the shed. 'Why on earth did someone have to decide to clean it today, of all days?'

'Well, we have half an hour free this afternoon,' said Katie. 'We can try again then.'

But once more the girls' plans went awry, as they had to spend their free half hour explaining the disappearance of some new stockings to Matron.

'Perhaps we should slip out tonight, when everyone is asleep,' said Daffy. 'At least we know that no one will be sweeping the landing then, and we will be safe from Matron!'

But Katie had made up her mind that she was going to think twice before becoming involved in any more of her friend's madcap schemes, and she said firmly, 'No! We will just have to wait until tomorrow.'

'No, we won't!' said Daffy suddenly. 'Why, we don't have to get Willow back into the box-room ourselves at all! We will send Violet an anonymous note, telling her that Willow is in the shed. Then she can do it herself.'

'Yes!' cried Katie. 'Why didn't we think of that before?'

That afternoon, while the two first formers composed a carefully worded note to Violet, Felicity was leaving the San, having paid a visit to Alice.

'Thank goodness you have brought me something to keep me occupied,' Alice had said, taking the book that Felicity had brought her. 'I have slept nearly all day, and I'm quite sure that I shall be awake all night.'

'Well, don't let Matron catch you reading late at night,' Felicity had warned with a laugh. 'Or you'll be for the high jump!'

'Felicity!' called out Matron as she saw the girl leave Alice's room. 'Will you take some mending back to Amy for me, please? Why the silly girl persists in darning brown stockings with coloured wool I don't know, for she knows I will only return them to her. Go and wait in my room, while I just give the youngsters their medicine, and I will be with you in a moment.'

Felicity went into Matron's cosy little room, grimacing as she looked at the big bottles of medicine that stood neatly on the shelves. Matron also had lots of photographs pinned up on her walls, of various forms at Malory Towers throughout the years. Felicity smiled as she saw a photograph of her sister, Darrell, and June's cousin,

Alicia, when they had been first formers. And, heavens, there was a photograph of Felicity and her friends when they had been in the second form. How young they all looked! Suddenly, Felicity's glance rested on someone in the front row of the photograph and her smile froze, as she gave a gasp. She took a step forward, to get a closer look, her heart beating fast. It couldn't be – could it? But it was, there was no doubt. Now Felicity knew exactly who Alice was!

A most dramatic night

Daffy and Katie had put the note they had written to Violet in the girl's desk.

'She will find it tomorrow morning,' said Daffy. 'And will rush off to get Willow at lunchtime. Then all our problems will be at an end.'

But Daffy was wrong, for Violet slipped into the empty class-room before tea, to get a book that she needed for prep, and found the note then.

Who on earth could it be from, the girl wondered, ripping open the envelope and pulling out the sheet of paper inside. Her heart pounded, as she read:

Come to the disused shed behind North Tower at 12. Come alone, do not tell ANYONE where you are going, and you will get your cat back.

Violet gave a gasp. Why, it sounded almost like a ransom note – except that whoever had written it had not demanded money.

Of course, Daffy hadn't expected Violet to find the note until tomorrow, and meant her to go to the shed at lunchtime. But Violet thought that she was supposed to be there at midnight tonight!

The thought of going out alone at midnight to meet

the kidnappers was very frightening indeed. Heavens, what if the person who wrote the note was waiting for her? What if she ended up being kidnapped as well? Violet hastily stuffed the note into her pocket, and went to tea, slipping into her seat beside Faith.

She longed to confide in the girl, but it was too dangerous. The kidnappers had said that she wasn't to tell ANYONE.

I know what I shall do! thought Violet. I will write Faith a note and put it on her bedside cabinet, before I go out to meet the kidnappers. Then, if I don't come back, she will read it in the morning and raise the alarm.

Poor Violet felt so scared that she could hardly eat any tea. But, although she was very frightened, the thought of not going never even occurred to her. All that mattered was getting her precious Willow back.

At the sixth-form table, Felicity also had something on her mind, and Susan, who had spoken to her twice without getting a reply, said, 'Felicity, what on earth is the matter with you? You've been in a perfect daze since you went to visit Alice.'

'Sorry,' said Felicity with a rueful smile. 'It's just that I found something out, and I'm rather puzzled about it.'

'Well, are you going to tell me what it is?' asked Susan curiously.

'Yes, but I need to tell the others as well,' said Felicity. She raised her voice, and said, 'Listen, everyone! Please can you all come to my study after prep? There is something that I need to talk to you about.'

Everyone agreed at once, and wondered what it was that Felicity had to say to them. She looked awfully serious!

It was very crowded in Felicity's study that evening as the sixth formers poured in, all of them feeling very curious indeed. Felicity opened the drawer of her desk and pulled out a photograph, which she placed on the desk.

'I borrowed this from Matron,' she said. 'Take a look.'

'My goodness, it's us when we were second formers!' gasped Nora.

'Look, June, there you are in the back row,' said Freddie. 'You've hardly changed a bit.'

But June wasn't looking at herself. She was looking at a plump girl in the front row and, as the truth dawned, her eyes met Felicity's.

'This is all very nice,' said Julie. 'But I don't understand why you have asked us here to look at an old photograph.'

'I do,' said June. 'Take a look at the girl next to Pam, in the front row.'

'I remember her!' said Susan. 'Josephine Jones. What a horrible girl she was. I remember . . . Oh, my goodness! It's her, isn't it? It's Alice!'

'Of course it's not Alice!' scoffed Delia, looking over Susan's shoulder. 'That girl is plump and Alice is thin. And she is fair, while Alice has brown hair.'

'People can lose weight,' said Bonnie, looking at the photo critically. 'And change their hair colour. But they can't change their faces, and that is most definitely Alice's face.'

'There's no doubt about it,' said Gillian. 'Just look at the eyes. It's Alice, all right.'

'Of course, that would explain why she wore glasses with plain glass in them!' said Felicity. 'To try and disguise herself a bit.'

'I don't understand,' said Amy, with a puzzled frown. 'Are you saying that Alice and this Josephine are one and the same? If that is true, why would she try and disguise herself and change her name?'

'Because she knew that we wouldn't want her back here,' said Nora rather scornfully. 'Of course, you girls who joined us higher up the school won't know the story, but Jo was an awful girl – conceited, boastful and thought that she could do as she pleased. She was expelled in the end, after running away and taking a first former with her.'

'My goodness!' said Lucy, looking most astonished. 'That doesn't sound like Alice at all.'

'I don't understand why Jo – Alice – whatever you want to call her, would want to come back here,' said Pam. 'She didn't fit in, and no one liked her. It doesn't make sense.'

'It makes sense to me,' said Felicity, looking thoughtful. 'Bonnie, you were quite right when you said that Alice felt ashamed of herself and wanted to make amends. That is why she has come back to Malory Towers.'

'The locket!' cried Susan suddenly. 'Felicity, that

locket that we found, with the initials JJ engraved on it – I bet that it belonged to Alice!'

'Of course!' said Felicity. 'And it explains how she knew the end of Miss Grayling's speech – because she had heard it before, when she was in the second form!'

'Are you going to tell Miss Grayling?' asked Freddie, who had been listening open-mouthed. 'I shouldn't think that she would want a girl here who has already been expelled once.'

'I would be very surprised if Miss Grayling – and some of the other mistresses – don't already know who Alice is,' said Felicity. 'The Head must have agreed to take her back, and if she was willing to give her another chance I think that we should too.'

Most of the others agreed with this, though June wasn't convinced, saying in a hard voice, 'A leopard doesn't change its spots. As far as I am concerned, Jo has been putting on an act, trying to convince us that she is someone she isn't. Until we speak to her, and she explains her reasons for coming back to Malory Towers, I don't know whether I can trust her.'

'Are you going to tell her that we know her secret, Felicity?' asked Julie.

'Yes, for now that we know I think that it is better if we bring it all out into the open,' said Felicity. 'I will go and see her tomorrow.'

In the first-form dormitory, all was silent, for most of the girls were fast asleep. Only Violet was wide awake, for she meant to slip out of the dormitory shortly before midnight. The time seemed to creep by very slowly indeed, but at last it was ten minutes to twelve, and Violet got out of bed. It was a bitterly cold night, but the girl didn't want to get dressed, in case one of the others woke and saw her. So she put on her warm dressing-gown and outdoor shoes, placed the note that she had written to Faith on the girl's bedside cabinet, and slipped quietly from the room. A floorboard creaked as she tiptoed along the landing, and Violet stopped, her heart in her mouth. But no doors flew open and no mistress appeared on the scene, so the girl carried on down the stairs.

This is all very strange, she thought to herself. Here I am going out to rescue a cat – and perhaps meet a desperate kidnapper – dressed in my pyjamas!

A nervous giggle rose in her throat, but Violet quelled it, silently opening the big door that led into the garden. She shivered as a blast of cold air hit her, and suddenly realised that it was pitch black outside, with no moon to light her way.

'Why didn't I think to bring a torch with me?' thought Violet. 'Ah, I wonder if there is one in the cupboard!'

The big cupboard at the bottom of the stairs was home to all kinds of odds and ends, but there was no torch there. However, Violet did find an old-fashioned oil lantern and a box of matches. With a trembling hand, she struck a match and lit the wick, before stepping out into the cold and shutting the door softly behind her.

Violet felt very nervous indeed, trembling with cold and fear as she made her way to the big shed at the bottom of the garden. What if the kidnapper was inside, waiting for her? Oh, how she wished Faith was with her!

A sudden sound from inside the shed almost made her jump out of her skin, then she realised what it was. It was Willow mewing! Screwing up every ounce of courage she possessed, Violet pushed open the door, holding the lantern aloft as she peered inside. Relief made her go weak at the knees as she realised that there was no kidnapper there, only her own, beloved Willow. A rickety wood table stood in the middle of the shed, and Violet placed the lantern on it, before rushing to pick up Willow. The little cat had been rather cross with her mistress for neglecting her, but all that was forgotten now, and Willow purred in delight, rubbing her silky head against Violet's chin. As for Violet, she forgot that she was cold, forgot that she had been frightened, forgot *everything* except that she had found Willow!

'I had better get you back indoors,' said the girl at last. 'I shall have to carry you, so please don't wriggle!'

But Willow had decided that it was time to stretch her legs, and she suddenly jumped from Violet's arms, landing on the rickety table. The table wobbled dangerously, which Willow didn't like at all, and she leapt off at once, but the lantern that Violet had placed there fell to the floor, smashing and sending a sheet of flame across the dry wooden floor.

Snatching up Willow, Violet screamed, wondering if she dared run through the flames, which were between

419

her and the door. But, even as she hesitated, the fire was spreading, the table alight now and flames shooting up the walls.

Violet coughed and choked, tears streaming down her cheeks, as she looked round desperately for a way out. But the only window in the shed was on the other side of the flames. She screamed again, as loudly as she could, praying that someone would hear her, but it was hopeless, for the thick, dark smoke was choking her. She was trapped, and no one was going to rescue her!

But Violet was wrong. Alice, feeling very restless from having slept so much during the day, simply couldn't sleep. Gingerly, for the girl still felt a little weak, she got out of bed and went across to the window. From her room she had an excellent view of the garden, and she started in fright as she spotted someone carrying a light darting across the lawn. Why, it was that first former, Violet! What mischief was she up to now? If she was caught out of her tower in the middle of the night, the girl would be in big trouble!

As a sixth former, it was up to Alice to see that she went back to bed, so the girl pulled on her dressing-gown and put on her slippers.

In the main San, one of the second formers was awake, and she whispered, 'Where are you going, Alice?'

'Never you mind,' said Alice. 'I shall be back shortly.'

The girl went quietly past the room where Matron slept and down the stairs, but as soon as she stepped outside, she smelled smoke.

'How odd!' she thought. 'It's a bit late for one of the gardeners to be having a bonfire. I wonder what it could be?'

As Alice came round the corner of North Tower, she was left in no doubt as to where the smell was coming from. The shed was ablaze! The shed that she had seen Violet enter a few minutes ago. Alice ran towards the fire, heart pounding and her mind racing. Was Violet still in there, or had she managed to get out? Then she heard a muffled scream, and knew the dreadful truth – Violet was trapped in the burning shed.

There was no time to raise the alarm or fetch help. Alice knew that she had to act quickly. Glancing round, she spotted a water butt nearby and, heedless of the cold, she pulled off her dressing-gown, soaking it in the water. Then, wrapping part of the dressing-gown round her hand, to protect it from the heat, she pulled open the shed door, the force of the blaze making her reel.

It was impossible to see anything because of the smoke and flames, and Alice called out, 'Violet, where are you?'

'Here!' croaked Violet. 'At the back of the shed.'

Then Alice did a very brave thing. She pulled her wet dressing-gown over her head, making sure that it covered as much of her as possible. And she ran through the flames to Violet.

The first former was sobbing with terror now, her face streaked with black, and she was still clutching Willow tightly. There was no time to enquire what the girl was doing with a cat, and Alice, with more courage than she felt, said, 'I'm going to get you out of here. Do exactly as I say, and don't hesitate. Now, put the cat in the front of your dressing-gown quickly!'

Violet did as she was told, then Alice put her own dressing-gown over both their heads, took Violet's arm in a firm grip, and shouted, 'RUN!'

The heat was almost unbearable as the two girls ran through the blaze, and Alice felt an agonising burning sensation to her hand. Their escape took only seconds, but to Violet and Alice it seemed like hours until they were outside, both of them collapsing on to the grass, coughing and choking.

Then there was a commotion, and the sound of raised voices, and Violet looked up to see Matron, Miss Grayling, two gardeners and several mistresses running towards them.

Matron had been woken by one of the second formers having a coughing fit, and had looked in on Alice only to find that she wasn't there. Then she had seen the blazing shed from the window, and raised the alarm.

'Good heavens!' she cried, as she saw the two girls lying on the ground, taking in their blackened faces and charred clothing. Then her sharp eyes spotted the burn on Alice's hand and she called out, 'Miss Grayling! We need to get Alice to hospital at once. She has a very bad burn and needs more expert treatment than I can give.'

'I shall telephone for an ambulance at once,' said the Head, going back into the school.

Miss Potts and Mam'zelle Dupont were also on the

scene and, as Matron carefully checked the two girls over, Mam'zelle stood wringing her hands, and moaning. Miss Potts was more practical, saying, 'Is there anything I can do to help, Matron?'

But, before Matron could answer, Mam'zelle suddenly spotted Willow, and cried, 'A cat! Why does Violet have a cat in her dressing-gown?'

Of course, Matron and Miss Potts had also noticed Willow, and Miss Potts said drily, 'We are all wondering that, Mam'zelle, but I am afraid that such questions will have to wait. The immediate need is to tend to the girls.'

Suddenly there came the wail of a siren, and everyone knew that the fire engine had arrived.

The two gardeners, who had been training hoses on the fire, stopped what they were doing, and went round to the front of the school to direct the fire engine.

Of course, the siren woke many of the girls up, and they looked out of the windows to see what was going on. They gasped when they saw the fire, and the people rushing about outside, most of them thinking that it was rather a thrill. Some of them made their way outside, not wanting to miss the excitement, and soon quite a crowd had gathered.

'Heavens, look at the old shed! It's been burnt to the ground!'

'Someone's been hurt! Look, it's Alice, of the sixth form.'

'And Violet! Goodness, I hope they aren't seriously injured.'

'Girls, do go back inside!' called out Miss Potts.

But, for once, no one took any notice of Miss Potts, and soon more girls came down, several of the first formers among them.

Daffy turned white when she took in the scene and saw the two girls lying on the ground, their faces black. And Willow was there too! For a moment she felt quite sick, but she simply had to find out what had happened, and whether Violet or Alice was badly hurt. So Daffy made her way across to where Miss Potts was bending over the girls, saying, 'Miss Potts, what happened?'

'As you can plainly see, Daphne, the shed caught fire,' said Miss Potts with sarcasm. 'How it caught fire is something we have yet to find out. Now, please get out of the way, for the ambulance will be here shortly.'

The ambulance arrived a few moments later, and everyone watched gravely as Alice was lifted on to a stretcher and put into the back. Violet had been lucky, as she had not suffered any burns at all, and did not need to go to hospital. But she had inhaled a large amount of smoke, and Matron took her to the San.

'Though that cat most certainly can't come,' she said sternly. 'Daffy Hope, make yourself useful and take it to the stables.'

'Yes, Matron,' said Daffy meekly, coming over and taking Willow from Violet.

'Oh, but she can't go to the stables!' Violet protested, her voice little more than a croak.

'Don't worry,' said Daffy in a very solemn whisper.

'I'll let Matron think that's where I'm taking Willow, but really I shall put her back in the box-room. And I shall take the greatest care of her, Violet, I promise.'

'Thanks, Daffy,' said Violet, rather surprised that Daffy was being so nice. It was probably just because she, Violet, had been in the fire and Daffy felt sorry for her. No doubt tomorrow, the girl would be back to her old, hostile self again!

With the two casualties gone and the fire almost out, there wasn't much left to see, and when Miss Potts again raised her voice and commanded that everyone go back to bed, she was obeyed.

Most of the girls were far too excited to sleep, though. Heavens, what a night it had been!

Daffy learns a lesson

The sixth formers hadn't heard the fire engine, as their dormitory was on the other side of North Tower, so they didn't hear the news until the following morning.

Mam'zelle Dupont, rather excited to be first with the news, stopped by the sixth-form table at breakfast, and told the girls of the dramatic events that had unfolded last night.

They listened in astonishment, and June said, 'Well! So Alice saved young Violet's life!'

'Ah, she is a heroine, that girl,' said Mam'zelle. 'The poor Violet was scarcely able to talk, but she managed to tell Matron that Alice ran through the flames to save her.'

'How brave of her!' said Susan. 'I'm not sure that I would have had that kind of courage.'

'Yes,' said June as Mam'zelle moved away. 'Anyone who shows the kind of bravery that Alice did last night has more than made amends for anything they did in the past. I wasn't sure about giving her another chance last night, but I jolly well am now! I vote that, when she comes back, we give Alice a hero's welcome.'

Everyone agreed at once, for all of them felt intensely proud of Alice.

'I wonder when she *will* be back,' said Bonnie. 'Mam'zelle said that she had burned her hand quite badly and, of course, she must have inhaled a great deal of smoke, just as Violet did.'

In fact, Alice returned to Malory Towers that very afternoon, but none of the sixth formers saw her, for Matron whisked her straight off to the San. The girl's hand had been bandaged, and she had a very sore throat, but she protested strongly.

'Matron, I feel quite well,' she said in a rather croaky voice. 'Really, I would far rather go back to the others.'

But Matron insisted, saying, 'You can join the others tomorrow, provided that you don't have a relapse. Come along now.'

And Alice, realising that it was quite useless to argue with Matron, followed her meekly.

Daffy, meanwhile, was in turmoil. Her conscience had kept her awake the night before, and she felt that she was to blame for everything that had happened. It was quite clear now that Violet must have found that note before she was meant to, and gone to the shed at midnight instead of midday. It was all because of her that Violet had been in the shed, and that Alice had been hurt. The first formers wondered why she was so subdued and unlike herself, but she refused to tell them. Katie guessed, of course, for she was also feeling very guilty at having gone along with Daffy's scheme.

'I wish that I had never let you talk me into it,' groaned Katie, for about the twentieth time that day as she and

Daffy walked through the courtyard after lunch.

'And I wish that I had listened to you,' said Daffy, sounding very miserable indeed. 'When I think what might have happened to Violet – and Willow – if Alice hadn't rescued her . . .' She broke off, giving a sudden sob, and Katie, who had never seen her friend cry before, realised how distressed she was.

'It's no good upsetting yourself,' she said rather awkwardly, giving Daffy a pat on the shoulder. 'Just be glad that Alice got there in time.'

'That's just it,' said Daffy, her voice almost breaking. 'I don't think that I shall ever feel glad about anything again until I get this off my conscience. I am going to own up to Miss Grayling.'

'Daffy!' gasped Katie. 'Are you sure?'

Daffy nodded firmly. 'I shan't mention your name, Katie, for you aren't to blame. You tried to talk me out of it, and I wouldn't listen.'

'Daffy, the Head is going to come down awfully hard on you,' said Katie, looking rather scared. 'She might even . . .'

The girl's voice tailed off, and Daffy said, 'Expel me? Yes, I know that.'

'But think how upset your people will be!' cried Katie.

Daffy's face quivered, but she took a deep breath, and said, 'The very last thing I want to do is hurt my parents. But I don't feel that I can stay at Malory Towers unless I own up, so either way I will have to leave.'

Katie understood this, and respected her friend for

making the difficult decision to tell Miss Grayling everything. All the same, she felt very unhappy as she watched her friend walk away, for the first form without Daffy just wouldn't be the same.

Miss Grayling had been to see Violet that morning and, although she had barely been able to croak, the girl had told her the whole story of how she had come to be in the shed, and how the fire had started.

When Violet had asked anxiously how she was to be punished, Miss Grayling had replied, 'Well, I think that what you suffered last night was punishment enough. And, as it is so close to the end of term, I shall allow you to keep your pet at school with you for the last few days. But please leave her at home next term, Violet, or I shall take a very dim view indeed!'

Violet, who had really feared that she might be expelled, felt most relieved, but the Head was far more worried than she had appeared, and later that day she sent for Miss Potts, to discuss the matter.

'I don't believe for a moment that the cat was taken by a kidnapper,' said Miss Grayling.

'I agree with you,' said Miss Potts. 'I think it is much more likely to have been one of the girls playing a trick.'

'Have you any idea who the culprit could be, Miss Potts?' asked the Head. 'After all, you know the first formers far better than I do.'

Miss Potts was just considering this when a knock came at the door.

Miss Grayling's voice was rather sharp as she called out,

'Come in!', for she was annoyed at being interrupted.

She frowned when Daffy Hope walked in, and said, 'Daphne, I am discussing something very important with Miss Potts at the moment, and must ask you to come back later.'

But Daffy was afraid that her courage might fail her if she went away, and she said, 'Please, Miss Grayling, I need to speak to you now. It is very important, for it is about the fire last night.'

Miss Grayling and Miss Potts exchanged glances, and the Head said, 'That is exactly what we have been talking about, so I suppose we had better hear what you have to say. Go on, Daphne.'

So, haltingly, with a great deal of prompting from the two mistresses, Daffy confessed to hiding Willow, and sending the note that had lured Violet to the shed last night. As she had promised, she kept Katie's name out of it and shouldered the whole blame herself. The Head and Miss Potts both looked extremely grave by the time she had finished, and Miss Grayling said heavily, 'You are very lucky, Daphne, that your prank did not end tragically.'

'I know that, Miss Grayling,' said Daffy, her voice trembling. 'That is why I had to get it off my conscience.'

'Well, that is to your credit, I suppose,' said the Head, looking very stern indeed. 'Though it doesn't alter the fact that you behaved very foolishly.'

Daffy hung her head, and Miss Potts asked, 'Daphne, why did you take Violet's cat?'

Daffy hesitated. She couldn't mention the feast, or all

of her form would be in trouble. So she said, 'I don't like her, Miss Potts. And I wanted to get back at her for something she had done to me.'

'I see,' said Miss Potts. 'So your motive was a desire for revenge.'

'Yes,' said Daffy, thinking that it sounded rather horrible when Miss Potts put it like that. 'I suppose it was.'

'Nothing good ever comes out of vengeance or vindictiveness,' said Miss Grayling. 'When a person is motivated by spite, someone always gets hurt. Sometimes it is the person who that spite is directed at, but often it hurts the person who is taking revenge just as badly. I trust that you have learned that, Daphne.'

'I have, Miss Grayling, and it is a lesson that I will never forget,' said Daffy with feeling.

Miss Grayling did not doubt the girl's sincerity. She had received a huge shock, and had shown great courage in owning up. But what she had done was so serious that it could not go unpunished.

An uncomfortable silence stretched, as the Head considered what she should do with Daffy. At last, the girl could bear it no longer, and she blurted out, 'Are you going to expel me, Miss Grayling?'

'I am not going to make that decision,' said Miss Grayling. 'Violet and Alice are. They both need to rest today, so I shan't tell them about your confession until tomorrow. But your fate is in their hands. You may go now.'

Daffy went, feeling sick at heart. She remembered the

time she had pulled Violet into the swimming-pool, and Alice had accidentally fallen in, too. The two of them were sure to want her expelled, and the girl couldn't find it in her heart to blame them!

Alice, meanwhile, was delighted to receive a visit from Felicity, who arrived bearing an enormous bouquet of flowers, which the whole of the sixth form had clubbed together to buy.

'How beautiful!' exclaimed Alice, thrilled. 'I really don't deserve them.'

'You most certainly do,' said Felicity, arranging the flowers in a vase that Matron had given her. 'You're a real heroine.'

'Nonsense,' said Alice gruffly, turning red. 'Anyone would have done what I did.'

'I'm not so sure,' said Felicity. 'Anyway, the point is, anyone *didn't* do it, you did, and we are all very proud of you.'

'How is Violet?' asked Alice, who was back in her little room and hadn't seen the girl since last night. 'And Willow, of course?'

'Both fine,' said Felicity. 'Violet escaped without any burns, though she has a very sore throat from all the smoke. As for Willow, Miss Grayling has allowed her to stay for the rest of the term, and she's having the time of her life being thoroughly spoilt by absolutely everyone!'

Alice laughed at this, which brought on a fit of coughing, and Felicity patted her on the back, saying, 'Poor thing! How is your hand?'

'Sore!' said Alice. 'But the doctor said it should heal nicely in time.'

Alice was so pleased to have company that she seemed to have lost some of her shyness, and chattered away. And, as Felicity listened, she could hear traces of Jo Jones coming through. Jo had been a dreadful chatterbox, bumptious, boastful and conceited. No one could call Alice bumptious, boastful or conceited, but she was gaining confidence, and that, thought Felicity, was a very good thing. She had made up her mind not to tell Alice that the sixth form knew her true identity just yet, for the girl had enough to deal with at the moment. But, in the end, Alice gave herself away.

The two girls were talking about June, and how great a success she had been as games captain. Alice, feeling more relaxed than she had since she started at Malory Towers, forgot to guard her tongue, and said, 'Who would have thought it? I remember her so well as a bold, mischievous second former . . .'

Then Alice's voice died away as she realised what she had said, and she turned pale. And Felicity knew that this was the time to bring Alice's secret out into the open.

'It's all right, Jo,' she said. 'We know who you are. By the way, which should I call you – Alice or Jo?'

Alice turned even paler, hardly able to speak for a moment, but at last she said in a strangled voice, 'Alice.'

'Very well,' said Felicity pleasantly. 'Alice it is.'

'How long have you known?' asked Alice, her voice

hardly more than a whisper, and her eyes wide behind the glasses.

'Only since yesterday,' said Felicity. 'Though you've had us puzzled for quite a while.'

She went on to tell the girl about the photograph she had seen in Matron's room, then asked, 'Why did you come back to Malory Towers, Alice? And why the change of name?'

Alice was silent for a moment, then she began quietly, 'I went to several schools after Malory Towers, you know. And at each one, I realised more and more what a splendid school this was, and what a marvellous opportunity I had wasted. And I began looking at my own behaviour, and realising why I didn't fit in here, and why people disliked me so. I decided that I didn't want to be Jo Jones any more, that I wanted to change myself completely.'

'Heavens!' said Felicity, listening to this in amazement. 'And how did your parents react to that?'

Felicity remembered the girl's parents well, especially Mr Jones, who had been every bit as loud and bumptious as Jo herself!

'Father didn't like it, of course,' said Alice. 'He liked me as I was, for I was just like him. And when I decided that I didn't want to be like him any more, he thought that it meant I was ashamed of him.' The girl took a deep breath, and said, 'Well, I *was* ashamed of him in many ways. You know what he was like, Felicity, always pushing himself forward and airing his opinions, and not showing any respect for people's feelings. I couldn't see it when I was younger, but I do now. Of course, I still love him dearly,' she added. 'I just wanted him to learn to be a little less full of himself, and more considerate of other people, as I was trying to be.'

'Well, you have succeeded very well indeed,' said Felicity. 'But what about your father?'

'He really has improved a lot,' said Alice with a smile. 'Remember I told you that he helped me to study for School Cert by asking me questions? Well, that was true. A few years before, he would have told me not to waste my time studying, for *he* never did. That just shows how much he has changed.'

'It certainly does!' said Felicity, astonished. 'Alice, how did you get Miss Grayling to agree to give you another chance at Malory Towers?'

'I telephoned her myself,' said Alice. 'I knew that it was no use asking Father to do it, for although he has changed a lot, he can still be tactless at times. Miss Grayling listened to what I had to say, though, and knew that I was sincere. So she agreed that I could join the sixth form at Malory Towers. Of course, she knew how unpopular I had been with you others, so she agreed to me using my middle name, Alice, and my mother's maiden name.'

'You have changed your appearance, too,' said Felicity. 'You were fair when you were in the second form.'

'Yes,' said Alice, flushing a little. 'That wasn't my real colour, though. I used to dye it! Shocking, wasn't it?'

'Shocking!' agreed Felicity with a laugh. 'And you have lost an awful lot of weight, too.'

'Yes, I was a tubby little thing in those days,' said Alice, grimacing. 'I feel much healthier now.'

Felicity looked hard at Alice for a few moments, then she asked suddenly, 'Are you happy, Alice?'

'I am happier than I was when I was cocky, conceited Jo,' answered the girl, after considering this for a minute. 'But I'm not *completely* happy, for I feel that I don't know who I really am. You see, Felicity, Jo wasn't the real me – although I thought she was at the time. But really, I was just acting the way that my father wanted me to act, trying to please him. Do you understand?'

'I think so,' said Felicity. 'But what about Alice? Isn't she the real you, either?'

'Parts of her are,' answered the girl. 'But, inside, I am not really as meek and timid as I have made out.'

'I can tell you one thing that is real,' said Felicity. 'And that is your bravery last night. You can't possibly pretend to have courage like that.'

'To be honest, I didn't know I had it in me to act like that,' said Alice. 'But once I knew that Violet was in danger, I didn't even stop and think that I might be hurt.'

'You probably have all sorts of hidden qualities, if only you will be yourself, and let them come to the fore,' said Felicity. 'I think that is what you should do, Alice – just be yourself.'

Alice felt as if a weight had rolled off her shoulders after her talk with Felicity. She hadn't felt comfortable about hiding her identity from the others, although she had done it with the best of motives.

Felicity had assured her that the others didn't think any the worse of her for her deception, adding honestly, 'June wasn't too sure at first, but your courage in saving Violet convinced her that you deserve to be given a chance. Everyone thinks you're a proper heroine.'

The girl felt warmed by these words, and found that she couldn't wait to get back to the sixth form tomorrow. And she was going to take Felicity's advice, and be herself!

Before she joined the others in class the next morning, Alice was surprised to be summoned to the Head's room.

Miss Grayling greeted her with a charming smile and said, 'How are you feeling today, Alice?'

'Much better, thank you, Miss Grayling,' answered the girl.

'I am pleased to hear it,' said the Head. 'My dear, your courage the other night averted a great tragedy, and I am very proud of you indeed.'

Alice, feeling as though she might burst with pride, turned very red, and stammered out a thank you.

'And now I am going to ask you to do something else, which requires a different kind of courage,' said Miss Grayling. 'I think that it is time for you to tell the others who you really are.'

'Oh, but they already know, Miss Grayling,' said Alice. 'Felicity came to see me yesterday, and she told me that – thanks to an old photograph in Matron's room – the girls had discovered my true identity.'

'Well,' said Miss Grayling. 'I always knew that the

sixth formers were very shrewd. They are very kind-hearted and just, too, generally speaking.'

'Felicity has already assured me that I will be welcomed back with open arms,' said Alice, smiling at the Head.

'I am glad to hear it,' said Miss Grayling, smiling back at the girl. 'But before I let you join them, I need you to make a decision, Alice. It won't be an easy one, for someone else's future rests on it.'

Alice looked very puzzled indeed, and rather alarmed, but before the Head could enlighten her, a knock came at the door and Miss Potts entered, followed by Violet and Daffy.

Violet looked just as puzzled as Alice felt, while Daffy looked very subdued and unhappy. The girl's eyes looked suspiciously red, as if she had been crying. But surely not, thought Alice. What could the happy, carefree Daffy have to cry about?

Miss Potts left to go back to her class, and Miss Grayling said seriously, 'Alice and Violet, Daphne has something to say to you both, and when she has finished I want you both to make a decision. That decision will be whether or not Daphne remains at Malory Towers.'

A marvellous end to the term

Unable to meet the eyes of the two girls, Daffy confessed to them, as she had confessed to Miss Grayling the day before.

Violet could not contain herself when she learned that it was Daffy who had taken Willow, and burst out, 'You mean beast! You knew how worried and upset I was. You could have put me out of my misery in an instant, but you didn't.'

'I'm sorry,' said Daffy, looking Violet in the eye for the first time. 'If I could only turn back the clock, I would. I have never felt so dreadful in my life as when I knew that the shed had caught fire, and that you and Alice had been hurt. And I hope that I never feel like that again. I've learned my lesson, but I shan't blame either of you if you want me expelled. I should probably feel the same if I was in your shoes.'

Miss Grayling, who had listened in silence, never taking her eyes off Daffy, turned to Alice and Violet now, saying, 'Well, girls?'

There was a moment's silence, then Alice said, 'Miss Grayling, when I was not very much older than Daffy, I was sent away from Malory Towers in disgrace. Only after I had left did I realise what a splendid school it is.'

Of course, this was news to the two first formers, who stared at Alice open-mouthed.

'I was lucky enough to be given a second chance,' the girl went on. 'Though I had to wait several years for it. So I am certainly not going to deny Daffy *her* second chance. I vote that she should stay at Malory Towers, and sincerely hope that she will come to realise what a marvellous school it is, as I did. And I also hope, Daffy, that – if you stay – you take the opportunity to show that you are truly sorry, and to do better in the future.'

Daffy felt a small – a very small – glimmer of hope. It was all up to Violet now.

The girl had listened intently to what Alice said, and now she turned to Daffy, as she began, 'Daffy, I think that what you did was low and mean and nasty,' she said. 'But, while I've been lying in the San, I have had time to think about my own behaviour. And I have come to realise that I can be a boastful, conceited little beast at times.'

Daffy gasped, while Miss Grayling and Alice exchanged an amused glance at Violet's frankness.

'I can understand why you wanted to take me down a peg or two,' went on Violet. 'Though the way that you went about it was quite wrong. But I am in no position to judge you, and I agree with Alice. I think that you should be given another chance at Malory Towers.'

'Thank you, girls,' said Miss Grayling. 'Daphne, I echo the words of Alice and Violet. You have been very lucky indeed, for few people are given the chance to start afresh. Make the most of it.'

'I shall,' said Daffy fervently, feeling quite weak with relief. She really had thought that she was going to be expelled, and the thought of leaving Malory Towers, and of her parents' pain and disappointment, had weighed heavily on her. 'Thank you, Miss Grayling. And as for you, Alice, and you, Violet . . . well, I can't find the words to tell you how grateful I am to both of you. I do realise what a fine school Malory Towers is, and I mean to make myself worthy of my place here. I shall own up to the others, of course, and I daresay they will send me to Coventry, for a bit, but –'

'Daphne, that isn't necessary,' interrupted Miss Grayling in a firm tone. 'You have owned up to the two people who were affected by what you did, and they have forgiven you. I see no reason for you to make your fresh start here difficult by setting the first formers against you.'

'Miss Grayling is quite right,' said Violet, as Daffy turned this over in her mind. 'I shan't tell any of the others, you may be sure of that.'

'Nor shall I,' said Alice.

'Then the matter is settled,' said Miss Grayling. 'There is no more to be said. You may go.'

'Miss Grayling, there is something else I would like to say, if I may,' said Violet. Miss Grayling nodded, and Violet turned to Alice.

'I haven't had a chance to thank you yet, for what you

did the other night,' she said. 'You risked your life to save mine and Willow's. Just saying *thank you* doesn't seem enough somehow.'

'It's more than enough,' said Alice, giving the girl a pat on the shoulder. 'And now, I rather think that Miss Grayling would like to have her study to herself.'

The Head fell into a reflective mood after the three girls had left. It had been a dramatic term, but, on the whole, a good one, she thought. Felicity Rivers had done a first-rate job as Head Girl, but then, Miss Grayling had never doubted that she would. And Alice – or Jo, as she had once been – had proved that she was a very worthwhile person indeed, with more in her than the Head had ever suspected.

The first formers had been very troublesome this term, but it looked as if Violet was beginning to see the error of her ways, and Miss Grayling hoped that it would help her to change them. According to Miss Potts, Faith, too, was changing, beginning to show signs of leadership, and the others were starting to respect her. The Head was very pleased, for this would stand Faith in good stead in the future. As for Daphne Hope – the girl had a lot of good qualities, and could do well for herself and the school. But she also had a lot of faults, and would have to strive to make the good cancel out the bad. She was a strong character, though, and Miss Grayling knew that – with a little guidance – she could do it. On the whole, decided the Head, things had worked out very well indeed.

The last week of term was a full one. Alice returned

to class after her visit to the Head's room and was given three rousing cheers by the proud sixth formers. Even the serious Miss Oakes beamed at the girl and patted her on the back.

Alice was the heroine of the school, for everywhere she went, girls and mistresses wanted to cheer her, or shake her good hand, and tell her how they admired her bravery.

'Heavens, I shall get a swollen head if this goes on for much longer,' said Alice, quite red-faced.

'No, *Jo* would have got a swollen head,' said June, clapping the girl on the shoulder. 'But *Alice* is far too decent a person.'

June hadn't been in the best of moods for the last few days, for she still hadn't solved the problem of how to replace those members of her lacrosse teams who had gone down with the flu – and the matches were to be played the day before term ended. Now, though, she had finally got to grips with things, and made some decisions.

At break-time she approached Felicity and Susan, and said, 'I have some news for you. You are both playing in the upper-school match against Marlowe Hall on Thursday.'

The two girls stared at June, quite speechless. At last, Felicity found her voice, and said, 'But, June, we have hardly played at all this term, because of the exams and our extra duties. What if we let you down?'

'As long as you try your best you won't let me down,'

said June. 'And I know that you will both do that. Can I count on you?'

The girls knew that June had been having difficulty making up her teams, and that if they didn't play, the match might have to be cancelled. That, of course, was quite unthinkable, and, with the honour of Malory Towers at stake, both of them chorused, 'Yes!'

'We shall have to spend the next couple of days practising like mad,' said Susan.

'Well, what are you waiting for?' laughed June. 'You are both free now until after lunch, so off you go to the lacrosse field!'

June then went in search of Daffy, and found her in the courtyard, chatting with Katie, Faith and Violet.

'Daffy!' she called. 'I want to see you at the lower-school lacrosse practice this afternoon.'

'Of course, June,' said Daffy, who had vowed to be on her very best behaviour from now on. 'I'll be there all right.'

'Good,' said June, 'because you are in the team against Marlowe Hall on Thursday.'

For a moment, Daffy thought that she hadn't heard June properly, then Katie gave a whoop of joy and thumped her on the back. 'Good show, Daffy! We shall be playing together. Isn't that marvellous?'

'I'll say,' said Daffy, her voice quivering with excitement. 'Thank you, June. I shall shoot *dozens* of goals, you see if I don't!'

As June walked away, Faith congratulated Daffy too,

but Violet said nothing. And Daffy, who felt that a new understanding had sprung up between the two of them, felt rather hurt.

Then Violet gave a haughty sniff and said, 'Of course, you know that June only chose you because so many of the others are ill, don't you?'

Daffy whipped round to stare at the girl, hardly able to believe her ears, then she saw that Violet was grinning.

'Only joking, old girl!' she laughed, giving Daffy a playful punch on the arm. 'I'm simply thrilled for you!'

Then Daffy laughed too, while Katie and Faith exchanged startled looks. Heavens, only the other day Violet and Daffy had been bitter enemies, and now they were on their way to being the best of friends! Whatever next?

Felicity, Susan and Daffy stuck to their word, all three of them spending every spare minute on the lacrosse field over the next few days. Then it was Thursday, and the teams climbed aboard the big coach that was to take them to Marlowe Hall.

The lower school played first, while the upper school watched and cheered them on.

'Daffy's going to have her work cut out,' said Felicity. 'The girl marking her is twice her size.'

'Yes, but Daffy is very agile and very fast,' said June. 'I don't think that her opponent will be able to keep up with her.'

And June was quite right, for as soon as Daffy got the ball into her net, she was off down the field like a streak of lightning, before passing to Katie, who was very near the goal. Katie aimed for the goal, but just missed, causing the watching Malory Towers girls to groan.

'Bad luck, Katie!' called out Susan.

The two teams were very evenly matched, but a few minutes later one of the Marlowe Hall girls broke away from the girl marking her and shot a goal. Then, just before the whistle blew for half-time, Marlowe Hall scored again!

June was in despair, but although she groaned inwardly, she sportingly applauded the girl who had scored, for it really had been a most spectacular goal.

The lower-school team looked rather dispirited as they sank down on to the grass to rest, and June ran on to the field.

'Cheer up!' she said. 'You're all doing splendidly and you mustn't lose heart. There is still a long way to go before the match is over.'

Her words put new heart into the girls, and they started the second half full of fighting spirit. And it paid off, for after only five minutes, Rita of the second form shot a goal. The team were inspired after that, and a little later Maggie also shot one.

Felicity and Susan hugged one another excitedly, while June cried, 'We're even! Come on, Malory Towers! Play up!'

And the girls did play up, putting every effort into stopping the Marlowe Hall girls from shooting any more goals.

Then, with only a few minutes of play left, Daffy found herself with the ball in her net and a clear shot at goal. The only trouble was, she was so far away that she wasn't certain if she could get the ball in. Rita, however, was closer, and if Daffy were to pass the ball to her, she was almost certain to score. Daffy hesitated for a moment. How marvellous it would be if she were the one to shoot the winning goal! And wouldn't it be something to tell the others when she returned to Malory Towers. But what if she missed? There would be no glory in that! Besides, if she passed to Rita, she would still have played a big part in scoring the goal. All of these thoughts ran through Daffy's head in an instant and, in that instant, Daffy got an inkling of what team spirit was all about. The ball flew from her net to Rita's, the second former caught it and flung it towards the goal, and then a great cheer went up, just as the whistle blew.

They had won! Malory Towers had won!

The upper-school team yelled themselves hoarse, thumping one another on the back, until June cried, 'I say! We had better go and get changed, for our match starts shortly. Come along, everyone!'

Then it was the turn of the lower school to cheer on the older girls, which they did with great enthusiasm.

'Good show, June!'

'Come on, Felicity!'

'Oh, rotten luck, Susan!'

Once again, the match was a very close and exciting one. Neither Felicity nor Susan shot a goal, though they tried their hardest, but June did, and won the match for her team.

As June shook hands with the captain of the opposing team, the younger girls jumped up and down, hugging one another in excitement.

And no one was more thrilled than Daffy, who felt as if she might burst from happiness. It just goes to show, she thought. There are other ways of having fun besides fooling around and playing jokes. All the same, I expect I *shall* get up to mischief occasionally, for it's in my nature. But, from now on, I shall think things through properly before I play a trick, and make sure that no one can be hurt, for there is nothing funny in that at all!

Daffy thought that the day couldn't get any better, but she was wrong, for June came and sat down beside her on the coach back to Malory Towers, and said, 'Well done, Daffy. You played jolly well today.'

Daffy turned red with pleasure, and said, 'Thanks, but I didn't do anything marvellous. Why, I didn't even shoot a goal.'

'No, but you made it possible for Rita to shoot one, and win the match for us,' said June. 'I was watching you, and saw you hesitate, wondering if you should try and aim for goal yourself.'

Daffy looked at June in surprise, wondering how on earth the games captain could have known what had been going through her mind.

June laughed, and said, 'I know exactly what you were thinking, because the same thoughts would have gone through my mind when I was your age. In fact, I was once in your position, but I decided to try and grab the glory for myself, and shot for goal.'

'What happened?' asked Daffy, her eyes wide.

'I missed,' said June ruefully. 'And our team lost the match. So you see, Daffy, you made the right decision. You have a lot more team spirit than I did when I was a youngster, and are a great deal more sensible.'

Sensible! What a horrid word, thought Daffy. She had made up her mind to turn over a new leaf, but she didn't want to go too far and become all sensible and dull and goody-goody. That would never do! What a pity that it was the end of term tomorrow and there wasn't time to plan another trick on Mam'zelle. Well, she would come back next term with plenty of tricks up her sleeve, and show everyone that, although the new Daffy was kind and thoughtful, she still knew how to make people laugh!

'Well, this has rounded off the term nicely,' said Felicity cheerily as the lacrosse teams arrived back at Malory Towers tired, untidy, hungry – and very, very happy.

'I should say,' agreed Susan. 'My word, I'm starving! Hope there's something good for supper.'

'There's sure to be, as it's the last night,' said June. 'Come on, there's just time to tidy ourselves up a bit and get changed before the bell goes.'

Of course, word had got round that both teams had won their lacrosse matches, and the players were absolutely thrilled when they entered the dining-room, and everyone got to their feet to applaud them.

'Very well done, girls,' called out Miss Potts. 'We are extremely proud of you all.'

Then everyone took their seats and tucked in for, as June had predicted, it was a most delicious supper.

There were fat, juicy sausages and fluffy mashed potatoes, all smothered in gravy, followed by treacle pudding with custard. And, if anyone was still hungry after that, they could help themselves to cheese and biscuits.

Everyone ate hungrily, and Felicity noticed that even Alice, who normally had a poor appetite, seemed to be enjoying the meal.

The girl seemed much more relaxed and less timid now that her secret was out, and Felicity was pleased to see her chattering happily to Nora as she ate.

'I say, Alice!' she called out. 'Will you be coming back to Malory Towers next term?'

'Yes,' said the girl, looking pleased. 'If things had gone badly for me this term, I probably wouldn't have, but as it is you've all been awfully decent to me.'

The others were pleased to hear this, for they had grown to admire Alice enormously, both for her ability to see her faults and change them, and for her courage.

'It's been a funny old term,' said Felicity. 'What with all the mystery surrounding Alice, and the trouble that the first formers have caused. As for Daffy Hope, I simply can't believe how mistaken I was in her character!'

'Well, you can hardly be blamed for that,' said Susan. 'Even her parents don't realise how naughty she is!

She had most of the mistresses fooled at first, too, with her innocent act, though Miss Potts saw through her fairly quickly.'

'She's not a bad kid at heart, though,' said Felicity, looking across at the first-form table, where Daffy was chattering nineteen to the dozen with her friends. 'And I shall certainly keep an eye on her next term!'

Many of the girls found it hard to sleep that night, for they were all excited at the thought of going home for the Christmas holidays. Even Felicity, quite worn out from her strenuous lacrosse match, found her mind racing as she thought of what fun it would be to spend Christmas with her parents and Darrell. At last, though, she dropped off, and didn't stir until the bell rang the following morning.

Even Nora, who normally hated getting out of bed, was up on time, for she was as excited about going home as anyone.

After breakfast, there was the usual last-minute panic as everyone packed their trunks and hunted for long-lost items.

'Oh, *where* is my hairbrush?'

'Pam, have you seen my slippers?'

'Lucy, why you are packing a photograph of *my* parents in *your* trunk, I don't know!'

Things were even more chaotic in the first-form dormitory, for Willow had been brought down from the box-room and thought that it was great fun to climb in and out of the open trunks.

'One of us is going to end up taking her home, if you don't keep an eye on her, Violet,' said Katie.

'No chance of that,' laughed Violet. 'I'm not going to risk losing her again.'

Daffy flushed a little at this, for she always felt uncomfortable when reminded of the time that she had taken Willow and, seeing this, Violet quickly changed the subject, saying, 'My goodness, won't it be fun to be at home for Christmas?'

Daffy threw the girl a grateful look. Violet really had changed a lot just lately, she thought, and had become a much nicer person.

At last it was time for the girls to gather in the hall. Some of them were being collected by their parents, while others were waiting for the coaches that would take them to the railway station.

Susan's parents were coming to drive her and Felicity home, and as the two girls waited patiently, Susan said, 'Heavens, what a din! And most of it caused by the first formers!'

'Well, we were just like them once,' said Felicity with a grin. 'And, one day, they will be just like us!'

'Only two more terms,' said Susan rather wistfully. 'And then we leave Malory Towers for good.'

'Yes, but we must try not to feel sad about it,' said Felicity, giving her friend's arm a squeeze. 'Otherwise it will spoil the time that we have left.'

'Yes, you're quite right,' said Susan, glancing out of the window. 'Oh good, Mother and Father are here.

Got your things, Felicity? Come along then.'

And, calling 'goodbye' to the others, the two girls walked out of the school, Felicity wondering what was in store for her during her final two terms at Malory Towers.

Plenty of fun, I expect, as well as some shocks and surprises. We shall have to come back and see!

Malory Towers

Goodbye

Written by Pamela Cox

Contents

Last term at Malory Towers

'Well, Felicity,' said Darrell Rivers to her younger sister. 'Your last term at Malory Towers. How do you feel?'

'My feelings are rather mixed, to be honest,' said Felicity, taking a sip of her tea. 'I feel excited about going to university, of course. But, at the same time, I shall be awfully sad to leave old Malory Towers. I have had so many good times there, and I shall miss my friends terribly.'

'Not all of them,' said Darrell. 'Susan will be going to university with you, won't she?'

'Of course! I couldn't possibly be separated from Susan,' said Felicity. 'June and Freddie are hoping to come to the same university as us too, and so is Pam.'

'That's good,' said Darrell. 'I remember how glad I was to have a few friends around me when I started university. It must be awfully daunting to go alone.'

'I wonder if Bonnie will want to carry on her education?' said Felicity thoughtfully. 'She did awfully well in Higher Cert, you know. And the only reason she decided to take the exams in the first place was to prove a point to June.'

'She's a funny girl,' said Darrell. 'Judging from what

you've told me over the years, there's a lot more to her than meets the eye.'

'There certainly is,' said Felicity, remembering some of Bonnie's exploits. 'I thought her terribly spoilt and tiresome at first, but actually she's a very strong character, and has grown stronger during her time at Malory Towers.'

'That's one of the marvellous things about going to a good school,' said Darrell. 'If you have a good character, and are willing to learn, it will bring out all your strengths and help you to conquer any weaknesses.'

'Very true,' said Felicity, buttering a slice of toast. 'I can't think of anyone who hasn't benefited from being at Malory Towers. Even June has changed an awful lot over the last few years, and has become much more steady and responsible since she was made games captain. And as for Jo Jones – or Alice, as she calls herself now – why, you wouldn't think she was the same person.'

'I was quite astonished when you told me that Jo had returned to Malory Towers, under a different name,' said Darrell. 'I remember her so well from her time in the second form – my word, what a little beast she was then. But if she has changed as much as you say, Felicity, I shall look forward to meeting her again.'

'Darrell!' cried Felicity. 'Does this mean that you are going to come with Mother and Daddy to see me at half-term? Oh, do say you will!'

'Who knows?' said Darrell teasingly. 'I might find time to visit, or I might not. You will just have to wait and see.'

'Of course, I suppose you will have to see if you can

get time off from this new job of yours, won't you?' said Felicity. 'Won't I boast about it to the others when I get back to school – my sister an ace reporter!'

'A very junior reporter!' laughed Darrell. 'I daresay I shall be running errands and making the tea to start with.'

'Not for long,' said Felicity confidently. 'You always did have a talent for writing, Darrell. Remember that super pantomime you wrote when you were in the fifth form?'

'Cinderella,' said Darrell with rather a wistful smile. 'Yes, I still have a copy of the script. What a happy time that was!'

Darrell seemed to grow rather quiet and thoughtful then and, at last, Felicity asked, 'Is anything wrong, Darrell?'

'Oh, I was just thinking about what you said earlier,' replied her sister. 'About not knowing anyone who hasn't benefited from being at Malory Towers. You see, I can think of someone.'

'Who?' asked Felicity, surprised and curious.

'Gwendoline Lacey,' answered Darrell. 'She was in my form all the way through the school. Remember her, Felicity?'

'Oh, yes, I remember Gwen, all right!' said Felicity. 'Of course, I didn't know her nearly as well as you did, but she seemed awfully spoilt and stuck-up. Sly, too.'

'Yes, that just about sums up Gwendoline,' said Darrell rather sadly. 'She had a great many hard lessons at Malory Towers, but never seemed to learn anything from them.'

'Wasn't her father taken ill suddenly?' said Felicity.

'That's right,' said Darrell. 'At one time it looked as if he wouldn't pull through, but fortunately he recovered, though he never regained his full health. Actually, I think that Gwen did learn something from that, for she was suddenly brought to realise what is truly important in life.'

'What a horrid way to learn it, though!' said Felicity with a shudder. 'Thank heavens that Mr Lacey recovered.'

'Yes, but he wasn't able to return to his job,' said Darrell. 'Which meant that Gwen and her mother had to learn to lead a much more simple life than they had been used to.'

'That must have been very difficult for them both,' said Felicity.

'Yes, but it may also have been the making of them,' said Darrell. 'I certainly hope so.'

'Do you still keep in touch with Gwen?' asked Felicity curiously.

'No,' said Darrell. 'For we weren't close friends. Well, Gwen didn't really have any close friends. We did exchange a few letters when her father was taken ill, and she left Malory Towers, but that sort of petered out after a while. I wonder what she is doing now?'

'Well, I know what you two should be doing now!' said the girls' mother, coming into the kitchen in time to hear this last remark. 'Darrell, it's almost time for you to leave for work. And Felicity, Daddy is just loading the car up, then it will be time for us to set off for Malory Towers.'

'Heavens, is that the time?' said Felicity, glancing at the clock on the wall, before getting up from the breakfast table.

Darrell remained at the table, a rather wistful expression on her face, and Felicity asked, 'What are you thinking?'

'I was just remembering my last term,' she said with a sigh. 'I wanted to savour every moment and make it last as long as possible, and store up every memory so that I could think of my time at school fondly. And that's just what I did. I really made the most of that last term, Felicity. All of us did – except poor Gwen, of course. We worked hard and played hard.'

'That's exactly what I'm going to do,' vowed Felicity, feeling a surge of excitement, as always, at the thought of being back at school. Her last term was going to be one to remember!

The journey back to Malory Towers was very long indeed, but, to Felicity, it seemed to pass more quickly than any of the previous ones.

When the family stopped for a picnic lunch, she said as much to her parents, and Mrs Rivers said, 'It is probably because it is the last time that you will be making this journey. I expect your last term will simply fly by as well.'

'No, for I shan't let it,' said Felicity firmly. 'I am going to do as Darrell said, and make the most of every single minute – every single second!'

As the car drew closer to Malory Towers, Felicity sat up straight and gazed out of the window, drinking in every familiar landmark. There was the first glimpse of the sea in the distance, clear and blue, with the sun reflecting off its surface. And now she could see the cliffs, along which she had enjoyed so many happy walks. Then, as the car rounded a bend in the road, Felicity could see Malory Towers itself, grand and imposing, with its four towers – South, East, West and North Tower, the best one of all, for it was the one that she belonged to. And now she was going back there for the last time. As usual, on the first day of term, there was a great deal of hustle and bustle, the grounds full of people, as girls said hallo to their friends and goodbye to their parents. A big coach had just pulled up in the drive and girls poured out, most of them first and second formers.

'Oh, there's little Daffy,' said Mrs Rivers, as a small, dark girl sprang down from the steps of the coach and began chattering nineteen to the dozen with her friend. 'Doesn't she look sweet?'

'Yes, she looks sweet, all right,' murmured Felicity drily, for she knew that Daffy's looks were deceptive and hid a very naughty streak indeed. The girl had got into so much trouble in her first term that she had come very close to being sent away from Malory Towers in disgrace. The shock had been so great that Daffy had mended her ways a little, and become a lot more thoughtful and considerate. But she still had a mischievous nature, and enjoyed playing tricks, especially on poor old Mam'zelle Dupont, one of the school's two French mistresses.

As Felicity and her parents got out of the car, Daffy raced across the lawn to greet a group of her friends, all of them making a great deal of noise.

Felicity had spotted a group of her friends, too, but, as Head Girl, she couldn't sprint across to greet them as Daffy had done, much as she wanted to. Instead, she turned to her parents, saying, 'Well, dears, I shall see you both at half-term. And I shall write every week, of course.'

'See that you do,' said Mr Rivers gruffly, giving her a hug.

'Yes, for I so look forward to your letters,' said Mrs Rivers. 'Do have a good term, dear – and don't forget your night case.'

Felicity hugged her mother, picked up her night case and said goodbye, feeling glad, as she walked across to join a group of sixth formers, that her parents were sensible, and had never been the kind to indulge in long, emotional farewells.

'Felicity, you're back!'

'Nice to see you again! Had good hols?'

'Isn't it grand to be back?'

Felicity beamed round at the others – Pam, Nora, Bonnie, Amy, June, Freddie, Alice – and, of course, her best friend, Susan. How good it was to see them all again! Even the snobbish Amy looked pleased to be back.

'I say, you've had your hair cut, Amy!' said Nora, admiring the girl's sleek, golden bob. 'Very smart, I must say!'

'Are we all here?' Felicity asked. 'Oh, no, Julie and Lucy are missing. I daresay they are down at the stables.'

'And I suppose you've heard that Gillian and Delia aren't coming back?' said Susan. 'Gillian decided to take up a place at music college, and Delia is going with her so that she can have her voice trained.'

'Yes, I had a letter from Delia in the holidays and she told me,' said Felicity. 'I shall miss them both, but it's a marvellous opportunity for them.'

Gillian was a very talented musician, while her friend, Delia, had an excellent singing voice, and both girls had been very popular with the others.

'I wonder if we will have any new girls this term?' said Pam. 'Probably not, for it would be most unusual for someone to change schools in their last term.'

But, as it turned out, the girls *were* to have a new addition to their form, as they found out when they went to Matron's room to hand in their health certificates.

'Well, girls!' said Matron in her crisp tone. 'This is the very last time that I shall ask you for your health certificates. And my word, won't I be glad to see the back of you, for you've been an awfully troublesome lot!'

But Matron was smiling, and the girls knew that she was joking.

Making her eyes wide and innocent, June said, 'Matron, you surely aren't suggesting that I have been troublesome! Why, I have been as good as gold.'

'June, you are responsible for more of my grey hairs than any other girl in the school!' said Matron, shaking her head. 'And your cousin, Alicia, was just as bad in her day. I'm just thankful that you don't have a younger sister to follow in your footsteps! Now, let me have your health certificates and you can go and unpack. You are all in the same dormitory, along with Julie and Lucy, and Lizzie Mannering.'

'Lizzie Mannering?' said Nora, puzzled. 'But she's a fifth former, Matron.'

'Not any more,' said Matron. 'Miss Grayling has decided to put her up into the sixth form a term early.'

'How odd!' said Freddie as the girls made their way to the dormitory. 'I know that Lizzie is supposed to be awfully clever and studious, but it seems rather strange to separate her from her friends and put her with us.'

'Actually, I don't think that Lizzie has many friends among the fifth formers,' said Felicity. 'She was head of the form, you know, and she took it all a little too seriously for their liking.'

'That's right,' said Bonnie. 'I remember Elsie of the fifth saying that Lizzie is frightfully domineering, and doesn't care for fun and jokes.'

'Apparently she used to spend all of her spare time in the common-room studying,' said Nora. 'Imagine! And she was most disapproving of the others when they chose not to follow her lead and wanted to relax and have a little fun instead.'

'She sounds like a bit of a wet blanket,' said June, pulling a face. 'Just what we need in our last term!'

'I don't think she will try throwing her weight around with us, as she did with the fifth formers,' said Felicity. 'For we are all older than her and have been in the top form for two terms already.'

'She had better not!' said June, rather belligerently. 'Or she'll be sat on, good and hard.'

Lizzie was already in the dormitory when the others arrived and, looking at her hard, Felicity thought that she didn't look domineering at all. In fact, she looked rather scared and nervous.

Lizzie was a tall, slim girl with long, dark hair, which she wore in a thick plait over one shoulder. She had clear skin and bright blue eyes, and would have been very pretty indeed if only she didn't look so terribly serious all the time.

The girl had been arranging some things in her bedside locker, but straightened up as the others entered, looking at them rather warily.

'Hallo, Lizzie,' said Felicity in her friendly way. 'Welcome to the sixth!'

The others welcomed her too, and Lizzie said, 'Thank you. I feel awfully honoured to be here.'

'Why *are* you here?' asked June rather bluntly. 'I mean to say, what made Miss Grayling take you out of the fifth form a term early?'

'She said that, as my work was so far in advance of the others, she thought that it would do me good to go up into the sixth,' said Lizzie. 'I must say, I'm very pleased that she did, for you all seem so much more mature and sensible than the fifth formers.'

'Appearances can be deceptive,' murmured June to Freddie. Aloud, she said smoothly, 'What a shame that the fifth formers didn't live up to your high standards. I hope that we don't let you down, Lizzie.'

Lizzie was unsure how to take this, and looked a little puzzled, so Felicity stepped in, saying, 'Let's unpack quickly, girls, before the bell goes for tea. I don't know about you, but I'm starving!'

Since everyone was very hungry, they obeyed at once, and when Lizzie went to the bathroom to wash her hands, June gave a grimace. 'Lizzie might have given up her domineering ways, but she's awfully prim and proper,' she said. 'I don't like her.'

'Oh, June, do give her a chance!' said Pam. 'Why, you've only known the girl for two minutes.'

'That's long enough,' said June. 'She's the sort of person who makes me want to act all childish, and do stupid things like sticking my tongue out at her, or pulling faces.'

The others laughed, but Alice said rather hesitantly, 'I do think that Pam is right, though, and we should give Lizzie a chance. After all, you were decent enough to give me one.'

This made the others think, for Alice had first joined

Malory Towers in the second form, as the unpopular and unpleasant Josephine Jones, and had ended up being sent away. Two terms ago, she had persuaded Miss Grayling to let her join the school again, and had proved beyond doubt to the others that she had changed her ways for good.

Felicity looked at Alice, who appeared quite different now that she no longer wore glasses. Her confidence had grown too, and she was no longer the nervous, timid girl who had first joined the sixth form. Well, thought Felicity, perhaps Lizzie could change too, and realise that it was possible to take life a little too seriously at times, and there was no harm in having a little fun now and again.

The new mistress

Felicity was most surprised when, as she finished breakfast the following morning, Miss Potts, the stern head of North Tower, came over and told her that Miss Grayling would like to see her. Wondering what the Head wanted, Felicity went along to her room at once, and tapped on the door.

'Come in,' came Miss Grayling's clear voice, and Felicity entered, relieved to see that the Head was smiling.

'Well, Felicity,' said the Head, after inviting her to sit down. 'It is the beginning of your final term at Malory Towers, and I am very pleased indeed with the way that most of you sixth formers have turned out. You are, on the whole, good, kind, responsible young women, who have got the most out of your time at Malory Towers and learned all that it can teach you.'

Felicity knew very well that the Head did not just mean the lessons that could be learned in the classroom, and she flushed with pleasure.

'But there are always new things to learn,' Miss Grayling went on. 'That is why this term I have arranged some special classes for the sixth form, which I hope that you will enjoy, and which I think will be of benefit to you as you prepare to go out into the world.'

Of course, Felicity was very excited and curious indeed. What could the Head be talking about?

'A new teacher will be starting at Malory Towers this term,' said Miss Grayling. 'And she will be teaching you sixth formers such things as deportment, etiquette and so on.'

'The kind of things we would learn at a finishing school, Miss Grayling?' said Felicity, sounding most surprised, for she certainly hadn't expected this.

'That is right,' said the Head. 'I realise that some members of your form may not take to the idea as readily as others, but I would like them to attend the classes anyway, for it is always good to be open to new ideas and different ways of doing things.'

'Of course, Miss Grayling,' said Felicity rather faintly, for she wasn't too sure whether she was keen on the idea of these new classes herself!

'There is one other thing that you should know,' said Miss Grayling. 'The name of your teacher is Miss Lacey. Miss Gwendoline Lacey.'

For a moment Felicity thought that she hadn't heard the Head correctly, then she gave a little gasp.

'Gwendoline! How odd. You see, Miss Grayling, Darrell and I were talking about her only yesterday, and wondering what had become of her.'

'Well, now your curiosity has been satisfied,' said the Head with a smile. 'I realise that Gwendoline – or Miss Lacey, as you must call her now – was not the most popular of girls when she was a pupil here, but I trust that you and the others will put that behind you and treat her with the same respect you would show any other mistress. She is certainly very well-qualified to teach you in matters of etiquette and so on, for she went to a very fine finishing school herself.'

Felicity frowned at this, saying, 'I thought that Gwen – Miss Lacey – was unable to go to finishing school after her father was taken ill.'

'Fortunately her uncle stepped in and paid for Miss Lacey to take a course,' said the Head. 'Though she had to go to a school in England, and not one abroad, as she had hoped.'

'I see,' said Felicity, wondering how the others would take this news. Some of them – notably June and the tomboyish Julie – would be less than thrilled, she felt, both at the idea of having to attend the classes, and at being taught by Gwen, of all people!

But it seemed that Miss Grayling had finished with the subject, for she had now begun talking about Lizzie Mannering.

'I daresay that you were surprised to find that I had put Lizzie up into the sixth form,' said the Head.

'Yes, we were, to be honest,' said Felicity. 'I know that she is a very clever girl, but . . .'

Her voice tailed off, for she could hardly tell Miss Grayling that she thought her idea had been a strange one!

But the Head seemed to realise her dilemma, for she

smiled, and said, 'Normally I would not consider such a thing at this late stage in a pupil's education, but I considered it would be good for Lizzie, and good for the others in the fifth form.'

Miss Grayling paused for a moment, considering her words, then she went on, 'Lizzie has many good qualities, but she was not popular with the others in the fifth form because of her strictness and very serious nature. Succeeding at her studies means everything to Lizzie, and it is stopping her from growing into a well-rounded person. Also, I feel that she lacks tolerance and understanding at times. Because of this, she has not been entirely successful as head of the form, which is a shame, because I feel that she has the makings of a very worthwhile person. Perhaps she could even be a future Head Girl of Malory Towers, but only if she learns those things that she needs to learn. That, Felicity, is why I have put her into the sixth form.'

'You think that we may be able to teach her these things, Miss Grayling?' said Felicity, looking most surprised.

'I hope so,' said the Head. 'It would have been more difficult for her to learn them in the fifth form, where the girls have already formed an unfavourable opinion of her. But among new people, who are a little older and wiser than she is, and whose opinion she might value more than that of the fifth formers, I feel that she might do better. Then, when the rest of the fifth form join her next term, they will have had a break from her, and, hopefully, they will see changes in her.'

'Well, we will certainly do our best, Miss Grayling,' said Felicity.

'I know that I can rely on you,' said the Head. 'It might help if you, or one of the others, can encourage Lizzie to open up to you a little. You see, Felicity, I know a little about her home life, and I know that things haven't been easy for her. Of course, it would be quite wrong of me to say any more, but if Lizzie chooses to tell you herself, that is quite a different matter.'

Felicity was deep in thought as she made her way to the class-room, for Miss Grayling's words had brought to mind a little incident that had occurred earlier that morning.

The sixth form had been making their way to the dining-room, when they were overtaken by three giggling first formers – Daffy Hope, her friend Katie and a new girl. Daffy whispered something to the new girl that made her squeal with laughter, and Felicity, walking next to Lizzie, felt the girl stiffen beside her. Then Lizzie called out sharply, 'Edith, come here at once!'

The little first former turned, her face a picture of dismay as she walked over to Lizzie, and the sixth formers watched in astonishment as Lizzie took the girl aside and began to scold her roundly. None of them could hear what she was saying, but it was obvious from Lizzie's expression, and her tone, that she was very angry indeed, and when the first former went off to join her new friends, it was with a very subdued air.

'I say, you were a bit hard on that new kid, weren't you, Lizzie?' said Lucy. 'All the poor thing did was laugh!'

'Lizzie doesn't much care for the sound of laughter,' said June with a touch of malice. 'Do you, Lizzie?'

'That's enough, June,' said Felicity, seeing Lizzie turn red. 'All the same, Lizzie, Lucy is quite right. If you come down too hard on the youngsters over petty little things they will soon grow to resent you.'

'Yes, but you see, Edith isn't just any first former, as far as I am concerned,' said Lizzie a little stiffly. 'She is my sister, and I intend to see that she doesn't waste her time here at Malory Towers playing the fool.'

'Poor Edith!' said June, raising her brows. 'She has my sympathy, for she's not going to have much of a time of it here with you watching her every move.'

Most of the others felt the same, and Susan said, 'But she didn't do anything wrong, Lizzie. All of the youngsters get a bit over-excited on the first day of term, and even the mistresses make allowances for them, so I think that we should too.'

'Besides, your sister has to learn to stand on her own two feet and make her own mistakes,' said Pam.

'And she won't thank you for it if you keep ticking her off in front of her friends,' put in Nora. 'Take my word for it.'

'I don't mean to be hard on her,' said Lizzie, looking rather hounded. 'But I promised that I would look out for her, and I don't want to see her getting into bad company. Daffy Hope . . .'

Felicity frowned at this, for her family had been friends with the Hopes for a number of years, and she said firmly, 'Daffy is a good kid at heart. She can be a bit naughty at times, and is fond of jokes and tricks, but there is no harm in her. Anyway, there is no time to discuss it any further now, or we shall be late for breakfast, and I am sure that you don't want to set a bad example to your young sister, Lizzie.'

Felicity had glanced across at the first-form table as she ate her breakfast. She could clearly see the resemblance between Edith and Lizzie now, for the first former had the same thick, dark hair and bright blue eyes as her sister. She noticed too that the girl's blazer was a little too large for her, and the collar was beginning to fray slightly, while the skirt she wore had obviously been shortened to fit her. Were they Lizzie's hand-me-downs, Felicity wondered? Lizzie hadn't started at Malory Towers until the third form, which would explain why her old uniform was too big to fit her first-form sister.

It was clear that Edith was fast becoming friends with Daffy and Katie, for the three chattered away together over breakfast. But, Felicity noticed, Edith often looked across at her sister, a wary expression on her face, and if Lizzie was watching her, she soon fell silent.

Now, Felicity wondered if Edith had something to do with the difficult home life that Miss Grayling had hinted at, and she knew that she would have to tread very carefully indeed if she was to gain Lizzie's confidence.

Felicity was so lost in thought that, coming round a corner, she almost collided with one of the school maids.

'Oops, sorry, Daisy!' said Felicity. 'I was in a world of my own just then.'

'Oh, you did give me a start, Miss Felicity,' said Daisy, putting a hand to her heart.

Felicity hoped that the maid would not keep her talking too long, for Daisy was a great chatterbox and loved nothing more than a good gossip. Today, though, she seemed to be in a rush and hurried off without saying any more.

As she went on her way, Felicity greeted Miss Potts, who was leading a group of new girls from North Tower down the corridor, and she guessed that the mistress was taking them to see Miss Grayling. Edith Mannering was among them, looking rather nervous, and Felicity gave her a smile, which she returned shyly.

For a moment, Felicity felt wistful, wishing that she was one of the new girls, just starting out at Malory Towers, instead of finishing off. Then she remembered Darrell's words, and gave herself a shake. She mustn't waste a minute on being sad, or wishing for things that couldn't be. She had a whole term to fill with good memories for the future.

'Sorry I'm late, Miss Oakes,' said Felicity to the sixth-form mistress as she slipped into the classroom. 'Miss Grayling called me to her study.'

'Yes, Susan told me,' said Miss Oakes. 'We are just making out the time-table, Felicity, if you would like to copy it down from the blackboard.'

Felicity got out a pen and sheet of paper, and set to work. The first day of term was always nice, for there were no proper lessons. Instead, books were given out, and time-tables and lists of classroom duties were drawn up.

The sixth form seemed to have quite a lot of free periods, and Felicity guessed that some of them would be taken up by the Finishing School classes that Miss Grayling had discussed with her. Heavens, she couldn't wait to see how the others took the news when she told them at break-time.

As the sixth form were busily making out their time-tables, a taxi pulled up outside the main entrance of the school, and a young woman got out. She was well-dressed, though in rather a fussy way, a floaty scarf trailing from her neck and a huge brooch adorning her dress. As for the big, flower-trimmed hat she wore, it was really more suited to a garden party than a girls' school.

This seemed to occur to the young woman, for she hesitated outside the door and removed it, a rather apprehensive look in her eyes as she smoothed down her fluffy golden hair and picked up her suitcase.

Miss Gwendoline Mary Lacey had returned to Malory Towers.

Settling in

It was a gloriously sunny morning, and, at break-time, the sixth formers went outside and sat on the lawn, where Felicity broke the news to them about the Finishing School classes. As she had expected, reactions were mixed.

'Oh, how super!'

'What a waste of time! Who needs to learn stuff like that?'

'I think it will be jolly good fun!'

'Well, I don't. I can think of a dozen things I would rather be doing.'

'I find it quite laughable that we are supposed to learn anything from Gwendoline, of all people!' said June scornfully.

Felicity looked sharply at June, and said pointedly, 'Miss Grayling expects us to treat *Miss Lacey* with the respect that she deserves.'

'And that is exactly how I shall treat her,' retorted June. 'With the respect that she *deserves*.'

'I don't understand,' said Amy with a frown. 'Who is this Gwendoline Lacey?'

'Oh, of course, she was before your time,' said Susan.

'A few of you others won't have had the pleasure of meeting her, either.'

'Gwen was in the same form as my cousin, Alicia, and Felicity's sister, Darrell,' said June. 'And she is a sly, spiteful snob.'

'She *was*,' Felicity corrected her, with a stern look. 'She may have changed completely now, for she did go through a terrible time when her father was ill.'

'Perhaps,' said June, not sounding very convinced. 'But it sounds like she still got her way and went to finishing school, as she had always wanted. Surely, if she had been so concerned about her father, she would have stayed at home and helped her mother to care for him.'

'I quite liked the idea of Finishing School classes,' said Nora. 'Until I learned that Gwendoline was going to be taking them. I remember her making me learn a poem once, when she was in the fifth form, because she thought I had been pulling faces at her.'

'Nora, you *had* been pulling faces at her,' laughed Susan, much amused.

'Well, yes,' said Nora. 'But she could have made allowances for my youthful high spirits!'

'Gwen never made allowances for anything, once she took a dislike to someone,' said June. 'She punished me several times for the most trivial misdemeanours, but the truth of the matter was that she was using me to get back at Alicia. The two of them never got on, you know. Alicia was always making digs at Gwen, but Gwen was too afraid of my cousin's sharp tongue to retaliate.'

'I remember Gwendoline,' said Alice. 'But she may have changed, you know. It is possible for unlikeable characters to become likeable.'

'Well, you've certainly proved that,' said June, clapping the girl on the shoulder. 'But, as far as Gwen is concerned, I will believe it when I see it.'

'She sounds awful,' said Freddie, who hadn't known Gwendoline. 'But, at the same time, I'm dying to meet her just to satisfy my curiosity.'

'Yes, it will be interesting to see how she has turned out, and if she *has* changed at all,' said Pam. 'I wonder when she will arrive?'

None of the girls realised that Gwendoline was already at Malory Towers, for she had gone straight to Miss Grayling's study, where she had had a long talk with the Head.

'Well, Gwendoline,' Miss Grayling had said. 'I am pleased to welcome you back to Malory Towers as a member of staff.'

'Thank you, Miss Grayling,' Gwendoline had answered politely. 'I am very pleased to be here, and very grateful for the opportunity you have given me.'

Miss Grayling had looked at her hard, thinking that, outwardly, Gwen had not changed a great deal since her days as a pupil at the school. She was a little slimmer, and the long, golden hair, of which she had been so proud, had been cut into a more grown-up style, but apart from that she looked like the same old Gwendoline.

Had she changed inwardly, though, wondered the Head. That was what really mattered.

As their talk continued, it became apparent that Gwendoline still had the same airs and graces that everyone had disliked in her so much as a pupil. But the shrewd and wise Miss Grayling saw through them, and realised that, beneath them, was a worried and nervous young woman, striving to make her own way in the world. If only Gwendoline would stop putting on an act, how much easier she would find it! Perhaps, in time, she would come to realise that the girls would respond to her better if she dropped all her posing and behaved in a more natural way, as the other mistresses did. Gwendoline had come to Malory Towers to teach, but how marvellous it would be if she learned something as well.

Miss Grayling rang a bell on her desk and, a few moments later, Daisy, the maid, appeared.

'Daisy, please show Miss Lacey to her bedroom, so that she can unpack,' said the Head.

'Yes, Ma'am,' said Daisy, politely, before stooping to pick up Gwen's night case. 'Come this way, please, Miss Lacey.'

'Well, Daisy, so you are still working at Malory Towers,' said Gwen as she followed the maid up the stairs. 'You must have been here for quite a few years, for I was in the fifth form when you first started.'

'That's right, Miss Lacey,' said Daisy. 'I was the same age as you were then, when I began work.'

But Daisy must have led a very different life from

hers, thought Gwen, considering it for the first time. There had been no boarding school or finishing school for her, instead she had had to work, to help her family. Just as she, Gwen, was doing now. Looking at the girl, dressed in her neat, plain black dress and white apron, which all the maids wore, Gwen suddenly realised that she should be grateful for the good education she had received, for it meant that she did not have to undertake the same kind of menial work as poor Daisy. Perhaps she wasn't so badly off, after all.

Amy and Bonnie were simply thrilled at the thought of the Finishing School classes, while most of the others thought that, although they sounded like rather a waste of time, they might be good fun. Four girls, however, were very much against them. One, of course, was June. Quite apart from her dislike of Gwendoline, as games captain of the whole school she was very busy indeed and would much rather have spent the time coaching the youngsters at tennis, or arranging matches with other schools. Julie and Lucy, both of whom were rather tomboyish, couldn't see that the classes would be of any use to them at all. As Julie said, 'Why do I need to learn to walk like a fashion model when I shall be spending most of my time on horseback?'

The fourth was Lizzie, who was quite horrified that she would have to give up precious time that could have been devoted to studying.

'I will be going in for Higher Cert next year,' she said. 'And I was rather hoping that by coming up into the sixth this term I could get a head start.'

'Well, Lizzie, if you ask me, you spend far too much time poring over your books as it is,' said Felicity. 'It will do you good to think about something else. Besides, the rest of us have already taken Higher Cert, so this term is bound to be a slack one, as far as work is concerned.'

Lizzie was dismayed to hear this, and began to wonder if coming up into the sixth form had been such a good idea. She had liked being head-girl of the fifth, and had enjoyed the sense of importance and responsibility it had given her. Even if the others hadn't always seemed very grateful when she had tried to advise or guide them. But among the sixth formers she felt very small and insignificant indeed. The others were all older than she was, and there were several very strong characters in the form. Lizzie was bossy by nature, but the very thought of trying to take the lead over people like June, or Felicity, made her shake in her shoes, for she knew that they simply wouldn't stand for it and would put her very firmly in her place.

Still, there was one person at Malory Towers that she could offer guidance to – her young sister, Edith. Although Edith never seemed very grateful either!

Lizzie bit her lip as she thought of her encounter with the girl that morning. She hadn't meant to be hard on her sister, but Edith was young, and silly at times, and didn't fully realise how lucky she was to be at a good school like Malory Towers. It was vital that she made the most of the opportunity that she had been given and worked hard, and Lizzie intended to see that the girl didn't waste her time playing the fool with Daffy Hope and her friends. It was all very well for the other sixth formers to criticise, and say that she should leave Edith alone, but they didn't understand the situation, and didn't know what it felt like to be kept at Malory Towers by charity.

'I think that the classes are a marvellous idea,' said Amy. 'Don't you, Bonnie?'

'I certainly do,' said Bonnie. 'Miss Lacey will be able to teach us all sorts of things that will come in useful when we leave school.'

'Just what do you mean to do when you leave school, Bonnie?' asked Susan, curiously. 'Are you coming to university with us?'

'No, Amy and I have made a plan of our own,' said Bonnie. 'We are going to open our own dress shop. A very exclusive one, of course. Amy's father is going to lend us the money, I shall design the clothes, and Amy and I are going to run it together. With my skills and her connections I don't see how we can fail.'

Nor did the others, for Bonnie was very skilled indeed with her needle, and designed and made most of her own clothes. She was also very determined when she set her mind to something, and the girls felt certain that her venture with Amy would be a success.

'Well, I shall know where to come when I want a new dress,' said Nora. 'I wish that I had a talent like yours, Bonnie, but there's nothing that I'm particularly good at.

Mother wants me to go to secretarial college when I leave Malory Towers, but I haven't quite decided yet.'

'Well, I have decided what I am going to do, once I leave university,' said Pam. 'I would like to become a teacher.'

'Good for you, Pam!' said Julie, clapping her on the back. 'I'm sure you'll make a first-class one. And, who knows, you may end up teaching here at Malory Towers.'

'What about you, Julie?' asked Felicity. 'I bet you and Lucy both want jobs that have something to do with horses.'

'Well, my father breeds horses, as you know,' answered Julie. 'So Lucy and I are both going to work for him.'

'I'm so looking forward to it,' said Lucy, her eyes shining. 'Julie and I will be able to live together, and work together, and –'

'And eat, sleep and breathe horses!' said June, with a laugh. 'It will suit you both down to the ground. I'm hoping to train as a games teacher after I've been to university.'

The others stared at her, remembering the bold, bad, careless June who had first joined Malory Towers. Who would have thought then that she would one day want to become a teacher? The girl had had some grave faults in her character as a youngster, but she had overcome them, and, although she would probably always have a malicious streak, June had learned the meaning of responsibility and team spirit. If she had gone to another school, thought Felicity, one that wasn't as good as Malory Towers, she could have turned out very differently indeed.

Guessing at some of her friends' thoughts, June grinned, and said, 'I know, unbelievable, isn't it? But this last couple of years as games captain has pointed me in the right direction and shown me what it is I really want to do with my life.'

'Well, I can't think of anyone who would make a better games teacher,' said Felicity warmly. 'You've always been excellent at coaching, and bringing out the best in people. And, of course, none of your pupils will get away with playing any tricks on you, for you will be able to spot them a mile off, being such a joker yourself!'

Everyone laughed at this, and Pam said, 'Will you be following in Darrell's footsteps, Felicity?'

'No, because I don't have her talent for writing,' answered Felicity. 'I've always been better at things like Science and Biology. I would like to follow in my father's footsteps instead, and become a doctor. Not a surgeon, like he is, but a family doctor.'

The only one of her friends to whom Felicity had confided this ambition was Susan, and the others stared at her now, realising that the girl had chosen exactly the right career for herself. Felicity had always been kind and compassionate, and these qualities had grown within her over the years, and were just what a good doctor needed.

'How wonderful to have found your vocation,' said Alice.

'Yes, you're just the kind of doctor I would like to see if I was feeling under the weather,' said Nora. 'Always so calm and reassuring.'

'I'm hoping to enter the medical profession, too,' said Susan. 'But as a nurse. I say, Felicity, wouldn't it be marvellous if we could both do our training at the same hospital?'

'I wish I knew what I wanted to do,' said Freddie with a sigh. 'Still, I shall have a few years at university to think about it.'

'I'm undecided too,' said Alice. 'But I shan't starve, for Father will give me a job in his business while I think about it.'

Felicity was just about to ask Lizzie what she planned to do when she left school, but the girl suddenly spotted her young sister walking across the courtyard, and got to her feet, saying, 'Excuse me, I must just have a quick word with Edith.'

Edith was on her way to join Daffy and Katie, and her shoulders slumped as she heard her name called and saw Lizzie approaching.

'Come to tell me off again?' she said, a hint of defiance in her tone.

'Of course not,' said Lizzie, keeping her tone light. 'Why should I? Have you been up to mischief?'

'No,' answered Edith. 'But I hadn't been up to mischief at breakfast time either. That didn't stop you scolding me, though.'

'Oh, Edith, I didn't mean to scold,' said Lizzie, laying

a hand on her sister's arm. 'I promised Mother and Uncle Charles that I would look out for you, that's all.'

Lizzie had always looked out for her younger sister, and Edith had always looked *up* to her. But, after the incident at breakfast time, Daffy had said, 'I never let my big sister scold *me* like that! If you want to get the most out of your time at Malory Towers, Edith, you need to show Lizzie that you mean to stand on your own two feet and not allow her to boss you around all the time.'

'Daffy is quite right,' a girl called Ivy had put in. 'I have a cousin in the fifth, and she thought that she was going to queen it over me when I started here. But I soon set her straight and now she leaves me alone.'

Edith had realised that she was going to have to stand up to her sister if she was to win the respect of her fellow first formers. It wasn't going to be easy, for Lizzie had always ruled the roost at home, but Edith was determined, though her voice sounded more sulky than defiant as she said, 'You're just trying to spoil my fun.'

'You're not here to have fun,' said Lizzie sharply. 'You are here to work, and get good results. You know how important it is that we do well, for we can't let Uncle Charles down. It's thanks to his kindness and generosity that we are here, remember.'

'His charity, you mean,' said Edith, scowling at her sister. 'As if I am ever likely to forget.'

'Hush, Edith!' said Lizzie, as two girls walked by. 'Don't talk so loudly. We don't want everyone to know our business.'

'It's all right for you,' said Edith resentfully. 'Because you are the oldest, and bigger than me, you always have a new uniform each term, but I have to wear your ugly hand-me-downs. And they are so worn, and so ill-fitting that I shouldn't think it will be long before everyone guesses that we are poor.'

'Nonsense!' said Lizzie. 'Why, I am sure that lots of girls wear their big sisters' hand-me-downs.'

'Well, it's a pity that Uncle Charles's generosity didn't stretch a little further, so that I could at least have had a new blazer,' said Edith crossly.

'Edith, that's not fair!' said Lizzie. 'You know very well that Uncle Charles would have provided you with a complete new uniform, if it had occurred to him. But it didn't, and he has already been so kind, paying our fees, that Mother didn't like to ask him.'

Seeing that Edith looked as if she was about to argue, Lizzie went on quickly, 'Anyway, that is beside the point! You can work just as hard in a second-hand uniform as in a brand-new one. But not if you allow yourself to be distracted by the antics of Daffy Hope.'

'I like Daffy,' said Edith firmly. 'And Mother may have asked you to keep an eye on me, but she didn't say that you could choose my friends for me, Lizzie.'

'I can see that Daffy has had a bad effect on you already,' said Lizzie harshly. 'You would never have spoken to me like that before, for you always used to respect my opinion.'

'I still do,' said Edith in a more gentle tone, for she

was really very fond of her big sister. 'In some things. But how am I ever to learn to make my own decisions if you won't let me stand on my own two feet?'

Since Lizzie couldn't think of anything to say to this, it was as well that the bell which signalled the end of break-time rang.

But, as her sister ran towards the school, Lizzie stared after her, a bleak expression on her face. She simply couldn't allow Edith to waste the marvellous opportunity she had been given, and she was going to make jolly sure that the girl toed the line!

Good news for Edith

Felicity was the first of the sixth formers to meet Gwendoline. The girl was on her way to the library later that day, to return a book, when she spotted someone walking towards her. At first she didn't recognise Gwen, but as the young woman drew closer, Felicity suddenly realised who she was.

'Gwen!' she cried in surprise. Then she stammered, 'I beg your pardon! I mean, Miss Lacey.'

Gwen frowned, then her brow suddenly cleared and she said, with a smile, 'Why, it's Felicity Rivers! I hardly recognised you, for you were just a little second former when I left Malory Towers. Heavens, you're quite a young lady now.'

Felicity gave a laugh, and said, 'Well, perhaps I will be when I have attended some of your classes.'

'I certainly hope so,' said Gwen. 'Tell me, how is Darrell?'

'She's very well, thank you,' said Felicity. 'She has just started working as a reporter on a newspaper, you know. Goodness, she will be surprised when I tell her that you are teaching here.'

Felicity had been pleasantly surprised, for Gwen had

seemed quite friendly and natural. But now she gave a laugh which, to Felicity's ears, sounded rather false, and said, 'I expect that she will be. I have so much, so I wanted to do something to help others, and give something back to dear Malory Towers, as Miss Grayling has always urged us to do. The finishing school I went to was a first-rate one, you see, and I would like to put what I learned there to good use. Do give my regards to Darrell when you write, won't you, Felicity? Tell her that I'm sorry I didn't keep in touch, but I daresay she knows how it is – one is always so very busy!'

And with another, rather false laugh and a toss of her golden head, Gwen went on her way.

'It sounds as if she hasn't changed much,' said Nora, when Felicity told the others of the encounter at teatime.

'I don't know,' said Felicity thoughtfully. 'When I first bumped into her, she seemed very friendly and open. Then she suddenly put on this stuck-up act, just like the old Gwen.'

'More likely the friendliness was an act, knowing Gwen,' said June scornfully. 'I say, there she is now! She has just come in, with Miss Nicholson, the new Geography mistress.'

'What *is* she wearing?' asked Freddie with a giggle. 'Heavens, I've never seen so many bits and pieces! And that brooch she has on is the size of a dinner plate!'

'Gwen is getting more and more like her mother,' said Susan, smiling. 'I remember how Mrs Lacey always used to turn up at half-term, with scarves and veils flying everywhere.'

'I hope that Miss Grayling doesn't expect us to copy her style of dress,' said Amy, looking at the new teacher with disdain. 'I think that she looks rather vulgar.'

'Well, let's give her a chance,' said Felicity fair-mindedly. 'And her classes. Who knows, they might turn out to be good fun.'

The younger girls stared at Gwen unashamedly, for they had never seen a mistress quite like her before, and a flurry of whispering and giggling broke out.

Gwen was aware of it, turning a little pink, but she held her head high and appeared quite unconcerned as she and Miss Nicholson took their seats at the mistresses' table.

In fact, she felt very nervous indeed, particularly as many of the fifth and sixth formers remembered her from her time as a pupil at Malory Towers. And Gwen knew that their memories of her were not likely to do her any credit!

She had been very relieved indeed when Miss Grayling had told her that she was to share a study with Miss Nicholson, who, as well as being new, was young and very jolly. Gwen had dreaded that she might have to share with one of the mistresses who had taught her as a pupil, for she would have found that very awkward indeed!

She had already encountered several of the mistresses, including the stern Miss Potts, and they had welcomed her politely, but coolly, for all of them remembered the sly, stuck-up Gwendoline they had once taught. Only Mam'zelle Dupont had greeted her with warmth, for she had never seen through Gwen as the others had.

But, as silly as she was, Gwen knew that if she was to succeed as a teacher at Malory Towers, it was the good opinion of the girls that she had to win.

She felt heartened when Felicity caught her eye and gave her a smile, which she returned with genuine warmth. The others saw it too, and it made them think – perhaps Gwendoline really *had* changed for the better!

The late afternoon sun was pleasantly warm and, when she had finished her tea, June said, 'I'm off for a quick dip in the pool before prep. Anyone else fancy coming?'

Felicity, Susan and Freddie accepted this invitation eagerly, and the four girls hurried off to fetch their swimming costumes.

There were several younger girls in the pool by the time the sixth formers had got changed, and June's keen eye was caught by one of them in particular.

'My word, who's that?' she asked as the girl moved swiftly and gracefully through the water, effortlessly overtaking anyone in front of her.

'I don't know who she is, but she's jolly good,' said Felicity, watching in admiration. 'Fast, as well. I wouldn't be surprised if she could beat some of us sixth formers in a race.'

Then the swimmer climbed out of the pool, pulling

off her tight bathing cap, and Susan said, 'Why, it's young Edith Mannering!'

June was at the girl's side at once, saying, 'Edith! I was just watching you swim and you really are very good.'

Edith, quite overawed at being addressed by the games captain of Malory Towers, flushed with pleasure, and said, 'Thanks, June. I absolutely adore swimming.'

'Then I have some good news for you,' said June, grinning. 'For I want you to put in as much practice as possible. There is a swimming gala coming up in a couple of months, against four other schools in the area. And you, my dear Edith, are going to take part. Can you dive?'

Speechless with delight, Edith could only nod, and June said, 'Well, see that you practise that as well.'

Then she gave the girl a careless pat on the shoulder, before getting into the pool herself. Edith was surrounded at once by a group of first formers, all eager to offer their congratulations.

'Well done, Edith!' cried Daffy, clapping her on the back. 'June told me last term that she wants me to take part in the gala too, so we shall be able to practise together.'

'You must be frightfully bucked!' said Katie. 'I say, won't this be a bit of good news to give that sister of yours?'

'Yes, she'll be awfully proud of you,' said Ivy. 'After all, it's not everyone who has the honour of being chosen to swim for the school – and on your very first day, too!'

This hadn't occurred to Edith, and her face lit up now at the thought of how pleasant it would be to win back Lizzie's approval.

'I think that I shall go and tell her as soon as I have changed,' she said.

'Well, be quick,' said Katie. 'It will be time for prep soon!'

Edith changed quickly, then sped along to Lizzie's study, her cheeks flushed and eyes sparkling as she tapped on the door.

'Come in!' called out Lizzie, her expression most astonished as her young sister pushed open the door. 'Edith! What are you doing here? Has something happened?'

'Yes, the most marvellous thing!' said Edith, coming into the room. 'Lizzie, what do you think? June has chosen me to take part in the swimming gala! Isn't it wonderful?'

Eagerly, Edith waited for her sister's congratulations and words of praise. But they didn't come. Instead, Lizzie frowned and said, 'That's very nice, of course. But June will expect you to put in a lot of extra practice, and think how that will affect your studies. You will have to tell her that you can't do it.'

Edith's face fell as she stared at Lizzie in disbelief. 'You want me to turn down an honour like that?' she said. 'Lizzie, most girls would give anything to be chosen to swim for the school!'

'I daresay,' said Lizzie. 'But you aren't most girls,

Edith, and you don't have time for such things.'

For a moment Edith stared at her sister, then she burst out, 'I don't know why I expected you to be pleased for me! You have no time for the jolly, fun things in life, and you don't seem to care much for the honour of the school, though you should, for you have been here far longer than me. Well, I *shall* take part in the gala, Lizzie, for June is in charge of games, not you!'

With that, the girl flounced out of the room, slamming the door behind her, and Lizzie sighed heavily. This was just what she had feared, that something would happen to distract Edith from her work – but she hadn't expected it to happen quite this soon! Well, if Edith refused to back down, she, Lizzie, would just have to speak to June about it, and ask her to drop the girl from the swimming team.

It wasn't a task that she relished, however, and it took Lizzie several days to work up the courage to approach June.

Before that, there came the excitement of the sixth formers' first Finishing School class.

Miss Grayling had arranged for a disused room on the ground floor of North Tower to be cleared out so that Gwen could use it for her classes, but the door had remained locked and the sixth formers were very curious to see inside. There were to be separate classes for each tower, Miss Oakes had told the girls, for Miss Lacey felt that it was very important that she was able to give each pupil enough individual attention.

The North Tower girls felt very honoured that the new class-room was in their tower, of course.

'It makes it seem as if it belongs to *us*, somehow,' as Nora said. 'Though we shall have to let the girls from the other towers borrow it sometimes.'

They were also delighted to find that they were to be the first to use the new class-room, and all of them felt very curious indeed as they poured in on Friday afternoon. Gwen was already there, and she smiled to see the looks of astonishment on their faces as they walked in. For this was no ordinary class-room. Instead of desks and hard wooden chairs, there were sofas and armchairs. Large plants in big pots were dotted around, green velvet curtains framed the windows, and, in the corner of the room, there was a big dining table, surrounded by chairs. The room had been freshly painted in a lovely pale green, and framed pictures hung on the walls. The only thing that made it look slightly like a class-room was the large blackboard on one of the walls.

Of course, everyone was thrilled at the thought of taking lessons in such pleasant surroundings, though Amy said with a sniff, 'This furniture is awfully shabby. And the curtains have been darned.'

'I expect the room has been furnished from odd bits and pieces that have been lying around for years,' said Felicity. 'It would have cost a fortune if Miss Grayling had bought everything new.'

'Well, I believe that if a thing is worth doing it's worth doing properly,' said Amy in her haughty manner.

'Second-hand furnishings and a second-rate teacher don't bode very well, if you ask me!'

Felicity looked round sharply at Gwen, for Amy hadn't troubled to lower her voice, but she was plumping up one of the cushions and didn't appear to have heard the girl's cutting remarks.

Gwen allowed the girls a few minutes to wander round and inspect everything, then she clapped her hands together, and called out, 'Sit down, please, girls.'

At once the girls sat down, some on the sofas, others in the armchairs, several of them glancing curiously at Gwen as they did so. Most of them thought that she looked very confident and poised, but Felicity saw a hint of uncertainty and anxiety in the young woman's eyes, and realised that Gwen was not quite as sure of herself as she wanted everyone to believe. Felicity wondered if she was the only one who noticed the slight tremor in the new teacher's voice, as Gwen said, 'Well, that was your first test. Some of you passed, while others didn't.'

The sixth formers looked at one another in puzzlement, and Gwen went on, 'Pam, you flopped down on that sofa like a sack of potatoes – not very elegant! And Julie, please will you sit on the seat, not astride the arm. You are not riding a horse now!'

And so Gwen went round the class, telling this girl to sit up straight, and that one not to stick her feet out. Only Nora and Bonnie came in for wholehearted praise, Gwen telling them that they had both sat down very gracefully – 'As ladies should.'

There was one girl that Gwen didn't speak to at all, her eyes merely flicking over her coldly before moving on – and that was Amy. The girl had taken her seat every bit as elegantly as Nora and Bonnie, but not a word of praise came her way. Felicity realised then that Gwen *had* overheard the girl's remarks, and been hurt by them. Amy realised it too, and knew that she had made a bad start with the new teacher, but she shrugged it off. There was nothing that Miss Lacey could teach *her*, of that she was quite certain.

On the whole, though, most of the girls found the lesson far more amusing than they had hoped, particularly when each girl had to walk round the room, a book balanced on her head.

'Keep your back straight, Susan!' called out Gwen. 'June, don't walk quite so quickly. Oh dear, Lucy, you're supposed to glide, not stomp!'

Even Nora, Bonnie and Amy, all three of whom were naturally very graceful, couldn't manage to balance the book on their head all the way round the room, but they did very much better than the others. Again, though, while Nora and Bonnie were singled out for praise, Gwen simply ignored Amy.

'Oh dear,' thought Felicity. 'Gwen really does have it in for Amy. I do hope that it's not going to lead to any trouble.'

Felicity knew that Gwen had used spiteful and underhand methods to get back at those she disliked when she had been a pupil at the school. Surely, she wouldn't resort to such tactics now that she had grown up, and was a teacher?

Felicity spoke to Amy about it in the dormitory that evening, but the girl was unrepentant. She carried on brushing her silky, golden bob and said in a bored voice, 'I don't particularly care for Miss Lacey's opinion of me.'

'You'll care all right if she reports you to the Head,' said Felicity. 'You really shouldn't have said that she was a second-rate teacher, you know.'

Amy looked a little worried at this, for she was very much in awe of Miss Grayling, and certainly didn't want to be reported to her.

'Very well,' she said. 'I shall be all sweetness and light in the next class, and make it up to Miss Lacey.'

But alas for such good intentions, Amy had another encounter with Gwendoline the very next day.

The teacher was walking along the corridor, reading a letter, and she walked round a corner, colliding with Amy, who was coming the other way. Both the letter and the handbag that she was carrying flew from Gwendoline's grasp, the bag strewing its contents all over the floor, and she gave an irritated exclamation.

The mishap had not been Amy's fault, for Gwen had not been looking where she was going but, in an effort to make amends for her behaviour yesterday, the sixth former said politely, 'Oh, I'm so sorry, Miss Lacey. Are you hurt?'

Gwen wasn't hurt at all but, as she looked at Amy, and remembered the spiteful words that the girl had uttered yesterday, bitterness rose up within her. As it was Saturday, and the girls were allowed to wear what they pleased, Amy was dressed in a very expensive, but very simple, blue dress with a neat collar. She looked fresh and charming, and Gwen, with her frills and adornments, suddenly felt silly and over-dressed beside her.

'You silly, clumsy girl!' she snapped. 'Pick my things up at once!'

Now, Amy had been about to offer to do just that, in an effort to get into Gwen's good books, but the unfairness of the teacher's words, and her harsh tone, nettled her, and she said, 'I don't see why I should, Miss Lacey, for *you* walked into me.'

'How dare you?' gasped Gwen. 'I've a good mind to report you to Miss Grayling for insolence.'

But, even as she uttered the words, Gwen knew that she would do nothing of the kind. It would not reflect well on her, she knew, if she had to report one of the girls to the Head for cheeking her, for it might look as if she was poor at discipline.

So, instead, she said stiffly, 'I shan't report you on this occasion, Amy. But I want you to write out "I must always pay attention and look where I am going" fifty times. Bring it to my study after tea.'

Amy was simply furious at this, for she had been looking forward to a nice, lazy afternoon, and instead she was going to have to spend part of it doing a punishment that she hadn't earned at all. But she knew that to argue with the teacher might well result in greater punishment, so the girl gritted her teeth and said politely, 'Yes, Miss Lacey.'

But Amy did have the satisfaction, as she walked away, of looking back over her shoulder and seeing Gwen on her hands and knees as she picked up her belongings. Her feelings were soothed even further when she walked out into the courtyard and was greeted by Violet Forsyth of the first form. The plump little Violet had a great admiration for Amy, and she approached her now, saying breathlessly, 'Oh, Amy, how pretty you look today. That dress is so lovely.'

'Why, thank you, Violet,' said Amy, preening a little. It was a pity, she reflected, that she couldn't say the same for the first former, who was wearing a frilled, flounced creation that her mother had bought her, and which didn't become her at all. Violet, who was beginning to grow out of the fussy dresses that she had once loved, also realised that the style did not suit her and, rather nervously, she said to Amy, 'I wonder if you would mind telling me where you got the dress?'

Amy, who loved nothing better than to bask in flattery and admiration, was only too happy to give Violet this information, adding kindly, 'If you don't mind me saying so, Violet, I think that this style would suit you perfectly. Perhaps you could ask your mother to buy you something similar?'

Violet was simply thrilled at the interest that Amy had taken in her, and ran off to the first-form common-room at once, to write a letter to her mother, asking for a new dress. Her parents were very wealthy, and never refused their daughter anything, and Violet knew that it would not be long before a parcel containing the coveted dress arrived for her. Perhaps she could stop curling her hair every night, too, and have it cut into a bob like Amy's. My word, that would certainly make the others sit up and take notice!

Gwen's missing letter

Lizzie had settled into the sixth form in her own way, finding most of the girls pleasant and easy to get along with. There were a few that she was a little wary of, though, like the snobbish Amy, who seemed very grand indeed to Lizzie, and the sharp-tongued June, whom she was secretly a little afraid of.

Which was why Lizzie felt very nervous indeed now, as she knocked on the door of June's study, before gingerly pushing open the door. As always, June's desk was littered with papers, and the girl was frowning heavily at a list that she held in her hand. She didn't look up, and Lizzie gave a cough.

'What is it?' asked June impatiently. Then she glanced up, saw Lizzie hovering uncertainly in the doorway and her brow cleared.

'Sorry,' she said. 'I didn't mean to sound unfriendly, I was just absorbed in making out this rota for swimming practice. What can I do for you, Lizzie?'

'I wondered if I might have a word with you,' said Lizzie.

'Of course,' said June, putting down the list she had been holding. 'Come in and pull up a chair.'

Lizzie did so, but before she could speak, June said, 'My goodness, that young sister of yours swims like a fish! She's causing me some dreadful problems, though.'

'Oh?' said Lizzie hopefully, thinking that if Edith was causing problems for June, the games captain might be thinking about dropping her from the gala. Her hopes were dashed, though, when June said, 'Yes, you see she is superb at diving and swimming, so I'm really not sure which to enter her for in the gala. It's a pity that she can't do both, but I don't want her splitting herself in two, so to speak, for then I shan't get the best out her. It will be far better if she just concentrates on one or the other. Though perhaps she would want to do both? Oh, sorry, Lizzie, once I start talking about the swimming gala, I can't seem to stop! Now, what was it you wanted to say?'

Lizzie looked at June for a moment, sizing her up. She was a very downright person, who always said exactly what was on her mind, and Lizzie decided that the best way to tackle her was by being just as downright herself. So, hoping that she didn't sound as nervous as she felt, Lizzie took a deep breath, and said, 'I know that this will seem strange, but I want you to drop Edith from the gala.'

June raised her eyebrows at this, and said, 'Do you, indeed? May I ask why?'

'It's very important that Edith concentrates on her schoolwork,' said Lizzie, looking June in the eye. 'The swimming gala is a distraction.'

'Most girls seem able to fit in their schoolwork and

make time for sports and other hobbies,' said June, staring hard at Lizzie. 'And it is quite right that they should, for it is important to get a proper balance between work and play. Is this Edith's decision, or yours?'

'Mine,' answered Lizzie coolly. 'You see, June, my mother is relying on me to make sure that Edith knuckles down, and I feel that dropping her from the gala would be for the best.'

'Well, I'm sorry to disappoint you,' said June, equally coolly. 'But I have no intention of doing such a thing.'

'I am Edith's older sister,' said Lizzie, her temper rising. 'And I insist –'

But she got no further, for June was on her feet, eyes blazing. 'How dare you?' she said, her tone icy, and as stern as that of any mistress. 'You might be Edith's older sister, but I am games captain, and you don't have the right to *insist* on anything. I don't allow anyone to interfere with my decisions. Edith is taking part in the gala, and that, my dear Lizzie, is that.'

'I shall go to Miss Potts!' said Lizzie, feeling very angry herself now. 'She will back me up, I am sure.'

'And I am quite sure that she won't,' said June flatly. 'Go to the Head herself, if you wish, Lizzie, but it won't do any good.'

The two girls glared at one another for a moment, then Lizzie left the room, resisting the impulse to slam the door behind her. She went straight to Miss Potts's room, where the mistress was busy marking the first form's maths prep, and tapped on the door.

Mam'zelle Dupont, who was also there, shouted out, '*Entrez!*' and the girl went in.

'Ah, Lizzie!' cried Mam'zelle as the girl entered. Then she peered closely at the girl's pale, serious face, and said kindly, 'Is anything wrong, *ma chère*?'

'Not exactly,' said Lizzie. 'Actually it was Miss Potts I wanted to speak to.'

'What is it, Lizzie?' asked Miss Potts, looking up from her work.

Quickly, Lizzie explained the matter to Miss Potts, who, as well as being in charge of North Tower, was also the first-form mistress.

Miss Potts listened, a serious expression on her face, then she said, 'Lizzie, I can't possibly interfere in any decision that June makes as games captain. Besides, your sister is not behind in her studies in any way, so there is no reason at all why she can't take part in the swimming gala.'

'This is very true,' said Mam'zelle. 'The little Edith is excellent at French. Besides, what is it they say? Ah, I have it! *All work and no play makes Jack a dull boy!*'

Miss Potts's rather stern features relaxed into a smile at this, and she said to Lizzie, 'Mam'zelle is quite right. It wouldn't hurt you to take up some kind of sport, or hobby, Lizzie, for you are growing one-sided. I really think that you should give it some thought.'

Lizzie couldn't very well argue with Miss Potts, so she agreed that she would, then left the room – only to walk smack into June!

'So, you went to Miss Potts, after all,' said June. 'What did she say? Is she going to tell me that I can't have Edith for the swimming gala?'

Lizzie didn't reply. She didn't need to, for her flushed face and downcast eyes were answer enough, and June smiled.

'Well, I did warn you,' she said, before going on her way, whistling an annoying little tune that made Lizzie clench her fists angrily.

Dispiritedly, the girl went back to her own study, sitting down at the desk and resting her chin in her hands. A cleft appeared between her brows as she wondered what to do next. She could always write to her mother, of course, or Uncle Charles. But Mother had quite enough on her plate at the moment, and if Uncle Charles got it into his head that Edith was wasting her time at Malory Towers, he might refuse to continue paying the fees.

Suddenly, Lizzie heard footsteps in the corridor outside, followed by the sound of voices.

It was Felicity and Susan – and a thought came to Lizzie. Perhaps June would listen to Felicity. After all, she was Head Girl, and the two of them had known one another for years. Getting up, she opened the door and put her head out. 'Felicity!' she called. 'Could you spare me a moment, please?'

'Of course,' said Felicity. 'Susan, I'll meet you down at the tennis court in ten minutes.'

Then she followed Lizzie into her study, saying, 'You

really shouldn't be indoors on a glorious afternoon like this, you know. Why don't you join Susan and me for a game of tennis? I'm sure that we can find someone to make up a four.'

'Thanks,' said Lizzie with rather a strained smile. 'But I don't go in for games much.'

'Well, perhaps you should,' said Felicity, looking hard at the girl. 'You need more fresh air, for you look awfully pale. I say, is something up?'

'Sort of,' said Lizzie. And, yet again, she told the tale of what had taken place between her and June.

Felicity listened attentively, then said roundly, 'Lizzie, you're an idiot. Don't you realise what a tremendous honour it is for a first former – and a new girl at that – to be chosen for the swimming team? Edith will resent you dreadfully if you try to take this opportunity away from her, and what's more I don't blame her. You really must learn to leave her alone a bit and let her find her feet.'

Lizzie felt disappointed and let down, for Felicity was well-known for her sympathetic nature. Rather stiffly, she said, 'With respect, Felicity, you don't understand what it's like to be the eldest sister.'

'No, but I know what it's like to be the youngest,' retorted Felicity swiftly. 'My sister Darrell was in the fourth form here at Malory Towers when I started. And I know that if I had come to her and told her that I was to be in the swimming gala, she would have been as pleased as punch, and would have backed me up like anything.'

Lizzie turned red, and said, 'Believe me, Felicity, I

have Edith's interests very much at heart. I just want her to do well at Malory Towers.'

'She *is* doing well,' said Felicity. 'For she has thrown herself into life here. Not just lessons, but taking part in games and making friends. She is enjoying her time at school, and that's as it should be. I would like to see *you* taking a leaf out of her book, Lizzie. Now, I must dash, for Susan will be waiting for me. Are you quite sure you won't join us?'

'Quite sure,' said Lizzie, sounding so prim and so serious that Felicity felt quite exasperated.

What on earth was wrong with the girl? she thought, as she made her way down to the tennis court. Still, Miss Grayling felt that Lizzie was worthwhile, and Felicity had never known the Head to be wrong in her summing-up of people. As she walked through the grounds, Felicity spotted Alice in the distance. As Alice had no particular friend of her own, she and Lizzie had been thrown together a good deal, pairing up whenever any activity took place for which a partner was needed. The two girls seemed to get along well together, and Felicity wondered whether Lizzie had confided in Alice at all. She resolved to ask Alice, but there was no time now, or she would be late for tennis. Heavens, there was always so much to do at Malory Towers!

While the girls made the most of the fine weather, Gwendoline was in the study that she shared with Miss Nicholson, frantically rummaging through the drawers of her desk.

'Lost something?' said Miss Nicholson.

'Yes, a letter from home,' said Gwen, frowning. 'I had it this morning, and simply can't think where I've put it!'

'It will turn up,' said Miss Nicholson in her cheerful way. 'These things always do. Have you looked in your handbag?'

At the mention of her handbag, Gwen suddenly remembered bumping into Amy that morning, and of the letter and the bag flying from her hand. She *thought* that she had picked everything up, but just suppose that she had overlooked the letter? It was a very personal one, from her parents, and the thought that one of the girls could have found it, and perhaps read it, was a distressing one.

Quickly, Gwendoline made for the door, saying over her shoulder to Miss Nicholson, 'I have just thought of somewhere I might have dropped it! I'll be back shortly.'

Gwen went back to the corridor where she had bumped into Amy that morning, but the letter was nowhere to be seen, and, frowning, she retraced her steps. What if Amy had come back and picked up the letter? She was certain to be sore with Gwen for giving her lines, and might decide to get her own back by showing it to the others.

'Hallo, Gwen,' said a cheery voice. 'Hallo, *Miss Lacey*, I should say.'

Gwen looked up, startled, for she had been so lost in her thoughts that she hadn't even heard Matron approaching. She returned her greeting, and said, 'I say,

Matron, I don't suppose that anyone has handed in a letter that they have found to you?'

'No,' said Matron. 'Today I have had a purse, a hair-slide, and – of all things – a very grubby handkerchief brought to me, but no letter. Why, have you lost one?'

'Yes,' said Gwen. 'It was from my parents, and I don't like to think that someone else might have got hold of it.'

'Well, I am sure that most of the girls here are far too well-brought-up to think of reading someone else's letters,' said Matron reassuringly. 'If one of them had found it they would have given it back to you, or handed it in to me. I daresay you've put it in a safe place and forgotten where it is!'

Gwen agreed with this and went on her way, but inwardly she felt very uneasy, for she knew that she hadn't put the letter in a safe place at all.

'No luck?' said Miss Nicholson sympathetically, seeing Gwen's downcast expression when she went back to the study. 'What a shame!'

The mistress spoke sincerely, for she knew that letters from home were very important, both to the girls and to the teachers.

'Buck up!' she said. 'You'll find it in-between the pages of a book, or something – that happened to me once. Listen, why don't the two of us pop into town for a spot of tea? That should cheer you up.'

Gwen looked into Miss Nicholson's friendly, open face and felt warmed. The other mistress was a downright, no-nonsense young woman – not the kind of person that the old Gwen would have wanted as a friend at all. Now, though, she smiled, and said, 'That would be very pleasant indeed.'

And, as the two young women walked out of the gates of Malory Towers together, Gwen reflected that she had never had a real friend in all her years as a pupil at the school. Perhaps, now that she had returned as a teacher, she had finally found one.

Amy's admirer

Gwendoline's missing letter did turn up, several days later. She and Miss Nicholson went into their study, and Gwen gave a cry as she saw the letter lying on her desk.

'Someone must have put it there while we were out,' she said. 'I wonder why whoever found it didn't return it to me immediately.'

'Oh, you know how forgetful these schoolgirls can be at times,' said Miss Nicholson. 'I expect one of them picked it up and put it into her pocket, meaning to give it to you when she saw you, and then forgot all about it.'

'Probably,' said Gwen, relaxing a little.

She had asked Amy directly if she had picked up the letter when the girl had handed in her lines on Saturday afternoon.

'Of course not, Miss Lacey,' Amy had said, getting on her high horse at once. 'If I had done so I should have given it back to you straight away.'

Gwen hadn't known whether to believe the girl or not. She had certainly *sounded* sincere, but then people who were good at telling fibs usually did.

Amy, for her part, had been most annoyed at being accused – as she put it – of taking Miss Lacey's letter, and had complained bitterly to Bonnie about it later.

'Well, to be fair, Miss Lacey didn't exactly *accuse* you,' Bonnie had pointed out. 'She merely *asked*.'

'You like her, don't you?' Amy had said, sounding rather accusing herself.

But Bonnie had merely shrugged, saying, 'I neither like nor dislike her. But I do enjoy her classes, and think that I can learn a lot from them. So I intend to stay on the right side of Miss Lacey.'

Amy smiled to herself now, as she walked to her study and remembered the conversation, for Bonnie never had any trouble in staying on the right side of people, flattering them outrageously and 'turning on the charm', as Freddie called it. And it certainly seemed to work with Miss Lacey, who was fast making a favourite of Bonnie.

Amy heard herself hailed as she opened the door, and turned to find young Violet Forsyth standing there – wearing an exact replica of the dress that she had so admired on Amy the other day.

'Look, Amy,' she said, beaming. 'I wrote to Mummy and sent her a drawing of your beautiful dress, and she managed to find one exactly like it. Isn't it super?'

'It suits you much better than all those frills,' said Amy, approvingly. 'You look very nice, Violet.'

Of course, Violet was absolutely thrilled by this praise, and she said happily, 'And Mummy's going to try and find me a bracelet like the one you wear. We shall be just like twins.'

'Well, not twins precisely,' said Amy, looking at Violet's short, plump figure and her long ringlets. 'Let's say that you will look like my younger sister.'

June and Freddie came out of June's study in time to hear these remarks, and both of them grinned broadly.

'What's this, young Violet?' said Freddie. 'A new dress?'

'Yes, and it's exactly like Amy's,' said Violet.

'Very pretty,' said June, her lips twitching with amusement. 'But I should go and get changed, Violet. It's not the weekend, you know, and if Matron or Miss Potts sees you out of uniform they're likely to take a dim view.'

'Of course,' said Violet at once. 'I just wanted Amy to see it.'

As the first former walked away, June said, 'You seem to have an admirer, Amy.'

'I know that Violet looks up to me enormously,' said Amy rather loftily. 'So, of course, I am happy to help if she asks my advice on fashion and so forth.'

'The best advice you could give her would be to work harder at tennis and swimming, and lose some weight,' said Freddie, watching Violet critically as she went downstairs. 'She would look much nicer then, and feel better.'

'Perhaps Amy doesn't want Violet to lose weight,' said June slyly. 'Imitation is the sincerest form of flattery, they say, but it won't be very flattering if your little copycat starts to look better than you do, will it, Amy?'

Amy scowled at June, while searching her mind for a withering retort, for the girl was quite right. Amy found the fact that Violet admired her so much that she wanted to copy her very flattering indeed. So much so that she was positively revelling in it! At last she said scornfully to June, 'Well, I shouldn't think anyone would ever want to imitate *your* style of dress, June. Why, sometimes you look more like a boy than a girl.'

'Oh, I don't mind that,' said June cheerfully. 'I would far rather be admired for my achievements than my looks.'

And with that, she smiled sweetly at the seething Amy, tucked her arm into Freddie's and walked away.

Violet, meanwhile, couldn't resist showing off her finery to the others, and popped into the common-room on her way to get changed.

'Violet!' said her friend Faith. 'Why are you wearing that dress? You'll get into awful trouble if one of the mistresses sees you.'

'Oh, I just wanted to try it on,' said Violet airily. 'Mummy sent it to me in the post today.'

'Very nice,' said Daffy, walking slowly around the girl. 'Er, doesn't Amy of the sixth form have a dress very similar to that one?'

Violet's worship of Amy was a great source of amusement to the first formers, and they grinned at one another. Violet, however, didn't notice, and said, 'Actually, it was Amy who told me that this style of dress would suit me. She takes *such* an interest in me, and always gives good advice.'

'I don't like her,' said Katie, wrinkling her nose. 'She's awfully stuck-up, and never even says "hallo" if she sees me, just walks by with her nose in the air.'

'Really, Katie,' said Violet, with a laugh. 'You can't expect someone like Amy to take notice of a mere first former.'

'Well, *you're* a mere first former, and she takes notice of you,' said Daffy.

'Yes, but that's because we are so alike in so many ways,' said Violet, rather smugly. 'Both of us are interested in fashion, and appreciate the finer things in life.'

'You mean that you're both a couple of vain, spoilt little snobs,' said the forthright Ivy, and some of the others laughed.

Violet scowled, but there was no time to retort, for at that moment Matron put her head round the door of the common-room, and said, 'Faith, I wanted to see you about –'

Then her eyes fell on Violet, standing in the middle of the room in her blue dress, and Matron's lips pursed, her brows drawing together in a frown. 'Violet, why are you out of uniform?' she snapped.

The girl opened her mouth to explain, but Matron swept on, 'You know very well that you are only allowed to wear your own clothes at weekends. Now, go and get changed at once, and this had better not happen again, or it will mean an order mark!'

With that she put her hand on Violet's shoulder and

steered her from the room, the others grinning as they heard Matron's voice continuing to scold as she followed the girl upstairs.

'Poor old Violet!' said Faith with a laugh. 'I must say, I can't see why she thinks Amy is so marvellous. If she has to worship one of the sixth formers, why can't she pick someone *worth* worshipping – like Felicity, or June or even Bonnie?'

'Because she's too silly to realise that their good qualities are far more important than things like wealth and good looks,' said Ivy scornfully. 'Violet is quite right, she and Amy *are* alike in some ways.'

'Well, I hope that Amy becomes bored with Violet, for she's awfully bad for her,' said Daffy. 'She was starting to behave quite sensibly last term, like an ordinary, jolly schoolgirl, but now she is slipping back into her old ways.'

Daffy and Violet had been arch-enemies when they had first started at Malory Towers, two terms ago. Daffy had hated Violet's stuck-up ways and conceit, while Violet had resented Daffy's popularity.

But then Daffy had got into serious trouble, and Violet had saved her from getting expelled, and since then the two girls had got on very much better together, a mutual respect springing up between them. The two still quarrelled at times, but without any of the bitterness they had felt before. Both of them had also been brought to see the flaws in their own characters, and had been doing their utmost to put them right.

Of course, thought Daffy, neither of them would change completely. She would always have a mischievous streak in her nature, and would always love to play tricks. But she was much more thoughtful now, and no longer played the kind of tricks that could hurt people. And Violet would never be completely without vanity, or conceit, but she had certainly improved a great deal over the past few months and the others had grown to like her much more than they had at first.

What a shame it would be if her foolish admiration of Amy undid all of that.

But, as the weeks went on, Violet continued to copy Amy in any way that she could.

If Amy had a new pair of shoes, Violet would be wearing an identical pair a few days later. When Amy appeared in the dining-room wearing a blue Alice band in her hair, Violet insisted that Faith accompany her into town on Saturday so that she could buy the very same one. And when Amy began to part her hair on the side, instead of in the middle, Violet also followed suit.

'If Amy came down to breakfast barefoot and dressed in a sack you would copy her,' said Katie, scornfully, when the first formers were in their common-room one evening.

'I wonder that you don't have your hair bobbed like Amy's, as well,' said Ivy with a sniff. 'I notice that you have stopped curling it every night.'

Violet had. She had also started brushing her hair one hundred times each night, as Amy had told her to, in the hope that it would shine like the sixth former's.

She turned a little red now, and said, 'Actually, I *am* going to get my hair cut like Amy's. As soon as my people send me some more pocket money, I shall go to the hairdresser's shop in town. But they are away on holiday at the moment, so I have to wait for them to come back before they can send me any money.' The girl sighed. 'How I wish that I didn't, for I would so like to have it cut now.'

'I bet I could cut it for you,' said Edith, looking up. 'My aunt has a hairdressing shop and I have often watched her cut people's hair. I daresay I could do it just as well as she could.'

Violet looked rather doubtful, but Ivy produced a pair of scissors from her work-basket, saying, 'Come on, then. Violet, you sit on that chair over there, and Edith can set to work.'

Violet hesitated. She wasn't entirely convinced of Edith's skill, but the girl *sounded* confident. And how wonderful it would be to go down to breakfast in the morning with a sleek, shining bob, just like Amy's, and see heads turning towards her in admiration.

So Violet sat on the chair and removed the ribbon that tied her golden hair back, while Daffy hurried to the bathroom, coming back with a towel, which she arranged over Violet's shoulders like a cape.

'So that the hair doesn't go down your back and make you itch,' she explained.

Then, under the fascinated eyes of the first formers,

and with a look of great concentration on her face, Edith began snipping away at Violet's long hair.

Alas, the girl soon discovered that it wasn't as easy a task as it looked, and as Violet's golden tresses piled up on the floor, the first formers began to look at one another uneasily.

Edith had cut quite a lot off, but instead of the neat bob Violet had wanted, her hair looked uneven and ragged, one side slightly longer than the other.

Blissfully unaware, Violet said eagerly, 'What does it look like? Is it like Amy's?'

'Er . . . sort of,' said Daffy faintly. 'Edith, I really think that you had better stop cutting now.'

Edith put down the scissors and stood back to survey her handiwork, her face falling as she realised that Violet's hairdo really didn't resemble Amy's very much at all. In fact, it looked most peculiar.

'Oh, I can't wait to see it!' said Violet, pulling off the towel and jumping to her feet.

As the first formers waited with bated breath, Violet skipped happily over to the mirror that hung on the wall.

Her happy expression turned to one of horror, then she gave a piercing shriek, crying, 'My hair! Oh, Edith, what have you done?'

'I'm sorry,' said Edith, quite aghast. 'It looked all right when I was cutting it. It was only when I stood back that I realised . . .'

Her voice tailed off as Violet wailed, 'What am I

going to do? I can't possibly go round looking like this! Everyone will laugh at me.'

'You could wear a hat,' suggested Daffy.

'Don't be ridiculous,' snapped Violet. 'I can't possibly wear a hat indoors. Potty would only make me take it off, anyway. Edith, I shall never forgive you for this.'

'Violet, I truly am sorry,' said Edith again, sounding very contrite. 'Look here, if I can just snip off that little bit of hair that is sticking up at the back, it might look better.'

She picked up the scissors again and advanced on Violet, who squealed and backed away. 'Don't you dare come near me with those scissors!' she cried.

'I think that Violet is right,' said Faith, removing the scissors from Edith's hand. 'The only thing for it is to visit the hairdressing shop and have it put right. Edith, you should really pay for it, seeing as you messed up Violet's hair in the first place.'

'Well, I can't,' said Edith bluntly. 'You know that I don't get an awful lot of pocket money, and at the moment I'm completely broke.'

'Then what's to be done?' said Violet in despair. 'I shall be the laughing stock of the whole school.'

But help was at hand. Lizzie, walking down the corridor near the first-form common-room, had heard Violet's squeals and shrieks, and been most alarmed.

Now she burst into the common-room, taking in Violet's strange hairdo, her tearful expression and the crowd of girls gathered around her.

'Violet!' cried Lizzie in horror. 'What on earth have you done? Don't tell me that you have been foolish enough to cut your own hair?'

'It wasn't me,' said Violet sullenly. 'It was –'

Then she stopped, for even silly Violet knew that it simply wasn't done to sneak, and everyone was aware how hard Lizzie could be on her young sister.

But Edith stepped forward herself, a rather defiant expression on her face as she turned to Lizzie, and said, 'It was me.'

'Well, of all the idiotic tricks!' scolded Lizzie. 'I thought that you had more sense than that, Edith. I think it's jolly mean of you to ruin Violet's hair, simply for a prank.'

'It wasn't a prank!' said Edith hotly. 'I meant to cut it properly, and I really did think that I could make a good job of it, for I have watched Aunt Mary do it so many times.'

'Well, perhaps I can tidy it up,' said Lizzie, lifting a strand of Violet's golden hair. 'I have sometimes helped Aunt Mary in the shop, for extra pocket money, and she says that I am quite good at cutting hair. Sit down, Violet.'

Violet looked very nervous indeed at the thought of another of the Mannering sisters cutting her hair, but she didn't dare disobey a sixth former, and sat obediently.

'Lizzie really is very good,' said Edith reassuringly. 'She cut Mother's hair for her in the holidays.'

Certainly, Lizzie seemed a lot more skilled than her young sister as she set to work tidying up Violet's hair, snipping off a bit here, and a bit there. At last she was finished, and Lizzie clapped her on the shoulder, saying, 'All done. Go and have a look in the mirror.'

Once again, rather apprehensively, Violet went over to the mirror and looked at her reflection. What she saw there made her want to burst into tears. Lizzie had certainly done a good job, and the girl's hair looked very neat and tidy. But, because Edith had cut it so raggedly, Lizzie had had to cut it very much shorter than Violet wanted, in order to get it even.

Hardly able to get the words out for the lump in her throat, she said tonelessly, 'Thank you, Lizzie.'

'That's quite all right,' said Lizzie. Then she turned to her sister, and said sternly, 'I hope that this has been a lesson to you, Edith. If you had been occupied with something useful, such as studying, you wouldn't have had time on your hands to make such a mess of Violet's hair.'

Then she went from the room, closing the door behind her.

'Take no notice of her,' said Daffy, patting Edith on the arm. 'I know that she's your sister but, my goodness, she's awfully domineering.'

'Don't I know it!' said Edith ruefully.

Then Daffy turned to the unhappy Violet, saying, 'Cheer up! It suits you much better than those long curls. You look like a proper, sensible schoolgirl.'

'But I don't *want* to look sensible,' moaned Violet. 'I want to look –'

'We know!' chorused the others in exasperation. 'Just like Amy!'

Lizzie makes a friend

Of course, somehow the story of how Edith had ruined Violet's hair, and Lizzie had come to the rescue, soon flew round the school, and poor Violet had to endure a great deal of good-natured ribbing when she came down to breakfast the following morning.

She felt rather hurt when Amy herself teased her about it. But, seeing that the girl was upset, and not wanting to lose her faithful admirer, Amy quickly said, 'It might not look exactly like mine, but it will soon grow. I think that it would look better if you clip the front back with a hair-slide. I have a very pretty one that would be just right, so if you would like to come to my study later, I shall give it to you.'

So, thrilled at the thought of getting a present from Amy, Violet soon cheered up, and didn't even mind too much when Mam'zelle Dupont exclaimed over the loss of her beautiful golden curls.

One good result of the affair was that Lizzie went up a little in the estimation of the sixth formers, for dealing so well with the situation.

'It was jolly decent of you to step in,' said Alice to Lizzie, in the courtyard on Saturday afternoon. 'Though

I must say, I should have liked to see Violet's hair after your young sister had cut it. My word, she must have looked a fright!'

Even Lizzie couldn't suppress a grin at this, as she said, 'She did. It's just lucky that I happened to be near the kids' common-room and heard all the commotion.'

Alice glanced at Lizzie, pleased to see her smile for a change.

The other day, Felicity had spoken to Alice, and asked her how she got on with Lizzie.

'All right,' Alice had replied with a shrug. 'She is very difficult to get to know, for there is something rather stand-offish about her. She never talks about her home, or her people, and even in her spare time she would rather sit with her head in a book than do something just for fun.'

'Do me a favour, would you, Alice?' Felicity had said. 'See if you can bring Lizzie out of herself a bit, and see if you can get her to think of something other than work for a change. I really think that it would do her the world of good.'

'I shall do my best,' Alice had said, feeling rather proud that Felicity had entrusted her with the task of befriending Alice, and she had sought the girl out several times. Lizzie, who knew very well that she wasn't enormously popular, had been surprised to find that Alice wanted her company. Her responses to Alice's attempts at conversation were not very encouraging, however, for although Lizzie was always perfectly polite, she always managed to give the impression that she was in a hurry to get back to her books.

Encouraged now by Lizzie's smile, Alice said, 'It's a simply glorious day. How about coming for a walk along the cliffs?'

'That sounds nice,' said Lizzie, politely, 'but I have some reading that I must be getting on with. Miss Oakes told me that we will be studying the Tudors for Higher Cert next term, so I am getting a head start on the others who will be coming up into the sixth next term.'

'I didn't go in for Higher Cert myself,' said Alice. 'I don't have the brains for it, you see. But I did help some of the others study, and I remember copying down reams of notes on the Tudors for Felicity. I wonder if she still has them, for I am sure you would find them most useful.'

'Oh, it would be marvellous if she would lend them to me!' said Lizzie eagerly.

'Well, I shall ask her,' said Alice. 'But you must do something for me in return. Slack off a bit this afternoon and come for a walk with me.'

Lizzie bit her lip. A walk in the sunshine would be very pleasant, and if Alice really could get hold of Felicity's notes for her, they would come in very useful. So she nodded, and said, 'Very well. If I can get hold of Felicity's notes it will save me an awful lot of trouble in the long run, so I daresay that I can spare a little time.'

Felicity, watching the two girls walk towards the gates a few minutes later, was pleased. What an achievement for Alice, to get Lizzie away from her books for a while!

Most of the sixth formers were outside, making the most of the good weather. Julie and Lucy had gone horse-riding, June and Freddie were down at the pool, coaching the first and second formers, while the others lazed on the grass.

Only Amy and Bonnie were indoors. Bonnie was in her study, engrossed in a tablecloth that she was embroidering for her mother, and humming softly to some music on the radio as she worked. Amy, meanwhile, was making her way to Miss Lacey's class-room, a large bunch of sweetly scented flowers in her arms.

Miss Lacey had been showing the girls how to arrange flowers in vases, making use of ferns and foliage to create an artistic effect, and it had been decided that, each week, the girls would take turns to do a flower arrangement for her class-room.

It had been Bonnie's turn last week and, as the girl had a flair for such things, her arrangement had been very pretty, and Miss Lacey had been pleased with it. This week, though, it was Amy's turn, and the teacher had condemned her effort as very poor indeed.

'It doesn't look as if you have even attempted to create anything pleasing to the eye, Amy,' Miss Lacey had said with a sniff. 'You have simply stuck the flowers into the nearest available vase, without any thought of arranging them prettily.'

In fact, this was exactly what Amy *had* done, for she found flower-arranging a dreadful bore and simply couldn't see the point of it!

'When you are married, and have your own home, you will want it to look nice, won't you?' Miss Lacey had said.

'Of course,' Amy had replied, in her haughty way. 'But I shall have a housekeeper to see to such dull chores as arranging flowers.'

Miss Lacey had looked simply furious, two spots of red darkening her cheeks, as she glared at Amy, but before she could vent her anger on the girl, Bonnie said in her soft voice, 'Oh, Amy, flower-arranging isn't a chore! Why, it's an art, isn't that so, Miss Lacey?'

Bonnie's words, her soft voice and the way she looked admiringly at Miss Lacey, soothed the teacher a little.

'I am glad that there is someone in the form who realises that,' she said, giving Bonnie a warm look. Then her voice hardened as she turned back to Amy, and snapped, 'This won't do at all. Amy, I must insist that you pick fresh flowers and make a new arrangement tomorrow.'

Amy had scowled, and as Miss Lacey moved away Bonnie hissed under her breath, 'Idiot! Why do you persist in getting on the wrong side of Miss Lacey? You know that she will only end up punishing you.'

'I don't care,' said Amy with a shrug. 'At least I don't suck up to her like you do.'

'You can think yourself jolly lucky that I stepped in just then,' said Bonnie severely. 'If I hadn't, I think you might have got a worse punishment than just having to do the flowers again!'

Amy was forced to admit that this was true. She also knew that she was only hurting herself by antagonising Miss Lacey, but somehow she couldn't seem to stop herself, for her dislike of the young teacher grew more intense with every day. But the feeling was entirely mutual, for Miss Lacey didn't like Amy, either, and showed it very plainly.

Now, as Amy went towards Miss Lacey's class-room, she saw Violet Forsyth approaching, and smiled at the girl.

'Hallo, Amy,' said Violet. 'My word, what lovely flowers.'

'Yes, it is my turn to do the flowers for this week,' said Amy. 'But my efforts at arranging them didn't meet with Miss Lacey's approval, so I have to do them all over again. It's utterly pointless doing them on a Saturday, for by the time the class-room is used again they will be all wilted. It's just spite on Miss Lacey's part, so that I have to give up part of my weekend.'

'What a shame that I can't help you,' said Violet. 'I sometimes help Mummy to do our flowers at home, and I have quite a knack, you know.'

Amy looked down into Violet's eager face, and a thought occurred to her. Miss Lacey's classroom was strictly out of bounds to all but the sixth formers, and it was kept locked when there were no classes taking place. Amy had got the key from Daisy, the maid, so that she could do the flowers. But it had suddenly occurred to the girl that she could finish her task much more quickly with Violet's help.

So she leaned forward, and said in a conspiratorial whisper, 'Violet, how would you like to see inside Miss Lacey's class-room?'

Violet, of course, was simply thrilled, for she – like the rest of the first form – was very curious indeed to see inside the locked room. How marvellous to be able to boast to the others that she had actually been inside!

This hope was dashed, though, when Amy held up a warning finger, and said, 'You mustn't let anyone know that I have taken you in there, or I would be in the most awful trouble! It must be our secret.'

Violet was disappointed that she wouldn't be able to tell the first formers of her adventure but, in a way, it would be just as nice to have a secret from them, something that only she and Amy knew about.

So the girl promised solemnly that she would not tell anyone at all, and Amy gave her the flowers to hold while she quickly unlocked the door. Then – after glancing swiftly up and down the corridor, to make sure that no one was about – she ushered Violet inside, closing the door.

Violet had never seen a class-room like this one before, with its armchairs and sofas, and the elegant velvet curtains hanging at the windows.

'How marvellous!' she breathed, gazing around her.

Amy, extremely gratified at the younger girl's reaction, quite forgot that she had criticised the furnishings as being shabby and said airily, 'Much nicer than an ordinary class-room, isn't it?'

'I should say!' breathed Violet. 'Amy, do you think I might try one of the sofas? They look so comfortable!'

Amy looked on indulgently as Violet tried the sofas and the armchairs, pronouncing that they were very comfortable indeed, and so much more elegant than the hard chairs in the first-form class-room. Then Amy glanced at her watch, and said, 'I suppose we had better get on and arrange these flowers. Violet, be a dear and fetch a vase from that cupboard, would you?'

Violet did as she was asked, then Amy sighed, and said, 'Oh dear, how difficult it is to know where to start! I really have no talent for this sort of thing at all.'

'Let's start by putting the taller flowers in the vase,' said Violet, picking one up. 'Then we can arrange the smaller ones around them.'

The first former proved to be surprisingly nimble-fingered, and Amy soon found that she had nothing to do but stand back and watch, which – of course – suited her perfectly.

Violet, meanwhile, was in her element, for not only was she doing something which she genuinely enjoyed, but she was spending time with Amy, revelling in the honeyed words of praise that fell from the sixth former's lips.

'That ought to please Miss Lacey,' said Amy as Violet put the finishing touches to her arrangement. 'How disappointed she will be not to have an excuse to scold me!'

'You know, Amy, I wouldn't be a bit surprised if Miss

Lacey wasn't jealous of you,' said Violet. 'She always tries hard to look fashionable and elegant, yet somehow she never manages to look as nice as you do. In fact . . .' Violet gave a little giggle. 'The way that Miss Lacey dresses rather reminds me of my mother.'

Amy laughed at this, pleased with both the compliment, and the dig at Gwendoline.

But before she could reply, the door suddenly opened and Daisy stood there. 'I came to see if you had finished, Miss Amy,' she said. 'So that I can take the key back to the housekeeper.'

Then she spotted Violet, and said, 'Miss Violet, you know that you shouldn't be in here! This room is for the sixth formers only.'

'Oh, Daisy, do be a sport and don't sneak on us!' said Amy, giving the maid a pleading look. 'Violet wasn't doing any harm, really she wasn't.'

'I really should report this to Miss Potts,' said Daisy, looking stern. Then, looking at the two rather scared faces before her, she relented and said, 'I'll let you off this time – mind, it's only because I'm scared of that Miss Potts, and I don't like talking to her if I don't have to. Now be off with you, Miss Violet, and don't let me catch you in here again!'

Relieved, Violet scuttled away, while Amy said to Daisy, 'Thanks awfully. You're a good sport, Daisy.'

'That's as may be,' said the maid with a sniff. 'But you're old enough to know better than to break the rules, Miss Amy. What Miss Lacey would say if she knew about all this, I don't know.'

The snobbish Amy didn't at all care to be scolded by a maid, but it wouldn't do to upset Daisy, so she said meekly, 'You are quite right. I shan't let Violet in here again.'

Daisy seemed satisfied with this, and she and Amy left the room, Amy locking the door behind her and handing the key to the maid. Then the two of them went their separate ways, Daisy to return the key to the housekeeper, and Amy to go in search of Bonnie.

Lizzie, meanwhile, was finding her walk with Alice unexpectedly enjoyable.

'Do you know,' she said to Alice, 'I have been at Malory Towers for two whole years, and yet I have never walked along the cliffs before!'

'Well, now that you know how enjoyable it is, I hope that you will make the time to do it more often,' said Alice.

The two of them had found a sunny spot overlooking the sea and were sitting on the grass.

'My word, only two weeks until half-term,' said Alice. 'I can't believe how the time has flown. Will your parents be coming, Lizzie?'

'There is only Mother,' said Lizzie. 'For Father died when Edith was small, you know. I doubt very much that she will be able to come, because she had to take a job when Father died and she works so terribly hard all the time.'

Alice was very sorry to hear this, but she was also rather curious, as she knew that the fees at Malory Towers were expensive, and it sounded as if Lizzie's mother was not terribly well-off. So how on earth did she manage to keep two girls at Malory Towers?

Almost as though she had guessed what Alice was thinking, Lizzie said, 'Our Uncle Charles pays our school fees, Edith's and mine. He is Father's older brother, and we are very grateful to him.'

'I should think you must be,' said Alice. 'It's awfully generous of him.'

Lizzie gave a tight little smile, but said nothing, and rather an uncomfortable silence fell.

Alice broke it by saying, 'Shall we make our way back to school now? I don't want to be late for tea, for this fresh air has given me such an appetite!'

Lizzie agreed at once, and the two girls took the cliff path back to Malory Towers, coming out near the swimming-pool.

'It looks as if June is still coaching the youngsters,' said Alice, putting a hand up to shield her eyes from the sun as she watched some of the first and second formers climb out of the pool. A lone diver stood poised on the topmost diving-board.

'I say, isn't that your young sister up there, Lizzie?' Alice asked. 'I've heard that she's absolutely marvellous at swimming and diving. Let's get a closer look.'

As they moved nearer, Edith launched herself from the diving-board, doing the most beautiful swallow dive, and entering the water with barely a splash. She really was very graceful to watch, and the spectators, who had all stood in enthralled silence as Edith dived, now burst into a round of spontaneous applause.

Edith turned red with pleasure as she climbed out of the pool, and June went across to clap the girl on the back, crying, 'Jolly well done, Edith! My word, you will certainly shine at the gala. You really are a wonder!'

Lizzie, overhearing, felt a pang. There was such pride in June's voice, and in her face. And Edith, thrilled, was hanging on the games captain's every word, looking up at her in the same worshipful way that she used to look at her older sister.

Oh, it just wasn't fair, thought Lizzie bitterly. She almost felt as if June had stolen Edith away from her, for the girl obviously looked up to her no end, while she, Lizzie, had become almost an enemy. Out of the corner of her eye, she could see Alice watching her, a curious expression on her face, and Lizzie knew that the girl was wondering why she didn't go and make a fuss of her young sister, and tell her how well she had done.

The odd thing was that as Lizzie had watched Edith glide gracefully into the water, she *had* felt proud of her – intensely proud. But she couldn't bring herself to go to the girl and tell her that, for to do so would only encourage her to waste even more time on swimming and games. And, no matter how good she was, Edith would never be able to make a career out of swimming, and earn good money at it, and that was what mattered.

Just then Edith turned, and saw Lizzie watching. She smiled at her big sister, hoping that she would come across and speak to her. But Lizzie merely waved, before turning away and saying to Alice, 'Come on, let's go and wash our hands before the bell goes for tea.'

Edith's shoulders slumped, some of the joy fading from her face, and several of the others noticed it.

'Never mind about Lizzie!' said Daffy, giving her arm a squeeze. 'I know that she is your sister, but she really is a misery!'

June had noticed too, and she stared after Lizzie and Alice as they walked away, a hard expression on her face.

If Lizzie wasn't very careful indeed, she thought, she was going to end up pushing her young sister away completely.

Daisy is very sly

There were three letters beside Gwendoline's plate when she came down to breakfast on Monday morning, and Miss Nicholson exclaimed, 'Heavens, someone's very popular! Don't tell me that it's your birthday?'

'Oh, no,' said Gwen, picking up the envelopes as she sat down. 'This one's from Mother, and this is from Miss Winter, my old governess. I recognise their writing.'

Then she frowned as she picked up the third one. 'The writing on this one looks vaguely familiar too, but I simply can't think whose it is.'

Gwen read her mother's letter without much enthusiasm as she ate her scrambled eggs. Mrs Lacey had never fully adjusted to the more simple way of life that the family had adopted since her husband's illness and, as Gwen had expected, her letter was just a list of complaints and grumbles.

Gwen sighed as she laid it aside and opened Miss Winter's, which was much more cheerful in tone. The young woman smiled fondly as she read it, for she had grown to appreciate Miss Winter far more in recent years than she had as a spoilt schoolgirl. The old governess really had been a tower of strength to the whole family, particularly to her mother, since Mr Lacey had been taken ill. Not that Mother would ever admit that, of course!

Gwendoline herself often felt ashamed when she thought of how, as a young girl, she had rather despised poor, plain Miss Winter, and taken her adoration for granted. Now, though, she understood her situation a great deal better, and felt very grateful indeed for the woman's affection and friendship.

It took Gwen a while to read Miss Winter's letter, for it was a long and chatty one, but at last she finished and slit open the third envelope. Then she gave a gasp.

'Anything wrong?' asked Miss Nicholson, looking up sharply from her plate.

'No, not at all,' said Gwen. 'It's just that this letter is from someone I haven't heard from in simply ages. One of the girls who used to be here, at Malory Towers with me, in fact.'

The letter was actually from Darrell, for Felicity had told her sister that Gwen was now teaching at the school. Gwen was surprised at how pleased she felt to hear from Darrell, for the two of them had never been close friends. But Darrell had been kind to her when her father had been taken ill, something which Gwen had never forgotten.

Her letter was packed with news, and it was obvious that Darrell was leading a full and enjoyable life, making the most of every moment, just as she had when she had been at Malory Towers. There was also news of some of the other Malory Towers girls who had been in her form

– Sally, Alicia, Irene, Belinda, Mavis and Mary-Lou, and Gwen began to feel quite nostalgic as she read it. Then, at the end of the letter, Darrell had written something that brought a wide smile to Gwendoline's face.

Oh, my goodness! thought Gwen. How marvellous! How simply splendid! I shall write back to Darrell this very evening!

Over at the sixth-form table, Felicity had also received a letter from Darrell, and she read parts of it out to the others.

'Darrell is simply thrilled that I am to be in the swimming gala,' she said. 'Oh, how super, she's promised to take me out to tea in the holidays if I do well.'

'How marvellous!' said June. 'Of course, Darrell is the kind of sister who would always back you up in whatever you chose to do.'

June flicked a glance at Lizzie as she spoke, and the girl, knowing that the words were aimed at her, flushed.

'Alicia is just the same,' went on June. 'Though, of course, she is my cousin, and not my sister. But she was terribly proud of me when I became games captain, and sent me such a nice, encouraging letter.'

Susan, not realising that June was getting a dig in at Lizzie, said, 'How nice it must be to have an older sister – or cousin, in your case, June – to look up to and share good news with. I have often wished that I had one.'

'I'm sure that you are not alone in that wish, Susan,' said June smoothly.

Lizzie scowled at June. Since she had tackled June

about dropping Edith from the swimming gala a few weeks ago, Lizzie was not in as much awe of her as she had been. But she was still a little afraid of June's sharp tongue and sharp wits, for it was rare indeed for anyone to get the better of the girl in an argument.

So Lizzie held her tongue and said nothing, though it was really very difficult, especially when she saw June go up to her sister after breakfast and lay a friendly hand on her shoulder, while Edith looked up at her admiringly. Daffy and Katie were there too, and it was plain that they both thought that June was a most wonderful person as well. As the three first formers moved away to go to their first lesson, Lizzie called out Edith's name, but her sister did not turn round.

Lizzie was quite convinced that Edith had heard her, though, and was simply pretending not to because she didn't want to talk to her. Lizzie felt hurt and angry, for although she knew that she was sometimes hard on Edith, she was very fond of her younger sister, and everything she did was for the girl's own good. What a beastly day this was turning out to be!

But someone else was having an even worse day than Lizzie. Gwen was in a good mood as she unlocked the door of her class-room that morning. The letter she had received from Darrell had cheered her up enormously, and she was pleased to see that the West Tower sixth formers had arrived early for their class and were waiting for her to unlock the door. She greeted them brightly, for they all looked keen and that boded well for the lesson.

But when Gwen unlocked the door and stepped inside, she gave a little groan, putting her hand up to her throat.

'What is it, Miss Lacey?' asked a plump, kindly girl called Christine.

'See for yourself,' said Miss Lacey in a trembling voice, standing to one side.

The West Tower girls poured inside, and a collective gasp went up. For the flowers that Violet had so carefully arranged two days ago had been taken from their vase and strewn higgledy-piggledy about the room. Some had been thrown on the chairs and sofas, others were on the floor, and still more had been thrown on to the big table. The water from the vase had been poured over Miss Lacey's desk, ruining some papers that she had left there. And the lovely glass vase, one that Gwen had brought herself from home, had been thrown against the wall and was smashed to smithereens. The West Tower girls exclaimed in horror.

'Who on earth could have been mean enough to do this?'

'Could it have been meant as a joke, do you suppose?'

'If it is a joke, it's not very funny.'

'This is no joke, it's sheer spite! Anyone can see that!'

'Well, let's set to work and clean up,' said Christine briskly, seeing that Miss Lacey was in a state of shock, and taking charge. 'Vera, Joy and Nancy, you begin picking up the flowers,' she went on. 'Jane, can you clear the papers from Miss Lacey's desk, and I will sweep up the broken glass.'

Gwen, who hadn't moved or spoken since she had seen the damage done to her lovely class-room, sank down into an armchair, looking very pale, and Christine said, 'Tessie, can you fetch Miss Lacey a glass of water, please?'

'Of course,' said Tessie, hurrying from the room.

Miss Potts, who happened to be walking down the corridor, spotted her, and called out, 'Where are you off to in such a hurry, Tessie? Shouldn't you be in Miss Lacey's lesson?'

'Yes, Miss Potts,' said Tessie. 'But something terrible has happened, and I am just going to get some water for Miss Lacey. She really does look as if she might faint, you know.'

Heavens, what on earth can have happened? thought Miss Potts, frowning, as Tessie continued on her errand. I had better go and investigate.

The mistress walked into Miss Lacey's class-room, her lips pursing as she took in the scene before her. Girls bustled about, clearing up the mess, while Miss Lacey sat huddled in an armchair, looking – as Tessie had said – as if she might faint at any moment.

The girls stopped what they were doing when Miss Potts entered, standing politely to attention, and the mistress said, 'Carry on, girls.'

Then she sat down next to Miss Lacey, and said in a low tone, 'What has happened here?'

'I don't know,' said Gwen in a tremulous tone. 'The room was like this when I unlocked the door this morning. I simply can't think who could have done this, or why.'

'The door was locked, you say?' said Miss Potts.

'Yes, it is always kept locked when it is not in use,' said Gwen. 'Only myself and the housekeeper have keys.'

'Well, I hardly think that the housekeeper would have done such a thing,' said Miss Potts, looking very puzzled indeed. 'I wonder if anyone else could have got hold of her key?'

Suddenly Gwen remembered something, and gave a gasp. 'Amy had the key on Saturday! It was her turn to do the flowers for the room, and she was going to get the key from the housekeeper.'

'Then we had better speak to Amy,' said Miss Potts, looking rather grim as she stood up. 'I shall tell her to come to my room at break-time.'

Amy was puzzled, and a little alarmed, to receive a message saying that Miss Potts wanted to see her at break-time. Oh dear, what if Daisy had broken her word and told the mistress that Violet had been in Miss Lacey's room on Saturday? Not only would she be in trouble with Miss Potts and Miss Lacey, but the rest of the form would be angry with her too.

When the bell went for break, she made her way to the study that Miss Potts shared with Mam'zelle Dupont. Mam'zelle was not there, but Miss Lacey was seated next to Miss Potts, looking very upset.

'Sit down, Amy,' said Miss Potts, sounding very stern. Then she went on to tell Amy of the damage that had been done to Miss Lacey's classroom.

'I am not accusing you of anything, Amy,' she finished. 'I am simply giving you an opportunity to own up if you do know anything.'

'Miss Potts, the room was in perfect order when I left it,' said Amy, looking the mistress straight in the eye, and sounding rather dignified. 'That is the truth. Why, I would never dream of doing such a thing.'

Miss Potts believed the girl at once. Amy could be spiteful at times, but her spite usually took the form of making cutting remarks about the others. She had never been one for playing mean tricks on people. Miss Lacey, however, was not so convinced, and she said, 'Is there anyone who can confirm that?'

Amy hesitated for a moment. Violet could confirm it, of course, but Amy couldn't possibly tell the two mistresses that she had allowed the first former into the classroom, for then both of them would be in trouble. Then she remembered that someone else had been there.

'Yes,' she said. 'Daisy, the maid, came along just as I was finishing off. We left the room together, then I locked the door and handed her the key, to give to the housekeeper. She will be able to tell you that I left the room as I found it.'

'Good,' said Miss Potts, sounding relieved. It didn't solve the mystery, but at least Amy's name would be cleared. 'I shall send someone to fetch Daisy.'

'I can go and find her, Miss Potts,' said Amy, for a thought had just occurred to her. Daisy had given her word that she would not sneak, but she had not known then that she would have to face the stern Miss Potts. It would be as well to have a quick word with the maid before she was questioned, decided Amy, to make absolutely sure that she didn't give the game away.

A third former told Amy that she had just seen Daisy making her way up to the dormitories with a pile of clean linen, and the girl quickly caught up with her.

'Daisy!' she said. 'I must speak with you at once.'

'Why, whatever is the matter, Miss Amy?' asked Daisy, startled.

'Come in here, where we shan't be overheard,' said Amy, taking the maid's arm and pulling her into the sixth-form dormitory.

Quickly she told Daisy of what had happened. The maid's eyes were big and scared as she said, 'And now Miss Potts wants to question me?'

'That's right,' said Amy. 'But all you have to do is tell her that the room was neat and tidy when I locked the door, which is perfectly true.'

'Yes,' said Daisy hesitantly. 'But what if it comes out that a first former was in there with you?'

'Daisy!' gasped Amy, shocked. 'You promised that you wouldn't tell.'

'I won't,' said Daisy. 'Well, not on purpose, anyway. The thing is, you see, that Miss Potts frightens the life out of me, with her stern voice, and her cold eyes, and that way she has of looking at you over the top of her glasses. She gets me that flustered, there's no knowing what I might say!'

Daisy had moved across to the little cabinet that stood beside Amy's bed as she spoke, and she picked up a bottle of perfume that stood there, taking out the stopper and sniffing at it. 'My, this is lovely,' she said. 'No wonder you always smell so nice, Miss Amy. How I wish that I could afford expensive perfume, but there's not much chance of that on the wages I earn.'

'Look here, Daisy,' said Amy. 'If you promise to keep your nerve when Miss Potts questions you, and not to mention Violet, I shall give you the perfume to keep.'

Daisy's eyes lit up, and she said eagerly, 'Do you mean that, Miss Amy?'

'Yes,' said Amy. 'But you must keep your part of the bargain, see, otherwise I shall take the perfume back.'

'Oh, I won't sneak, no fear of that,' said Daisy, slipping the perfume bottle into the big pocket of her starched, white apron. 'I shall run along to see Miss Potts this very minute.'

The maid almost skipped from the room, and Amy watched her go, a frown coming over her face. She regretted having to give her lovely perfume away, but that wasn't what was troubling her. It seemed to Amy that there had been rather a sly look on Daisy's face when she picked up the perfume. Had that been the maid's intention all along – to get an expensive present from Amy, in return for her silence?

A bad time for Gwen

Word of the damage that had been done to Miss Lacey's classroom soon spread around the school, and the North Tower sixth formers, in particular, felt very dismayed when they heard the news.

'I know it's silly, but I feel as if that room belongs to us more than any of the others, because it is in our tower,' said Nora.

'I wonder who can have done it?' said Pam with a frown.

'Someone with a very mean, spiteful streak, obviously,' said Susan scornfully. 'I hope that whoever it was feels thoroughly ashamed of herself.'

The girls were sitting on the grass outside, enjoying the brilliant sunshine, and Freddie, who had been lying on her back, shielding her eyes with her hand, suddenly sat up and, lowering her voice, said, 'Of course, you know that Miss Lacey suspected Amy, don't you?'

'Yes, I had heard a rumour,' said Felicity. 'But Daisy was able to clear her name, fortunately.'

'I can't say that Amy has ever been my favourite person,' said June. 'But I don't think that she would stoop to that kind of low trick.'

'Nor do I,' said Felicity. 'It's rather horrible to think that it must have been a sixth former, though.'

'What makes you say that?' said Alice, startled.

'Well, obviously someone has a grudge against Miss Lacey,' said Felicity. 'And as we are the only form that she teaches, that rather rules out the lower forms, for none of them know her well enough to have taken a dislike to her.'

'That's very true,' said Susan. 'I wonder if it could have been someone from another tower?'

'Well, I know that Jane from West Tower doesn't like Gwen,' said June, who steadfastly refused to refer to the new mistress as Miss Lacey. 'And that South Tower girl, Elspeth, dislikes her heartily.'

'And let's not forget that you aren't too keen on her either, are you, June?' said Lizzie with a little laugh. 'I don't suppose it could have been you, could it?'

It was said lightly, but everyone knew of the animosity between Lizzie and June. Felicity braced herself to intervene, as they all waited with bated breath for June's withering retort. But, to the surprise of the sixth formers, the girl merely laughed, and said, 'Actually it could easily have been me. Or you, Lizzie, or Felicity, or Susan – or any one of us.'

'Don't!' said Nora with a shudder. 'It's horrible to think that we are all under suspicion.'

'Well, we are,' said June bluntly. 'For the key to Gwen's class-room hangs on a hook in the housekeeper's room. It would have been an easy matter for anyone to slip in while she was out and take it. Why, even one of the mistresses could have done it.'

Freddie gave a laugh, and said, 'Who do you suspect, June? Mam'zelle Dupont, perhaps?'

The others laughed too, as they pictured the plump little French mistress sneaking into Gwen's class-room and wreaking havoc. Then June said, 'Probably not, for she never saw through Gwen and I believe that she is quite fond of her. But there is no denying that she wasn't popular with most of the mistresses when she was a pupil here.'

'Oh, I simply can't believe that any of the mistresses would do such a thing!' exclaimed Felicity. 'Why, most of them have been here for years!'

'Miss Nicholson hasn't,' said Alice thoughtfully.

'No, but she and Miss Lacey seem to be good friends,' said Susan.

'Yes,' said June. 'But perhaps that is Miss Nicholson's way of trying to avoid coming under suspicion.'

'I refuse to listen to any more!' cried Nora, clapping her hands over her ears. 'It's simply horrible to think that someone as downright and jolly as Miss Nicholson could play mean tricks on someone who is supposed to be her friend.'

'Of course it is!' said Felicity. 'We shall probably never find out who was responsible, so let's just hope that whoever wanted to get her own back on Miss Lacey will think that she has done enough and won't take things any further.'

But Miss Lacey began to go through a most annoying time over the following week. A photograph of her mother, which she kept on the desk in her study, was removed from its frame and torn into tiny little pieces. Then someone cut the flower off her favourite hat when she left it on a bench in the courtyard one day. And worse was to come.

Going into her bedroom one Saturday afternoon, Gwen was horrified to discover that her chest of drawers had been ransacked, the contents strewn about the bed and the floor. She gave a little cry of horror, the tears that had always come so readily when she had been a schoolgirl starting to her blue eyes. But Gwen blinked them back resolutely, gritting her teeth as she began picking up stockings and handkerchiefs, and putting them away tidily again. Someone obviously had it in for her, and was trying to make her time at Malory Towers as miserable as possible – perhaps they even meant to drive her away. But they would not succeed. Gwen could not let them succeed, for she needed this job and the money it brought in, and so did her family. Then as Gwen put her scattered things away, she made an unpleasant discovery. A pair of cufflinks that she had bought her father for his birthday, and hidden in one of the drawers, was missing. A lump rose to her throat, for she had badly wanted to buy her father something special, and had been putting a little money aside each week, picturing his surprise and delight when he opened her gift. As she fought to control her tears, a cheerful whistling came from outside, and Gwen, recognising it, pulled open her bedroom door and said, 'Miss Nicholson! Come here a moment, would you?'

Miss Nicholson entered the bedroom, frowning as she saw her friend's distressed expression.

Quickly, Gwen explained what had happened, her voice breaking slightly as she told the other mistress about the missing cufflinks.

'This is quite dreadful!' exclaimed Miss Nicholson, sounding most concerned. 'The other things that have happened to you – as horrible as they are – can be dismissed as mere spite, but this is theft. You must report it to Miss Potts, or even to Miss Grayling, at once.'

But Gwen was strangely reluctant to do this, and, when pushed by Miss Nicholson, she admitted, 'If I tell Miss Grayling about the cufflinks, all the other things will come out too.'

'Well, that's a good thing, if you ask me,' said Miss Nicholson stoutly. 'It's about time that the person who is playing these beastly tricks knew that we are taking it seriously, for it might make her think twice before playing the next one.'

'Yes, but don't you see?' said Gwen, a bleak look on her face. 'If all of this comes out, Miss Grayling might decide that it is too much trouble to keep me on here as a teacher. Oh, I know that the girls play tricks on the staff sometimes, just as they did when I was a pupil here. But it is all done in good humour, and this is quite different, for there is so much spite in it! Whoever heard of a teacher who was so unpopular that someone hates her enough to steal from her, and spoil her things?'

'Well, if you refuse to report it, we shall just have to do our utmost to thwart whoever is doing this ourselves,' said Miss Nicholson, a very determined expression on her round face. 'You must make sure that you lock your bedroom door from now on, every time you leave it.'

'That's just it, though, I thought that I *had* locked it,' said Gwen with a puzzled look. 'But I suppose I must have been in such a hurry that I forgot. I saved so hard for those cufflinks too.'

'Look here,' said Miss Nicholson gruffly, laying a hand on Gwen's shoulder. 'I can lend you the money if you want to buy another pair, and you can pay me back a little at a time.'

Gwen flushed, deeply touched by her friend's offer. But she had been brought up not to borrow or lend money, and she said, 'It's awfully kind of you, but I simply couldn't. I'm afraid that Father will have to be content with a set of handkerchiefs.'

'Just as you like,' said Miss Nicholson. 'But the offer stands if you change your mind. Now, let's put the rest of your things away and go down to tea. And this time, make sure that you lock the door behind you!'

Lizzie, meanwhile, had been pleasantly surprised when her young sister had agreed to take a stroll with her.

'I went along the cliffs with Alice the other day,' she

said. 'And the views are simply marvellous. Do let's, Edith! It seems such a long time since we spent some time together.'

Edith had looked a little doubtful, and, seeing her expression, Lizzie had laughed, and said, 'I will promise not to mention the swimming gala, or June, or your friendship with Daffy.'

'All right,' Edith had said with a grin. 'I shall hold you to that.'

And the two sisters had talked and laughed together as they strolled, making it seem quite like old times.

'How the weeks have flown,' said Lizzie, as the two stood looking out to sea. 'Next weekend it will be half-term.'

'How I wish that Mother could come,' said Edith, rather wistfully.

'So do I,' said Lizzie, squeezing her sister's arm. 'Still, it won't be so very bad. At least we will have one another, so we shan't be quite alone.'

Edith bit her lip, and cast a sidelong look at Lizzie.

'Actually,' she began, rather hesitantly. 'Actually, Lizzie, Daffy has asked me to go out with her and her people. And I – I said yes.'

'Oh!' said Lizzie blankly. She had pictured herself spending the day with Edith, trying to make up to her for their mother's absence. And now it seemed that the girl didn't need her after all!

'I'm sorry,' said Edith, hanging her head. 'I was so thrilled to be asked that it never even occurred to me that you would be alone too. Of course, I shall tell Daffy that I can't go with her.'

But Lizzie, looking down at her sister, took a sudden, noble resolve, and said, 'You'll do nothing of the sort!'

Edith looked up in surprise, and Lizzie went on, 'As if I would ask you to give up such a treat! Of course you must go with Daffy. Don't worry about me, for I will be quite all right.'

'Are you sure?' said Edith, her brow clearing. 'Oh, of course you will be all right! One of the sixth formers is sure to ask you out. In fact, I thought that you would probably have had one or two invitations already.'

'Oh, I have,' said Lizzie airily. 'I turned them down because I didn't want to leave you on your own, Edith, but now that I know you are going out with Daffy I shall be able to accept one of them. It looks as though we are both going to have a marvellous half-term.'

Lizzie spoke cheerfully, for she didn't want to dampen her sister's spirits, but actually no one had asked her to go out with them at half-term. In fact, Alice was the only one who knew that Lizzie's mother wasn't coming, and she had assumed that the girl would not want to leave Edith on her own, so had not bothered to invite her out.

Normally, the thought of an extra day to herself, to pore over her books, would have been a very welcome one, but it would be hard to think of studying when the others were all having a happy time with their families. Suddenly Lizzie began to feel very lonely, and to realise that the others had a point when they said that there was more to school life than studying. If only she hadn't cut herself off from the others quite so much, she might have more friends, and wouldn't be facing the bleak prospect of a lonely half-term.

This thought was on Lizzie's mind when she went into tea and, seeing her miserable expression, Alice said in a friendly way, 'Is something the matter, Lizzie?'

'No, nothing at all,' said Lizzie, forcing herself to smile, for she was far too proud to admit to Alice that Edith had been asked out at half-term.

'Well, you look as if you have all the cares of the world on your shoulders,' said Susan. 'For goodness' sake, cheer up! There's only a week to go until half-term.'

'Perhaps that is what's upsetting Lizzie,' said June smoothly. 'We all know how she hates to tear herself away from her books. And heaven forbid that she should actually have some fun!'

Lizzie couldn't even bring herself to retort to this, but Alice said rather sharply, 'Oh, do be quiet, June. I'm sure that Lizzie is looking forward to spending the day with her sister just as much as the rest of us will enjoy being with our families.'

Felicity threw Alice an approving look, and said, 'Oh, isn't your mother coming, Lizzie?'

'No, she can't get away,' said Lizzie, trying her hardest not to sound too mournful.

'What a shame,' said Pam. 'But it's a good thing that you will have Edith to keep you company.'

Lizzie could have told the others then that Edith was

spending half-term with Daffy, but somehow she couldn't bring herself to say it. Alice, or one of the others, might feel sorry for her, and feel obliged to invite her to go with them. And Lizzie didn't want anyone's pity. So she merely nodded, and said, 'Yes, it should be a pleasant break.'

But Alice, who knew the girl a little better than any of the others did, was puzzled. Something was definitely bothering Lizzie. And Alice found out what it was quite by accident.

She was in the changing-room after tennis practice one afternoon when Daffy and Katie came in. Neither of them saw the sixth former, for she was seated behind a row of lockers.

'I'm so excited about half-term!' said Katie. 'Father said that my older brother may be coming as well, and I can't tell you how much I'm looking forward to seeing him again.'

'Yes, it will be fun,' said Daffy. 'Edith is coming out with my people, for her mother can't come, you know.'

'I don't think that Mrs Mannering is terribly well off,' said Katie. 'For Edith told me that she can't afford the train fare to Malory Towers. Still, I'm sure that she will have a marvellous half-term with you.'

'I suppose anything is preferable to being with that miserable, domineering Lizzie,' said Daffy. 'Although I must say, she seems to have taken the news that Edith won't be able to spend half-term with her jolly well. I think that several of the sixth formers have invited her to go out with them.'

The two first formers chattered for a few more minutes as they changed, then they left, their voices fading away.

Alice, who knew very well that no one had invited Lizzie to go with them, sat deep in thought. So, Lizzie had pretended to her sister that she had plans of her own, so that Edith could go off and enjoy herself without feeling guilty. Well, that was all very fine and noble, but why on earth couldn't Lizzie just come out and admit that she felt upset about spending half-term on her own? If Alice had known that Edith was going with Daffy, she would have asked Lizzie to join her people. And, no doubt, a few others would have extended invitations too, for the sixth formers were a good-hearted lot, on the whole. Lizzie must have known that.

She *did* know it, thought Alice, suddenly realising what was preventing Lizzie from telling the others that she would be on her own. It was foolish pride, pure and simple. Alice remembered the way that Lizzie had suddenly seemed to close up when she had been talking about her uncle paying her school fees, and Edith's. The girl didn't like to think that she was at Malory Towers because of someone else's charity, and she didn't want the others to know it either. And what had Katie said? Mrs Mannering couldn't afford the train fare to the school. Yet Lizzie had told Alice that her mother couldn't come because she was too busy – her pride again. And she didn't want the others pitying her, and feeling that they had to ask her to join them, that was why she hadn't told anyone that Edith would be going out with Daffy and her people at half-term. Alice gave a sigh. It was very good to have pride, of course – pride in one's school, one's family and one's self. But the kind of pride that Lizzie had was just foolish, and was going to make her very unhappy in the long run. Alice was quite determined that Lizzie wasn't going to spend half-term alone, but she knew that she would have to approach the girl very carefully. How was she to go about it, though?

A super half-term

Alice wracked her brains, and at last she came up with a plan for inviting Lizzie out, without revealing that she knew Edith was spending half-term with Daffy.

Lizzie spotted Alice going into her study one evening, looking rather preoccupied, and, remembering how kind the girl had been to her, she went across and said, 'Anything wrong, Alice?'

'Oh, hallo, Lizzie,' said Alice. 'Well, nothing is wrong, precisely, it's just that . . .'

She paused, looking up and down the corridor, then went on, 'Look here, can you come into my study for a moment? I don't want to be overheard.'

'Of course,' said Lizzie, surprised and a little alarmed. Whatever could Alice have to say to her?

The two girls sat either side of the desk in the little study, then Alice leaned forward and said in a confiding manner, 'The thing is, Lizzie, I'm absolutely desperate to find someone who will come out with me and my people at half-term, and I just can't think of *anyone*! Julie's parents can't come, but she has already arranged to go with Lucy, and Nora thought that her people might be busy, but it turns out that they are going to be able to come after all. Oh dear, what am I to do?'

'But, Alice, I don't understand,' said Lizzie with a frown. 'Why is it so important that someone comes along with you at half-term?'

'So that I can convince my mother and father that I have settled down here and made friends,' explained Alice. She looked Lizzie in the eye, and said, 'It's no secret that I was once sent away from Malory Towers, when I was in the second form.'

Lizzie nodded, for although she had not been a pupil at the school in those days, she had heard the story.

'It was partly because my parents didn't back me up in the right way,' Alice continued. 'And partly because I was such a horrid little beast that no one wanted to be my friend. But now that I have turned over a new leaf, my parents have done the same, and they are keen to come along and see how I am doing. Mother wrote and said that she would be so thrilled if I could bring a friend along with me at half-term. I know that it would help convince her that I really am doing well at Malory Towers now.'

Lizzie bit her lip. She had grown to like Alice very much, and it would certainly be much more pleasant to go out with her and her people at half-term than to stay at Malory Towers alone, watching everyone else enjoying themselves.

Alice sensed that she was wavering, and said, 'It's a shame that you will be with Edith. I would really have liked you to come with me, Lizzie, for Mother said that she would like to meet my best friend. And I suppose that *you* are my best friend, for I seem to spend more time with you than with anyone else.'

This was all that Lizzie needed to hear, and, turning red with pleasure, she said, 'Well, actually, Alice, I won't be with Edith, for she has been invited out by Daffy Hope and her people.'

'Really?' said Alice, sounding most surprised. Then she sighed, and said, 'I suppose that I am too late, though. No doubt someone else has invited you to go along with them.'

'No, no one has,' said Lizzie. 'And I would simply love to come out with you and your people, Alice.'

'Would you?' said Alice, with a smile. 'Good, well, that's settled then.'

The next few days simply flew by, and the girls grew very excited indeed as half-term drew closer and closer.

The younger ones, in particular, became very boisterous, but most of the mistresses were lenient, and made allowances for their high spirits. Even Miss Potts let Daffy, Katie and Edith off with the mildest of scoldings when the three of them skipped the whole length of the corridor, almost knocking over one of the maids, who was carrying a tray of crockery to the kitchen.

At last the big day arrived, and soon cars lined the driveway, and the school became a hive of activity as girls greeted their parents and eagerly showed them around.

Felicity was delighted to see her mother and father,

of course, but she was a little disappointed that Darrell was not with them.

'I did think that she might be,' she said to June, who was standing nearby. 'For she said to me as I left that she might see me this term.'

'That's funny, Alicia said something similar to me when I saw her in the hols,' said June. 'I half expected her to turn up as well, but there's no sign of her.'

But despite Darrell's absence, Felicity enjoyed a marvellous half-term, going out for lunch on both days with her parents, taking part in the diving exhibition, and going to bed thoroughly worn out, but very happy.

All of the sixth formers were very curious to see Alice's parents, particularly her father, who they remembered very well from her time in the second form.

Alice's father had been a very loud, ill-mannered individual indeed, and although Lizzie had never met him, the others were full of stories, and she felt rather nervous.

But it seemed that Mr Jones had changed his ways, for the man who greeted Alice with a hug was polite, quietly spoken and rather subdued.

He and his wife took the two girls for a picnic on the beach on Saturday, and to a very nice restaurant on Sunday. The restaurant was a rare treat for Lizzie, whose mother had little money to spare for such luxuries, and she enjoyed herself enormously, and thanked Alice and her parents profusely when half-term was over.

The first formers, of course, had had a whale of a

time, and as several of them had birthdays coming up, some of the girls came back with money or gifts.

'My parents have given me some money so that I can have some sort of party,' said Katie.

'And mine,' said Ivy. 'And my grandmother has promised to send me a big birthday cake.'

Violet also came back with a hamper full of goodies, even though it wasn't her birthday. But, as Daffy said, Violet's parents never seemed to need an excuse to spoil her!

'Look at this!' said Violet in the common-room on Sunday evening as she pulled one thing after another from the magnificent hamper. 'Tins of prawns and pineapple, chocolate, shortbread biscuits – oh, and a gingerbread cake!'

'How super,' said Edith enviously.

'We really should have some sort of feast, you know,' said Daffy. 'It's your birthday soon, Katie, and Ivy's. We could make it a joint celebration.'

This suggestion found instant favour.

'Oh yes, do let's!'

'My word, wouldn't that be wonderful!'

'We really should. It must be at least two terms since we last had a feast.'

'When and where, though?' said Katie.

'Well, your birthday is next Saturday, Katie,' said Ivy. 'And mine is the following Monday, so why don't we have it in the middle – on Sunday?'

'Marvellous idea!' said Faith. 'I suppose we could have

it in the dorm, though it's a little cramped in there.'

'The common-room would be better,' said Edith. 'Though it's a little close to the study Mam'zelle and Miss Potts share, and I know that Mam'zelle often sits up late at night.'

'Oh, it would simply ruin things if Mam'zelle heard us,' said Daffy. 'I say, what about having it outside? I remember my sister, Sally, telling me that the upper fourth had a feast by the pool once. They went for a swim, as well.'

'How super!' said Ivy, her eyes lighting up.

'Well, it would have been,' said Daffy. 'Only it began to rain, so they had to go back indoors after all.'

'I really think it would be safer to hold it inside,' said Faith. 'I suppose it will have to be the dorm.'

'Perhaps not,' said Violet, who had been listening to all of this with a thoughtful expression. 'I know of somewhere else we might be able to go.'

'Where?' asked everyone eagerly.

Violet, however, adored being mysterious and having a secret, and refused to say any more for the time being. But she had thought of a rather daring plan, one which she was quite certain even Daffy would not have come up with, and she was certain that she would go up in the estimation of the first formers when they learned what it was.

For Violet intended to get hold of a key for Miss Lacey's class-room, and hold the feast there. It was far enough away from the studies or dormitories for any slight noise to go unheard, and they would be able to have their feast in elegant surroundings. What could be better? Of course, Amy had told Violet about all the fuss there had been when the flower arrangement had been smashed, so the girl knew that they would have to be very careful and clear away any mess after they had finished. And she also knew now that the key was kept on a hook in the housekeeper's room, so it should be quite simple to sneak in and borrow it.

So the first formers went ahead with their plans for the feast, trusting Violet to find a safe place for them to hold it. There was a large cupboard in their common-room, and Violet placed her hamper on the big bottom shelf.

'With the things Ivy and I will buy with our birthday money, there should be more than enough for everyone,' said Katie.

'Well, we others will contribute something too,' said Faith. 'It's only fair, as you two – and Violet – are being generous enough to share with us.'

Over the coming days, the cupboard filled up as the first formers stored their contributions to the feast. Edith managed to save a small amount from her meagre pocket money, and bought two tins of condensed milk. But as she was on her way to the common-room with them, who should she bump into but her sister, Lizzie.

'Hallo, Edith,' said Lizzie. 'It's not like you to be indoors on a glorious day like this.'

At once, Edith flushed guiltily, and she quickly hid

the bag containing the tins behind her back. But Lizzie's sharp eyes spotted the movement, and the guilty look, and she said, 'What are you up to, Edith?'

'N-nothing,' stammered poor Edith, doing her very best to look as innocent as possible. 'I just need to fetch something from the common-room.'

'What are you holding behind your back?' asked Lizzie sharply. 'And don't say "nothing", for I can see quite clearly that you have something there.'

'Just a little shopping,' said Edith, feeling that it was terribly bad luck that she should have run into her sister.

'Oh?' said Lizzie. 'I'm surprised that you have any money to go shopping, Edith, for I know exactly how much pocket money you have, don't forget.'

'Well, I managed to keep a little back, so that I could buy some things that I needed,' said Edith. 'Some shoelaces and a new hair ribbon.'

'Let me see,' said Lizzie, growing more suspicious by the second. Edith's manner was so very odd.

'No!' said Edith defiantly. 'What I choose to spend my pocket money on is none of your business, Lizzie.'

She stepped forward, determined to put an end to the conversation, but as she did so, the paper bag containing her purchases slid from her grasp, and the two tins of milk rolled across the floor.

Swiftly, Lizzie stooped and gathered them up, her mind working quickly, then she glanced at her sister, who had turned very red indeed, and said, 'These are the funniest looking shoelaces I have ever seen. You first formers are planning a midnight feast, aren't you?'

Edith knew that there was no point in denying it, for her face gave her away. If Lizzie had been different, she could have told her all about it, and although her big sister might have pretended to look stern and wagged her finger, there would have been a twinkle in her eye, and they could have laughed about it together. But there was no twinkle in Lizzie's eye, and Edith began to feel angry, as she said, 'What if we are? It has nothing to do with you.'

'Well, that's just where you're wrong,' said Lizzie in a harsh tone. 'I am a sixth former, and it is my duty to see that the rules of the school are kept.'

Edith gave a gasp, and cried, 'But what harm are we doing? It's only a feast.'

'Which means that you will be tired the following day, and unable to concentrate on your lessons,' said Lizzie severely. 'You can't possibly expect to work well if you are up half the night.'

'Do you mean to say that you would get the whole of the first form into trouble just to make me knuckle down?' asked Edith, looking her sister in the eye.

Lizzie hesitated. *Was* she prepared to go that far? The truth was that she simply didn't know, but she wasn't prepared to make an empty threat. So she said heavily, 'I shall have to think about this, Edith. I will let you know what I decide.'

And with that, Lizzie turned on her heel and walked away, leaving her sister staring after her in dismay.

Of course, Edith had to tell the others, for she had to warn them that there was a chance Lizzie might sneak on them, so a meeting was called in the first-form common-room that evening.

'Blow!' said Ivy when Edith broke the news. 'If it had been any other sixth former, I daresay they would have been decent about it and turned a blind eye. Not Lizzie, though, mean beast.'

Edith flushed, for it was not pleasant to hear her sister spoken about in this manner.

'Lizzie *might* not tell,' she said.

'Might isn't really good enough,' said Daffy crossly. 'We need to be absolutely certain that Lizzie won't sneak on us.'

'Edith, please tell me that you weren't silly enough to tell your sister *when* we are holding the feast,' said Katie.

'Of course I wasn't!' said Edith hotly. Then, in a more subdued tone, she added, 'Not that it matters. Lizzie will be watching us like a hawk now.'

'Oh well,' said Ivy with a sigh. 'I suppose that settles it. The feast is off.'

'It doesn't have to be cancelled altogether,' said Faith. 'We can hold a party at teatime, instead.'

But this idea found no favour with the first formers at all.

'Where's the fun in that?'

'It just won't be the same!'

'Sneaking out of our beds at midnight is what makes the party special.'

'No, the midnight feast *will* go ahead!' said a very determined voice, and everyone was surprised to see that it was Edith who had spoken. She got to her feet now, and said, 'I will see to it myself that Lizzie doesn't interfere. Even if it means missing the feast so that I can keep an eye on her.'

The first formers, who had all felt a little cross with Edith, immediately thawed towards her, and Faith said, 'Well, that's awfully decent of you. I must say, it would have been terribly tame if we had had to hold the party at teatime, instead of at midnight.'

'Well, you won't,' said Edith firmly. 'I shall make sure of that.'

Violet plays a trick

Two days before the first formers' feast, Miss Nicholson walked into the study that she shared with Miss Lacey, looking very pale and heavy-eyed.

'My goodness, you look dreadful!' exclaimed Gwendoline. 'Whatever is the matter?'

'Toothache,' groaned poor Miss Nicholson, putting a hand to her jaw. 'I've scarcely slept a wink.'

'Well, you had better go and visit the dentist in town as quickly as possible,' said Gwen.

'I can't,' sighed Miss Nicholson. 'I am taking the first formers for the next lesson. Not that I shall have much to do in the way of actual teaching, for I have set them an essay to write. But I daren't leave them to work unsupervised, for there are far too many scamps in that form!'

'If it is merely a matter of supervising them, surely I could do that,' said Gwen. 'Then you can pop into town and see the dentist.'

'I say, would you?' said Miss Nicholson, brightening. 'That would be awfully good of you. Just watch out for young Daffy Hope and her friend Katie, for they are always up to mischief.'

Then she handed Gwen a sheet of paper, and said, 'This is the essay I would like them to write. It should keep them safely occupied for the whole of the lesson.'

So, while Miss Nicholson went off to find Miss Potts, and explain that she had to rush off to see the dentist, Miss Lacey made her way to the first-form class-room.

The teacher was considerably softer-footed than Miss Nicholson, and the first formers did not hear her coming, so she walked into a scene of disarray. All of the first formers were chattering away like mad, Ivy and Edith were squabbling over possession of a ruler, and Daffy was standing on a chair, trying to attract the attention of someone outside the window.

For a moment, Miss Lacey wished that she had not made her generous offer to Miss Nicholson. The sixth formers were far too dignified and well-mannered to behave badly, but the first form was a very different kettle of fish. Then she pulled herself together, deciding that a few small girls certainly weren't going to get the better of Gwendoline Lacey!

'Girls!' she said, raising her voice. 'Quiet, please!'

Immediately the noise ceased, Daffy got down from her chair, and Ivy and Edith subsided.

Everyone stood, silently, and Miss Lacey, clearing her throat, said, 'Please sit down. Unfortunately, Miss Nicholson has had to go to the dentist, but she has left clear instructions for an essay that she wishes you to write.'

Daffy nudged Katie and whispered, 'Do you suppose that Miss Lacey will leave us to get on with it alone, or do you think that she will stay and supervise us?'

'Daffy!' said Miss Lacey sharply. 'Is there something you wish to say?'

'No, Miss Lacey,' said Daffy meekly, but with a glint of mischief in her eye.

'Then kindly keep quiet,' said the teacher, thinking how unlike her sister, Sally, the girl was. 'Now, you are to write an essay on the rivers of South America, which you may illustrate with maps, if you wish. Please get on with your work quickly and quietly, and if anyone wishes to ask anything, she must put her hand up.'

Though hopefully no one *would* ask anything, for Miss Lacey knew practically nothing about the rivers of South America!

Violet, watching the teacher closely, saw the flicker of uncertainty in her face, and smiled to herself. Amy didn't like Miss Lacey. And, because Amy didn't like her, Violet didn't like her either. How marvellous, she thought, if she could humiliate the teacher, and make her look small. Amy would be most impressed.

The girl wasn't brave enough to be openly rude to Miss Lacey, but halfway through the lesson, when they all had their heads down and were busily working away at their essays, Violet put her hand up and said, 'Miss Lacey, my pen has stopped working.'

'It probably needs some more ink,' said Miss Lacey, looking up.

'Oh no, for I filled it just before the lesson started,' said Violet, looking at her pen with a puzzled expression. 'I simply can't think what's the matter with it.'

'Well, you will have to borrow mine,' said Miss Lacey, rising and picking her pen up from the desk. 'But please make sure that you give it back to me at the end of the lesson, Violet.'

'Thank you, Miss Lacey,' said Violet demurely as the teacher walked towards her. 'I shall remember to give it back to you. I really don't understand why mine has suddenly decided to stop working, though!'

Then, as Miss Lacey leaned over to place the pen on her desk, Violet suddenly shook her own pen violently, and a shower of ink flew from it, leaving dark blue spots all over Miss Lacey's frilly white blouse.

'Oh!' cried the teacher, jumping backwards. 'Violet, you careless girl! Look what you have done. My blouse is quite ruined.'

Some of the first formers had to hide their mirth, for Miss Lacey really did look funny, standing there covered in ink.

'Miss Lacey, I'm so terribly sorry!' said Violet, looking and sounding most contrite, though the first formers had seen her smirk triumphantly. The teacher, however, hadn't, and she said, 'Oh well, I suppose accidents will happen. Now, I am putting you all on your honour to carry on with your essays and behave yourselves, while I go and get changed.'

'Yes, Miss Lacey,' chorused the first form.

But, of course, as soon as she was out of earshot, a perfect babble broke out.

'Violet, you did that on purpose!'

'Yes, you did, I saw the look on your face when the ink splattered Miss Lacey's blouse.'

'And your pen didn't stop working at all,' said Faith, who sat next to Violet. 'That was a fib. Why, Violet?'

'I know why!' said Daffy, suddenly. 'You're getting back at Miss Lacey because your precious Amy doesn't like her.'

'Violet, is that true?' gasped Faith, quite shocked.

'Of course it's true,' said Katie. 'Violet would do anything to score points with Amy. She already follows her around like a little puppy dog.'

'No, I don't!' said Violet hotly. 'Amy is my friend, and she enjoys my company. Why should any of you mind, anyway? At least I got Miss Lacey out of the room for a while.'

'I don't mind at all,' said Daffy with a shrug. 'Actually, I thought it was rather funny. But you are kidding yourself, Violet, if you think that Amy really sees you as a friend. Why on earth would a sixth former want to bother with a kid like you? She just enjoys having someone to worship her, that's all.'

Violet turned an angry red and, anxious to avert a quarrel, Faith said hastily, 'Miss Lacey is taking simply ages. I wonder where she has got to?'

'Perhaps she has gone to report Violet to Miss Potts,' suggested Edith slyly, grinning as Violet turned pale.

But Gwen hadn't done anything of the kind. Hurrying to her bedroom, so that she could change her clothes, she was spotted by Daisy.

'Good heavens, Miss Lacey!' cried the maid, looking at Gwen's ink-stained blouse in astonishment. 'Whatever has happened to you?'

'An accident,' sighed Gwen. 'Oh dear, I do hope that the ink will come out, for this is one of my favourite blouses.'

'Now, don't you worry about that, Miss,' said Daisy soothingly. 'I have something that will get the ink out in a trice. You go and get changed, then bring the blouse to me, and see if I don't have it looking as good as new for you.'

Then she peered closely at Gwen, and said, 'There's a little spot on your skirt, too, so I'd better have that as well. Once I've got the ink stains out, I'll wash and iron them for you, and you shall have them back in a few days.'

'Thanks awfully, Daisy,' said Gwen, sounding more cheerful. 'I really am most grateful.'

Of course, as soon as she had time, Violet rushed off to find Amy, and told her all about the incident.

Amy laughed, and patted Violet's golden head, saying, 'Well done, Violet. Oh, how I wish that I had been there to see that horrid Miss Lacey covered in ink!'

Violet giggled. The two of them were standing outside Amy's study, and the first former looked at the closed door with longing. She had never been invited into

Amy's study, and she would have so loved to go inside. Amy had such lovely things and such marvellous taste, Violet was quite certain that her study would be much nicer than any of the others. How thrilling it would be if Amy were to ask her in, so that they could sit and chat cosily together, perhaps over tea and biscuits. Violet would really feel that she had made a friend of Amy then.

Alas for such grand plans! Bonnie came along at that moment, and Amy said, 'Oh, there you are, Bonnie! I was just going to put the kettle on, and I have some delicious ginger biscuits that my grandmother sent. Will you join me?'

Bonnie accepted the invitation at once, and Violet continued to hang around, quite certain that Amy would ask her in for tea as well. But, instead, the sixth former turned to her, and said, 'You had better run along now, Violet. I daresay that your first-form friends will be wondering where you have got to.'

Violet was bitterly disappointed, and her mood was not improved when she spotted Edith coming out of Lizzie's study.

'It's all very well for Edith,' the girl thought, scowling. 'I bet she is always being invited into her sister's study for cosy chats.'

But Violet was quite wrong, for Edith had been summoned, rather than invited, and her chat with Lizzie had been far from cosy.

'I have come to a decision,' Lizzie had said heavily,

and Edith's heart had sank. Then it lifted again, as Lizzie said, 'I am going to give you a chance. I will turn a blind eye to the first-form feast and allow it to go ahead.'

'Oh, thank you, Lizzie!' said Edith, a smile lighting up her face. 'You won't regret it, I promise! We will be very careful, and –'

But Lizzie held up her hand, and said, 'I haven't finished yet, Edith. The feast can go ahead – provided that you give up any idea of taking part in the swimming gala.'

For a moment, Edith stared at her older sister as if she couldn't believe her ears. Then she cried, 'But you can't ask that of me, Lizzie! It's just not fair!'

'I'm sorry that you feel like that,' said Lizzie. 'But it is up to you to decide.'

'Well, I shan't!' said Edith, her cheeks flaming. 'You have no right to give me such an ultimatum, and I refuse to accept it. I *will* take part in the swimming gala! And if the first formers decide to hold their feast, you won't stop it!'

'I wouldn't be too sure of that, Edith,' said Lizzie, a hard look in her eyes. 'I shall be watching you all very carefully.'

Not trusting herself to say any more, Edith stalked from the room, resisting the impulse to slam the door behind her. Blow Lizzie! Why did she have to interfere all the time?

Then an idea came into her head, and she hurried off to find Daffy and Katie.

The two girls were in the courtyard, and Edith ran across to them.

'Hallo!' said Daffy. 'I say, whatever's up? You look awfully miserable!'

Quickly, Edith told the two girls of Lizzie's ultimatum, and they were quite outraged.

'Who does she think she is?'

'Thank goodness you stood up to her and told her what you thought!'

'Yes, but suppose Lizzie really does carry out her threat to stop our feast?' said Katie. 'Why, she could be sneaking on us to Miss Potts as we speak!'

'I don't think she would be foolish enough to do that,' said Daffy. 'She doesn't know when or where we are having the feast, so she wouldn't be able to give Miss Potts much information. Besides, Potty doesn't much care for sneaks and I think she might send Lizzie away with a flea in her ear.'

'And Potty can hardly punish us for *thinking* about having a feast,' said Edith. 'Why, even if she found our store of food, we could always say that we were planning a teatime party. No, Lizzie means to catch us in the act, then Miss Potts can't doubt her word.'

'Well, unless she stays up and sits outside our dormitory every night, I don't see how she *can* catch us out,' said Katie.

'That's the thing, though,' said Edith with a grimace. 'Lizzie is so persistent, and so used to having her own way, that she is quite likely to do just that!'

'Then what are we to do?' asked Daffy blankly.

'Well, that is where you and Katie come in,' said Edith. 'I'm going to throw Lizzie off the scent, and I want her to overhear the two of you talking about our feast on Sunday night. But I want you to say that we are having it by the pool, and going for a midnight swim too. If I know my sister, she will come outside well before midnight, and lie in wait for us.'

'So she will be out of the way when we leave the dormitory and have our feast indoors,' said Daffy thoughtfully. 'Which is all fine, but when we don't appear at the pool, she's sure to investigate. And she'll no doubt start by taking a look in at our dormitory, which will be empty!'

'Oh no, she won't!' said Edith grimly. 'I gave you my word that I would keep Lizzie out of the way, and I shall.'

'How?' asked Katie.

But Edith refused to tell, and would only say, 'The less you know about it the better.'

Daffy and Katie had the chance to put their plan into action that very evening as they strolled through the grounds before prep.

Coming round a corner, Daffy almost walked right into Lizzie, but the sixth former had her back turned, and didn't see the two first formers. Daffy swiftly retreated back round the corner and, winking at Katie, she raised her voice and said, 'My word, I can't wait until Sunday evening, Katie.'

'Nor can I,' said Katie eagerly. 'A midnight swim, followed by a picnic at the pool. It's going to be super.'

'Yes, we will have to come down at about a quarter to twelve, I should think,' said Daffy. 'For we shall need to get changed into our swimming costumes first.'

The two girls continued to chatter, talking in detail about the feast, but Lizzie, just around the corner, had heard enough. She knew all that she needed to, and now she hurried back to her study to make plans.

So, the first formers were holding their feast by the pool on Sunday night, were they? Well, they could jolly well think again! She, Lizzie, intended to find a good hiding place by the pool, and be there ready to surprise the first formers. The rules about girls leaving their tower at night were very strict indeed, and Miss Potts would take a dim view. A pang of conscience smote Lizzie then, for although she wanted to stop the feast, she didn't want to get her young sister into trouble. Or the other first formers, for that matter. But it was quite Edith's own fault for being so obstinate. If only she had agreed to give up her place in the swimming gala, the first form could have enjoyed their feast in peace. Lizzie still disapproved strongly of such things as midnight feasts, of course, but she had been prepared to compromise a little. In the long run, one late night was going to do less harm to Edith's studies than this swimming nonsense, which took up far too much of her time. Lizzie really did think that she had been very fair and reasonable in saying that the feast could go ahead, but her sister had thrown it back in her face. Miss Potts was sure to punish the first formers severely, but if it made Edith knuckle down, and realise that school wasn't all fun and games, it would be worth it.

Midnight feast

Lizzie told no one about her plans to sneak on the first formers, for she knew that the others would disapprove most strongly.

Alice, however, realised that the girl was preoccupied and did her best to find out what was troubling her.

'Oh, it's nothing,' said Lizzie, when Alice asked her what was wrong. 'I've just had a silly quarrel with Edith, that's all.'

But Alice watched Lizzie closely, and it seemed to her that there was more on her mind than just a silly quarrel. Lizzie did not confide in Alice, though, which was disappointing, for Alice had begun to feel that the two of them were growing closer since half-term.

As Sunday dawned, the first formers were very excited indeed about their feast.

'What a super day it's going to be,' said Ivy happily. 'No lessons, just a glorious day in the sun and a midnight feast to finish off with.'

But that afternoon a thought occurred to Katie as the first formers lazed on the grass, and she sat bolt upright.

'We don't have anything to drink!' she cried. 'I meant to get some bottles of ginger beer yesterday, but June called an extra tennis practice, so I didn't get the chance to go into town.'

'Blow!' said Faith. 'We simply must have something to drink.'

'I suppose we could drink water,' said Violet, wrinkling her nose. 'But it just won't be the same.'

'Water?' said Daffy, looking horrified. 'We can't possibly drink water at a midnight feast! No, I'm sure I can talk one of the kitchen staff into supplying us with something better.'

The first formers thought that this was a marvellous idea, for the angelic-looking Daffy was a great favourite with the kitchen staff. The girl leaped to her feet at once, and raced to the kitchen.

Cook wasn't there, but Daisy was, sitting at the big scrubbed table and drinking a cup of tea.

'Hallo, Daisy,' said Daffy. 'Sorry, I didn't mean to interrupt your break. Is Cookie about?'

'No, she's gone for a bit of a lie-down, for this heat doesn't agree with her,' said Daisy. 'Is there something I can do for you, Miss Daffy?'

Daffy hesitated, looking at the young maid. Then Daisy grinned, and Daffy saw the twinkle in her eye, and decided that she could be trusted.

'The thing is, Daisy,' said Daffy, shutting the kitchen door behind her. 'I wondered if there was any chance of you sparing a couple of jugs of lemonade for a little party that we first formers are planning tonight.'

'Oho!' said Daisy, with a knowing look. 'And would

this party happen to be taking place at midnight, Miss Daffy?'

'Yes,' admitted Daffy. 'But please don't tell anyone, Daisy, or it will all be spoiled.'

'You can trust me,' said Daisy, her grin broadening. 'There's no harm in you youngsters having a bit of fun, that's what I say. I shall leave two jugs of lemonade in here for you tonight, and I shan't say a word to anyone.'

'Thanks awfully, Daisy,' said Daffy happily. 'You're a good sort. I'll see if we can save you a piece of birthday cake!'

Then she went to report back to the others, and Katie said, 'Hooray for Daisy! Violet, you still haven't told us where we are having the feast.'

'All in good time,' said Violet airily. 'I shall tell you tonight.'

Violet had planned to go along to the housekeeper's room that evening and take the key from her room, but she had had an extraordinary piece of good luck. Earlier that day, she had passed the study that Miss Lacey and Miss Nicholson shared. The door was ajar, and Violet could see that it was empty. And there, on the desk, was the key to Miss Lacey's classroom! Violet hesitated. Dare she sneak in and grab it? It was Sunday, so Miss Lacey would not need to use the key today, and the chances were she would not even miss it. Quickly, before she could change her mind, Violet darted into the little study and snatched the key up from the desk, stuffing it into the pocket of her blazer before dashing out again. She felt horribly guilty, but it wasn't as if the first formers were going to leave the room in a mess. They would tidy up after themselves, then she, Violet, would find an opportunity to slip the key back on Miss Lacey's desk before she had even missed it.

Now, as she sat outside with the others, Violet patted the pocket of her blazer, feeling the key safely nestled inside. Oh, what a marvellous night this was going to be!

Lizzie had also made her plans. She intended to go to bed early, and was going to set her little alarm clock for quarter past eleven. That would give her time to dress and slip outside, so that she was there when the first formers came outside for their feast. She had found the perfect hiding place, for there was a small shed down by the pool, where life-belts and the like were stored. If she crouched down beside it, she had a clear view of the pool and the path leading down from the school. Oh, those first formers had a shock coming to them tonight!

Alice put her head round the door of Lizzie's study that evening and said, 'I was just about to have a mug of cocoa. Do you fancy joining me?'

'Thanks, Alice,' said Lizzie. 'But I was just about to turn in. I've got a bit of a headache, and I'm hoping that a good night's sleep will cure it.'

'I thought that you didn't seem yourself,' said Alice. 'Oh well, you get to bed then, and if you're no better tomorrow, perhaps you had better go along and see Matron.'

Lizzie promised that she would, but when she was alone once more, she sighed heavily. The girl had grown very fond of Alice, for she had proved to be a good friend – and now Lizzie had repaid her kindness by lying to her. But she would make it up to Alice somehow. The girl would receive her meagre pocket money from home in a day or two, and she vowed to spend every penny of it on treating Alice to tea in town, even though it meant that she would be broke for the remainder of the month. Her conscience slightly eased by this decision, Lizzie went up to bed, and was fast asleep when the others came up.

The first formers were only too keen to go to bed for once, and there were none of the usual groans and grumbles when the bell sounded.

'I am going to stay awake until eleven o'clock,' said Katie. 'Then I will wake Daffy, and she will sit up until midnight.'

'Then I will have the unenviable task of rousing the rest of you,' said Daffy wryly. 'Violet, I warn you, if you don't get out of bed as soon as I wake you, we will start the feast without you!'

'Don't worry, Daffy,' laughed Violet. 'I wouldn't miss this feast for the world!'

'Daffy, don't forget that you have to wake me before the others,' said Edith. 'I have to go and see what my dear sister is up to.'

'Oh, I almost forgot!' said Daffy. 'Thank goodness you reminded me. Edith, I do hope that your plan to keep Lizzie out of the way works. It will be too bad if you have to spend the whole night leading her on a wild goose chase, and miss the feast.'

'Don't worry, it will work, all right,' said Edith. 'But I can't join you others at the feast if I don't know where it is! Violet, do stop being mysterious and *tell* us!'

'Oh, very well,' said Violet rather grudgingly, for she had planned on keeping her secret until the very last second, and had pictured herself leading the others to Miss Lacey's classroom, and hearing their gasps of amazement as she produced the key and unlocked the door with a flourish.

So she was determined to extract every ounce of drama from the situation now, and, climbing out of bed, she reached into the pocket of her dressing-gown and produced a key, which she held up so that everyone could see it.

'This,' she announced, looking round at everyone, 'is the key to Miss Lacey's class-room. And that is where we are having our feast.'

There was a very mixed reaction indeed, for while some of the girls were thrilled at the thought of having their feast in the 'forbidden' class-room, others thought that Violet had gone too far.

'How exciting!'

'Oh, Violet, dare we?'

'Of course we dare! I've been simply dying to see inside that room.'

'Yes, but if we are caught we will get double the punishment you know!'

'Pooh! We shan't get caught.'

'Violet, do you mean to tell me that you took the key from the housekeeper's room?' asked Faith, looking quite horrified.

'Oh, no,' answered Violet, putting the key back in her pocket and climbing into bed again. 'I took it from Miss Lacey's study.'

Everyone stared at Violet in silence, then Daffy burst out laughing and said, 'I take my hat off to you, Violet! I didn't think you had it in you!'

'It's not funny!' said Faith severely. 'Violet, you have stolen Miss Lacey's property from her study.'

Violet looked rather taken aback at this, for she had not even considered that. Then she said stoutly, 'Nonsense! I haven't stolen it, merely borrowed it. I shall take it back as soon as I can, and she will be none the wiser.'

'I hope she won't, for your sake,' said Ivy.

There was a little more chat, and Miss Potts, making her way along the corridor outside, frowned as she heard the sound of voices coming from the dormitory. She put her hand on the doorknob, but before she turned it, Faith's clear voice came to her ears, saying, 'Quiet now, girls! Let's all try and get some sleep.'

Pleased, the mistress turned and walked away. Faith had turned out to be a very good head-girl, firm and fair. And it was just as well, for the first formers could be a little unruly at times, and they needed someone who was able to keep them in order.

Excited though they were, most of them fell asleep at

once, all except for Katie, of course. She had brought a book to bed with her, to while away the time, and she read it beneath the covers, with the aid of a torch. Even so, the time seemed to pass very slowly, and Katie felt her eyelids drooping several times. But at last it was eleven o'clock, and she padded across to shake the sleeping Daffy.

Daffy sat up at once, blinking a little and wondering why she was being woken in the middle of the night. Then she remembered – it was the night of the feast, and there was only one hour to go!

As Katie snuggled down in her own bed and dropped off to sleep, Daffy sat hugging her knees, her eyes shining in the darkness. She simply couldn't wait for midnight!

A short while later, Edith, who had only slept fitfully, began to stir. As she got out of bed and put her slippers on, Daffy whispered, 'Edith, do take care, won't you? Keep to the shadows, and make sure that none of the mistresses see you.'

'Don't worry about me,' Edith whispered back. 'I shan't get caught.'

And, quickly, the girl slipped on her dressing-gown and tiptoed softly from the room.

It took moments to reach the bottom of the stair, and let herself out of the side door that led into the garden. Then, heeding Daffy's advice, she kept to the shadows, making her way to the cliff path that led down to the pool.

The moon was very bright that night, and Edith hid

behind a large tree, looking all around. Everything seemed quiet and peaceful, with nothing to be seen. Then, suddenly, a small movement over by the old shed caught Edith's eye. Someone was hiding there, and that someone was Lizzie, she was certain of it!

But, before Edith could move, she suddenly saw another figure coming down the cliff path, and her heart leaped into her mouth. Could someone have followed her – and, if so, who?

Hardly daring to breathe, Edith flattened herself against the broad trunk of the tree as the figure drew closer. Then it walked straight past, without having spotted Edith, and the girl let out a little sigh of relief. Edith peered round the trunk of the tree, and saw that the mysterious person was making her way to the shed. Then she frowned. There was something awfully familiar about the person, the way that she walked, her clothes . . . Edith gave a gasp as she realised who it was. Miss Lacey! But what on earth was she doing out here at this time of night?

Lizzie, hiding beside the shed, also watched Miss Lacey approaching, and didn't quite know what to do. Should she make her presence known, and tell the mistress that she was waiting to catch the first formers out? Or should she simply keep quiet and wait to see if Miss Lacey went away?

Alas for Lizzie, she had no choice in the matter, for all of a sudden she felt a terrific tickle in her nose and, quite without warning, she sneezed suddenly.

Miss Lacey, almost at the door of the shed, stopped dead in her tracks, and looked in the direction from where the sneeze had come. Of course, she spotted Lizzie at once, and gave a gasp.

Caught out, Lizzie could do nothing but stand up, and stammer, 'M-Miss Lacey, I daresay you wonder what I am doing here at this hour. The thing is, you see –'

But she got no further, for Miss Lacey suddenly put a warning finger to her lips, and beckoned Lizzie forward.

How odd, thought Lizzie, moving to Miss Lacey's side. The teacher was wearing a hat with a little veil, which covered the top part of her face. What a very strange thing to wear for a late-night stroll in the grounds.

'I thought I heard a noise in the shed,' whispered Miss Lacey, her voice sounding rather hoarse and strained. 'Lizzie, open the door and take a look.'

Lizzie hadn't heard a sound, and said, 'There can't be anything or anyone in the shed, Miss Lacey, for the door is locked from the outside. See? The key is still in the keyhole.'

'I tell you, I heard something,' insisted Miss Lacey, still in the same hoarse voice. 'Open the door at once. '

So Lizzie turned the key and pulled open the door, wrinkling her nose at the musty smell that came from the old shed. It was very dark and gloomy in there, and Lizzie could hardly see a thing as she poked her head inside.

Then, suddenly, she felt a hand between her shoulder blades, propelling her forwards, and she was thrust into the shed, only just managing to keep her balance as the door was pushed shut behind her.

'Miss Lacey!' cried poor Lizzie as she heard the key turning in the lock. 'Miss Lacey, let me out at once!'

Bewildered, angry and a little frightened, Lizzie beat at the door with her fists, but the mistress did not answer. Poor Lizzie did not even know if she was still there, or if she had gone away.

Edith, who had watched the whole astonishing scene from a safe distance, ducked down behind a hedge as Miss Lacey walked back up the cliff path and went towards the school. Then, once the mistress was out of sight, she stood up and looked towards the shed, from which she could hear Lizzie's faint cries.

The girl didn't have the slightest idea why Miss Lacey had imprisoned Lizzie, and she supposed she really ought to go and let her sister out. But the fact was Miss Lacey had done exactly what she, Edith, had planned to do herself! The first former had been quite determined not to let her older sister spoil the feast, and she had decided to somehow lure her to the shed, then lock her in.

Oh dear, thought Edith, as she stood at the bottom of the cliff path, wringing her hands. What a dreadful dilemma! It was one thing for her to lock Lizzie up, to prevent her from ruining the feast. But it was quite another for Miss Lacey to do it, for her own mysterious purposes! In fact, it was quite dreadful. Whoever heard of a mistress doing such a thing? And what on earth could Miss Lacey be up to? But Edith had no time to ponder that now, for the others would be wondering what had happened to her. She gave a last, regretful look over her shoulder at the shed as she walked up the cliff path. It was most unfortunate, but it wouldn't do Lizzie any real harm to spend an hour or so in the shed, and Edith would make sure that she was released once the feast was over. Perhaps, thought the girl, it might even teach her a lesson, and she would think twice before spying on the first formers in future!

A most dramatic night

'I wonder where Edith has got to?' said Faith rather worriedly as the first formers finished setting out the food on the big table in Miss Lacey's class-room.

'I daresay she will be here at any moment,' said Ivy. 'Do try not to fret, Faith.'

'Isn't it marvellous to be able to have our feast in such splendour?' said Daffy. 'And to set the food out on the table, rather than the floor, and sit on chairs to eat.'

'Yes, you've done us proud, Violet,' said Katie, clapping the girl on the shoulder. 'What gave you the idea of using this room?'

Violet had meant to keep her visit to the room with Amy a secret but, basking in the others' praise, she couldn't resist boasting a little.

'Amy brought me in here once,' she said. 'Of course, you mustn't say a word to anyone else, for the other sixth formers are so stuffy that I don't suppose they would like it at all if they knew that Amy had let me into their precious drawing-room.'

'I should think they would be furious with her,' said Faith, staring at Violet in wonder. 'Amy really is the limit!'

Violet was about to leap to Amy's defence, but suddenly Daffy hissed, 'Hush! I can hear footsteps outside.'

As the others fell silent, they could hear the footsteps too, then they froze as the door was pushed open.

Everyone groaned with relief as they realised that it was Edith who stood there, a smile on her face.

'Don't stand there grinning like an idiot!' said Daffy, grabbing her arm and pulling her into the room. 'Let's get this door shut, before anyone sees the light.'

'Was Lizzie lying in wait for us?' asked Katie anxiously. 'Did you manage to get rid of her?'

'I can promise that Lizze won't be sneaking on us tonight,' said Edith, quite truthfully.

She would have dearly loved to tell the others of the strange events that had taken place by the swimming-pool, but one or two of the girls might feel a little uneasy if they knew that poor Lizzie was imprisoned in a shed! It would ruin things if Faith decided to go and let her out! They might also feel uncomfortable if they knew that Miss Lacey was on the prowl.

Edith had kept a wary eye out for the mistress as she walked back to the school, but there had been no sign of Miss Lacey. At one point, Edith had felt sure that she was being followed, but, glancing nervously over her shoulder, she had been relieved to see that no one was there, and had hurried back indoors as fast as she could.

Then she put Miss Lacey to the back of her mind, for there was no way that she could have heard about the first formers' feast, so Edith felt quite certain that, whatever the mistress was doing, she wasn't out to make trouble for them. All the same, she turned to Violet, and said, 'It might be an idea to lock the door. That way if anyone does come prowling around, they won't be able to get in.'

'Good idea,' said Violet, going across and doing just that.

'And, now that we are all settled,' said Daffy, 'let the feast begin!'

The girls sat round the big table and tucked in, feasting on tinned prawns and sardines, pork pie and sausage rolls. Then there were ripe, juicy strawberries, biscuits, chocolate – and a simply enormous birthday cake, which Ivy and Katie had bought between them.

'It's so beautiful that it's almost a shame to cut it,' said Faith, looking at the pink and yellow sugar roses that decorated the cake.

'We'll have to cut it if we are to enjoy it,' said the ever-practical Ivy, beginning to slice the cake. 'Help yourselves, everyone, with good wishes from Katie and me.'

'Happy birthday to you both!' chorused the girls as they raised glasses full of lemonade.

'Yes, even though yours was yesterday, Katie,' said Daffy.

'And mine isn't until tomorrow,' said Ivy.

'No, it is after midnight,' pointed out Violet. 'So your birthday is today.'

'So it is!' said Ivy happily, taking a sip of lemonade. 'Well, this is a jolly good start to it, I must say.'

'What a super night this is,' said Faith with a contented sigh. 'I really don't think that anything could spoil it.'

But she was wrong. Something could – and something was just about to!

Miss Potts was roused from a deep sleep shortly after one o'clock. She sat up and switched on her bedside lamp, wondering what it could have been that had woken her so suddenly. There were no strange noises to be heard, but *something* had disturbed her, so the mistress put on her glasses, which were on the bedside table, and went to look out of her window. It was a perfectly still summer night, with no wind and no rain, and there was nothing to be seen outside. Puzzled, the mistress had just decided to go back to bed, when a floorboard creaked outside her room, and there came a sharp rapping at her door.

Miss Potts jumped, and went across to the door, pulling it open. But there was no one to be seen there, either. How very odd! Miss Potts looked along the corridor, just in time to see a figure disappearing round the corner. Who it was she didn't know, for she only had the briefest glimpse. But whoever it was must be the person who had knocked on her door.

Most annoyed at being disturbed, the mistress quickly put on her dressing-gown and slippers, before setting off in pursuit of the culprit. It was probably one of the younger girls, dared by another to play a prank. But Miss Potts did not care for pranks, especially in the middle of the night, and woe betide the girl when she caught up with her!

The mistress went round the corner where she had seen the figure disappearing. And now she seemed to have vanished completely, for there was no sign of her – how annoying! But then Miss Potts peered over the banisters, just in time to see someone going towards Miss Lacey's class-room, and she made her way quickly down the stairs.

Now Miss Potts was in luck, for when she reached the corridor where the class-room was, the person was standing right outside, as if wondering whether to go in. Why, it was Miss Lacey! But what on earth was she doing wandering round the school at this late hour? Miss Potts wondered if she could be sleepwalking, but no, she was fully dressed – why, she was even wearing a hat!

'Miss Lacey!' hissed Miss Potts in a low voice, for although they were away from any bedrooms and dormitories, she didn't want to risk disturbing anyone.

Miss Lacey turned sharply and, for a moment, Miss Potts thought that she was going to say something. But then she scuttled away down the corridor, leaving Miss Potts feeling most exasperated. What on *earth* was she playing at?

The mistress was about to follow, when she heard a sound coming from the class-room. The unmistakable sound of girls giggling. She pursed her lips. Really, the whole school seemed to have gone quite mad tonight!

The first formers, busily clearing away after their feast, hadn't heard anything at all outside. So it came as a terrible shock to them when someone tried the handle of the door.

Katie dropped the plate that she was holding, and the thud it made as it landed on the carpet sounded very loud indeed in the still of the night.

'Idiot!' hissed Ivy, giving her a push.

'Hush!' whispered Faith. 'Let's try to keep calm until we know who is there.'

Then Miss Potts knocked smartly on the door, making everyone jump again.

'Who do you think it is?' whispered Violet fearfully, clutching at Daffy's arm.

'I don't know,' Daffy whispered back, trying to sound brave. 'But whoever it is, it means trouble for us!'

Then Miss Potts spoke, sounding very angry indeed. 'I know that there is someone in there, and I insist that you open this door at once!'

'Oh, help, it's Potty!' groaned Edith. 'Now what are we to do?'

'There's only one thing we can do,' sighed Faith. 'Open the door and face the consequences. Blow!'

'Your sister must have sneaked, after all,' said Ivy, to Edith, looking cross.

'She didn't,' said Edith shortly. 'Whoever told Miss Potts that we were in here, I can assure you that it wasn't Lizzie.'

Faith, meanwhile, had unlocked the door, with trembling hands, and now she opened it and stood aside to let Miss Potts in.

At once, everyone fell silent, their heads bent and eyes downcast, as Miss Potts's keen eyes took in the remnants of the feast and she saw at a glance what had been going on.

'Well!' she said in a stern voice. 'Not content with breaking one school rule by holding a midnight feast, you have broken another by holding it in a room that is out of bounds. Have you anything to say for yourselves?'

As head of the form, Faith stepped forward and said, 'We are awfully sorry, Miss Potts. But you see, it was Katie's birthday, then Ivy's, and –'

'And you thought that was a reasonable excuse to flout the rules,' said Miss Potts scornfully. 'I am very disappointed in you all.'

The girls hung their heads, then Miss Potts said, 'How did you manage to get hold of a key to this room? I suppose that you took it from the housekeeper's room?'

There was a long silence, and Violet's knees began to tremble.

'Well?' said Miss Potts sharply. 'I am waiting for an answer.'

'You'll have to own up, Violet,' whispered Daffy. 'It can't be helped.'

So, feeling quite faint, Violet said, in a shaking voice, 'I took the key from Miss Lacey's study, Miss Potts.'

The mistress stared at Violet incredulously. Then she said, 'This just becomes more and more serious! Well, it is too late to deal with you now. Go back to bed, all of you, and report to Miss Grayling's office immediately after breakfast tomorrow.'

'But, Miss Potts, we haven't finished clearing up,' ventured Daffy in a small voice.

'You will give up your break and do it tomorrow,' said Miss Potts severely. 'And see that you make a good job of it! Now, off to bed with you at once. Edith, why are you standing rooted to the spot?'

'You see, Miss Potts,' said Edith hesitantly. 'There is something else. My sister, Lizzie, is locked in the shed down by the swimming-pool, and I really think that someone should go and let her out.'

Miss Potts stared at Edith as if she couldn't believe her ears! Had her form taken leave of their senses tonight?

The first formers looked at one another in surprise too, for it was the first they had heard of Lizzie being locked in the shed!

'Am I to understand, Edith, that you locked your sister in a shed?' asked Miss Potts in a carefully controlled tone.

'Oh no, Miss Potts,' said Edith, shaking her head. 'It wasn't me. I meant to, for I knew that she intended to spoil our feast but, as things turned out, I didn't need to. You see, it was Miss Lacey who locked her in. I saw her.'

For a moment, Miss Potts wondered if Edith was

being foolish enough to try to make a joke. Then she looked at the girl's earnest expression, and realised that she was serious.

Faintly, the mistress said, 'Miss Lacey locked Lizzie in the shed.'

'That's right, Miss Potts,' said Edith. 'I know it sounds quite incredible, but please believe me, for it's the truth.'

Well, Miss Lacey had certainly been behaving very strangely a little while ago, thought Miss Potts, on whom the evening's events were beginning to take their toll. Perhaps she had taken leave of her senses, and really *had* imprisoned Lizzie.

'Very well,' she said wearily. 'Edith, you come with me to the swimming-pool, and the rest of you get to bed.'

'Yes, Miss Potts,' chorused the girls, sounding very subdued.

'And if there is one more sound from your dormitory tonight, whatever punishment Miss Grayling gives you tomorrow will be increased ten-fold,' she said firmly. 'Violet, please give me the key to this room, so that I can lock the door when everyone has left.'

Meekly, Violet handed over the key, and everyone left the room, the first formers trooping silently back to their dormitory, while Miss Potts and Edith made their way down to the pool.

There wasn't a sound coming from the shed, and Edith wondered if her sister had fallen asleep in there. Not that it would be a terribly comfortable place to sleep, for there was only a hard floor, and Edith wouldn't be at all surprised if there were spiders in there – and Lizzie simply hated spiders. Her conscience, which had been troubling her a little all night, now came fully alive. Poor Lizzie must have suffered quite an ordeal.

Miss Potts was turning the key in the padlock and, as she opened the door, Edith gave a cry – for the shed was quite empty! But how on earth could Lizzie have escaped, for there wasn't so much as a small window in the shed. Or had Miss Lacey returned and let her out?

Miss Potts turned her stern gaze upon Edith, who said hastily, 'Miss Potts, Lizzie really was locked in the shed, you must believe me!'

Miss Potts did, for it was quite obvious that the girl was telling the truth, and she said wearily, 'Well, she is not there now. Hopefully she is safely asleep in her dormitory. I shall go and check on my way back to bed. I trust that, in the morning, we will get to the bottom of all these strange events.'

Miss Potts escorted Edith back to her dormitory, then went to see if Lizzie was in her bed. Fortunately, the girl was, fast asleep and looking none the worse for her ordeal. Miss Potts was pleased, for she really felt quite exhausted now and didn't think that she could deal with any more extraordinary events that evening. But there was still one more thing that she had to do before she could finally retire. On the way to her own bedroom, the mistress stopped outside Miss Lacey's room and, very quietly and carefully, she pushed open the door.

Miss Lacey lay in bed, breathing deeply, her eyes

closed, and her clothes hung neatly over the back of a chair. That was odd, thought Miss Potts, frowning, for they weren't the clothes that Miss Lacey had been wearing a little while ago. But she was too relieved that the teacher had ccased her nocturnal wandering to worry about that now. Closing the door softly behind her, Miss Potts went back to her own bedroom and fell into an exhausted sleep, where she dreamed of midnight feasts, girls locked in sheds and sinister, shadowy figures who roamed the corridors at night!

Miss Lacey's strange behaviour

In fact, Lizzie had been released from her prison by
Felicity and Alice.

Alice had been woken by a ray of moonlight coming
in through a chink in the curtains. When she had got up
to close the curtains properly, she had seen that Lizzie's
bed was empty. Oh well, the girl had thought, perhaps
she had just gone to get a glass of water, for it was a very
warm evening. But, when Lizzie did not return, she
began to feel a little uneasy, and decided that she had
better go and look for the girl.

As she was donning her slippers and dressing-gown,
a voice in the darkness whispered, 'Alice, is that you?
What are you doing?'

'Oh, Felicity,' whispered Alice. 'Lizzie isn't in her bed,
and I'm going to look for her. I'm a little worried,
because I think she has had something on her mind the
last few days.'

'Well, you can't possibly go wandering round on your
own,' Felicity said, sitting up. 'I'll come with you. Go to
my bedside cabinet, Alice, and you'll find a torch there.
We'll take that with us.'

Soon the two girls found themselves at the little side

door, through which Edith had let herself out earlier. But, on letting herself back in again, Edith had been in such a hurry that she hadn't closed it properly, and now it stood ajar.

'This is very odd,' said Felicity, with a frown. 'The maids are usually so thorough about locking up at night.'

'I wonder if Lizzie could have let herself out though this door?' said Alice. 'But whatever can she be doing outside?'

'I don't know,' said Felicity. 'But we had better try to find her quickly.'

The girls' search eventually took them to the cliff path that led to the swimming-pool and, as they walked down it, Alice stopped suddenly, grasping Felicity's arm.

'Did you hear that?' she said. 'It sounded like somebody yelling. Listen! There it is again!'

'Yes, I heard it that time,' said Felicity. 'It seems to be coming from that shed. Come on, Alice, let's go and investigate.'

Lizzie could have almost wept with relief when she heard the voices of the two girls outside her prison, and she fell into Alice's arms as the door was opened.

'Lizzie!' cried Felicity in astonishment. 'What on earth happened?'

'She's frozen,' said Alice, chafing the girl's hands.

Indeed, Lizzie was shivering dreadfully, for although it had been warm earlier, the night had turned very chilly, and the dark little shed was cold.

'Let's go back to my study,' said Felicity. 'I'll make us all some hot cocoa, then Lizzie can get warm.'

The thought of hot cocoa was very welcome indeed to Lizzie, but she said, 'I must go and find Miss Potts first. You see, the first formers are having a midnight feast.'

'Do you mean to tell me it was one of those little first-form wretches who locked you in here?' said Alice angrily.

'No,' said Lizzie. 'It was Miss Lacey, though why she should have done such a thing beats me.'

Felicity and Alice exchanged glances, for Lizzie didn't seem to be making any sense at all.

'Lizzie, you are coming back to my study for a hot drink, and that's an order,' said Felicity firmly. 'Then you can tell Alice and me exactly what happened.'

Lizzie protested, but Felicity and Alice resolutely bore her up the cliff path and into school.

'Well,' said Alice, when the three of them were comfortably settled with mugs of hot cocoa. 'What's all this about, Lizzie?'

Lizzie told them the whole story, the two girls frowning in disapproval when she related how she had been lying in wait for the first formers to begin their feast. And when she told them that Miss Lacey had pushed her into the shed, their eyes grew wide with astonishment.

'Either you got hold of the wrong end of the stick, or the first formers were having you on,' said Felicity, when she had finished. 'There was no feast going on at the pool tonight, that much was obvious.'

'I know that they are having a feast,' said Lizzie stubbornly. 'Edith as good as told me so when I caught her hiding some food she had bought.'

'Well, what if they were?' said Alice. 'Goodness me, there's no harm in an occasional midnight feast! What a spoilsport you are, Lizzie.'

Lizzie turned red and said, rather stiffly, 'I think that there is a great deal of harm in it. Edith should be concentrating on her studies, not on pranks and feasts.'

'Lizzie, you really have got a bee in your bonnet about all this,' said Felicity, frowning at the girl. 'Midnight feasts are part and parcel of boarding school life. Yes, they are against the rules. But this is a rule that all schoolgirls break at some time or other, for it is just a bit of harmless fun.'

'Oh, you don't understand!' said Lizzie, becoming agitated. 'If Edith gets into trouble, or doesn't do well here, it could mean no more Malory Towers for both of us.'

'Whatever do you mean?' said Alice curiously. 'I say, Lizzie, this isn't something to do with that uncle of yours, is it?'

'What uncle?' said Felicity. Then she saw that Lizzie was looking uncomfortable, and said, 'Look here, Lizzie, if there's something you want to get off your chest, you may be sure that neither Alice nor I will betray your confidence. Isn't that so, Alice?'

Alice nodded emphatically and, at last, Lizzie said, 'As I told you, Alice, our uncle pays our school fees. But what I didn't tell you is that he expects Edith and me to repay him, once we are old enough and are making our way in the world.'

Neither Felicity nor Alice knew quite what to say to this, and Lizzie went on, 'Mother impressed on us that we had to work hard and pass all our exams well, for that is the only way that we will be able to get good jobs and pay Uncle Charles back when we are older. If he thinks either of us is wasting our time here, there is a good chance that he will refuse to continue paying the fees, then Edith and I will have to leave, and I will probably have to go out and find a job. But I know that I shall be able to get a much better one if I finish my education first.'

'Well, I see now why studying is so important to you,' said Felicity, frowning. 'And why you are so hard on young Edith at times. But I'm sure that your uncle wants you both to have fun here too, and be able to look back upon your time at Malory Towers with enjoyment.'

'Perhaps,' said Lizzie. 'You see, neither of us know Uncle Charles awfully well. He is Father's older brother, and he lives a long way from us, so we never see very much of him.'

'Personally, I always found it easier to study if I had a little fun and relaxation in between,' said Alice. 'You sort of come back to it with a fresh mind then, whereas if you sit poring over a book for hours on end, everything ends up getting all muddled in your mind. At least, it does in *my* mind.'

'Yes, I suppose you are right,' said Lizzie thoughtfully. Then she sighed, and said, 'I wonder where Edith and her friends are holding their feast tonight? I overheard Daffy and Katie talking about it, and distinctly heard them say that it was tonight, by the swimming-pool.'

'They probably knew that you were listening, and were leading you up the garden path,' said Alice drily.

'I wouldn't be at all surprised,' said Felicity. 'I must say, I'm much more concerned about Miss Lacey's part in this than anything the youngsters might be up to. Lizzie, are you absolutely certain that she was the one who locked you in the shed?'

'Absolutely,' said Lizzie firmly. 'She was acting awfully strange, and even her voice seemed peculiar – sort of hoarse.'

'You know that you will have to report it to Miss Grayling,' Felicity said soberly. 'And she will have to decide what is to be done, though I can't imagine her wanting to keep a mistress at Malory Towers who goes around locking up the pupils!'

'It's been a jolly odd sort of night,' said Alice, putting a hand up to her mouth to stifle a yawn. 'And now I suppose that we had better turn in, or we shall never be able to get up in the morning.'

The three girls made their way back to their dormitory, letting themselves in very quietly, so as not to disturb the others.

Alice and Lizzie fell asleep at once, but Felicity lay awake for a little while, puzzling over the evening's events, and Miss Lacey's part in them in particular.

'I remember Darrell saying that Gwen could be sly, and that she played some mean tricks on Mary-Lou when she was in the first form,' thought Felicity. 'But surely she has grown out of that kind of spiteful behaviour now? And what possible reason could she have for locking Lizzie in the shed?'

But Felicity couldn't come up with any reason at all for the mistress's extraordinary behaviour and, at last, she fell asleep too.

'Come on, sleepyheads!' said Susan, the following morning, as Felicity, Alice and Lizzie had great difficulty in getting out of bed. 'Anyone would think that the three of you had been up all night at a midnight feast, or something.'

'Nothing so jolly,' said Felicity, sighing as she left the comfort of her bed. 'Though we did have rather a disturbed night.'

'Do tell!' said Nora, who was standing in front of a mirror, brushing her hair.

So, with much prompting from Lizzie and Alice, Felicity told the sixth formers what had taken place last night. The others were very shocked and surprised, of course.

'Well! How very strange!'

'I've heard of girls playing pranks on teachers, but never teachers playing pranks on girls!'

'I would never have thought Miss Lacey capable of such a thing!'

'It doesn't surprise me in the slightest,' said Amy with a sniff. 'I always thought there was something rather odd about her.'

'Well, I think that Miss Lacey deserves a great big pat on the back,' declared June, giving Lizzie a scornful look. 'For she saved the first formers from having their feast ruined. You might call it looking out for your young sister, Lizzie, but as far as I'm concerned, you're no better than a sneak.'

Lizzie turned red, and Pam said hastily, 'My word, I wouldn't like to be in Miss Lacey's shoes when Miss Grayling hears about this. I wouldn't be a bit surprised if she is dismissed immediately.'

In fact, Miss Grayling already knew about Miss Lacey's behaviour, for Miss Potts had gone to the Head's study as soon as she was dressed and reported it.

'This is a very grave accusation, Miss Potts,' said Miss Grayling, looking at the mistress with a serious expression. 'You are quite certain that the person you saw in the corridor was Miss Lacey?'

'It certainly looked like her,' said Miss Potts. 'Edith actually saw her push Lizzie into the shed and lock the door. Apparently Miss Lacey spoke to Lizzie before she locked her in, though Edith was too far away to hear what she said. I haven't spoken to Lizzie myself yet, Miss Grayling, for I thought that you would want to do that.'

'Yes, and I will certainly need to see Miss Lacey,' said

the Head. 'That is not likely to be a pleasant interview, for if it is true that she imprisoned one of the girls I have no alternative but to send her away.'

'No, I don't suppose that you do,' said Miss Potts with a sigh. 'It is a great pity, though, for while I never had much time for Gwen when she was a pupil here, I was beginning to think that she had changed her ways and was actually making a go of things as a mistress.'

'Yes, so was I,' said Miss Grayling. 'How very disappointing it is to know that we were wrong! Miss Potts, send Miss Lacey to me at once, would you? I don't want her going into breakfast with the girls, for she must stay away from them until this matter has been resolved one way or another.'

'Of course, Miss Grayling,' said Miss Potts. Then she went off to knock on the door of Miss Lacey's bedroom.

The young mistress opened it, looking rather taken aback to see Miss Potts standing there at such an early hour. But she did not appear at all embarrassed or awkward, which, thought Miss Potts, was very odd, considering her strange behaviour of the night before.

'Miss Grayling would like to see you in her study at once, Miss Lacey,' Miss Potts said briskly.

'Before breakfast?' said Miss Lacey, sounding most surprised. 'Why, whatever does she want that is so urgent?'

'She will no doubt tell you that herself,' said Miss Potts. 'But I shouldn't keep her waiting if I were you, Miss Lacey.'

In the first-form dormitory, meanwhile, an air of gloom prevailed. All of the girls felt very tired indeed, and they had what was sure to be a pretty severe punishment to look forward to. Not even the fact that it was Ivy's birthday could cheer them up.

'I know it's got off to a rotten start,' said Katie dispiritedly, 'but happy birthday, Ivy, old girl.'

'Thanks,' said Ivy, doing her best to conjure up a smile. 'Oh well, at least things can only get better.'

And, for a while, things did get a little better, as the girls all gave Ivy presents and cards.

'You're all very decent,' said Ivy. 'This almost makes up for being caught out last night.'

Just then, like a small whirlwind, Daffy burst in and cried, 'I say, you'll never guess what I've just heard! Apparently it was Miss Lacey who split on us to Miss Potts. I just overheard Potty discussing it with Matron outside the bathroom, and it seems that Miss Lacey led Miss Potts right to our door.'

'How mean of her!' cried Violet. 'We weren't doing any harm. Amy was quite right about her.'

'But how did she know that we were having a feast?' said Ivy, wrinkling her brow.

'She probably just found out by chance,' said Edith. 'She was certainly prowling around last night, for she shut Lizzie in the shed, remember. She must have come along this corridor and heard the noise we were making.'

'It's all very strange,' said Katie. 'I wonder why she *did* shut Lizzie in the shed?'

'I can't imagine,' said Edith. 'I just hope that Miss Grayling gets to the bottom of it, and that she sends Miss Lacey away as soon as possible.'

Miss Nicholson saves the day

It was a very trying day for Miss Grayling, and one that was full of surprises.

When Miss Lacey came to her study, the Head wasted no time at all in getting to the point.

The mistress was most astonished to discover that she had been accused of imprisoning Lizzie Mannering, and she protested her innocence hotly. Miss Grayling watched her closely, and had to admit that, if Miss Lacey was lying, she was a remarkably good actress.

'But Miss Potts saw you as well,' said Miss Grayling. 'You led her to your class-room, where the first formers were having a midnight feast.'

'They were holding a feast in my class-room?' gasped Miss Lacey. 'I knew nothing at all of this, Miss Grayling, you must believe me. And I certainly wasn't wandering around last night, either in the corridors or down by the pool.'

The Head hardly knew what to say, for there were three witnesses who swore that they had seen Miss Lacey last night, yet the young woman seemed very sincere in her protestations of innocence.

Just then, someone knocked urgently at the door,

and Miss Grayling called out, 'Come in.'

Miss Nicholson entered the room and, not at all pleased at being interrupted, the Head said, 'Miss Nicholson, I am rather busy at the moment. Could you come back later, please?'

'I'm awfully sorry to interrupt,' said Miss Nicholson. 'But, you see, Miss Grayling, I know what Miss Lacey has been accused of, for the story is all over the school.'

'Well, I suppose it was only a matter of time before gossip began to spread,' said Miss Grayling. 'But I fail to see how it concerns you, Miss Nicholson.'

'Oh, but it does!' said the mistress. 'You see, Miss Grayling, Miss Lacey was with me last night. We sat up until very late in our study, chatting away about all sorts of things. Isn't that so, Miss Lacey?'

Catching the meaningful expression on her friend's face, Miss Lacey nodded and said, 'Er – yes, it is just as Miss Nicholson says.'

'Well!' said the Head, looking surprised. 'This puts a very different complexion on things. It seems that the person seen wandering around Malory Towers last night must have been someone else. Though how she came to be wearing your clothes is quite a puzzle!'

'Miss Grayling,' said Miss Lacey. 'What was the person wearing?'

'A white blouse and pink floral patterned skirt, according to Miss Potts,' said the Head. 'And, most unusually, a hat with a small veil.'

'Well, I certainly have an outfit like that,' said Miss

Lacey, frowning. 'But Daisy took the skirt and blouse off to be cleaned, because Violet accidentally splashed ink on them, and I haven't had them back yet. As for the hat – well, now that I come to think about it, I haven't seen it for a while.'

'This just becomes more and more mysterious!' exclaimed the Head. 'I shall have to speak to Daisy about the clothes, of course. Miss Lacey, you may go, and I am very sorry that you were unjustly accused. Oh, and you had better have this back, too.'

The Head took something from her drawer, and handed it to Miss Lacey. It was the key to her class-room.

'Miss Potts gave me this,' said Miss Grayling. 'It seems that Violet took it from your study yesterday. Needless to say, she will be punished for it.'

Well, really, thought Miss Lacey, it was just one thing after another! Murmuring a faint word of thanks, she took the key and put it in her pocket. Then she and Miss Nicholson went on their way, walking along the corridor in silence, each of them lost in her own thoughts. Only when they were safely in their own study, with the door shut behind them, did Miss Lacey break the silence, saying, 'You told the Head a lie to get me out of trouble. Why did you do that?'

Miss Nicholson turned a little red, and said gruffly, 'Because you are my friend, and I know that you didn't do what you were accused of. If it had just been Lizzie's or Edith's word against yours, the Head might have believed you. But Miss Potts also thinks she saw you, and you know how much Miss Grayling trusts her.'

Gwen looked at Miss Nicholson's round, rather plain face, and suddenly knew the meaning of true friendship. She thought back over the girls she had tried to befriend during her time as a pupil at Malory Towers, and then at finishing school. All of them had been wealthy, gifted or beautiful. Miss Nicholson was none of these things, but she was kind, loyal and good-hearted. And those were the things that really mattered in a friend. Gwen had been stupid not to see it years ago, she realised now.

'Thanks awfully,' she said in a low voice. 'I'll never forget what you did for me today.'

'Oh, think nothing of it,' said Miss Nicholson, going back to her usual hearty manner. 'What we have to consider now is that there is someone going around disguised as you.'

'Yes, and whoever it is is causing trouble in the hope that I will get the blame,' said Gwen, frowning. 'How I wish I knew who it was!'

Miss Nicholson said nothing, apparently lost in thought, then, abruptly, she said, 'You never told me about the incident with Violet and the ink.'

Gwen shrugged. 'It hardly seemed worth mentioning. I was a little annoyed at the time, but it was just an accident and there was no real harm done.'

'Are you quite sure that it was an accident?' asked Miss Nicholson.

'I think so,' said Gwen, puzzled. 'Why do you ask?'

'Because it suddenly occurred to me that young Violet

positively worships Amy of the sixth form, and would do anything for her,' said Miss Nicholson. 'And Amy's dislike of you is well-known.'

'What are you getting at?' asked Gwen, her brow furrowed.

'Well, Amy is about the same height as you, though a little slimmer,' said Miss Nicholson. 'And her hair is the same colour, so . . .'

As Miss Nicholson's voice tailed off, light suddenly dawned on Gwen. 'You think it was *Amy* who was masquerading as me last night!' she gasped. 'Oh, my goodness!'

Just then the two mistresses heard someone humming a tune in the corridor outside, and Miss Nicholson said, 'That's Daisy! She always hums while she works. Let's see if she can shed any light on who may have taken your clothes.'

She pulled open the door, calling, 'Daisy, would you come in here for a moment, please?'

Daisy entered the study, looking a little scared, and Gwen said, 'Daisy, what happened to the skirt and blouse that I gave you to wash for me the other day? I haven't had them back yet.'

'Why, Miss Lacey, I washed and ironed them, just as I said I would,' said Daisy. 'And I went to hang them up in your bedroom, but the door was locked, so I brought them in here. In fact, I hung them over the back of that very chair that you are sitting on, Miss Lacey.'

The two mistresses exchanged glances, and Miss

Nicholson said, 'When was this, Daisy?'

The maid thought for a moment, and said, 'It would have been while you were both at breakfast yesterday morning. I do hope that I haven't done anything wrong but, you see, the door was open, and –'

'No, you've done nothing wrong, Daisy,' said Gwen. 'Thank you, you may go now.'

The maid left, shutting the door behind her, and Miss Nicholson sat down in the chair opposite Gwen's, saying, 'That settles it then. Violet came in here yesterday and took your key. I'll bet that she saw your clothes on the chair and took those as well.'

'You think that she gave them to Amy, so that she could disguise herself as me?' said Gwen.

'That's exactly what I think,' said Miss Nicholson firmly.

'It's certainly possible,' said Gwen thoughtfully. 'And I have been thinking about my hat, and have realised that it must have been taken when my bedroom was ransacked. I didn't notice that it was missing at the time, for I don't particularly like it and I was thinking of throwing it away.'

'If that is so, then either Amy or Violet – or both of them – are responsible for ransacking your room,' said Miss Nicholson with a grim expression.

'Then there was the time that someone got into my class-room and did all that damage,' said Gwen, looking thoughtful. 'I was convinced that was Amy too, but Daisy was able to clear her name. Oh dear, how horrible it is! I really don't know what to think! Should we tell Miss Grayling of our suspicions?'

'No, for we have no proof,' said Miss Nicholson. 'I think we need to catch the two of them out ourselves.'

'Perhaps you are right,' said Gwen. 'And until we do, we had better make sure that we lock the study door whenever we leave it.'

'I don't think that we should,' said Miss Nicholson. 'We need to make it easy for Amy and Violet to play their tricks so that we can trap them somehow. All the same, we had better be careful what we leave lying around in here. And we must be sure not to let either of the girls think that we suspect them, for that will put them on their guard, you know.'

Violet, meanwhile, quite unaware that she was regarded with such dark suspicion by the two mistresses, was in the Head's study, along with the rest of the first form.

They had already endured a very severe scolding, and Miss Grayling finished off by saying, 'Although midnight feasts are against the rules, I am well aware that most schoolgirls take part in them now and again. But there are other things about this business that concern me greatly.'

She paused to look sternly at the first formers, all of whom were standing with bent heads.

'First of all, you held the feast in a room that was out of bounds,' went on Miss Grayling in a very serious voice. 'A room that you had been put on your honour not to enter. Faith, as head of the form, didn't you feel some sense of responsibility? Didn't it occur to you that you should – at the very least – have stopped the others from using that room?'

Faith bit her lip. It had occurred to her, briefly. But then she had got caught up in the excitement of it all, and had been as thrilled as the others at the thought of having the feast in Miss Lacey's class-room.

'No,' she said honestly, raising her head and looking Miss Grayling in the eye. 'But it should have. I am very sorry, Miss Grayling. We all are.'

'As for you, Violet,' said Miss Grayling. 'What you did was very wrong indeed. You had no right to go into the mistresses' study, never mind stealing Miss Lacey's key.'

The unfortunate Violet trembled like a leaf, and her voice shook as she said, 'I-I didn't think of it as stealing, Miss Grayling. It *wasn't* stealing, for I meant to return it to the study this morning.'

'I daresay,' said Miss Grayling. 'However, I trust that the punishment I give you will make you think twice before you decide to help yourself to someone else's property in the future.'

Miss Grayling looked at the row of bent heads before her, then said, 'You are all confined to school for the next two weeks.'

The first formers groaned inwardly, for this meant no walks on the beach and no trips into town to spend their pocket money. No one protested, though, for they all knew that they had well and truly earned the punishment.

'You, Violet, will apologise to Miss Lacey,' the Head continued, and Violet almost sighed with relief, for she felt that she had got off very lightly. But Miss Grayling hadn't finished.

'You will also go to bed an hour early every night for the next week. And I hope that you will use the time to reflect on what you have done.'

This seemed very harsh indeed to poor Violet. How horrid to have to go to bed when it was still light outside, and the others were in the common-room having fun. But she did not dare argue with the Head, and said meekly, 'Yes, Miss Grayling.'

Daffy, however, had listened to this with a frown and, as she was considerably bolder and more outspoken than Violet, she said, 'But Miss Grayling, didn't Miss Potts tell you that Miss Lacey locked Edith's sister in the shed last night? She doesn't deserve an apology, if you ask me. In fact –'

'I didn't ask you, Daphne,' said Miss Grayling, so coldly that the girl fell silent. 'So kindly keep your opinions to yourself until I ask for them. I have investigated the matter, and the person who locked Lizzie in the shed was most definitely *not* Miss Lacey.'

The first formers looked at one another in astonishment and, unable to hold her tongue, Edith said, 'But it was, Miss Grayling. I beg your pardon, but I saw her with my own eyes.'

'No, Edith,' said the Head. 'The person you saw was someone pretending to be Miss Lacey. Who it was, and what her motive was, I don't know, but I hope that we will get to the bottom of the matter eventually. Now, you may all go to your lesson. Miss Potts knows that you have been with me, so she will excuse you for being late. Edith, not you. I would like a word with you, please.'

As the others trooped out, Edith looked rather alarmed. And her heart sank when Miss Grayling looked at her coldly, and said, 'I find it quite extraordinary, Edith, that you watched someone lock Lizzie in a shed and, rather than letting her out, you simply left her there and went off to enjoy a feast with your friends. Hardly the behaviour of a loyal and loving sister.'

Edith turned red and said, 'I was going to let her out later. You see, Miss Grayling, she found out that we were planning a feast and she meant to sneak. So Lizzie isn't quite as loyal as everyone thinks either.'

'I see,' said the Head, rather shocked at the bitterness in Edith's tone. 'Why do you think that Lizzie intended to sneak?'

'Because she simply can't bear me to have any fun,' Edith burst out. 'She thinks that school is all about studying, and lessons, and exams and –'

'Well, these things are very important,' interrupted the Head.

'I know,' said Edith with a sigh. 'And I do want to do well at those things, Miss Grayling, really I do. But I also want to make friends and enjoy my time at school. But

Lizzie thinks that is wrong. Why, she doesn't even want me to go in for the swimming gala.'

'I see,' said Miss Grayling again, frowning. 'Well, I shall be seeing Lizzie shortly, for no doubt she will come along to report Miss Lacey to me. I will have a talk with her, Edith, and see if I can impress on her the importance of striking a healthy balance between work and play.'

'Thank you, Miss Grayling,' said Edith, though she didn't feel very hopeful. Lizzie had such very firm ideas about things. But if anyone could get through to her, Miss Grayling could.

Unexpected arrivals

'I can't believe that it is almost the last week of term,' said Felicity as she and her friends lazed on the grass one Saturday afternoon after an energetic game of tennis.

'I know, hasn't the time just flown!' said Susan. 'Soon we shall all be packing to go home.'

Never to return to Malory Towers. No one said the words, but they hung, unspoken, in the air, making everyone feel a little melancholy.

None of them wanted to talk about the prospect of not returning to school, so Julie said heartily, 'I'll bet the last two weeks haven't flown by for the first formers. They must be jolly glad that their two-week punishment is up.'

'Silly kids,' said June rather scornfully. 'Having a midnight feast is one thing, but to steal a mistress's key, then hold it in a room which is out of bounds is quite another.'

'That was a strange business,' said Pam. 'We never did find out who it was wandering around that night dressed in Miss Lacey's clothes.'

'I daresay that we never will now,' said Nora. 'A pity, because I hate unsolved mysteries. I always feel . . .'

Suddenly Nora's voice tailed off as she gazed towards the school, and Lucy gave her a nudge, saying, 'You always feel what?'

'I don't know,' said Nora distractedly. 'For I've completely forgotten what I was talking about. I say, Felicity, I've just seen someone go into the school who is the spitting image of your sister Darrell.'

'Darrell?' said Felicity, astonished. 'Oh, that's impossible! What would she be doing at Malory Towers?'

'I don't have the faintest idea,' said Nora. 'But if it wasn't her, it was her double.'

Intrigued, Felicity got to her feet and said, 'I'm going to investigate.'

'I'll come with you,' said Susan. 'It's awfully hot out here, and I need to get into the shade.'

As the two girls walked towards the front door of the school, a voice behind them called out, 'Excuse me, young ladies! I wonder if you might help me?'

Felicity and Susan both turned, to find themselves looking at a tall, distinguished-looking man, with a big moustache and twinkling grey eyes. He doffed his hat in a very gentlemanly manner and said, 'Could you direct me to Miss Grayling's study, please?'

'Of course,' said Felicity politely, wondering who the stranger could be. 'Please come this way.'

The distinguished-looking gentleman proved to be very chatty as he accompanied the girls to Miss Grayling's room.

'I do hope this headmistress of yours isn't a tartar,'

he said jovially, making both of them laugh.

'Not at all,' said Susan. 'She's very pleasant.'

'That's a relief,' said the man. 'For I've come to ask permission to take my two nieces out to tea.'

'Oh, who are your nieces?' asked Felicity. 'I daresay we know them.'

'Lizzie and Edith Mannering,' said the man. 'I meant to come and visit them at half-term, but what with one thing and another I couldn't get away. So I'm hoping that Miss Grayling will take pity on me and allow me to take them out for a treat today.'

'I am quite sure that she will,' said Felicity, trying not to stare at the man. So this was Uncle Charles! And he was very different from the dour, rather grumpy individual that she had pictured.

The two girls left him at Miss Grayling's door, where he thanked them politely, and went on their way. They didn't find anyone resembling Darrell, but, on the landing, Susan paused to look out of the window, and cried, 'My word! Isn't that Irene? And I do believe it's Belinda with her!'

Irene and Belinda had been in Darrell's form, and Felicity rushed to the window to take a look, but she was too late, for the girls Susan had spotted had disappeared from view.

'How odd!' said Felicity. 'First Nora thought that she saw Darrell, and now you have seen Irene and Belinda! What *is* going on?'

The girls found out as they went past the third-form

common-room, and heard a terrific racket coming from inside.

'My goodness!' said Felicity. 'Whatever are those third formers up to in there?'

'Nothing,' said Susan, a puzzled frown on her face. 'Miss Peters has taken them off camping for the rest of the term.'

'So she has!' said Felicity, remembering. 'Then who is in their common-room?'

Just as the girls were wondering if they should investigate, two figures came round the corner.

'Bill and Clarissa!' cried Susan. 'Hallo, you two! Are you here to see Miss Peters? I'm afraid you're out of luck, for she has taken her form camping.'

Bill and Clarissa were two old girls who ran a riding stables near Malory Towers, and they were great friends with the third-form mistress.

'No, we're here for the reunion,' said Bill with a grin.

'What reunion?' said Felicity, puzzled.

'Why, the old girls' reunion, of course,' said Clarissa, pushing open the door of the third-form common-room. 'And here they all are!'

Felicity and Susan stared as if they couldn't believe their eyes! There was Daphne and her little friend Mary-Lou, Irene and Belinda, June's cousin Alicia – and Darrell, with her friend, Sally.

'Felicity!' cried Darrell, coming over to give her sister a hug. 'How marvellous to see you!'

'Well, it's marvellous to see you, too,' said Felicity,

still feeling very surprised indeed. 'You didn't tell me there was going to be a reunion!'

'No, I thought I would surprise you,' laughed Darrell. 'This was all arranged with Miss Grayling at the end of last term. We asked her if we might hold a reunion here, and she said that we could use the third form's common-room and dormitory while they are away on their camping trip.'

'How's that cousin of mine, Felicity?' called out Alicia. 'Still causing trouble?'

'Oh no, June has settled down a great deal since she became games captain, you know.'

'I'm jolly glad to hear it,' said Alicia. 'Now, who's missing? Amanda, Gwen and Mavis.'

'Amanda can't come, for she is at college,' said Sally. 'And Mavis is going to join us later. As for Gwen, well, she is already on the premises, of course, and will be here soon. Miss Grayling has given her a few days off so that she can join our reunion.'

'Super!' said Irene happily. 'My goodness, I feel like a schoolgirl again. I say, wouldn't it be just wizard to have a midnight feast?'

'It's funny you should say that,' said Alicia with a grin. 'I feel just like playing a trick on Mam'zelle Dupont!'

'Yes, but we'd better not discuss such things in front of the Head Girl,' laughed Belinda, waving a hand towards Felicity. 'She might dish out a punishment!'

Felicity and Susan laughed, and Mary-Lou called out, 'Clear off, you kids, and leave us in peace!'

But she was smiling, so Felicity and Susan raised their hands in farewell and wandered off.

'Well!' said Felicity to Susan as they made their way back to their studies. 'The very last thing I expected was to see Darrell and all her friends back here at Malory Towers! That must be what she meant on the first day of term, when she said that she might see me here.'

'I say, let's go outside and give the others the news,' said Susan, slipping her arm through Felicity's. 'Won't June be surprised to learn that Alicia is here?'

Lizzie and Edith, meanwhile, had been startled to be summoned to Miss Grayling's study. They were even more surprised when they entered and saw their Uncle Charles sitting there.

Edith, who had been quite young when she last saw her uncle, was delighted to find that he wasn't nearly as alarming a figure as the one she remembered. As a small girl his booming voice and big moustache had frightened her, but now she simply couldn't understand why, for he seemed a very jolly character.

'Well, girls!' he said, getting to his feet, and enveloping them both in a hug. 'It's very good to see you again. Miss Grayling here has kindly agreed that I may take you out to tea.'

Both girls thanked him politely, then Uncle Charles turned back to Miss Grayling and, picking up his hat, he said, 'I will have them back here by six o'clock at the latest, Miss Grayling. You can rely on me.'

'I'm sure that I can,' said Miss Grayling with a smile. 'Enjoy your outing, girls.'

The sisters did, for Uncle Charles was very entertaining company, and he treated them to a slap-up tea at the little tea-shop in town.

'Super!' said Edith, her eyes shining at the spread that was laid out before them. There were dainty little sandwiches, jam tarts, biscuits and cakes of every kind.

'Tuck in, girls!' urged Uncle Charles, beaming, and the girls did not need to be told twice!

Lizzie was a little reserved with her uncle, but the more outgoing Edith very soon lost her shyness and chattered away to him about all her doings.

'I'm taking part in the swimming gala next week,' she said. 'Oh, Uncle Charles, it would be marvellous if you could come and watch. June – the games captain – thinks that I am certain to win my race. I've been training very hard for diving and swimming, spending every spare minute down at the pool.'

'Edith!' said Lizzie, sharply, shooting her sister a warning glance. Really, what a dreadful chatterbox her young sister was! At this rate, Uncle Charles would think that she spent no time at all studying.

Edith turned red and subsided, but Uncle Charles said, 'I'm jolly pleased to hear that you girls are enjoying yourselves at school. Swimming, eh? Well, I used to be quite a keen swimmer myself as a boy. I will certainly come along if I can. And what about you, Lizzie? What do you enjoy doing in your spare time?'

'Oh, I don't really have much spare time, Uncle Charles,' said Lizzie. 'I'm always busy studying.'

Uncle Charles frowned and said bluntly, 'Well, that can't be good for you! If I'd known that you were going to tire yourself out working all the time, I would never have agreed to pay your school fees.'

Lizzie and Edith looked at one another in consternation, and Lizzie said, 'We do appreciate you lending Mother the money for our fees, Uncle Charles, and –'

'Lending her the money?' said Uncle Charles. 'What nonsense is this? Anyone would think that I expected it to be paid back, and I most certainly don't. I have no children of my own, and I'm only too happy to do what I can for my nieces.'

'But I don't understand,' said Lizzie, looking most perplexed. 'Mother told us that we had to repay you.'

Uncle Charles frowned heavily, then his brow cleared and he gave a guffaw of laughter.

'My dears, your mother has got things quite wrong! I did say that I wanted you both to repay me, but I meant by making the most of your time at Malory Towers – and that means working hard and playing hard. It looks to me, Lizzie, as if you have been doing too much of one and not enough of the other.'

As Lizzie stared at her uncle in astonishment, it was as if a great weight had rolled off her shoulders. Her mother had completely misunderstood Uncle Charles, and because of it she had missed out on an awful lot of fun – and she had given poor Edith a bad time, all for nothing.

Uncle Charles was wagging his finger now, saying, 'I insist that you slack off a bit and have some fun this last week of term. Is that clear?'

Although her uncle's tone was stern, there was a twinkle in his eye, and Lizzie answered it with a broad grin, as she said, 'Perfectly clear, Uncle Charles.'

Edith, looking at her sister, marvelled at the sudden change in her. How much younger and prettier she looked when she smiled. And Edith had a feeling that she would be smiling a lot more from now on!

While the Mannering sisters were having tea with their uncle, Felicity and Susan were strolling along the cliffs when they heard footsteps behind them, and turned to see Darrell walking towards them.

'Hallo there, you two!' she called. 'Felicity, I was hoping to catch you.'

'Would you like to spend some time alone with Felicity?' asked Susan tactfully.

'No, you stay, Susan,' said Darrell. 'For you might be able to help me too. You see, it's about Gwen.'

The two sixth formers looked at Darrell curiously, and she went on, 'Gwen joined our little reunion soon after you two had gone. And it seems to me that something is troubling her. You were right, Felicity, when you wrote to me and said that you thought she had changed. She seems more humble and less boastful, somehow. But when she doesn't realise that anyone is watching her, there is a wistful, rather sad expression on her face.'

'Gwen hasn't had an easy time of it here,' said

Felicity. Then she and Susan went on to explain about the class-room being damaged, and about someone dressing up in her clothes to lock Lizzie in the shed and spoil the first formers' midnight feast.

'There's something else, too,' said Susan. 'I bumped into Daisy, the maid, in the hall a little earlier. You know how she loves a gossip! Somehow she had got to hear about poor Lizzie being locked in the shed, and she was digging for information, though of course I didn't tell her anything!'

'Heavens, is Daisy still here?' said Darrell. 'I remember her starting work at Malory Towers when I was in the fifth form.'

'Yes, but the thing is, Darrell, she told me something jolly interesting,' said Susan. 'Apparently Miss Lacey's room was ransacked a little while ago.'

'I know that,' said Darrell with a frown. 'You've just told me.'

'No, not her class-room – her *bed*room,' said Susan. 'She never reported it to the Head, though.'

'Well, this is certainly a piece of news!' exclaimed Felicity. 'I wonder how Daisy came to hear about it?'

'Oh, the domestic staff seem to hear about everything that goes on at Malory Towers,' said Darrell with a laugh. 'It has always been that way.'

Then her expression grew more serious, and she said, 'It certainly sounds as if someone has it in for poor old Gwen, though. Do you know if she has made any enemies here?'

'Well, a few of the girls aren't too keen on her,' said Felicity. 'But I don't think that any of them would go to those lengths to get back at her.'

'Well, what you have both told me has been very helpful,' said Darrell. 'I wonder if I can encourage Gwen to open up and tell us all of this herself. No doubt she has her own views on who is behind it.'

'I do hope so,' said Susan. Then she glanced at her watch, and said, 'Heavens, just look at the time! We had better turn back, or we'll be late for tea.'

'Are you old girls joining us in the dining-room?' asked Felicity. 'Or are you too grand for us?'

'Oh, we shall be there, all right,' laughed Darrell. 'We will be sitting at the third formers' table while they are away. I must say, I'm looking forward to sitting down and enjoying a Malory Towers tea again!'

Reunion at Malory Towers

There was a shock in store for Daffy as she went in to tea that afternoon.

'I say, where is Edith?' she asked the others, as they made their way to the dining-room.

'Oh, her uncle came to visit, and he has taken Edith and her sister out to tea,' said Ivy. 'Lucky Edith! I bet he will have taken them to that little tea-shop in town, where they do those marvellous chocolate cakes.'

'Well, I can't say that I envy her,' said Daffy, pulling a face. 'I wouldn't want to go out to tea with some stern old uncle and a bossy older sister.'

'Yes, Lizzie is rather a wet blanket,' said Katie. 'Though I must say, it's partly Edith's own fault for not standing up to her more.'

'Yes, I gather that Lizzie has always ruled the roost at home,' said Daffy. 'And Edith allowed her to get away with it. My goodness, I would never stand for it if my sister, Sally, spoke to me the way that Lizzie does to Edith. Sally's an awfully good sort, but she would boss me around too, if I let her, for that is what big sisters are like. I showed her right from the start that I wouldn't put up with that sort of nonsense, though. I told her –'

'Daffy!'

Hearing her name called from behind brought Daffy to a halt, and she turned sharply, her mouth dropping open when she saw that the person who had hailed her was none other than Sally.

'S-Sally!' gasped Daffy, staring at her sister as if she couldn't believe her eyes. 'What on earth are you doing here?'

'Why, I am here for the old girls' reunion,' said Sally, ruffling her sister's curly hair. 'Mother was going to write and tell you that I was coming, but I thought it would be a nice surprise if I just turned up unexpectedly.'

'Well, it's certainly a surprise,' said Daffy, who didn't quite know whether to feel dismayed or delighted.

She was terribly fond of her big sister, of course, but she certainly didn't want Sally keeping a watchful eye on her!

'Goodness me, Daffy!' said Sally, eyeing Daffy critically. 'Whatever have you been doing, with one sock up and one sock down? Do tidy yourself up!'

Hastily, Daffy bent over and pulled up the offending sock. Then, to the amusement of the watching first formers, Sally straightened the girl's tie, before standing back and saying, 'There, that looks much neater. Off you go now, or you will be late for tea, and that will never do!'

'Yes, Sally,' said Daffy meekly, her cheeks turning pink as she saw the others struggling to control their mirth.

Sally strode past the first formers and went to join

the others, who were already seated at the third formers' table.

Mam'zelle Dupont, quite overcome with delight at seeing so many of her old favourites again, was standing by Darrell's chair, her hand on the girl's shoulder and a beam of pleasure on her face.

'Ah, how good it is to see you again – and what fine young ladies you have all grown into!' she cried. 'But where is Mavis?'

'She will be along later,' said Irene. 'Of course, Mam'zelle, you know that our Mavis is now a great opera singer, don't you?'

'Yes, indeed,' said Mam'zelle. 'The dear girl sent me one of her records, and what pleasure it gives me to listen to her voice.'

'I bet that Mavis has gone all high-and-mighty boastful again now that she is famous,' murmured Alicia to Darrell and Sally.

'Well, if she has, we shall soon bring her back down to earth with a good dose of Malory Towers common sense!' said Sally firmly.

'I say, who is that young woman over at the mistresses' table?' asked Mary-Lou. 'She must be new.'

'Yes, she looks rather jolly,' said Belinda.

'Oh, that's Miss Nicholson,' said Gwen, helping herself to a slice of bread and butter. 'She is the Geography mistress, and a very good sort. She and I are the best of friends.'

The others looked at one another in surprise, for

the plain, sensible-looking Miss Nicholson was the very last person they would have expected Gwen to be friends with.

'Heavens!' whispered Daphne to Mary-Lou. 'Gwen really *has* changed!'

As it was such a warm and pleasant evening, many of the girls went for a stroll in the grounds after tea.

Darrell and her friends picked a sunny spot on the lawn near the big driveway and sat down.

'Your friend, Miss Nicholson, will be missing your company while you are with us at the reunion,' remarked Sally.

'Yes, though she quite understood that I couldn't pass up the opportunity to join in the reunion,' said Gwen.

'You must introduce us to her,' said Darrell, thinking that she might be able to get some information from Miss Nicholson. 'Perhaps she would like to join us in the common-room tonight? I am sure it will be much more pleasant for her than sitting alone in her study.'

'Oh, thank you,' said Gwen, flushing with pleasure. 'I will ask her, for I'm sure that she will enjoy the company.'

'Here, look what's coming up the drive!' cried Daphne suddenly. 'My word, did you ever see a car that size before?'

The sixth formers turned their heads, and saw a very long, very expensive-looking car making its way up the drive.

'Goodness!' said Mary-Lou, her eyes almost starting

from her head. 'Who on earth can this be?'

A group of sixth formers were standing nearby and they, too, wondered who the occupant could be.

At last, the car drew to a halt, and a uniformed chauffeur got out, opening one of the back doors.

The young woman who emerged drew gasps of admiration from the watching girls, for she was slim, elegant and *very* expensively dressed. Her red hair was piled up on top of her head, while diamonds glittered in her ears and at her throat.

'I know who that is!' cried Amy. 'It's Mavis Allyson, the opera singer. My parents took me to hear her sing in Rome during the holidays and she was simply stunning. Oh, I wonder if she would give me her autograph?'

Of course, Amy wasn't the only one to have recognised Mavis, and scores of eyes followed her progress as she daintily approached the old girls. Several younger girls would have liked to ask for an autograph, but Mavis looked so haughty and unapproachable that no one dared!

'Just as I thought,' whispered Alicia to the others. 'Fame has gone to Mavis's head.'

'Oh, what a shame!' replied Darrell in dismay. 'When she left Malory Towers she had really settled down and become one of us.'

'Well, she needn't think that she's going to queen it over us!' said Irene indignantly. 'Mavis isn't going to spoil our reunion.'

Mavis was almost upon them now, and she looked so

grand that, instinctively, Mary-Lou made to get up. But Daphne pulled her back down again, saying, 'She's not royalty, Mary-Lou – even though she might think she is.'

'How lovely to see you all,' said Mavis, in a bored, rather affected voice. 'Of course, I am dreadfully busy these days, but I managed to make time to fit the reunion in.'

'We're honoured,' said Alicia bitingly.

'I should jolly well think you are!' said Mavis. 'Don't you know that I'm an opera singer now?'

Then her face split into a broad grin, and – to the astonishment of the others – she threw her head back, roaring with laughter.

'Oh, your faces!' she cried when she had stopped laughing. 'I knew that you would be wondering if I had gone back to my old, unpleasant ways, so I thought I'd play a little trick on you!'

'You wretch, Mavis!' cried Darrell, also laughing.

'Yes, I must admit, one or two of us did wonder if fame would have changed you,' said Alicia, having the grace to blush a little. 'Do sit down – or don't you want to get that expensive-looking dress of yours dirty?'

'As if I care for that!' said Mavis, flopping down on to the grass beside Alicia. 'I say, isn't it marvellous to be together again?'

'Do you always travel by chauffeur-driven car, Mavis?' asked Daphne curiously.

'Of course not!' laughed Mavis. 'I persuaded the director of my opera company to lend me his car and chauffeur for the day, just so that I could make a grand entrance.'

'Well, you certainly had us fooled,' laughed Belinda.

'It's ten minutes to six,' said Sally, looking at her watch. 'You know that Miss Grayling asked us all to go to her study at six.'

'So she did,' said Darrell. 'Oh, won't it be wonderful to see her again?'

'I feel rather nervous about it,' said Mary-Lou with a little laugh.

'Nonsense, why should you?' said Alicia, giving her a little push. 'Just remember that you are a nursing sister now, Mary-Lou, not a schoolgirl. I'm sure that when you are at work you must be reliable, responsible and confident, or they wouldn't let you loose on the wards!'

'I am,' said Mary-Lou. 'It's funny, though, now that I am back at Malory Towers I feel like a timid little schoolgirl again!'

As it turned out, Mary-Lou wasn't the only one who felt as if she had gone back in time when faced with Miss Grayling.

There were some people, thought Darrell, as the old girls sat in the Head's study, who naturally commanded respect. And, unquestionably, Miss Grayling was one of them.

But the Head very soon put the girls at their ease, asking each of them in turn what paths their lives had followed. Irene, of course, had pursued a career in music, while Belinda was making a name as an artist. Daphne was working as a secretary in her father's office. Sally had just started teaching at an infants school and was loving every minute of it. As for the clever, quick-witted Alicia, she had found a career where she could put her brains to good use, and had surprised everyone by joining the police force!

'Well!' Darrell had exclaimed on hearing this piece of news. 'That's certainly something you can get your teeth into. It would take a jolly cunning criminal to outwit you, Alicia.'

'Gwen, I need not ask what you are doing, of course,' said the Head, with a smile. 'Or you, Bill and Clarissa. I am glad that you have managed to leave the stables for a few days to come and join us.'

'Two of my brothers are looking after things while we are here,' said Bill. 'We wouldn't have missed this reunion for the world.'

'Well, at least you can relax and enjoy yourselves, knowing that your horses are in good hands,' said Miss Grayling. Then she turned to Mavis, saying, with a smile, 'I imagine that everyone in the country must know your name by now. And Darrell, Felicity tells me that you are a reporter on a newspaper.'

'Yes, Miss Grayling,' said Darrell with a smile. 'I enjoy it tremendously, for I've always loved writing. In fact . . .'

She paused, for she had received a piece of very good news the day before. But perhaps mentioning it here, in front of the others, would seem like boasting.

Sally, who already knew what the news was, spoke

up, saying, 'Go on, Darrell. Tell everyone!'

The girls and Miss Grayling were all looking very curious now, and, clearing her throat, Darrell said, 'I have been writing a children's book in my spare time, and a little while ago I sent it off to a publisher. It was just a spur of the moment decision, and I never dreamed that anyone would be interested in it, but – well, they have decided to publish it.'

'My dear, that is marvellous news!' exclaimed Miss Grayling.

And the girls agreed, all gathering round Darrell to clap her on the back and offer their congratulations.

'Good for you, Darrell!'

'Just think, when you are a famous author we will be able to say that we were at school with you!'

'If anyone deserves success it's you, Darrell!'

'What is your book about?' asked Gwen.

Darrell laughed, a little self-consciously, and said, 'Well, actually it's about a girls' boarding school – not unlike Malory Towers.'

Everyone was simply thrilled to hear this, and Miss Grayling said with a smile, 'You will certainly have been able to draw on your personal experience for that, Darrell.'

The conversation continued for several more minutes, then the Head said, 'It is very good to have you all back here as responsible adults, even if it is only for a few days. I hope that you will have a pleasant reunion, and that it brings back many happy memories for you.'

'Well, we are very grateful to you for having us,' said Darrell.

The old girls made their way back to the common-room in a dignified manner, then, as soon as the door had closed behind them, Irene jumped in the air and cried, 'Hurrah, we're back at Malory Towers!'

Alicia grinned and shook her head. 'Honestly, Irene, I don't think that you will *ever* grow up and be a responsible adult!'

A shock for Gwen

Lizzie and Edith were delivered back to Malory Towers at six o'clock precisely, as their uncle had promised. Before the girls got out of the car, Uncle Charles took his wallet from his pocket and removed two notes, handing one to each girl.

Both of them gasped, and Lizzie said, 'Uncle Charles! We can't possibly accept this. Why, it's almost the end of term and we will never manage to spend this amount.'

'Well, if you have any left over you can spend it in the holidays,' said Uncle Charles firmly. 'I must have a word with your mother and see about making you both a proper allowance next term. And Edith, it looks as if you need a new uniform as well. Make sure that your mother gets you one, and tell her to send the bill to me.'

'Oh, but you've already been so generous!' said Edith. 'I couldn't let you –'

'Now, that's quite enough!' interrupted her uncle with mock sternness. 'My word, I've never known such argumentative girls, and very disrespectful it is too! All that you have to do, my dears, is say, "Thank you, Uncle Charles," and that is an end to the matter.'

The two sisters exchanged glances and smiled, then,

obediently, they chorused, 'Thank you, Uncle Charles!'

The two of them were chattering nineteen to the dozen as they entered the big hall, and Lizzie, spotting Alice, hailed her.

'Hallo!' said Alice. 'You two look as if you have had a wonderful time.'

'Oh, we have,' said Lizzie, her eyes sparkling as she put her arm through Alice's. 'Do come to my study and I will tell you all about it. Edith, off you go and have fun with your friends. I will see you tomorrow.'

Alice stared at Lizzie in astonishment. Why, she had never seen the girl look so relaxed and happy before! There was a kind of glow about her that made her look really pretty. And were Alice's ears deceiving her, or had Lizzie actually told her young sister to go off and have fun?

'Come along, then,' she said to Lizzie. 'I am simply dying to hear what you have been up to!'

In the third-form common-room, the old girls had been joined by Miss Nicholson, who had been delighted when Gwen told her that her friends wanted to meet her. She was about the same age as the others, and they soon warmed to her friendly, open personality.

'Gwen, I hope that we are going to see this marvellous class-room of yours,' said Darrell. 'Felicity tells me that it's quite magnificent.'

'Well, I don't know that I would go that far,' said Gwen. 'But it's certainly a little different from the other class-rooms in the school.'

'Will you be returning next term?' asked Sally curiously.

'I don't know yet,' answered Gwen. 'This term was a sort of experiment, to see how I fitted in and how the classes went. I shall have to wait and see what Miss Grayling thinks.'

She spoke airily, but, inside, she was very worried indeed that the Head might not want her to come back next term. The classes had gone well, on the whole – better than Gwen had expected, in fact. But she seemed to have been at the centre of rather a lot of trouble, even though none of it was her fault. Perhaps Miss Grayling might think that she was more trouble than she was worth!

'Well, I think you've done marvellously,' declared Miss Nicholson. 'Especially when one considers all the setbacks . . .'

But Gwen flashed her friend a warning glance. The others were doing so well in their chosen careers, and she still had enough pride not to want them to know of her problems.

Hastily, she said, 'I shall show you all the class-room tomorrow morning. I do hope that you will like it.'

Just then, there was a tap at the door, and Daisy entered.

'Excuse me, young ladies,' she said. 'The housekeeper wanted me to tell you that there are extra blankets in the big cupboard just outside your dormitory, just in case any of you should get chilly during the night.'

'Thank you, Daisy,' said Clarissa. 'It's quite warm though, so I am sure we will be fine.'

'Will you be sleeping in the dormitory too, Miss Lacey?' asked the maid. 'Or are you going back to your own room?'

'Oh, I shall be sleeping in the dorm, all right,' said Gwen. 'I should feel quite left out if I had to go to my own room.'

'What a pity we don't have an extra bed,' said Belinda to Miss Nicholson. 'Or you could have joined us too.'

Alicia was just about to ask Miss Nicholson how she liked it at Malory Towers, when she became aware that Daisy was still hovering, and said, 'Thanks, Daisy. You can go now.'

'Well, if you're sure there is nothing that you need,' said Daisy, seeming rather reluctant to leave. But, as Alicia had told her to go, she really had no choice.

'You were rather sharp with old Daisy, weren't you?' said Bill, once the door had shut.

Alicia shrugged, and said, 'I never liked her, even when we were pupils here. She's a great deal too nosy for my liking.'

'Oh, she's not a bad sort,' said Gwen.

Alicia laughed. 'You've certainly changed your opinion of her! I remember how spiteful you were to her when she first started here as a maid.'

'Me?' said Gwen, quite astonished. 'Oh, Alicia, I wasn't!'

'You were, Gwen,' said Mary-Lou. 'I remember it

well. You were always getting poor Daisy to run errands for you, and you would give her the most tremendous scolds if she made the slightest mistake.'

'Yes, you made the poor girl's life a misery, until Darrell stepped in and ticked you off,' said Belinda.

'Oh!' cried Gwen, pressing her hands to her hot cheeks as the memories flooded back. 'I had quite forgotten that! What a mean little beast I was!'

'Well, it seems that Daisy has forgotten it too,' said Miss Nicholson. 'Thank heavens she doesn't bear you any grudge.'

Just then Mavis put her hand over her mouth to stifle a yawn. 'Gosh, I'm tired after that long drive,' she said. 'If no one minds, I think I might turn in soon.'

She removed her diamond necklace and earrings as she spoke, dropping them into her handbag, and Daphne said, 'Mavis, you really ought to give your jewellery to Matron, to put in her safe. It looks awfully expensive.'

'It does, doesn't it?' laughed Mavis. 'But they are not real diamonds, you know. This is just cheap costume jewellery that I bought so that I could look the part of the great opera singer when I turned up here!'

The others laughed too, then Mavis, along with Daphne and Mary-Lou, who had also had long journeys, went off to the dormitory.

Presently, Miss Nicholson left too, and Darrell stared after her thoughtfully. She had seen the warning look Gwen had given her friend when she had mentioned something about setbacks. Perhaps, she thought, it might be helpful to talk to Miss Nicholson alone, and see what she could get out of her.

As things turned out, though, Darrell didn't need to speak to Miss Nicholson!

'Anyone fancy a swim after breakfast?' asked Lizzie over breakfast on Sunday morning.

The sixth formers looked up from their meal in surprise. It wasn't like Lizzie to suggest anything like that!

'Um – yes, I wouldn't mind,' said Felicity, feeling that the girl ought to be encouraged. 'What about you, Susan?'

'Yes, why not?' said her friend. 'It's far too nice a day to stay indoors.'

One or two others said that they would also enjoy a swim, while Alice, who wasn't fond of the water, said that she would come along and watch.

'Whatever has got into Lizzie?' Felicity asked Alice as the sixth formers walked down to the pool a little later. 'I've never known her be so friendly and jolly. Is this your doing?'

'I'd like to take the credit,' said Alice with a smile. 'But you must thank her uncle.'

And, quickly, Alice told Felicity the tale that Lizzie had related to her last night.

'Well!' exclaimed Felicity, at the end. 'So Lizzie got the wrong end of the stick. Or rather, her mother did. Thank goodness Lizzie has decided to slacken off a bit and enjoy the rest of the term.'

'Yes, and it will make life easier for young Edith, too,' said Alice. 'I think both of them are going to find their next term a lot more enjoyable.'

'Oh, don't talk about next term!' wailed Felicity. 'For we shan't be here, and sometimes it makes me feel so sad!'

'Then you must make the most of the little time you have left,' said Alice sensibly.

'Yes, that's exactly what Darrell said to me,' said Felicity. 'She was quite right, and so are you. Last one in the pool is a rotten egg!'

The sixth formers had a marvellous time, and no one enjoyed herself more than Lizzie.

'Why, you're almost as good a swimmer as your young sister!' exclaimed June, after narrowly beating the girl in a race. 'Fancy keeping that to yourself! If only I had known, you could have had a place in the gala too!'

'That's why I didn't let you know,' said Lizzie with a self-conscious little laugh. 'I was afraid that you might expect me to practise swimming when I wanted to study.' Lizzie paused for a moment, then went on, 'Look, June, I've been an idiot this term, trying to persuade you to drop Edith from the gala. I'm just glad now that you didn't take any notice of me. And I'm sorry.'

June had never cared much for Lizzie, but she admired her now for being able to own up to a fault. She clapped the girl on the back, saying, 'There's no need to apologise, for I see that you were doing what you thought was right. I'm just glad you have come to realise there is more to school than books. How about a race back to the other end of the pool?'

'You're on!' said Lizzie at once, her eyes dancing.

This was the scene that greeted the old girls as they walked down the cliff path to the pool.

'Gosh, Alicia, just look at your cousin June go!' cried Bill. 'She's awfully fast.'

'Yes, that other girl isn't far behind her, though,' said Alicia, watching critically.

'What luck that the swimming gala is taking place on Wednesday,' said Sally. 'I shall be able to cheer on young Daffy, and Darrell and Alicia can support Felicity and June.'

'I say, who is that seated at the side, watching?' asked Mary-Lou. 'I can't quite place her.'

'Why, that must be Jo Jones – or Alice, as she is known now,' said Darrell.

Almost as though she knew someone was talking about her, Alice turned her head. She got politely to her feet as the old girls approached, feeling rather apprehensive. The last time she had seen any of them was when she had been in the second form, and her behaviour then had left a lot to be desired. But, thanks to the sixth formers, Darrell and the others knew that Alice had changed, and all of them were prepared to let bygones be bygones. They greeted her in a friendly manner, and stood chatting to her until Daphne said, 'Mavis, that girl is at the top of the cliff path. The one who was waiting for you when you came out of the dormitory.'

'Oh, she wanted an autograph,' said Mavis with a laugh. 'Which I was quite happy to give her, of course.'

'Why, that's Amy, from our form,' said Alice, shielding her eyes from the sun as she looked at the figure standing at the top of the cliff path. 'I wonder what she is doing here, for she's not a great one for outdoor life!'

In fact, Amy was suffering from a bad dose of hero worship, and was following Mavis around in much the same way that Violet had been following her all term!

The girl had been up and dressed at a very early hour, and had waited outside the third-form dormitory for Mavis to come out, so that she might get her autograph. Mavis had been very chatty and friendly and, remembering how grand and aloof she had seemed when she arrived, Amy assumed that the young opera singer had taken a liking to her.

Now an idea had come into her head. Her mother was giving a grand summer party in the holidays. How marvellous it would be if she, Amy, could persuade Mavis to be the guest of honour, and perhaps sing at the party. Her mother would be delighted, of course. Amy could almost hear her saying, 'Well, of course, Miss Allyson is a great friend of my daughter's, you know, and she agreed to sing at my party as a favour to her.'

Goodness, wouldn't that make everyone sit up and take notice!

So, as the old girls reached the top of the cliff path,

on their way to Miss Lacey's class-room, Amy was lying in wait.

'Oh, Miss Allyson,' she breathed. 'I wonder if I might have a word?'

But Mavis's attention was being claimed by Daphne, and she didn't even hear Amy.

The sixth former trotted along patiently behind the old girls, until they were almost back at North Tower, then at last her chance came, and she said, 'Miss Allyson!'

Mavis turned, and said, 'Why, hallo again, Amy. Don't tell me that you want another autograph?'

'Oh, no,' said Amy. 'I just wanted to ask –'

'Hurry up, Mavis!' called out Alicia. 'We have to go and say hello to all the mistresses, and Gwen is simply itching to show us her class-room.'

'I'm coming!' called Mavis. Then she turned back to Amy, patting her on the arm and saying, 'Excuse me, Amy, but I really must go. Perhaps we will have the chance to talk later.'

As Amy stood gazing worshipfully after Mavis, she, too, was being watched. Violet and Faith, sitting on a bench nearby, had witnessed the whole thing.

'Well!' laughed Faith. 'It looks as though Mavis has got herself an admirer.'

Violet, who had been quite horrified by the little scene, said nothing. She had set Amy up on a pedestal, and to see her trotting after someone else with an adoring expression on her face just didn't seem right somehow.

'Now you see how silly *you* look,' said Faith unkindly.

'What nonsense!' said Violet sharply. 'I don't talk in that silly, breathless voice, and make my eyes as big as saucers when I am with Amy.'

'Oh yes, you do, my girl,' said Faith with a grin.

'Do I really?' asked Violet, shocked.

Faith nodded, and, quite suddenly, Violet *did* see how silly she had been. And, just as suddenly, her admiration for Amy completely disappeared, as though it had never existed. Amy wasn't some marvellous, extraordinary person, she was just an ordinary schoolgirl with rather a high opinion of herself. And, by hanging around after Mavis, she had fallen off her pedestal, and Violet had seen her quite clearly.

The old girls, meanwhile, were having a marvellous time. They had already spoken to Mam'zelle Dupont, of course, and now they went to visit Mam'zelle Rougier, Miss Potts, Miss Linnie, the art mistress – and last, but not least, Matron.

'Well, well, well!' said Matron, beaming at them. 'How grown-up you all look. It's nice to be able to welcome you back here without having to warn you against having midnight feasts, or asking for your health certificates!'

'Matron, have you been dyeing your hair?' asked Alicia cheekily. 'I'm sure you had more grey hairs last time I saw you.'

'The grey has slowed down a little since you left, Alicia,' retorted Matron. 'Although that cousin of yours has done her best to take over where you left off. Thank heavens she's settled down a bit now that she is in the sixth form!'

Then, of course, the girls had to see Gwen's classroom. Gwen unlocked the door, and stood back for the others to go in before her.

They exclaimed over the furnishings and ornaments, then Clarissa said, 'It looks as if you have forgotten to clean the blackboard after your last lesson.'

'Oh no, that's impossible, for Bonnie cleaned it for me.'

'Well, there's certainly something written here now,' said Sally, going up to the blackboard. Then she turned pale, and, as the others gathered round and read what was written there, a shocked silence fell.

The words were chalked in big, capital letters, and said:

'HALLO, OLD GIRLS. I'M SURE THAT MISS LACEY DOESN'T WANT TO SPOIL YOUR REUNION BY TELLING YOU WHY SHE WAS DISMISSED FROM HER LAST POSITION, SO I WILL. MISS LACEY IS A COMMON THIEF.'

A very successful gala

The silence was suddenly broken by the sound of sobbing, and everyone turned, horrified to see that Gwen had burst into noisy tears.

Darrell took charge at once, leading Gwen to a sofa.

'I'm not a thief,' Gwen sobbed piteously. 'I'm not.'

'Of course you're not,' said Mary-Lou, who always hated to see anyone upset. 'We know that, and I can't think why someone would write such a thing.'

Some of the others, however, weren't so sure, and they exchanged glances. Gwen had played some mean tricks during her time as a pupil at the school, and her nature had been a sly and spiteful one. Perhaps she hadn't changed so much after all.

'Gwen, dear,' said Darrell, sitting down beside the young woman and taking her hand. 'You must tell us what this is all about. I may as well tell you, I know that someone has been playing horrid tricks on you since you came back to Malory Towers. Is this another of them?'

Gwen produced a dainty handkerchief from her bag and blew her nose, before looking round at the watching girls.

'Yes, it is,' she said. 'But it's true. I was dismissed from my last post for stealing.'

A gasp went round, and Gwen said defiantly, 'But I was falsely accused, and stole nothing.'

'What happened, Gwen?' asked Sally. 'It might help if you tell us.'

'Very well,' said Gwen, giving a sniff. 'But would one of you fetch Miss Nicholson, please? She has been a true friend to me, and I would like her to hear this too.'

'I'll go,' said Mary-Lou at once, dashing from the room.

There was an awkward silence while the others waited for Mary-Lou to return with Miss Nicholson. Fortunately, as it was Sunday, she had no classes to teach, and Mary-Lou soon found her in her study, where she told her what had happened.

Gwen had composed herself a little by the time they returned and, once everyone had seated themselves on the chairs and sofas, she began, 'After I left finishing school, I took a job as companion to an elderly widow, Mrs Carruthers. She was a friend of Mother's, you see, and I thought that she would treat me as one of the family.'

'But she didn't?' prompted Alicia as Gwen's eyes began to fill up again.

'No, she made it clear that she thought she was doing me a great favour by giving me the job,' said Gwen. 'She even hinted that she was doing Mother a favour by not ending their friendship once Father was taken ill, and we were no longer wealthy.'

'What a horrible woman!' cried Miss Nicholson.

'Yes, she was horrible,' said Gwen, managing a little smile. 'She treated me like dirt, expecting me to be at her beck and call at all hours. Then one day a valuable antique vase went missing from her drawing-room, and I was accused.'

'But why did she think it was you, Gwen?' asked Mavis.

'Because the cook and the maids had worked for Mrs Carruthers for years,' said Gwen. 'And nothing had ever gone missing before. Besides, she knew that my family had fallen on hard times, so I suppose she thought that gave me a motive.'

'And she dismissed you?' said Sally.

Gwen nodded, and said bitterly, 'She searched my bedroom first, but even though the vase wasn't there, Mrs Carruthers refused to believe in my innocence. I was sent packing, without a reference or the wages that she owed me, and was told that I was lucky the police hadn't been called.'

'Well!' said Irene, shocked. 'I wonder who did steal the vase, then?'

'That's just it,' said Gwen. 'No one did. Miss Winter, my old governess, bumped into Mrs Carruthers' cook about a month after I had been dismissed. It turned out that one of the maids had broken the vase and been afraid to own up to it straight away. She was away visiting her family when I was accused, but when she came back and heard what had happened she was awfully upset, and admitted breaking the vase at once.'

'I see,' said Belinda. 'And did Mrs Carruthers offer you your job back?'

Gwen shook her head. 'No, not that I would have accepted the offer. She didn't contact me at all, or apologise, or send me the wages I was owed. In fact, if Miss Winter hadn't bumped into the cook that day, I would never have known that my name had been cleared.'

'Well, it sounds to me as if you are well out of it,' said Darrell. 'Gwen, does Miss Grayling know about this?'

'Yes,' said Gwen. 'I had to explain why I didn't have a reference, you see. And I wanted to be honest about it from the start. But I asked her not to tell anyone else, for I know that there are always some people who will say that there is no smoke without fire.'

'I am quite sure none of us think that,' said Miss Nicholson, looking round the room.

Everyone agreed at once, for even those who had doubted Gwen believed her now.

'The question is, who wrote that message on the blackboard?' said Miss Nicholson. 'For whoever it is must be the person who has played those other beastly tricks on you.'

'What other tricks?' asked Daphne, her eyes wide.

Aided by Miss Nicholson, Gwen told the others of the things that had happened to her.

'We think that Amy of the sixth form might be responsible, for it's no secret that she dislikes me intensely,' finished Gwen.

The girls were very shocked, of course, and there were a great many exclamations of disgust. One person who said nothing, however, was Alicia, who sat gazing thoughtfully into space. As Alicia was someone who usually had plenty to say for herself, Darrell asked, 'What are you thinking, Alicia?'

'I'm thinking that perhaps Amy isn't the culprit,' said Alicia, frowning. 'There's another person whose name seems to come into this rather a lot – Daisy. She took Gwen's clothes to be cleaned, and it was her word that proved Amy wasn't responsible for damaging the flower arrangement.'

'Well, one thing is for certain,' said Bill. 'Whoever wrote that message on the blackboard had a key to this room. And I would imagine that it would be an easy matter for Daisy to get hold of the key.'

'Yes, but it would be quite an easy matter for anyone to get hold of it,' pointed out Miss Nicholson. 'The housekeeper has the key on a hook in her room, it would only take an instant to slip in and get it while she wasn't there.'

'Yes, but how could Daisy – or anyone else, for that matter – have known about Gwen being dismissed from her last position?' asked Belinda.

'I never thought of that,' said Gwen, looking puzzled. 'I can't imagine . . . yes, I can, though! Shortly after I arrived here I had a letter from my mother, and it went missing. Mother mentioned Mrs Carruthers and the whole incident in the letter. That was why I was so concerned when it disappeared, for I was worried that it would fall into the wrong hands.'

'And it seems that it did,' said Miss Nicholson gravely.

'Susan told me yesterday that Daisy was trying to get information out of her,' said Darrell, rubbing her nose. 'She was talking about the time Lizzie was locked in the shed, and the time someone got into Gwen's bedroom . . .'

'But Daisy didn't know about that,' Miss Nicholson interrupted. 'No one did, apart from Gwen and me, for she didn't report it.'

'Then the only way Daisy could have known about it is if she was the culprit,' said Darrell heavily. 'That settles it.'

'It seems that I was wrong,' said Miss Nicholson, looking upset. 'Daisy *has* been holding a grudge.'

'And she has slipped up by telling Susan about the bedroom incident,' said Belinda. 'Well, if she has slipped up once, she can slip up again.'

'Yes, but we can't leave it to chance, with only a few days to go until the end of term,' said Alicia. 'Daisy must be *made* to slip up.'

'But how, Alicia?' asked Sally.

'I think those very valuable diamonds of Mavis's might provide the answer,' said Alicia.

'But they're not valuable, Alicia,' said Mavis, puzzled. 'I told you, they are just paste.'

'My dear Mavis,' said Alicia, going across and laying a

hand on the girl's shoulder, 'you are quite mistaken. That jewellery is very valuable indeed – worth a fortune, in fact. And we are going to use it to bait a trap for Daisy.'

'I think I see what you are getting at,' said Mary-Lou excitedly. 'We know that Daisy has stolen once, for she took the cufflinks that Gwen had bought for her father. And if she has stolen once, she may do so again.'

'Especially if temptation is put in her way,' said Alicia with a grin.

The last week of term was a very busy one. There were desks and cupboards to clear out, trunks to be packed, and – of course – the swimming gala to look forward to. June was very wrapped up in the organisation, for it would be her last duty as games captain, and she was determined that it should go smoothly. Felicity and Susan, as well as taking part, were helping her, but June always seemed to find something to worry about.

'What if more parents than we expect turn up?'

'What if no one turns up at all?'

'Felicity, have you had the programmes printed yet?'

'Susan, can you check that the life-belt has come back from being mended?'

'Do stop fretting,' said the placid Pam. 'I'm quite sure that everything will go – er – swimmingly.'

Everyone groaned at this but, as June had feared, things did not go quite as swimmingly as she had hoped!

'Disaster has struck!' she cried, bursting into Felicity's study on the day before the gala.

'Heavens!' said Felicity, who had been enjoying a chat with Susan. 'What on earth has happened, June?'

'Cathy of the fifth form has gone down with chicken pox and been sent home,' said June, sinking down into a chair and burying her face in her hands. 'And she was taking part in the senior backstroke race tomorrow.'

'Call on one of the reserves,' said Susan sensibly.

'They have both gone down with chicken pox too,' said June glumly. 'There seems to have been an outbreak in the fifth form. Oh, what am I to do?'

While the others considered this, someone knocked on the door, and Lizzie came in, saying in a breezy manner, 'Has anyone seen Alice? We were supposed to be going for a walk together.'

No one had, but a light came into June's eyes as they rested on Lizzie, and she leaped up with a cry that made the others jump.

'Never mind going for a walk, my girl,' said June, taking Lizzie by the shoulders. 'You are going to get some swimming practice in, for you're taking part in the gala tomorrow.'

'Am I?' said Lizzie, startled.

'You are,' said June firmly. 'And you need to practise your backstroke. Any objections?'

'None at all,' said Lizzie. 'My uncle may be coming to watch, and it will be nice for him to have both nieces taking part.'

'I simply can't get over the change in Lizzie,' laughed Felicity, when June had led Lizzie off to the pool.

'What a pity that her uncle didn't turn up earlier in the term!'

There was a surprise in store for the Mannering sisters on the day of the gala, for not only did Uncle Charles turn up, but he brought their mother with him!

'Mother!' cried both girls, flinging their arms around her. 'What a wonderful surprise!'

'Well, when your uncle telephoned and offered to drive me to the school, I simply couldn't resist,' said Mrs Mannering, a pretty woman, who looked very like her daughters. 'I thought that it would make up for missing half-term. Edith, darling, I am simply dying to watch you swim.'

'Oh, it's not just me that you will be watching,' laughed Edith. 'Lizzie is in one of the races as well.'

'Oh, that's marvellous!' cried Mrs Mannering, looking hard at her older daughter and feeling pleased that she had lost her rather serious expression, and now seemed like a happy, carefree schoolgirl. She blamed herself for the strain that Lizzie had placed herself under, and now, as she put an arm about each girl's shoulder, she said, 'My dears, I can't tell you how sorry I am for misunderstanding what Uncle Charles said to me. I can't believe that I was foolish enough to think that such a generous man would really expect us to repay him for your school fees.'

'Now, that's quite enough of that!' said Uncle Charles, turning a little red. 'This is supposed to be a happy occasion for us.'

'Yes,' said Lizzie, squeezing her mother's hand. 'It was just a mistake, Mother, so let's forget all about it.'

In the end, despite June's misgivings, the gala went off very well indeed. Mrs Mannering had the thrill of seeing Edith receive a standing ovation for her graceful diving, while Lizzie finished a very honourable second in her race.

Neither Felicity's parents nor June's had been able to come, but Darrell applauded wildly at Felicity's impressive diving, while Alicia yelled herself hoarse as June streaked the length of the swimming pool, narrowly beating her opponents. Sally was there to spur Daffy on, too, of course, her heart in her mouth as she watched the girl poised on the topmost diving board. How tiny she looked, all the way up there! Sally squeezed Darrell's hand involuntarily as Daffy launched herself into the air, turning a perfect somersault, before stretching out her arms and legs and diving cleanly into the water.

'That was simply marvellous!' said Alicia, clapping June on the back when everyone went in to tea afterwards. 'To think that my don't-careish cousin was responsible for organising all that!'

'I'm not *quite* so don't-careish now, if you don't mind, Alicia,' said June with a grin. 'But I mustn't take all the credit, for Felicity and Susan were an enormous help to me.'

'You were excellent too,' said Darrell to Felicity. 'I was proud of you. And I managed to get some decent photographs, so Mother and Daddy will be able to share your moment of glory as well.'

All of the Malory Towers girls went to bed without protesting that night, tired but happy. Only the old girls – along with Miss Nicholson – sat up late.

'Well, today has been fun,' said Clarissa. 'But tomorrow is not going to be fun at all.'

'I just hope that everything goes according to plan,' said Mavis, looking worried.

'As long as everyone plays their parts, nothing can go wrong,' said Alicia, confidently. 'Everything will be all right, you'll see.'

'Oh, I do hope so,' said Gwen, wringing her hands. 'Miss Grayling hasn't said anything yet about me coming back next term. If she does, I would very much like to accept her offer, but I don't feel that I can if Daisy is still here, planning and plotting against me.'

'She won't be,' said Darrell, a grim expression on her face. 'Dear Daisy is in for a shock tomorrow!'

Goodbye Malory Towers

As the old girls had already discovered, Daisy was on duty in the dining-room at breakfast time, and they spoke freely in front of her.

'So, we are agreed,' said Sally. 'We are all going to the cinema tonight?'

'Yes,' said Darrell. 'The film starts at eight o'clock, so we should be back shortly before half past ten.'

'Are you wearing your famous diamonds, Mavis?' asked Daphne.

Mavis laughed. 'I think that they may be a little showy for a small cinema,' she said. 'I'd better leave them behind.'

'Well, for heaven's sake give them to Matron for safe-keeping,' said Gwen. 'It makes my blood run cold to think of them lying around in the drawer of your cabinet.'

'Oh, they have been perfectly fine there all week,' said Mavis, lightly. 'And they will be perfectly safe there tonight, as well.'

But the girls didn't go to the cinema that night. Instead they sat in the common-room, as quiet as mice, so that if Daisy happened to pass she would not know they were there. All except for Alicia, Darrell and Gwen, who were upstairs. Alicia lay hidden under her bed, which was opposite Mavis's, so that she had an excellent view if anyone came in. And jolly uncomfortable it was too! Darrell and Gwen, meanwhile, sat on a window seat in an alcove in the passage outside the dormitory, hidden from view by a heavy curtain.

The time seemed to pass very slowly indeed for all concerned, as there was nothing they could do to occupy themselves, not even talk! But, just as the three upstairs were beginning to wonder if Daisy was going to take the bait, they heard the sound of feet padding softly up the stairs. Gwen clutched at Darrell's arm, and Darrell patted her hand reassuringly, holding a warning finger up to her lips.

In the dormitory, Alicia tensed as she heard the door open, then blinked rapidly as the light was switched on. Hardly daring to breathe, she watched as a pair of legs, clad in black stockings and sensible black shoes, came into view and made straight for Mavis's bed. The intruder had her back to Alicia now, so the girl took a chance and stuck her head out so that she could get a good look. Yes, it was Daisy all right! And she was helping herself to Mavis's 'diamonds'!

Quickly, Alicia drew her head back in, then Daisy switched off the light and went out, closing the door behind her. Instantly, Alicia emerged from her hiding-place, yelling at the top of her voice, 'DARRELL!'

This was the signal that they had agreed on, to let Darrell and Gwen know that Daisy had taken the jewellery, and both girls jumped out from behind the curtain, confronting the startled Daisy.

The maid hardly knew what to think for a moment. That yell had come from the dormitory, but there had been no one in there a moment before. And what were two of the old girls doing up here when they were supposed to be at the cinema? Then Daisy heard a door open behind her, and saw Alicia coming out of the dormitory, a grim expression on her face and, all at once, she realised the trap she had fallen into.

'Let us see what you have in your pocket, Daisy,' demanded Darrell.

'W-why, nothing,' stammered Daisy, trying to bluff it out.

'Don't lie, Daisy,' said Alicia. 'You have Mavis's jewellery in there, for I saw you take it.'

'I – I was taking it to put in Matron's safe,' said the girl, sounding desperate now. 'You see, I overheard you talking at breakfast, and –'

'Don't lie!' said Gwen scornfully. 'You were stealing them, just as you stole the cufflinks I bought for my father.'

Daisy turned pale, and suddenly all the fight seemed to go out of her. Then she glared at Gwen and hissed, 'Yes, I took the jewellery. But I wasn't going to keep it for myself, oh no. I was going to plant it in your room, so that it looked as if *you* had taken it, then Miss Grayling would have had no choice but to dismiss you – the high-and-mighty Miss Lacey! But you're not so high-and-mighty now, are you?'

Gwen shrank back as though she had been slapped, quite sickened by the hatred in the maid's voice.

Seeing that Gwen looked as if she was about to faint, Alicia said to Daisy, 'Be quiet! You're coming along to Miss Grayling's study with us, right now.'

Daisy did not protest, for she knew that the game was up, and walked along sullenly with the three girls to the Head's room.

Fortunately, Miss Grayling had not yet gone to bed, and she called out, 'Come in!' when Darrell tapped on her door.

She raised her brows when the three girls, accompanied by a reluctant Daisy, entered, and asked, 'Is something the matter?'

'I'm afraid that there is,' said Darrell. 'We have just caught Daisy stealing Mavis's jewellery.'

There was no need for the Head to ask Daisy if this was true, for guilt was written all over the girl's face. Miss Grayling felt shocked and dismayed, for Daisy had been at the school for a number of years, and although she was a little too fond of gossiping at times, the Head would have sworn that she was of good character. It saddened her deeply to find out that she had been mistaken.

'There is more, I am afraid, Miss Grayling,' said Gwen, and she went on to tell the astonished Head mistress the other things Daisy was suspected of doing.

Really, thought the Head, it seems quite unbelievable

that all this has been going on under my nose, and I didn't have the faintest idea!

'But Gwen, my dear, I don't understand,' she said. 'Why on earth didn't you report the loss of your cufflinks?'

'I – I didn't want to make a fuss,' said Gwen, looking down at the carpet. 'I thought that if I caused trouble, you might not want to keep me on here.'

'I see,' said Miss Grayling quietly. Then her expression hardened as she turned to Daisy, and said, 'Please hand over the jewellery that you stole.'

Red-faced, Daisy put her hand into the big pocket of her apron, and pulled out Mavis's necklace and earrings, placing them on the Head's desk.

Miss Grayling glanced at them, then said, 'And you intended to plant these in Miss Lacey's room so that I would dismiss her. All because she treated you unpleasantly many years ago. What a low and spiteful act, Daisy.'

Both Daisy and Gwen turned red at this, for Gwen did not like to be reminded of how mean she had been to Daisy.

'And am I to understand that you also masqueraded as Miss Lacey, and locked poor Lizzie Mannering in the shed?' asked the Head.

'Yes,' admitted Daisy. 'I knew that the first formers were having a feast, you see, for they had asked me to provide them with lemonade. And I knew that Miss Lizzie would be snooping around, for I overheard them discussing how to get the better of her. I already had Miss Lacey's clothes, for I had washed them for her, and I had taken the hat from her room when I stole the cufflinks. All I had to do was borrow a wig from the costume box behind the stage that is used for plays and concerts.'

'You seem to have done quite a bit of snooping around yourself,' said the outspoken Alicia in a hard voice. 'You were outside our common-room the other night, weren't you, and heard us talking about visiting Gwen's class-room the following morning. So you were able to sneak in first and write that horrible message on the blackboard.'

Daisy hung her head but said nothing and, at last, Miss Grayling said, 'Daisy, you will pack your bags tonight and leave Malory Towers tomorrow morning. But first, I must insist that you give Miss Lacey her cufflinks back.'

So the three old girls, Daisy and Miss Grayling went along to the maid's room, up in the attics. There, Daisy produced a rather battered suitcase from under her bed, and threw open the lid to reveal a small jewellery box containing the cufflinks, Gwen's hat, a blonde wig and a bottle of very expensive perfume.

'Is this yours, Gwen?' asked Darrell, holding up the bottle.

'No,' said Gwen, puzzled. 'I have never seen it before.'

'I took it from Miss Amy,' said Daisy. 'Oh, I didn't steal it from her, but what I did was just as bad. I made her give it to me in return for keeping quiet about something. I shan't tell you what.'

'Well, I'm glad to see that you still have *some* decency,' said Alicia scornfully.

Suddenly, Daisy's legs began to tremble, and she sat down abruptly on her bed, looking up at Miss Grayling, and saying in little more than a whisper, 'Will you have to call the police?'

The Head looked at Gwen, and said, 'That is for Miss Lacey to decide, as she has borne the brunt of your spite.'

'I don't want the police involved,' said Gwen at once. 'Daisy, you have behaved very badly indeed, but I am partly to blame because of the shameful way I treated you all those years ago. I think that losing your job and being sent away from Malory Towers is punishment enough.'

'A just decision, I think,' said Miss Grayling. 'Daisy, you will remain here until morning. I shall inform the housekeeper that you are leaving in the morning because of some family crisis. Any wages that you are owed will be sent to your home.'

'Thank you, Miss Grayling,' said Daisy, feeling quite light-headed with relief that the police weren't going to be called. Then she looked at Gwen, and said, 'Thank you as well. I'm sorry, but it should comfort you to know that I have hurt myself far more than I have hurt you.'

'It doesn't,' said Gwen quietly. Then, followed by Miss Grayling and the others, she turned and left the room.

'Phew! Thank goodness that's over!' said Darrell,

when they were all out on the landing.

'Well, I am thanking goodness that I allowed you girls to hold your reunion here,' said Miss Grayling. 'But for you, we might never have got to the bottom of this, and Daisy could have continued persecuting Gwen next term.'

'Next term?' said Gwen, hardly able to believe her ears. 'Miss Grayling, do you mean . . .'

'Yes, Gwen,' said Miss Grayling with a smile. 'I would like you to return to Malory Towers in September and teach the girls who will be moving up into the sixth form.'

'Marvellous news, Gwen!' cried Darrell, patting the girl on the back.

'Simply super!' said Alicia. 'Come on, girls, let's go back to the common-room and tell the others everything that had happened.'

'Oh, I've still got Amy's perfume,' said Darrell, suddenly realising that she was clutching the bottle.

'Well, you can give it to her tomorrow,' said Alicia, grabbing Darrell's arm and pulling her towards the stairs. 'Come *on*! The others must be on tenterhooks!'

Miss Peters and the third formers arrived back at school on Friday morning, the last day of term. Fortunately, the third formers had packed their trunks before leaving for their camping trip, so they had nothing to do but wait for their parents to arrive.

For everyone else, though, it was a bustle of last-minute activity as trunks and night cases were packed.

'This quite takes me back,' said Irene, haphazardly stuffing things into her night case. 'I can almost imagine that I am a first former, going home for the holidays.'

'Yes, you tried to steal my pyjamas then!' said Alicia, snatching them back from Irene.

'Thank goodness we only have night cases to fill this time, and not trunks!' said Daphne. 'How I do hate packing!'

In the sixth-form dormitory, meanwhile, Felicity went up to Amy and said, 'I almost forgot! Darrell came up to me after breakfast, and asked me to give you this.'

'My perfume!' cried Amy, absolutely delighted to have it back again.

'Yes, it was found in Daisy's room,' said Felicity, and Amy flushed a little as she remembered giving it to the maid in return for her silence.

The news of Daisy's disgrace had flown round the school, of course, but with the excitement of the last day of term, no one had said very much about it.

At last, the sixth formers were packed, and they carried their night cases down to the big hall, all of them feeling rather solemn suddenly.

The old girls were already there, and Darrell smiled at Felicity as she saw her coming down the stairs.

'How do you feel?' she asked when Felicity came up to her.

'Excited, sad – all mixed up, really!' laughed Felicity.

'Just the way I felt on my last day,' said Darrell.

All the mistresses, as well as Matron, had gathered in

the big hall, for everyone wanted to say goodbye to the old girls, as well as to the departing sixth formers.

Mam'zelle Dupont grew quite tearful as she hugged everyone in turn, and Nora disgraced herself by bursting into tears too, though everyone assured her that it was quite understandable.

At last the big coaches that would take the train girls to the station arrived, and there were a great many emotional farewells.

The hall seemed a great deal bigger and emptier once they had left, and Felicity said to Darrell, 'I do hope that Mother and Daddy don't arrive too soon. I want to make my last moments at Malory Towers last as long as possible.'

'They may not be your very last moments,' said Sally, overhearing this. 'Who knows, you may want to arrange a reunion of your own in a few years.'

'Yes, that would be fun,' said Felicity, brightening a little. 'It makes me feel less sad to think that I might come back one day.'

Just then, Daffy came running up to Sally, grabbing at her sleeve. 'Mother and Daddy are here!' she cried. 'Do come on, Sally. Goodbye, Darrell! Goodbye, Felicity!'

'These youngsters just have no sense of occasion,' sighed Sally, shaking her head. 'I shall see you both in the holidays, I expect. Yes, Daffy, I'm coming!'

'Do you mind if we wait outside, Darrell?' asked Felicity. 'I think the sunshine might cheer me up a little, and I'd like a last look at the grounds.'

'Good idea,' said Darrell.

So the two sisters made their way outside to wait for their parents, each lost in her own thoughts as they looked at the gaily coloured flower-beds, and well-kept lawns.

Then, all too soon, Mr Rivers's car could be seen winding its way up the drive, and it was time to leave.

Felicity and Darrell climbed into the back seat and, as the car pulled away, both of them turned and looked back – and said a silent goodbye to Malory Towers.

Have you read the first Malory Towers story?

Enid Blyton

Malory Towers

First Term

Darrell's looking forward to starting at her
new school, Malory Towers. She's packed her
tennis racquet and her toothbrush, but has she
remembered a lid for her fiery temper?
A trunkload of trouble awaits ...

Look out for more classic school stories from

ST CLARE'S

Schooldays at St Clare's are never dull
for twins Pat and Isabel O'Sullivan
and their friends.

There's mischief at St Clare's!

More classic stories from the world of

Enid Blyton

The Naughtiest Girl

Elizabeth Allen is spoilt and selfish. When she's
sent away to boarding school she makes up her mind
to be the naughtiest pupil there's ever been! But
Elizabeth soon finds out that being bad isn't as
simple as it seems. Thre are ten brilliant books
about the Naughtiest Girl to enjoy.

Enid Blyton

is one of the most popular children's authors of all time. Her books have sold over 500 million copies and have been translated into other languages more often than any other children's author.

Enid Blyton adored writing for children. She wrote over 600 books and hundreds of short stories. *The Famous Five* books, now 75 years old, are her most popular. She is also the author of other favourites including *The Secret Seven*, *The Magic Faraway Tree*, *Malory Towers* and *Noddy*.

Born in London in 1897, Enid lived much of her life in Buckinghamshire and adored dogs, gardening and the countryside. She was very knowledgeable about trees, flowers, birds and animals. Dorset – where some of the Famous Five's adventures are set – was a favourite place of hers too.

Enid Blyton's stories are read and loved by millions of children (and grown-ups) all over the world. Visit enidblyton.co.uk to discover more.